Cartim......

To Brenda

Best Wishes

Georgina
Hutchison xc

Cartimandua

Georgina Hutchison

This edition published 2012 by Belgarun
Typesetting by Gatecutter
Belgarun is an imprint of BGU Limited

BELGARUN
THE NEW FACE OF PUBLISHING

Belgarun, Huddersfield, England
www.belgarun.com
ISBN-13: 978-1-84846-019-5

Belgarun is a trademark of BGU Limited.

For Octavia and Ophelia

and

for Phu, who believed in me

PROLOGUE - AUTUMN AD 70

The bruise-coloured sky hangs still overhead, dark birds swirling in the twilight while a mist settles on the valley floor. Ahead, the path is lined with gorse so thick it claws our legs and ankles as we wade through it. This is good, I think to myself. When they attack us, the gorse will slow them down. As if that matters.

In front of us rises a sanctuary, a monolithic hill fort, overgrown and ancient, ascending from the valley in a spiral of forgotten ramparts. I remembered this place when Antikia, my loyal aunt and royal advisor, asked where we should take refuge. I saw it in my mind, like glimmering hope above the dark and monstrous battle.

As we climb, I recall from previous visits the way through the carefully placed breaks in the hill's earthworks, built here by my ancestors hundreds of years before. We come to the summit of the fort and I'm the first to walk through the gouge in the huge ramparts which rise to twice my height, like the shoulders of some giant, half-buried guards. I can tell that the atmosphere of this hill has awed my band of warriors and advisers. They follow me onto the flat central section of the hill's plateau, from where they gaze to the south west peak with its far-reaching vista and to the north east section, where the ground slopes away more steadily. Some are nodding as they look around, happy to be in a place of relative safety at last; others are dropping their crimson-tinged weapons and are busying themselves tending the livestock and building rough shelters and fires.

Antikia joins me, standing close by my side and squeezes my hand briefly to give me strength. She is my father's sister, my most senior adviser and if any other person could tell this tale as faithfully as I, it would be Antikia.

My name is Cartimandua.

I am the tribal chief of the Brigantes and I rule over all the hills, moors, valleys and waters of the north.

I am the beating heart of Brigantia, grand-daughter to the man who allied all this vast territory and made it great. This is my story, spun down through time, woven in the winds for anyone who will listen, before it is lost forever, before my courage and memory fade.

WINTER AD 28

A thin plume of smoke spilled continuously from the roof of the royal house, disappearing into the cold, misty sky. I trod with the exaggerated care of the sneaking little child that I was, across the frosted mud and away from the sleeping woman, Mandulay, who had been trusted to keep watch over me. The enclosure was quiet; all of the senior council were ensconced in the large central roundhouse, and the only sounds came from the birds and other wildlife in the woods beyond. I held my thick woollen skirt up out of the puddles of slush where the ice had melted. I was a slim girl then, with dark brown hair and brown eyes and a straight little nose that sat plainly between my high cheekbones.

Heavy drapes of tanned hides had been lowered over the south-east facing entrance of the imposing dwelling, so I skirted the structure to a section at the side where the daub had thinned and a small peep-hole existed. With my cold hands pressed flat to the twiggy surface to protect my face, I leaned my forehead onto the backs of them, eyes to the hole. Inside, the central fire gave off a warm glow, lighting up the faces of those who sat round it, holding wooden bowls of hot soup or trenchers of roasted pork with barley while they warmed their legs. My mother's face shone clearly, framed by her light brown hair, blue eyes glinting with reflected amber flecks from the fire and soft mouth held in a tight little smile. She kept staring down into her broth as though it fascinated her deeply and I could tell she was agitated. A cool wind nipped at my ankles and I longed to be on the inside, sitting with my family and the senior advisers and elders. I forced my feet to stay put and tried to ignore the cold. I knew this was an important meeting and I believed I should be present. I would have been too, had my mother, Metassia, not been so adamant that I be kept away. Of course, that only increased my interest and as I had reached seven full turns of all the seasons, I felt amply justified in disobeying her and making

3

myself party to whatever business my father was doing with the strange man from the north who currently sat with his back to me.

My father, Kesaven, sat at a quarter turn from his guest, so I could see his familiar profile, rectangular and chiselled like the crags on the hills, with high cheekbones and dark deep-set eyes. Unlike my mother's pursed mouth, his smile was genuine. I knew it from the way the lines around his eyes multiplied as though the creases were a measure of his good humour. I had seen him smile without those lines on several occasions, his teeth bared but his eyes blank, and it had always proved ominous for the recipient. Now he was laughing easily, listening to the north man who leaned forward as if telling a good joke. There were several conversations going on and at first it was difficult to pick out what anyone was saying. I stomped my feet quietly, in frustration and to ward off the biting feeling in my toes. Eventually the voices thinned out until just one remained. I listened to the rich tones of the north man as he addressed my father.

"Thank you, Kesaven," he said, "for this welcome. It's been too long indeed since we last shared a meal and our news." He paused and I wondered if this was a veiled reproach, but my father was nodding amiably.

"There isn't much news," Tyrius went on, "except to say that the same old disputes continue and, as always, there is the constant worry about attacks from the Selgovae, though these are few in number and mostly trivial. The Carvettii are generally well and settled."

"That's good to hear," Kesaven said. "As ever, the real threats seem to come from the south, not the north."

"Ah, I said the Carvettii were generally well and settled, my friend. There are stirrings however. The same old discontent rumbles on."

There was a pause, some low murmuring, and I noted that

my aunt, Antikia, had fixed a piercing stare on the north man. She was a noble woman of the Brigantes and one of the youngest of the council members. If I have worked it out correctly, she would have been about nineteen turns of the wheel back then. Years; I should call them years or I will lose you. I remember how I watched her through my little peep-hole, my toes aching with the cold, and wished I was as grown-up as her. With sleek dark hair a shade darker than my own, a curved slim nose and sharp cheekbones like my father's, she had a vicious kind of beauty that reminded me of the eagle a neighbour's boy had once brought to show me. When her charcoal eyes burned into you, it was either with smouldering fascination or bitter disdain, since she rarely wasted her time being indifferent. While the circle of people shifted and mumbled, and the stranger took a sip of his soup, her gaze never left him. Just as I thought no one was going to speak, her voice rang out playfully.

"And those doing the stirring, who would they be?" She cocked her head on one side and smiled. My father interjected before the stranger could reply.

"I'm sure whoever they are, the Carvettii council has them under control, Tyrius?"

"Our alliance could be made stronger. The council would have less trouble if our links were forged of a stronger metal. In this way we could stave off the unrest."

"There is unrest in the south also, Tyrius, and we have no bond or alliance to protect us there. The southern war hounds creep slowly north, the sun dog and his brother respect no boundaries."

Listening to their words, I struggled to keep up. I had heard of Cunobelinus, the sun hound, who led the ferocious Catuvellauni but I had always thought they were far away, too far to threaten us. As for Tyrius's words of forging a stronger alliance, I had no idea what he meant. The Carvettii were a part of the Brigantes, under rule of my father, Kesaven, and always had been. Always in my lifetime anyway, and that seemed a very long time to me.

"The Catuvellauni will never make it this far," Tyrius said, shaking his head so that his dark, jaw-length hair flew up and the longer plaits within it shuddered. I caught a glimpse of the side of his face, pale and square, with a short dark beard and thick lips. "The Corieltauvi flank our rear, and besides that, they cannot afford to over-stretch themselves."

"Cunobelinus has three sons." My father looked up slowly as he spoke, his face thoughtful and I saw Tyrius straighten his back. I wished very much that I could see his face.

"Aye, almost grown and cruel like their father, some say." Tyrius let the words hang and I saw my mother biting her lip, still looking anxious but now also confused. I tried to understand the hidden meaning behind their conversation and cursed my own ignorance. "Anyway, none of them has an army and even if they did come north, better they meet a solid resistance. An allied Brigantia would force them back to their own lands."

My father nodded and I thought I saw a mischievous smile creeping into the corner of his mouth. There were further murmurings and one of the advisers, a cousin of my father, broke some bread into pieces and dished out more soup with a wooden ladle. My stomach rumbled so loudly I worried they would all hear it. I toyed with the idea of strolling in and joining them, since I guessed my parents would not want a scene and would have to let me stay. As I worked up my courage, my mother's voice interrupted.

"How are your family, Tyrius?" She enquired, her voice higher than usual.

"They are all well, Metassia, and send their greetings. Risha would have joined me but for the demands of our children. Venutius is well and Iticus strives to grow as big as his older brother."

"They are still so young; you must hate to be away from them."

"It's true, I'm happiest when they're close to me. You must feel the same about your daughter. How is Cartimandua? I thought I'd see her here."

I flinched at his use of my name. How could this stranger know me and yet I knew nothing of him? My unease grew as my mother replied in clipped tones.

"My daughter is too young for serious meetings such as this."

I gasped in annoyance, then my aunt cut in.

"Yet I think she would have enjoyed it. Cartimandua is advanced for her age and takes a strong interest in her future role and the issues facing our tribe." Antikia cast her arm out expressively as she spoke and aimed her comments directly at Tyrius, pretending not to notice the grimace on my mother's face. I grinned behind my peep-hole, thankful to my aunt for rescuing my dignity.

"Perhaps you would like to meet her later, she would be interested to know more about the Carvettii," said my father and Tyrius nodded and said he would like that very much. I flushed and was nervously pondering what I would say to Tyrius to live up to my aunt's high praise of me, when I caught sight of her, head on one side sharp as a hawk, staring straight at me. I jumped away from the wall of the roundhouse and set off running back across the frosty ground of the enclosure.

It was not long before Antikia found me, kicking aimlessly against the stump of a long-since rotted tree at the side of the small hut where I was supposed to have remained all morning. She swept across the crisp mud and grasped my elbow.

"Come with me, child, we need to talk."

We walked towards the woods, Antikia loosening her grip on me once we were out of sight of the roundhouse. I kept my mouth shut as I expected to be in big trouble for listening to the council meeting.

"How much did you understand?" She asked as we came

to a stop under the cover of oaks and silver birches. I shrugged, unwilling to reveal my lack of knowledge. When I was young, I was always keen to impress my aunt. She waited and I twiddled with my thumbs. Eventually I spoke.

"I didn't get the bit about forging with a stronger metal," I admitted, "or why everyone was going on and on about Cunobelinus's sons."

"You recognise the threat from the Catuvellauni, though?"

"Oh yes, big threat," I said knowledgeably, "Very nasty tribe."

My aunt laughed and then bit her lip.

"Your mother didn't want you at the meeting. She thought you were too young."

"Well I'm not too young, I'm old enough now and even Tyrius thought so and he hasn't even met me and you said so yourself so," I paused for breath, "you can't be angry with me for listening in." I folded my arms and tried to appear regal. My aunt was looking amused.

"We were talking about you, Cartimandua. Tyrius wants you to marry his son, Venutius."

"But I'm only little!" I gasped, horrified and my aunt burst out laughing. She quietened when she saw my bottom lip quivering and put her arm round me.

"He doesn't want you married yet, silly. He wants a betrothal. Tyrius and his family rule the Carvettii, though they in turn are ruled by your father. Brigantia is such a large territory we have to rely on all the tribes within it to keep their allegiance. It's good for them too, in case other, bigger tribes threaten them, because we all come together to protect each other. What Tyrius was doing, albeit very clumsily in my opinion, was to threaten a Carvettii rebellion if we didn't agree to you taking his son."

"They'd turn against us?"

"No, I don't think so. It was just a threat. Leaders play games like this all the time."

"What was all that about the Catuvellauni?"

"Ah, we all have to be wary of them. Their hunger for other people's lands knows no bounds. Your father implied that he might try to marry you off to one of the Catuvellauni boys to create some kind of peaceful alliance."

"He won't do that, will he?" I cried

"And have those bloodthirsty fighters salivating over our lands? No, you'll marry Venutius," she answered.

"Why?" I was confused.

"Because there are greater threats than a disgruntled Carvettii council, greater threats even than a rampaging Cunobelinus. The real danger lies over the water and when that danger comes, we really will need a unified Brigantia."

I had heard of the Romans, of course. My mother told the tale of the mighty Caesar who crossed the dark seas to our ancient island in the time of my grandmother's mother. When I was very small, she told the funny story of how his ships approached the shores and were driven away, all the way back to his homeland by our bad-tempered god of the winds. As I grew a little older, I heard the more frightening epilogue; how he returned a year later with even more legions and chased the southern chief, Cassivellaunus, northwards. Only the increasingly militant Vercingetorix, supreme warrior of the Gauls, had drawn Caesar away from our island and back across the waters to fight battles on another front. We all knew what had happened to Vercingetorix in the end – taken to Rome in defeat and humiliation and strangled to death, a warning to all who would oppose the might of Rome.

Yet for so many years, we had heard little from that strange and distant power. The southern tribes had closer contact – the Trinovantes in particular had been indebted to Caesar after he helped restore their leader, Mandubracious, whose father Cassivellaunus had killed. Rome hated Cassivellaunus and his tribe, the ones who would later be called the Catuvellauni. Caesar put his faith in Mandubracious, proclaiming him the strongest of the British chiefs, which in my opinion goes to show how little he understood of our world and what a tiny part of our lands he had seen. Anyway, only a few generations later, around the time my mother was born, Cunobelinus rose to glory when he brought the Trinovantian empire under Catuvellaunian control. Fortunately for him, Rome is a fickle creature and they even ratified the take-over.

Occasionally we received goods from Rome, traded on the east coast and brought to us by Parisi merchants but trade contact was the only kind we had and for all we knew, Rome had never heard of Brigantia. To hear Antikia talk of this foreign stronghold as an imminent threat disturbed me greatly, such that I could not even form any questions or sensible response and instead stood silently at her side as she rubbed her hand over the bark of a tree and fixed her gaze on our enclosure of huts. Over in the pastures I could see the licks of bright orange flames from one of the grain pits that was being burned clean. Presumably satisfied that I had grasped the political situation and the need for marriage with Venutius, Antikia finally took me back to the big roundhouse.

Inside, my mother and father were arguing. Several others remained; nosy elders who could justify their presence because of the implications of the issue for the whole tribe. Tyrius had apparently gone in search of our metal-worker, whose weapons were much prized among our people.

"Can't you at least keep it hidden?" My father was saying. "The man must know how much you dislike him and that doesn't help our position."

"I hope it doesn't," my mother retorted, "if our position is to marry Cartimandua off to that family of thugs."

My father shook his head and I could tell the argument had probably lasted a long time and gone round in circles. It was a familiar pattern and one which infuriated them both. Metassia came from a family of cloth workers and her simplistic and fateful attitudes often exasperated my father, whose diplomacy and quiet intelligence she often purposefully ignored. Antikia coughed and they looked around. My mother held her arms out to me.

"Come here, my love," she said and I went to her side.

"Are they really thugs?" I asked, holding my mother but speaking to my father.

"No, they are not," he said, "They are good and loyal members of our tribe who have worked hard to maintain and defend our northern borders."

"You mean their northern borders," my mother spat and I felt her arm tighten around me. "They work only to protect their own interests and their only interest in our daughter is to make their son a chief."

"That may be so, Metassia, but Cartimandua will be chief and Venutius would be her husband. I would never let it be any other way."

"You won't always be here," my mother said.

"She'll always have the council," Antikia pointed out, "and there really is no other option. We cannot afford to lose the Carvettii. If things were different, maybe she would marry for love as you two did, but the world is moving on and we need our tribe to stay strong."

My mother stared over Antikia's shoulder, to the flames of the fire that was still burning. I could see that deep down she had already given up. As so often seemed to happen, Antikia and my father had out-numbered her. She stroked my hair.

"I know what you both think we need," she said, her voice slow and quiet, "but the world is indeed moving on, and it will keep moving regardless of what marriage we make for Cartimandua. All the might of Brigantia cannot keep the foreign tide from rolling in."

Antikia bit her lip and I saw that both she and my father had

11

underestimated my mother's grasp of the situation.

"I'll ask the great goddess to make this young Venutius attractive at least," she whispered in my ear, and at last gave a smile.

When Tyrius returned, he smiled to see me waiting with my mother. She introduced me and he took my arm in a full warrior's greeting, which flattered me no end since I was still too young to routinely carry weapons. His hand grasped my arm just below the elbow and I wrapped my own tiny hand around his bulky forearm, in the polite search for a hidden knife. I sneaked a sideways grin at my mother who rolled her eyes ever so slightly. She saw the gesture for what it was; an affirmation from Tyrius to Kesaven that he respected me as rightful heir to the position of chieftain. He sat close to me, and, leaning down as though to make our conversation more private, he said he had been greatly impressed to hear how wise and strong I was for my age.

"It is true I have mastered the short bow for killing small animals," I nodded, "and my father often speaks to me of tribal matters." I kept my head up and held my hands steady on my lap. I was trying to think of other examples of my wisdom and strength, but I saw Antikia in the shadows, pretending not to watch us, raise a forefinger to her lips and brush them slowly. Don't speak too much, she was telling me, draw the words from him instead.

"I've no doubt that Kesaven finds yours a wise shoulder to lean on." There was a glint in his smile that I didn't quite care for, one that said he wasn't taking me seriously, that he thought me just a silly little girl. I bit the inside of my cheek and stayed silent.

"My son is not far off your age. Perhaps you would like to meet him? He would love to go hunting with you."

"What does he look like?" I couldn't help myself. My

mother's earlier words had set my mind wandering.

"Like me, people say. He has my dark hair and my eyes. His nose belongs to his mother though. It is far slimmer than my own," and he wobbled his wide nose with a fingertip and made his eyes go cross-ways. I laughed. He winked at me and I blushed.

"I'd like to take Venutius hunting," I said. "When can he come and visit?"

Tyrius paused at this, and I knew then that the north man was hoping that once a deal was done, he could cart me away to his homeland, a prize for his young son. He'd had no desire to send his own boy to us. I tipped my head on one side expectantly, imitating the playful manner my aunt had adopted earlier when she asked who the trouble-makers in the Carvettii council were. My father, who had until now kept his distance, joined us.

"He's welcome any time, Tyrius. Bring him next time you travel here." And with those vague words, my future marriage was agreed.

SUMMER AD29

I remember the summer I met Venutius, not just for that event itself, but because the weather was the hottest I had ever known. The winter mud of our enclosure had baked into a dry brown crust that crumbled underfoot and we lit the fire only for cooking food and driving away the flies. In the green, swaying canopy of the woods I found some relief from the stifling heat and I would walk out to where a small stream wound its way downhill, to spend my time skimming stones, collecting round pebbles for Mandulay to use as pot-boilers and threading wild flowers into necklaces. Sometimes I went alone, sometimes after my betrothed arrived, I took the little boy with me, but thankfully I had left him behind on the day I saw his father there, the day I stayed hidden and witnessed something I shouldn't have.

I liked Tyrius. When he sent word to say he would come in the summer, my family were apprehensive, having expected another year or so to pass, but I was looking forward to seeing him again and meeting this boy who would be my husband. My mother had feared I was too young to understand the implications of my betrothal, but in fact it was surely better that way, for if I had been older I might have rebelled and caused problems. As it was, I felt excited and grown-up, in the short-sighted way that only innocent children can. Before they arrived, my mother cut the straggly ends from my hair with a specially sharpened knife, and then rinsed it through with sage water. She made me a spectacular new summer dress in a fiery autumn leaf colour that tied at the waist with a leather strap and a circular silver buckle. Her sister's daughter had sent the cloth, made by herself and dyed by her husband, from her home in the Latenses territory. Like all the tribes in Brigantia, the Latenses came under the central control of our family. My mother's parents, both now dead, had worked cloth all their lives and Metassia had learned the skill before she joined with my father. She sometimes sat spinning yarn for pleasure, one of the serving girls having cleaned and combed the wool for her so she could take out her little hand spindle that she weighted with a whorl of stone. Watching her spin would send me into a quiet reverie, her long, plump fingers moving rhythmically and magically making a line of yarn appear. She knew how to weave and once showed me on her cousin's loom, an upright, warp-weighted machine that parted the warp so the wooden shuttle could sneak through, carrying the weft in its wake. My mother still had her own beautifully carved weaving comb that she had used in her youth for tamping down the weft but she kept it idle, wrapped in a leather and stored with her jewellery. She didn't weave any more, but she could turn a thread with the best of them and she had cut and sewed my new dress herself, stitching away all of her worries about my match as she pushed her thin bone needle through the material. It was no plain tube of fabric such as I was used to, but a shaped and flattering garment that flared with thin gores that she had sliced out carefully with her sharpest knife and inserted.

I tried the dress on and told her it would look better if I had breasts like hers to fill the top half of the dress and she chuckled and said I would have to wait a few years for that. Then she became very serious and asked how much I understood of relations between a man and a woman.

"The night-time stuff? Oh I know all about that," I answered. We lived in a roundhouse after all, with tanned hides separating the sleeping areas, and though it was relatively private, I had sometimes heard light moans in the dark, and even glimpsed my parents, naked and intimate. That kind of cuddling was what adults did, when they were bound together and sometimes even when they were not. It was, however, the last thing on my mind when I met Venutius.

He stood before me, his big eyes wide and vulnerable and his cheeks flushed to a rosy red from the journey. Dark hair, just like his father's curled around his face and he looked about him with a natural curiosity. He was very small, only four years to my eight and I expected that he would be quite boring. But I also thought that he must be a bit scared so I stepped forward after my parents and his father had all greeted each other, and kissed Venutius's cheek and asked him if he would like to come and play with me. He nodded and so I led him out into the meadow to collect flowers.

"We have these flowers at home," he said after a while. "But it smells different here. I can't smell the sea."

"That's because the sea is a long way away from here," I announced.

"I like the sea, it's blue and green and splashy."

"We've got a stream." I said, feeling defensive because I had never seen the sea and didn't know what it looked like.

"Can we go paddling?"

"Not now, maybe another day." I didn't want to share everything with him at once, but I was enjoying having someone to show off to. I didn't have any siblings – unless my older sister counted, but she died when I was still very young so I had no real memories of her save for the bitter-sweet tales my mother occasionally told. From the start, Venutius was like a younger brother to me and I was happy that summer to have him to play with, especially since he was not as boring as I had expected and could even handle a small bow and arrow, but some days I still wanted to be by myself and so that is why I was walking alone in the woods when I saw his father.

Tyrius and Venutius slept and ate in our roundhouse, which was particularly large since we were the chief tribal family. Most nights, Venutius actually crept in with me and I made up silly stories to help him get to sleep, since his mother was not there to comfort him. Tyrius entertained us both at mealtimes with his fanciful tales of the peculiar tribes of the far north and their terrifying ways while my mother tutted disapprovingly but secretly revelled in the flirtatious deference he was careful to show to her. My father included him in many aspects of tribal business and accepted his help with some of the more mundane work required to keep our home functioning well. Tyrius was a good hunter and we all cheered whenever he brought home a deer or a wild pig. He understood livestock too, and was happy to ride around the extensive lands on which our herds roamed, checking fences and ditches. To my aunt, he was always very polite and proper and she returned this demeanour. Antikia was a fiery woman and her apparent coolness when he was near led me to believe she didn't like him very much. I worried about this, as it suggested to me that she had seen some unpleasantness of character that we had all missed.

One morning, when my father was away to deal with some territory dispute with the Parisi, and Venutius was walking with my mother, playfully gathering herbs and leaves in the fields, I went walking by myself. The sun blazed down and my scalp felt red hot so I headed for the shade of the woods and the cool of the stream. I waded up through the water, which came only to my knees in most places, picking up any very round pebbles, or stones in nice colours. Every so often a rustling in the undergrowth alerted me to a squirrel or hare but otherwise the woods were still and silent in the heat. I kept walking, deeper into the woods, feeling the air grow cooler as the green canopy overhead became thicker. As I came to a place where the stream cut deeper into the ground and the banks were too high to see over, I started to climb out, grasping at big tufts of tall grass to haul myself up. As I did, I heard noises. I peered over the grass and, seeing movement, I instinctively dropped back down. The noises came in waves, moaning and whispering. I looked again, crawling up a little higher, and in the shorter grass of a clearing under a willow tree some twenty wheels from me, I saw two figures lying on the ground, one on top of the other. The one on top was naked and male, his buttocks clenching and rising and falling. Underneath him was a woman, her dress pulled open and her legs slightly raised. I could see one of her brown-tipped breasts wobbling as the man rode her.

As I have said, living in a roundhouse it was fairly apparent to me that certain carnal things went on under cover of darkness, but this was a sunny day, out in the open and I was both drawn and a little repelled by their display. Some moments later, I realised who the couple were. My aunt's dark hair and distinctive profile gave her away and then the man turned his head and I saw that it was Tyrius, kissing her neck and biting her ear. I ducked away and set off back downstream, wading as quietly as I could until I was sure I was out of earshot. Then I ran, the cool water splashing all up my thighs, until I reached a place to sit down and think.

That evening I said nothing about what I had seen, although I desperately wanted to tell someone. But I understood that since Antikia was going to such lengths to hide her true feelings for Tyrius, there must be a good reason for the secrecy.

SUMMER AD31
TO SPRING AD35

After I had seen Antikia and Tyrius deep in the woods, my life changed subtly and forever. Perhaps I came of age in that moment, understanding for the first time something of the darker passions and desires that men and women hold secret. After that hot summer morning, I conspired to be near when they spoke together, feigning childish interest and I crept out of my furs at night in an attempt to catch them together. Mostly I failed, but one time, just before Tyrius was due to leave with Venutius, I found my aunt and her lover, curled up in his area of the roundhouse. They were speaking in tiny whispers, barely audible, but I stole close and picked out some of their words.

"She's a hard woman, good with the boys, but full of ideas," he said. "If it hadn't been for her pushing, I doubt I'd be here with Venutius at all."

"Well then I have something to thank her for," my aunt breathed, "but be careful when you go back. We cannot afford for Risha or anyone else to find out yet. You must be with her as you were before."

"That will be difficult, given the way I feel about you."

When Tyrius and Venutius left, I watched him, and I watched my aunt and I believed I was the only one who saw the sparks of fire in their eyes, the only one who knew their secret. She looked wistful after his horse had disappeared on the north-western way, kicking up dust in its wake.

For a few years, I reverted to acting just like a small child again, ignoring my deeper understanding of the adult world and clinging to the freedoms which I understood would soon give way to huge responsibilities. I spent my days caring for my pet goose, playing in the fields with my bow and building dens out of tree branches and mud. I loved the autumn, when the golden leaves fell knee-deep and I could pile them into great heaps and fall backwards into them. I used to go collecting acorns in the woods, filling baskets and bringing them them back to tip into the feed stores for the pigs. Each year, and especially in summer, I explored a little further into the woods, passing the point where I had seen Antikia and Tyrius and following the stream all the way to a small waterfall that splashed over smooth brown rocks. My mother taught me more ways to braid and pin my hair and my father gave me my first sword, bronze and lethal, for which he had traded ale with a Parisi merchant.

When I was ten, my father asked me to accompany him on one of his trips away. We rode south, following a great river and stopping at various roundhouses and small settlements along the way. My father knew practically all the people by name, hailing them as he approached. Each time we came near a homestead, he would draw his horse close to mine and say, "this is Banata's home, where the river bends east past three birch trees," or "Costeni lives here, but he is often south, trading with the Corieltauvi."

He knew them all, not just their names, but what they did, who they were related to and who their parents had been. It daunted me to realise that I would have to build up this same familiarity with my disparate and isolated tribe, but I threw myself into conversation at each roundhouse we passed and tried hard to remember all the details my father gave me about each family. Unlike some of the other tribes, particularly those in the south, our clan preferred to live in very small groups. At most, a settlement might consist of three or maybe four dwellings, but the usual situation was to have a single roundhouse, perhaps with a small hut or two for storage, passing traders or women in childbirth. Though our territory was the largest held by a single tribe, it held relatively fewer people. The high hills and bleak moors were beautiful to me, but they hardly held appeal to those not born there, with the heavy snows and strong winds that made life so hard. Whilst people occasionally left our lands to make their fortunes elsewhere, few entered our territory out of choice. With so much land to choose from, Brigantians seemed to have a natural tendency to live in seclusion.

We rode along the borderlands where our territory stretched south in a sharp point, my father being careful not to take us too near any Corieltauvi settlements. I found one of their coins as we crossed a marshy tract of land, the shiny metal glinting at me from the ground.

"What is this?" I asked. My father shook his head in a dismissive manner.

"It's a coin, for paying for goods."

"How? What I mean is, why would anyone want this, what does it do?" I rolled it between my fingers. My father tried to explain currency to me, how the coin had some kind of inherent value and you could use it instead of bartering with goods to get the item you wanted. I asked where the coins came from in the first place and he told me that the leaders of a tribe issued them and no one else could make them or it would disrupt the whole system.

"But what's to stop anyone making their own?"

My father shrugged and took the coin from my hand. He looked at the inscription for a moment, and then flung it far away into the muddy grass.

"Nothing," he answered, "It's a ridiculous way of trading."

Despite agreeing with him, I was disappointed he had discarded my souvenir. I wanted to save it for Venutius next time we met so he would know how far I had travelled.

The Corieltauvi were a troubling lot, apparently friendly but really an unknown quantity, which was why my father was keeping his distance. We used to be bordered by smaller tribes who traded peaceably with us and perhaps even counted themselves part Brigantian, but before I was born the smaller tribes banded together into a much larger confederacy, and recently they had even managed to maintain a system of dual rulers. A bordering group with that level of proven stability was obviously a threat, even if they remained peaceful, but we were always confident since our tribe still outweighed theirs and my father had in the past met with one of the rulers who had appeared to be a reasonable man.

Heading back in a north-west direction, my father told me of the far western tribes, the Silures and the Dematae, as well as the closer ones, the Deceangli and the Ordovices, who were our friends and with whom we had an agreement of peace and protection. I could see the tips of their mountains, bluer and stranger than our solid dark hills. We didn't go as far as the coast but I could smell salt in the air and I understood what Venutius had meant when he said our home smelled different to his.

"Over the water in that direction lies Mona. Has anyone talked to you about that island?"

"No," I said, my head still buzzing with all the things I was supposed to remember about the Ordovices and the Deceangli and the route we had taken since the last stop.

"Mona is where the Druids live. It's an island but when the tide is back you can wade to it. Sometimes, though, you can't even see it at all because the mists surround it like a blanket."

"An invisible island!" I said, delighted. "Are the Druids invisible too?"

"If they want to be," my father said with a grin so that I couldn't be sure if he was teasing me or telling the truth.

"I'd like to visit. Are they a friendly tribe?"

"They're different from all the others, including us. We don't know much about them, but they know every tribe in the land and what they do affects us all."

"How?"

"They are our link to the things we cannot see, they talk with the dead and they commune with the spirits of our land.

The work they do is crucial but they keep it well hidden in their huge oak groves. A trader once came through our homestead when you were only tiny. He was from the Gangoni, on the shores that look out over Mona and he said that sometimes you could hear chanting and screaming on the wind and it would make you feel in one moment the most horrified and frightened you could be, and in the next the most ecstatic and wise. Your grandfather went there at least once but he never spoke of it."

I wasn't so sure I wanted to visit them any more, but I wished we were at least on the shore, instead of so far inland, so that I could hear that chanting for myself.

"You should remember the druids always," added my father. "They hold a great deal of power and their wrath is terrible. Better to keep them as friends."

We altered direction after that point, heading now towards the north-east, along the ridge of hills that marked the backbone of the whole land, trekking over bare moorland of gorse and heather, the ground a strange mix of brown, purple and green with hidden dips and springs that we avoided by following a faint, flattened path. As we breasted one peak high above a deep valley shortly before stopping for the night, I saw a beacon of light straight ahead in the evening gloom. It topped a sharply defined hill that rose like a giant roundhouse from the valley floor.

"What is that?"

"That," my father said, reigning in his horse and pausing alongside me, "is the dun of Camulos. It is a shame we won't be visiting, but you'll no doubt have the pleasure at some point."

"Camulos? The war god?"

"The very same!" He laughed. "No one lives up there any more, but the hill of Camulodunum is famous. They built a massive homestead up there in ancient times. Can you imagine? A dun that sat astride the summit, protected on all sides by such a steep slope - except for the north-east side. You can't see it from here but it's a shallower drop. Even so, it would have taken a valiant army to survive that climb, through gorse and earthworks and no doubt being clobbered all the while by arrows and other missiles."

"It sounds perfect. Why does no one live there now?"

"The dun burned, a long, long time ago."

"Before Caesar?"

"Long before Caesar. When the fire took hold, it savaged the place so badly that no one wanted to go back. They say a dragon breathes under the hill and living there would tempt him out again. The local families use it as a meeting place, for drinking and fighting and all kinds of dubious entertainment," he looked at me with a raised eyebrow implying that he wasn't going to go into detail, "but no one lives there. The actual homesteads are down in the valley."

"Can't we go there tonight?" I tried, but he shook his head.

"Not a chance. They're a rough enough lot in daytime, never mind at night. Good people, but wild. When you're older you can see for yourself."

I bristled but kept my mouth shut. My father had the annoying habit of pointing out my chronological deficiencies just when I was beginning to feel his equal.

After that trip, I understood a great deal more of what my father's work entailed. I paid attention to everything and even tried to familiarise myself with the skills and crafts that provided our main trade. I sat with Jacavin a few times, watching the old metal worker beating and forging iron and I also spent time at the tanning pits, learning about how they were lined, and watching the leather workers stripping oak bark to go in the tanning liquid. I liked to watch them with the finished pieces, running their iron knives through the tough brown material, cutting out the shapes they needed and stitching them together with their ruthless bone needles and thick yarn. This was all work I would never need to do myself, but my father had shown me that you couldn't rule people without understanding them and, more importantly, without understanding the trades that maintained our wealth. I was old enough now to sit in on all council meetings, listening intently to my father, less so to the older members who rambled on. Antikia was keen to help me learn and she would quietly translate into my ear any confusing dialogue, where elders slipped into metaphor or talked of historical events of which I was unaware.

We all gathered one drizzly day for a council meeting to discuss safe trade passage for some of the merchants from neighbouring tribes who had suffered a number of violent thefts recently. There was talk of manning the hilltop paths from some of the younger men, whilst the older contingent cackled and made jokes about the silly fools freezing their what-nots off just to protect foreign traders to whom we had no duty anyway. Nobody was taking the issue very seriously until, in the midst of some good-natured banter, my father threw his mug down on the ground, the dark ale spilling out onto the rush matting.

"Enough!" He shouted, glaring around furiously. "A trader has died, and yes, he was a Parisi and not one of our own, but he was a good man and I had known him a long time. When these traders come travelling across our lands, or any others, they take a risk. They go where the trade is good and hope to meet with a friendly reception. They know that sometimes they might be accosted, but they take that chance. Do you expect them to keep coming if the chance turns into an inevitability? If this gets out of hand, traders will simply stop travelling through the dangerous areas. They'll go elsewhere to barter their goods - if they miss out on trade then that's still better than being murdered and having all their goods carted off regardless. And we'll be the ones that really miss out. This whole thing isn't about protecting members of other tribes, it's about protecting trade but perhaps you are all too stupid to understand that."

When he had finished, everyone was silently studying the floor, except for me. I stared open-mouthed at him, never having heard him yell at the council like that before.

"Can I take some people and track down the murderers?" a man named Tantoban asked, looking up. He had been one of those advocating manning the hill-tops and was probably happy to be vindicated after the teasing he had received, though he did not show any smugness.

"You certainly can. Hunt them down, chop off their heads and deliver them to the Parisi with our apologies. Baranak, you can travel direct to the Parisi borders and negotiate some kind of recompense for the losses that the other three traders have suffered – but no more. I'm not handing over prizes for every fool who's had a bag of grain stolen in the last season."

Baranak nodded, though he looked as if he would have preferred the job that the warrior Tantoban had requested. There was an uneasy atmosphere for the rest of that morning's business. My father had the ability to render grown adults into chastened children when he raised his voice berating their lack of understanding. Everyone had a high regard for his intelligence, something he had inherited from his own father, but his generally friendly manner made the occasional contemptuous outbursts shocking to those on the receiving end. So, for the rest of the meeting, everyone was on their guard, trying not to say anything that would betray their unequal intellect or inspire further animosity from Kesaven.

In honesty, I revelled a little in the way he had silenced the whole of his council. I had begun to understand that sometimes a leader has to be passionate, angry, harsh and even cruel with his own people. It's a way of reminding everyone of your power, but it's also a way of dispersing the burden of responsibility that comes with power. Every leader needs to let off steam now and then or they'd lose their mind. On that occasion, he was making what I felt was a valid point, but there were times I saw him turn on people for more trivial and even non-existent reasons, dealing either a verbal or physical blow when he felt he'd been provoked. Kesaven's skill was in maintaining a public image that clouded everyone's perception of his occasional petty viciousness, and I decided to watch him closely and learn how he did it.

Soon after I had seriously buckled down to study my father's work, my husband-to-be returned. He was now ten, and I was fourteen, but while I had developed curves and bodily hair and all the awkwardness of that in-between age, he was playful and unrestrained, still a child. Again, his father Tyrius travelled with him and I wondered if I would ever meet his mother.

"Ah, no Risha?" My mother enquired, apparently innocently and I listened to Tyrius smoothly explaining how she was busy overseeing his concerns in the north. Antikia glowed and preened more openly than before, so that I was concerned she would give herself away.

I played with Venutius in the fields when I could be bothered, shooting arrows at targets, fashioning the old style flint heads for spears we had whittled and carved. He wanted to wrestle and fight but with my changing body I avoided that kind of close contact. Mostly I was with Kesaven if he was home or travelling with him if he was away. Each day I learned a little more - what our crop supply from such a family was each year, which Parisi traders to deal with for silver and wine, even a few words of the far northern dialect of our bordering tribe, so foreign-sounding to my ears.

Venutius resented it all, even then. He wanted to join in too, but he always got bored and my father hadn't the patience to encourage him. While we were busy in whatever tasks were uppermost, Venutius would eventually slink away, mumbling about how bored he was and how no one wanted to play with him. He wished his younger brother was with him, but Iticus was at home, far away in the Carvetti territory with his mother. Even his father was remote, engaged as he was in his covert affair with my aunt. Tyrius lived with us for most of the first year Venutius was there and Antikia bloomed under the warmth of his attention. She even wore daisy garlands in her hair and the sharp granite glint in her eyes receded.

Venutius threw a terrible tantrum one fateful day. My father and I had returned from a visit to our borders with the Deceangli to the south west. They were a small tribe, pocketed in between us and the Ordovices and I had been learning all about how Brigantia had a policy of peace and protection towards them. My head was still full of all I had seen on our trip that I paid no attention to poor Venutius who was bored and frustrated. When he nagged and pulled on my arm, I pushed him away telling him to go and find something useful to do.

In the afternoon, my mother started to worry as no one had seen Venutius all day. Tyrius returned from a ride, smiling and flushed and had barely dismounted before Metassia hurried to him in case he knew where his son was. Worry turned to panic and as the pale cornflower sky sank into the streaky orange-pink horizon, leaving in its wake rapidly darkening blue, we all began to search, through huts, out in the meadows and fields, up into the woods. Presivin, whose father Binto sat on the council, had three big dogs who could track a scent better than any other. Tyrius found one of Venutius's tunics and let the dogs rub their muzzles into it.

Metassia was crying and I put my arm around her, realising how my mother had come to love Venutius, regarding him as practically her own son. Rather than making me at all envious, the realisation instead reminded me that Venutius was in fact family, and also how serious the consequences would be if we didn't find him well and unhurt. I imagined him lying on the ground, injured from a fall or an accident and a flash of pain struck through my chest, the same flavour of pain as I might have if I pictured my mother or father injured – a pain I had felt once before, when my sister died, though I kept my mind firmly barred to that. Venutius was small and annoying but he was like a brother to me and I couldn't stand the thought of him in distress. I wanted to search but instead Mandulay came and thrust her big arms round us, guiding my mother and I inside where we waited by the heat of the fire for news.

In the distance, the yaps and barks from the dogs mingled with the hoots of the night birds, the owls and the loons. The howl of a wolf broke into the night, threatening and taunting us. I arranged wood on the fire to keep my hands busy. Mandulay kept saying everything would be fine and he would turn up sooner or later, but her reassurances were hollow. She had nibbled the nail on one thumb until it bled.

I must have fallen asleep because shouting and cheering outside the roundhouse gave me a jolt and I couldn't think straight about what the commotion meant. Then people entered. My father, patting a boy on the back; Tantoban and his friend, Presivin, the owner of the dogs; Presivin's father, Binto, normally a reclusive man who only attended council meetings when my father absolutely insisted; then finally, Tyrius with Venutius in his arms.

"Venutius," I cried out, "You're alright!"

He gave me a weak and surprised smile. It shamed me that he had not expected me to care. I ran to him and hugged him while his father looked on approvingly.

Later, when all the hugs were done and everyone had downed a drink and had some food, Tyrius began a dramatic recounting of how they had found his son. He described the path they had followed, down the edge of the meadow, dipping in and out of the adjoining woodland. They walked so far that they couldn't believe the dogs had the right scent. The little boy had crossed the stream where it circled out of the forest and down further into the valley. Then he'd trampled on through gorse and heather, following the steady climb of the hillside and out towards where there were no paths or byways.

"And then my boy had become tired," Tyrius boomed, enjoying the drama of the tale, "and he had laid down to sleep, unaware of the danger that stalked him. As he slept, the wolves came upon him."

We all gasped. I looked at Venutius to remind myself that the story did in fact have a happy ending.

"Alone, defenceless, he didn't stand a chance against a pack of hungry wolves, their teeth sharp and bared. But then, as he dreamed, another person came upon the scene. Another young boy, only a little older than my son. The wolves were hungry and their blood was up but the boy had seen my son lying there so vulnerable and would not turn away. He picked up a rock and hurled it at one beast and as another leapt towards him he drew his dagger and ripped open the animal's side. So it was that when we arrived, we found one boy sleepy and shocked and another boy bloodstained, grazed and comforting him."

The boy who had returned with my father looked embarrassed and unsure, but Kesaven clapped him on the back again and we all applauded and cheered.

"I was just passing that way, collecting plants and fruit for my grandfather," mumbled the boy. It didn't occur to me until many years later that he was out terribly late for such a chore. Times must have been hard in his family home for him to have been scavenging the countryside in the late evening for such meagre pickings.

"What's his name?" someone asked.

The boy mumbled again, something I didn't catch.

"From now on, you can call yourself Vellocatus," Tyrius shouted, inspired by ale and the appreciation of his addled audience, "for you truly were better in battle than any could have imagined looking at you!"

More amused cheers followed but I didn't join in. I had

noticed how small and tired Venutius looked and how the corner of his mouth had turned downwards in misery when his father spoke.

SUMMER AD38

"Stop throwing grass at me."

"Stop being so boring then." Venutius hopped around me as we sunbathed in the meadow, taking advantage of the unusually warm April sun. Sheep that had crept closer to us sprang back away as Venutius pranced about.

"Let's go practice with our bows!" he yelled.

"Not now," Vellocatus groaned. He was eighteen years old, just one year older than me, with large hazel eyes that sat wide apart and dark gold stubble on his chin and upper lip the same colour as his hair which was shoulder length and wild.

"Or we could get the horses, go for a ride?"

Not much had changed since the day Venutius went off by himself. He still loved to play and always wanted company. Perhaps because he feared others would be disappointed in him, he was permanently cheerful and active as if to stave off their displeasure. Vellocatus and he had become good friends, spending all their time together, but now that Vellocatus was a man, pretending to be a child for Venutius's sake wore him down.

"Mother has some milk in the cold pit," I said, "run and get it will you?" Venutius sighed, but he ran off anyway and I grinned at Vellocatus. "Maybe that will wear him out a bit."

"He'll be back in no time, wanting to do something else," Venutius smiled. His mild irritation was good-natured. He owed a great deal to Venutius for it was in his friendship that Vellocatus had secured his own future. In reward for fighting off the hungry wolves, Tyrius had appointed Vellocatus as a full-time companion to his son, a position which, in the future, when Venutius was married, would bestow even more status since Venutius would rule at my side.

"Do you think we're cruel to him?" I asked.

"No, not really, we're just older." Vellocatus sat up. Seeds from the tall grass clung to the thin woollen tunic he wore. His dark blonde hair was ruffled at the back. He sat cross-legged, watching for Venutius to reappear. When the boy was out of sight he never relaxed.

"I hope he grows up before I have to marry him," I said. I was thinking aloud, but I was probing too, seeing if Vellocatus would react. He didn't. It was more than his life was worth.

"I'd better go and find him," he said, getting up and stretching his golden-brown arms. I watched him walk down the meadow, but he never looked around.

Since the day Tyrius and my father had brought Vellocatus back to our home, he had lived amongst us. Venutius was very sensitive about the incident which brought them together and after a few days, nothing more was ever really mentioned of it. If Venutius flinched a little when he heard a wolf howl in the evening, then we tactfully distracted him and hoped he would grow out of his fear. I spent more time with him, and the three of us became a happy little trio, exploring in the woods, hunting and playing together, at least on those days when I wasn't following my father around like a shadow. Vellocatus was a quiet boy with a serious attitude and he was very grateful to us all in those early days for taking him in and offering him such an exciting future. His grandparents were happy to see the good fortune he had encountered, though it must have pained them to let him go. Vellocatus had lived with them since his parents, of whom he had only the vaguest memories, had died. He visited them when he could and took food and gifts. Tyrius had provided the couple with a servant to take care of all the work Vellocatus would otherwise have done so they were well-cared for, but I knew Vellocatus worried about them.

"Grandma aches when it's cold," he fretted, during the first winter he lived with us.

"Old people always ache," shrugged Venutius. "It's just what happens when you get old."

"I hope that girl makes them a good fire, though. One that lasts all through the night and keeps them warm. I used to get up and check on it. I hope she does too."

I was touched by this boy my own age who was so used to putting other people's needs before his own. It was not something I ever had to do, except perhaps for Venutius, in whom I was investing more time and attention than before.

"Would you like to take her some rubbing ointment when you visit?" I asked him. "Mandulay always makes lots because she uses it herself. I'm sure she could spare some."

"Oh no, it doesn't matter," he said, still hesitant about taking anything from us, but I went and got him some anyway and Mandulay told him how it should be used so he could explain to his grandma when he saw her next. He thanked us very properly but there was a flush along his high cheekbones and when he smiled at me after that, it was with a more trusting warmth because I had shown interest in the people he loved.

My mother also liked him. She used to say, "Now where are my two boys?" when food was ready and Venutius and Vellocatus were still out roaming the woods and fields. Then they would arrive all dirty and worn out and she'd tut over the state of them, just like a mother with her troublesome sons. She fussed over them and made much of their achievements but, with me, she was always subtly different. She didn't have to talk so much with me, because we knew each other's thoughts so well. She would brush a hand over my shoulder softly or throw me a certain look and I would be reminded of the familial bond we shared that superseded any of the affection she showed to them. It stopped me from being at all jealous of the way in which Venutius and Vellocatus had inserted themselves into our family.

I think my mother welcomed the experience of having boys to care for, since she had none of her own and added to that she felt very responsible for my betrothed – a pressure that had only increased after Venutius's close encounter with the wolves. My father used to tell her not to bother so much about them - especially not to run around after Vellocatus since he was to all intents and purposes a servant - and that boys were supposed to be dirty, troublesome and covered in bruises, but she discharged her duties towards them with genuine loving care. Sometimes she admonished me about my behaviour with them.

"Cartimandua, you mustn't go leading those boys astray," she would say, tucking her straw-coloured hair behind her ears anxiously, "They wouldn't take such risks without you there to encourage them."

"They do what they want. I have nothing to do with it," I would shrug.

"They'd do anything for you. Don't take advantage of it," she would insist, but that only made me more curious to establish just how much control I really did have over them. Like most mixed-sex groups of children, the undercurrents of complicated emotions were starting to swell beneath the surface as we dipped our toes into early adulthood. When we were out hunting one time, and Vellocatus brought down his first deer, he threw himself into a manly embrace with Venutius and then slung an arm around me to give me a squeeze. The edge of his jaw, warm with the beginnings of a soft beard, brushed against my cheek. I could feel the impression on my skin even after he quickly released me and the sensation returned to me in several dreams afterwards. After that time, I started to notice how little Vellocatus and I touched in any way and that most often Venutius was between us, throwing his arm companionably around me or sitting close up to me. I loved him very much and was affectionate with him but for a time I craved the fuzzy, dizzy feeling I'd had when Vellocatus brushed against me. I shut myself off from that yearning and told myself that one day, I would feel that way about Venutius, if he ever grew up.

"Mandulay? Where are you, woman? Mandulay! Get in here now!" The urgent shouting woke me from a deep sleep and I rolled over on my hide-covered straw bed, pulling back the leather drape that separated my sleeping area from the main body of the roundhouse. Footsteps came rushing past, a stack of bowls clattered over in the dark. I got up and moved towards the just-visible embers of the fire to stoke them up. I was still half asleep and acting on instinct but then my father's voice, shrill and unusual with fear brought me up sharply.

"You've got to do something, give her something."

"I'll go and... yes, I'll bring a tonic." Mandulay sounded bewildered and scared. I grabbed a torch from its holster on a supporting pole and got it lit in the embers.

"What's going on?" I said, taking the torch to them. They were at my parent's area, a large section at the back. I looked from Mandulay's ghost-like face to my father who was gazing helplessly down at the bed.

My mother lay there straining for breath and twitching like a wounded rabbit. One of her hands was clenched into a white fist and a thin line of saliva trickled down the side of her chin. I thrust the torch to Mandulay and knelt down, wiping my mother's face with my sleeve. She gazed back at me, almost curiously, and as I took the unclenched hand, she squeezed mine softly.

"She's going," I said, not taking my eyes from hers. She squeezed her fingers on mine again and I kissed her cheek and stroked her hair then moved sideways to let my father be near her. He froze for a moment, then slumped down next to her, taking in a deep, ragged breath. I touched his arm, prompting him to take her hand as I had done. It's a curious thing that when people die we hold their hands, though often in life, once we are past childhood, we rarely hold hands with anyone.

We sat for only a short while, but it felt like a whole season had passed. My father whispered to her and I thought of all the things I should have said to her, regretted horribly that I had not, then trusted that being my mother she knew all those things anyway. My thoughts skittered around like sunbeams on ice and I had to drag my mind back to the dark, warm place where my mother was dying. It felt unreal, as if I had not woken up at all, but stayed in a sad, slow dream. The light, unsteady gasps of her breath punctuated the air, like a higher pitched harmony to the low, misery-stricken heave of my father's respiration. Then, finally, she went quiet and our home filled with the silence of death.

When we laid her body out two days later, many people came to say goodbye. Some of them approached me, touching my shoulder or trying to take my hands, telling me how they knew my mother, what she was to them. I don't remember their faces or their words. When they reached out to me, I smiled and nodded, stepping back, holding myself erect and aloof. I'm sure some of them thought I was cold, heartless even, but I couldn't be any other way.

Immediately after the life had passed from her body, my father had turned to me with his arms outstretched, but I fled outside in a stride breaking into a run, all the way up the meadow and into the dark, eerie woods, where the night birds tried their best to scare me but couldn't break through my grief. A long time afterwards, I knew that I had left my father alone in his grief – that he had reached out not for my sake, but for his own. I think after I had gone, Venutius awoke and went to my father for when I came back a long time later, the two were arm in arm around the fire.

Poor Venutius took it very hard. Not having his own mother near, he had relied heavily on my mother to care for him and when my father and I were busy together or away travelling, it was with my mother that he had spent a lot of his time. Vellocatus tried to console him but Venutius was ashamed to show his older friend the distress he was in. For perhaps the first time I felt a proper kinship with the boy, a bond that excluded all others as we sat together and cried or recalled memories of Metassia.

Although I was in a daze on the day we sent my mother to her goddess, I do remember one visitor very clearly. She arrived on a black horse with gold-coloured brocade, a party of riders following her. Tyrius was at her side and the two were close, conspiratorial even. He helped his wife dismount though she looked like she needed no help and he kept his arm about her as they walked towards us. Risha greeted me, not warmly, but appropriately. Her ash-brown hair was pinned up with a toothed comb made of some kind of bone and it revealed a plump face with greyish eyes that were far apart, separated by a long slim nose. Her eyebrows sat high on her forehead, giving her a wry expression.

In the days after she arrived, I watched her with Tyrius, taking his arm, preparing his food, hurrying him to bed. He was always respectful towards her, but more than that, he was affectionate. He didn't have the same passion in his eyes as when he looked at Antikia, but with Risha, although he appeared bound to her like a dog to its owner, he also had the same loyal attachment. He had to introduce his wife to Antikia. She told me about it afterwards.

"He called me the sister of Kesaven, couldn't even say my name and then she put her fat hand on my shoulder and said she hoped I would be a strong support to our chief in these difficult times. As if she was closer to Kesaven than I!" Antikia was fuming - flecks of spit flew from her lips as she spoke. "So I stayed very calm and said that myself and the whole tribal council were there to support him. And then she said I seemed a very loyal little sister. Little! And Tyrius just stood there mute!"

"Perhaps it wasn't an insult?" I ventured.

"That woman knows what she is doing. I've seen her doing it to everyone she meets, trying to put them in their place, assert her authority over them. I just never expected Tyrius to stand by and let her talk down to me like that."

Antikia was desperately hurt. I had no words of comfort ready for her as I'd had no idea she was so serious about her relationship with the Carvettii leader. Rolling around in the woods was one thing, but did she really expect him to put her before his wife? Yet it appeared that although Tyrius was quite coarse and simple in his daily life, he had been careful and cunning in his conversations with Antikia, implying that one day they would properly be together. How men can scheme when copulation relies on it! So it was a terrible blow for her to realise that had all been lies. I understand that now, but I must admit that at the time, I was a little impatient. My aunt was sister to the chief of the largest tribe in the land. Risha may have been an imposing woman back then, but she was wife to a man who was subservient to our whole family. I was a little annoyed that Antikia had not immediately put the woman back in her place. I had no experience of a love affair and did not appreciate how hurt Antikia was.

Tyrius was so busy attending to his wife that he barely noticed Antikia's reaction, an oversight that would be to his great cost later on. While she moped about, keeping away from everyone and barely raising a smile, he played intermediary between Risha and my family and council, whom he had grown close to in his time living with us. When he did see Antikia, or attempted to talk to her, he assumed her low mood was due to the loss of her sister-by-marriage, as did many others. We were all depressed and preoccupied, after all.

My father was walking about like a wounded animal, wary and pained, shunning help from anyone. Mandulay keened in the fields, the sing-song of her moans carrying in the wind. But underneath the deference and the mourning of the wider family and council was an unmistakeable sense of impatience. In my youth, our land and its people seemed gentle and loving to me. But growing up and working so closely with my father I had started to realise what a harsh place we lived in. This view was only reinforced by the contact I'd had with neighbouring tribes. In contrast, we lived far more isolated lives. While others, particularly the southern tribes whom I'd learned of but not yet encountered, lived in clusters, roundhouses side by side, we lived separately. Families kept themselves to themselves – even we lived in a very limited arrangement, with just a few other roundhouses nearby that contained close family and then some a little further away that constituted the closest thing we had to a village. The moors, the crags, the steep valleys and high hills were hard places to scratch a living and the people were similarly hardened. They could understand mourning the loss of a wife and mother, but they expected their leader to rise up and get on with his job.

And in my opinion they were right. I described earlier how I had set myself the task of understanding how my father inspired loyalty and respect in his tribe despite his capacity for cruelty and indifference. Well, I had learned this: that he did it by always moving us forwards. People knew him as a man who worked, who travelled, who made it his business to keep on top of what was happening in his territory. He negotiated when trade disputes flared up, stamped down hard on boundary incursions, encouraged reputable merchants and had miscreants manacled or put to death. His own father's awesome reputation as the man who made Brigantia by allying scores of smaller clans did help, but truthfully our tribe prospered because Kesaven never stood still. We might not have the luxuries that the southern tribes depended upon, but unlike many of them we were not at war with our neighbours and we maintained our grip on a huge amount of land.

I was seventeen, old enough to see all this clearly; young and selfish enough to let the immense tide of grief at my mother's passing wash over me. While my father was looking to the past and Antikia was caught up in her broken romance, I was looking to the future and my tribal inheritance. I rose from my sadness, just as I believed my mother would have wanted me to and grasped hold of power before anyone could object.

My first move was to call a council meeting. Only my father ever did this. I did it by speaking to just a handful of people, ensuring that they would pass on the call. I was lucky enough to have a good reason. A Parisi trader carrying swords and foodstuffs in from the eastern shore had seen a party of six armed Belgovae warriors just inside our borders. He had changed direction and travelled to our stronghold to give us this information rather than continuing north. Probably he did this to ingratiate himself with our family since traders usually liked to be suppliers to the chieftain or possibly he acted because it was in the interests of the Parisi to keep a strong Brigantian presence between themselves and the dark northerners. My father had not reacted to the news, other than to murmur that he'd look into it. But he'd forgotten all about it, lost in his misery as he was.

To me, it sounded like the Belgovae were gathering information since there were no reports of attacks. They were probably just watching their backs like we all had to if we wanted to keep our territory secure, but their warriors had been on our land covertly and I knew that ordinarily this was something my father would investigate. Fate had handed me the perfect reason to take the reins and I did so without hesitation.

I gave the summons then went to my father.

"I've called a council meeting," I said. There was no point beating around the bush. "It's about the Belgovae. You said we'd look into it."

He frowned at me for a moment.

"Yes, I did say that," he pondered. "You called a meeting?"

I didn't answer, just looked him straight in the eye with my head up and my arms by my sides, shoulders straight. If I believed

I had done the right thing, he would too. Or so I hoped.

"Fine, make sure we have enough food prepared." He was still frowning.

"I'll tell Mandulay," I said, determined not to be pushed into my mother's role of supervising the cooking. But then Kesaven surprised me.

"You'll do the talking. I'm not up to it. Speak to your aunt first and tell her to get that idiot man out of her head before the meet. If she wastes any more time on him, I'll flog the silly bitch."

I flinched both at his words and at the fact that he knew about Antikia and Tyrius. I knew she would be mortified but I was grimly pleased that I had this message to pass on. It would make clear to her exactly what the new hierarchy was.

"Get Tantoban to round up some muscle, you'll want to listen to what everyone says then order a band of men up there to check the lay of the land."

"I'll take them up there myself," I said.

He nodded. Finally his frown turned into the start of a smile and he gripped my shoulder.

"Don't mess this up," he said, "because everyone will be watching how you do."

They all expected that my father would take over. As they came in and sat down they were brief in their greetings, unsure whether to speak to my father or to me first. Mandulay hovered awkwardly. She had done her job of getting some food prepared and it seemed to have brought her almost back to her normal self. But she did not approve of what I was doing. In her eyes, I was still a child, even though I was seventeen.

I had been careful with my appearance. My brown hair, usually long and loose or tied in a simple tail, was scraped back at the sides and held in place with two of my mother's combs, the sharp teeth biting into my scalp. I wore one of my own dresses but I also wore an elaborate leather tunic over the top, one of my mother's from years ago that no one would remember, and two of her gold armlets, which they would. The tunic laced together at the front and the material was old and tough. My face was gaunt anyway but I added a little of the dark bluish powder my mother sometimes used, to make my cheekbones harsher, and I put a line of black soot powder on my eyes

As we sat there, Venutius watched me with some curiosity. He was old enough to understand the implications of what I was doing, but there was still a gulf between us in terms of maturity. I asked him to attend the meeting, which surprised him as my father had never had him present at one before. But rather than being delighted he was only vaguely interested. I remembered how I had secretly watched my first council meeting at half the age Venutius now was, standing outside the big roundhouse until my fingers turned blue with cold. I couldn't imagine Venutius ever doing that. He couldn't stand still for long enough, but more than that, he wasn't passionate about tribal matters. Perhaps it was because he didn't consider the Brigantes to be his tribe, even though his native Carvettii were under our rule, or perhaps it was because we hadn't included him enough. I was hoping it was the latter, which was why I invited him to the meeting. Vellocatus stayed outside somewhere. He had given me a cursory nod earlier but a shadow had passed over his face when he saw me and my stark attire. I felt a little hurt but I couldn't allow it to dent me. I was on my own, I had to accept that.

I couldn't even be sure that Antikia would support me. I had gone to her the day before, as my father asked me to. She was twisting some scrappy coppiced twigs, trying to make a basket.

"I've called a meeting," I said.

"So I heard. Kesaven will not be happy about that." She had a petulant little expression, her mouth set in a bitter line.

"I don't think you are in a position to tell me what Kesaven thinks," I replied "since you are too busy pining over Tyrius."

"I'm mourning your mother! Or had you forgotten?"

"Don't bother lying. We've all mourned for Metassia but now it's time to move on. Your problem is not grief, it's jealousy and wounded pride. Antikia, not many people know, but those who do are growing very displeased with the way you are behaving."

"The way I'm behaving? Get away from me, child, this is none of your concern."

"Oh I'll leave you alone," I said, careful not to raise my voice into a shout, "I'm too busy with council matters to worry about your hurt feelings. But if you keep this up, Kesaven has threatened to have you flogged back to your senses."

Her face turned pale.

"He wouldn't dare!"

"I don't know what he'd do. I don't care. I just need you back to your old self. You're supposed to be one of my main advisers, especially now Kesaven has authorised me to take control. Stay away from Tyrius and make sure you're at the meeting."

I walked away without another word, wanting the effect of what I'd said to sink in, wanting to be sure she understood I was taking my place as her leader. Even if she did think I was a foolish child, and looking back I suppose I was, she had to accept that I was going to be leader of our tribe. It appeared she had bowed to this, because she did arrive for the meeting. She was indifferent and aloof – to most of the people there she seemed, in fact, to be her normal self. She had raised her defences at last. I just hoped I wasn't going to be permanently shut outside them.

I couldn't think about that. Instead I had to focus on making the council see that I was competent enough to be in charge. I clapped my hands together and shouted above the noise of their conversations. They quietened down and watched me.

"This has been a difficult time for us. My mother is gone and we miss her very much. But the time for mourning is over. News has arrived of a threat to our northern border. Some of you may be aware of this."

There was a general muttering as those who were not aware grumbled to their neighbours and tried to find out more. Tantoban caught my eye and I gave him a tiny nod.

"Six Belgovae warriors have been sighted on our land by a trader from the East coast. The trader is a reputable man; we don't think he is mistaken." Tantoban looked around as he spoke.

"How far in were they?" asked Baranak, my father's cousin.

"The trader was passing close to the border. They were no more than a half-day's walk into our land," Tantoban answered.

"Far enough!" Baranak's son, Davit, called out and there was murmured agreement.

"If the Belgovae meant real harm, they'd have brought a lot more than six fighters and we'd have heard of attacks by now." That was Gorlensa, my great aunt, younger sister to my father's mother. Her hair was thin and silvery-grey around her wrinkled oval face.

"If they've murdered whole families, there would be no one to pass on the news to us!" Davit said, eager for a fight and almost gleeful at the possibility that blood had already been shed.

"Gorlensa is right, six fighters do not represent a real threat," I said, "However, these people have been on our land, uninvited and almost undetected. We need to make sure trouble is not brewing up there in the north. Tyrius, how well do you know the Belgovae?"

"We've had a few skirmishes, but mostly it's been the Novantae that we've encountered. The Tectoverdi could tell you more."

The Tectoverdi, like the Carvettii, were part of the Brigantes, but were a distinct group. Wherever our land met that of another large tribe, a sub-group had naturally developed, probably because these people on the borders had to fend for themselves, fighting off attacks and maintaining their ground. In the unification of Brigantia under my grandfather, these small tribes had become our front line and my family had understood for

45

generations that it was better to harness groups like the Carvettii and the Tectoverdi than to neglect them and see our borders begin to roll towards us as these groups became either hostile or defeated. Brigantia contained many other clans and tribes – the Gabrantovices on the east coast, the Setantii in the south west and the Latenses in the central south where my own mother was from, for example – but the northern fringes were where we saw the most serious incursion problems and therefore, where we had to provide the most assistance.

Tyrius was still sat forward, clearly frustrated that he could not be of more assistance in answering me. I decided then that I would make sure he came north with me – in that way I would kill two birds with one stone, since he was a fine fighter for one and it would also mean he was kept away from my aunt.

"We should travel north and speak with the Tectoverdi then," said Tantoban, looking at me and my father.

"Kesaven, I'll go with you," piped up Davit, his round, bearded face sincere and excited. He was just two years older than me though a skilled killer already. A hush fell. Up to that point, people had been addressing me, quick to see how Kesaven had stayed silent, his chin resting thoughtfully in his hand. The balance of power had shifted but Davit in his eagerness had not noticed. I paused, wanting to let my father reply since that was the courteous thing to do, but I dreaded in that moment that he would change his mind and decide suddenly that he did want to lead the party north after all.

"I won't be going. Cartimandua is in charge. I leave this expedition in her capable hands." He spoke quietly but clearly, and something in the lilt of his voice told me he was pleased with the way I had handled everything. I turned my attention back to the council, but avoided addressing Davit directly.

"I'll lead a party north tomorrow, at dawn. We'll travel light and I'm taking no more than ten people. We're checking on our borders but we don't expect to meet serious hostility and neither do we intend to start a war." Gorlensa nodded in approval and most of the others looked satisfied.

We discussed some other, smaller matters before the meeting broke up. Davit escaped as soon as he could looking embarrassed and I was just talking with Tantoban, confirming who we were taking with us when a sharp set of knuckles hit me on the arm. I wheeled round, ready to fetch a clout to Venutius who was the only person who ever dared hit me like that, but came face to face with Antikia.

"I'd like to come with you," she said, then added "if that's all right?" There was a trace of a smile on her face.

"I want you with me." I replied immediately, then remembered I had planned to take Tyrius especially to keep him from my aunt. I turned to see that Tantoban had already left my side to speak with him. Too late. I couldn't risk offending either of them by changing my mind. Perhaps it would not be such a bad thing anyway - Antikia would find a way of being near to Tyrius sooner or later, since we were as good as family.

Venutius was skulking around outside when I finally emerged from the roundhouse.

"Ooh, let me see your capable hands," he sniggered good-naturedly, and I aimed a punch to his head which he ducked easily.

"Can I come?" he said, taking me completely off guard. His face still bore a cheeky grin, but underneath the bravado I saw how vulnerable he was.

"Not this time. You need to stay with your mother and Iticus. It's bad enough I'm taking your father away when she sees so little of him. I can't take you as well."

He nodded and kicked at the ground.

"Iticus must be enjoying spending so much time with you. It's not often you two get any time together."

"Yes, he's good fun now he's grown a bit. Have you seen how good he is at climbing trees? He's faster than I was at his age.

And I want to teach him how to use a spear properly because he hasn't really practised with one yet." Venutius's face lit up as he talked, the trip north momentarily forgotten.

Iticus was only a little younger than him, but he worshipped the older boy and when I watched them mucking around together, I saw a different side to Venutius. As Iticus looked up to him and showed his obvious respect, Venutius in turn played up to the admiration and became far more mature. In the few weeks they'd had together, the two of them had played together most days and it had done them both good. I wondered how hard it would be for them when Iticus and Risha had to leave.

We followed the lines of the rivers, which were low since it was the end of a hot, dry summer. The land we passed through was beautiful; the purple heather swathed the hills and moors and the dry ground was easy for both travelling and making camp on. Tantoban was in good spirits and sometimes would sing loudly, making us all join in. Antikia was smiling and relaxed too, and Tyrius, who had never seemed to notice anything was wrong with her, was his usual easy-going self. When we made camp on the first night, we roasted strips of boar meat over the fire. Mandulay had packed them for us, along with a supply of hard little spelt flour cakes, and some salted beef. Fistoc, a small, muscular man with dark brown eyes and a hard mouth, told us all a story about the Druids and how they slaughtered children and animals on their sacrifice stones. I suspected it was partly made up, since very few people knew exactly what went on over on the dark isle of Mona. There were rules about who could enter their oak-covered island and what reasons they must have to do so. The Druids were free to travel across territories as they liked, but rarely did so, preferring to remain in their power base from where they cast their magic and passed on their learning through the generations. You could say the Druids were lucky to be born into such power, for they were respected as priests of knowledge and supernatural ability, or you could say they were fated to live a very restricted and hard life, full of personal sacrifice and important work. Whatever we thought of them, the Druids were the hard and vicious heart of all the tribes and if there was nothing else that the disparate people of our lands could agree on, we could at least agree that the Druids held a special power over all of us.

The night was warm and we drifted off to sleep near the fire with the sound of the river flowing nearby. I woke in the early hours while it was still dark, the crescent moon casting only a tiny amount of light. My back was aching even though I had a pile of furs to sleep on and I rolled over to get more comfortable. On the periphery of the glow cast by the fire's dying flames, I made out two figures curled together. That was not what I'd had in mind when I wanted my aunt to find a way to get on with Tyrius. I laid there watching them, wrapped around each other in sleep, and felt lonely. I was seventeen and I had never had that kind of closeness with a man. Instead, my years of turning into a woman had been spent waiting for Venutius to grow up as well. Added to the isolation I felt now my mother had gone and my father had turned inwards, it seemed so unfair. I rolled over again with a sigh that was almost a sob, tetchy and resentful.

"Are you alright?" The voice was a whisper, soft and deep. I looked over to Tantoban who was raised up on one arm, concern scored across his forehead.

"I can't sleep," I whispered back.

"Are you cold?" he asked, pushing some more kindling and branches into the fire and moving closer. He took his own blanket and threw it over me.

"You'll be cold now!"

He shrugged and laid back down, one bare shoulder catching the glow of light from the fire, the arm he was leaning on sinewy with muscle. He was in his thirties, perhaps even older, with a shaven head save for a thin warrior plait at the back; a man well accomplished in violence, who my father had always kept close but whom I had hardly paid attention to while growing up. He had the lines of age on his face, deep-set eyes that sparkled yellow-brown like tree resin and a lean body only just starting to sag with the rigours of the hard life he had lived. I glanced around. Everyone was sleeping, no one had moved from when I had first awoken. I reached my hand out to Tantoban and he came to me warily, laying down on my bed of furs while I pulled the blankets over him. He wrapped an arm around me, pulling me close in to him and the warmth of his honest body pressed up against mine, even though we were almost fully clothed, set a spark loose in me, made me realise that this closeness to a man was what I needed. He had closed his eyes, content to warm me with his hug. I stroked his face and they flicked open again.

"Are you really sure? I know that you're grieving, is that what this is about?" He asked and to my surprise I found that he had begun to shake and that his heart was beating hard enough in his chest for me to feel it against my cheek.

"It doesn't matter why, it's an order," I whispered, the new-found power of recent days going to my head, "and it's a safe time of the moon for me."

He loosened his own clothes and mine. I tried not to make a sound, pressing my mouth into the roughness of his neck and shoulder to quiet my breathing as his warm stomach pressed down onto my own and my breasts cushioned his hard chest. I thought of Venutius once, but pushed his face from my mind. He couldn't help being younger than me just as I couldn't help being older than him and having needs he couldn't yet fulfil.

Afterwards, Tantoban fell asleep at my side and I stroked his chest until the dark sky began to glow. Then I kissed him awake and he held me very tightly for a moment before returning to the patch of ground where he had first gone to sleep.

The Tectoverdi had heard we were on our way and they

were hospitable, at least as much as they ever were. They had been patrolling the border themselves since the sighting of the Belgovae but weren't worried since nothing further had happened. In the past, the Belgovae raiders had taken livestock, goods and, worst of all, people, but the raids had been less since the Tectoverdi became Brigantian under my grandfather's leadership. The Belgovae were more wary now of inflaming the large confederacy to their south. Even so with rumours circulating already about my father's grief-stricken state, the Tectoverdi didn't want their northern neighbours to get any ideas about about us being vulnerable or disorganised. I said we would stay for at least a few nights to show our presence and patrol along the borderline in clear sight.

Their council sympathised about the loss of my mother and asked about Kesaven.

"He'd be here himself but our settlement is packed full of visitors mourning my mother so he felt he should stay. You know my father though, he carries on with life, no matter what. His tribe comes first." I stuck to those sorts of blandishments whenever anyone asked about him and hoped that he was holding himself together at home.

The two days passed quickly and without much occurrence, apart from some useful relationship building with the main families living on the border. I took the opportunity to travel around several little settlements close by, learning the names of the people there. I met a renowned family of warriors, the eldest of whom remembered my grandfather and spoke a little of how he had seen the latter fighting and been very impressed. Unfortunately, he had little more to add, not being quite in his right mind any longer, but the rest of his family came out with us patrolling the borders. The grand-daughter, a woman a little older than me named Patissa with dark, slicked back hair and a pointed face, chatted with me while we rode, filling me in on some of the local politics, explaining the lay of the land and

51

giving me an overview of the tracks and pathways that bisected Tectoverdian territory.

The return trip was damp. The rains had started and we were a more subdued bunch. One or two were disappointed there had been no real action. Antikia and Tyrius were still sleeping together and I wondered at what point Tyrius had decided to throw caution to the wind, since he had been careful previously to keep their activities secret. I pulled Antikia to one side as we took a break from riding.

"I thought you and Tyrius were over," I said, balancing my concern for her and my slight irritation that she was caught up in him once more.

"We are over," she replied. "I loved him once, but not any more."

"So what are you doing?" I hissed.

"It might be useful to keep him on side. Haven't you studied Risha and the way she is? That woman thinks her family will rule. If she had her way, Venutius would take full control of Brigantia. She'll poison Tyrius until he finds a way to make that happen. On his own, he's not such a threat. Tyrius is loyal," She gave a bitter laugh, "to his chief, at least. But the rest of his family are dangerous. I'm doing this for you." She added.

I rolled my top lip between my teeth and sighed uneasily.

"Well, it does make sense. But Antikia, I don't want you to have to do this."

"Oh, it's no real hardship," she laughed. "I can't say I don't enjoy it. Don't worry, I have him under control. He won't hurt me again."

When we arrived home, Venutius greeted us, with his mother behind him. He took my hand as I dismounted and then pulled me into a clumsy embrace. I returned it, surprised, and tried not to feel Tantoban's eyes on my back. For a terrible moment it struck me how reckless I had been, and with Tyrius sleeping just footsteps away. It took all my effort not to blush. Risha stood like a black monolith with her usual prim smile and nodded to me. I nodded back, aware with a jolt that something had changed. Over near the roundhouse, breaking up wood for the fire, I could see Vellocatus. His face looked odd. As he turned to glance at me, I saw that one eye and cheek were blackened and swollen and a cut ran through his eyebrow. Risha followed my gaze then looked back to me with a broader smile that showed teeth, the pupils of her eyes like tiny, poisonous seeds as she placed a hand on her son's shoulder. I felt dizzy, like I had been taken into the woods I knew so well and spun around until I did not recognise the way back. His family are dangerous, I remembered.

AUTUMN AD40

Though none of us us were aware of it, time was steadily crunching on towards a whole new chapter in our lives. Before long, trouble would arrive to dwarf anything I had dealt with so far. But I wasn't looking to the future. I was trying to find a way to stall my father.

Kesaven had gradually pulled himself together following my mother's death, though he was a darker man, more prone to negative thoughts and aggressive action. Fortunately he had surrendered most of his authority to me, so I was leader, if not yet in name. No one saw me as a child any more, not even Mandulay who had smacked me when I was naughty and put me to bed more nights than I could remember. But given my age and status, my father saw no reason why I should postpone my joining with Venutius any longer. The problem was that I couldn't see an obvious reason either. I just felt uncomfortable about making the relationship official.

Venutius had grown up a great deal in the last two years and become more involved in tribal politics. He was taller than me now, by almost a head, and he had grown a beard and had parts of his hair plaited into warrior threads. The gesture wasn't just for show – Venutius had personally killed three men. One was a thief who had been attacking our traders as they crossed the high hills. The other two were part of a mob from the Novantae who had been involved in skirmishes with the Carvettii. His demeanour was unsettling – he could be sunny and energetic, just as he was as a child, but when he became angry, it was like a storm-cloud had settled on him and he thrashed out at whoever was closest. Vellocatus still attended him everywhere but the relationship between the pair had changed subtly. I knew that was Risha's doing.

When I had returned that summer day two years ago to see Vellocatus with his bruised face, I wondered for a while whether Risha herself had hit him for some reason. But Mandulay explained to me in dramatic whispers that Venutius had confronted Vellocatus himself.

"Called him arrogant and treacherous!" she said, "and then he hit him, a nasty little punch straight to the eye, that took his friend straight to the ground. Vellocatus, he never moved, just took it and wouldn't hit back, even when Venutius kicked him twice more."

"But why would Venutius say those things?" I asked, in sadness.

"He said Vellocatus thought he was the better man, just because he beat off those wolves. He said Vellocatus ought to remember his place and to stop behaving as if he were as important as him or you." Mandulay had screwed up her face as she strove to remember the words. "And his mother said..."

"Risha was there?"

"Oh yes, and she said Vellocatus had to promise absolutely to serve Venutius and be completely loyal to him if he wanted to keep his position."

The fury bubbled up inside me and I did my best to swallow it back down. Vellocatus had been the most faithful companion and friend that Venutius could have had and Risha had destroyed that. I couldn't understand why she had made Venutius treat his friend in that way, what threat she envisaged from a boy who only ever tried to protect her son. I remembered how he walked away from me that day in the sun, knowing that to become any closer to me would hurt Venutius.

"What are you going to do?" Mandulay had asked.

"Nothing."

"But it was so unfair, that poor boy-'

"-is a servant," I finished for her, "and no matter what I do, I can't undo the damage to their friendship. This is Venutius's mess. Let him deal with it."

I never mentioned it to Venutius. I suppose that was because I felt slightly guilty about what had happened with Tantoban and I didn't want to undermine him on anything. He wanted to spend more time with me than previously and gradually I found that wherever I went, Venutius would be there too. I didn't mind – after all, it was what had always been intended, that he should be at my side. I started to see him less as a younger brother and more as an equal, sharing my thoughts with him and even asking his opinion, which always made him happy.

In fact, a strong bond had grown between us and people sometimes treated us as a proper couple. When my father repeatedly asked why we couldn't just get the ritual out of the way, I was evasive. Antikia thought she understood. She believed I was worried about a battle for power and wanted to keep the upper hand by not marrying Venutius. Her reasoning was probably sound – had I been a little bit more tactical perhaps I would have felt that way. But it was nothing to do with power or tactics. I simply couldn't imagine bedding down with Venutius. I felt love towards him, but it was the type of love that comes from growing up around someone, a familiarity and level of intimacy that has nothing at all to do with passion. So I ducked my father's increasingly frequent questions and avoided discussing the matter with anyone. Venutius wasn't pressing me about it and I suspected maybe he felt the same as I did.

Something always happens to bring matters to a head, at least that's what I've learned over the years, and this marriage business was no different. Some of our Brigantians from the south came riding in on a crisp day, golden leaves crunching under their horses' nervous hooves.

"Cartimandua?" called one, dismounting as he did so and I came closer to the stranger. There were still so many of my own people that I didn't know, ours being such a large tribe, but they all seemed to know me now. My father joined me, striding out from the roundhouse where he had been resting.

"Have you news?" I asked, taking the man by the opposite arm in greeting.

"Important news, yes. Cunobelinus is afflicted. They say a demon took hold of his body and shook the sense right from him. Didn't kill him, oh no, left him alive and useless. One side of his body doesn't work at all, they say! And he can't speak."

"Cunobelinus is incapacitated? Who has taken control?"

"It's a messy situation. Togodumnus and Caratacus have moved as fast as arrows. They've taken Cantium already and Adminius is on the run."

"They'll be kept busy for a while with their own affairs," I said, turning to my father, "but this is like bloodthirsty dogs being set loose."

"It was bound to happen at some point," said my father, "Cunobelinus is an old man now, the sons had to rule one day."

We got some jugs of ale and sat out on logs in the weak afternoon sunshine to talk to our visitors. The southern tribes were a source of concern and gossip to our tribe. Sometimes it was hard to keep up with what our distant neighbours were doing, especially as most of our news came second-hand through Corieltauvi territory. Cunobelinus, the sun hound, had ruled the Catuvellauni for the past thirty years, and even before he ruled them he had made a name for himself by invading the Trinovantes and supplanting their leader. In doing this, he had been following the footsteps of his father who had tried the same thing years before. Cunobelinus was descended from Cassivellaunus, whom all the land remembered as the chieftain who turned back Rome from our shores. This heritage seemed to have instilled in Cunobelinus the belief that he was the centre of our world and he had raised in his sons this same sense of superiority.

The sons were a brew of strange flavours. The eldest was Adminius, ruthless and strategic but not as blunt or brutal as his brothers. He had a liking for the finer things in life and perhaps this is why he favoured a relationship with Rome, who could provide him with the oils and delicate cloths and other exotic goods he craved. Next was Togodumnus, a man who loved a good fight and had the broken nose and body full of scars to prove it. He was a man with no fear, or so we were told. Youngest of Cunobelinus's brood was Caratacus, the one made most closely in his father's image. He was a tactician, like his eldest brother, but a fighter too. He had the skill and reserve that his father had demonstrated through the years. The men who had brought news of Cunobelinus's demise had told us how the two younger brothers had quickly ousted Adminius, the eldest, from his seat at Cantium. No doubt Adminius was on his way to Rome already.

I had misgivings about that. There was a pattern of in-fighting within the southern tribes which led to ousted chieftains begging Rome for help, as if that far away place held any sway over our own lands! The Atrebates were as bad - long before I was born, their leader, Tincommius, had gone running to Augustus to complain of his nefarious brother, Eppillus. Yet Rome eventually accepted Eppillus as rightful leader. Dubnovellaunus of the Trinovantes had done the same, when Cunobelinus took his lands. And now Adminius was most likely about to complain to Caligula about his two brothers. It was as though Adminius, and Tincommius and Dubnovellaunus before him, would rather have Romans fighting on their land, than lose their own personal power. They didn't seem to see that once the Romans came, they would take all the power for themselves anyway.

I am rushing ahead of myself. At the time, I had misgivings, but I barely imagined the Romans would actually bother to invade again. Like most people, I clung to the image of how the sea had driven Caesar away, and how Cassivellaunus had fought him from our lands the second time. Who would waste the effort coming all that way again? Especially when, as far as I could see, there was little in the way of luxuries and bounty to tempt them.

So we didn't talk of the Romans at all. Instead we discussed what Togodumnus and Caratacus might do next. They held their father's lands which included the heartlands of their tribe and the old Trinovantian territory, not to mention the lands that their uncle, Eppaticus, had taken by force from the Atrebates before he died. And they held Cantium. Two brothers had their grip on most of the south-east. We had to hope that maintaining that grip would take up all of their time and attention. With every tribe that fell to the sun hound's old empire, the Catuvellauni would become a greater threat to us.

"It's time," said my father, later that evening, "you can't put it off any longer."

"I know," I sighed, "we should make the arrangements."

Cunobelinus's decline, and the rise of his warring sons, meant I could no longer postpone the marriage that would reinforce the ties within our tribe. Venutius studied my face when I went to him to say we should be married. I tried to smile, but it wasn't genuine and he knew it.

"What are you so worried about?" He asked, "Don't we get on?"

"Yes, of course we do," I stressed to him, "I wouldn't choose anyone else." It was true. Since Tantoban, I hadn't been with another and I never questioned the ultimate necessity of taking Venutius as my mate.

"Neither would I." Venutius appeared mollified and I stroked his cheek, hoping I hadn't hurt his pride. He was a good young man who tried so hard at everything he did. With his long, dark hair that waved where it wasn't held in plaits and his big brown eyes and square jaw covered in a soft brown beard, he was certainly attractive. He didn't deserve my lukewarm response.

He caught my hand and held it tight in his own.

"I don't want to be a brother to you any more," he said, his cheeks flushing with colour. "We should forget the past and treat each other as lovers, since that is what we are supposed to be."

I nodded, taken aback by his intensity. Gone was the little boy who wanted to play, here was a man who was deadly serious. He took my silence for acquiescence and pressed his lips hard to mine. Instead of the revulsion I had feared, I felt a warm rush of excitement. I kissed him back and laced my fingers behind his wide neck, under his hair and he pulled me tighter against him. I could feel the slight tremble in his arms as he held me.

I was glad I had done this before and was a little prepared, because Venutius was rougher and more urgent than Tantoban had been, being only fifteen years old and presumably inexperienced. He showed the same impatient energy in his coupling as he did in all other aspects of his life, but I didn't mind. In fact, as someone who was eminently practical, I appreciated the efficiency of his approach. When he pushed inside me that first time,   relief, as well as lust, flooded over me – relief that this joining was going to work despite all my doubts, relief that I could feel sexually attracted to Venutius and that I wouldn't have to spend a lifetime unable to enjoy this part of life and relief that I could fulfil the contract my father had made for me. It made me cling to Venutius all the more and when we finished, the bond was made, ceremony or no ceremony.

The joining itself took place on a frosty day late in the autumn. Venutius gave me some beautiful jewellery and invocations were sung to the gods and goddesses while sweet herbs were burned on an altar made of logs. There was a lot of ale and I wore a beautiful dress of soft leather with fur along the neck and hemline. The Carvettii sent gifts of wine they had specially imported, and ale they'd brewed themselves, as well as smoked fish and huge joints of meat cured in salt, a number of fine pieces of pork amongst them. We had musicians and dancing and a roaring fire that carried on until late into the night to take the edge off the chilly temperatures. Venutius and I danced for hours and I tried only to pay attention to him. His family were there, of course – little Iticus now a gangly young man, all elbows and knees. Risha was practically preening and I forced myself not to hear the constant boasting of how the Carvettii had provided so many wonderful gifts. She had complimented me earlier in the day, admiring my dress and the new hair grips I wore, carved into tiny ponies, but she managed to sound magnanimous with her praise. I didn't like her at all and the more I watched Tyrius with her, the more I suspected that he was not as decent and loyal as we had supposed. How could he be, whilst sharing intimacies and conniving with her?

Antikia danced and laughed, flirting with Tantoban and Fistoc and practically any other reasonably good-looking man in sight. She chatted to Iticus and must have been flirting a little with him too, because he looked decidedly flustered when she was with him. From Tyrius, she kept a careful distance, occasionally shooting him sympathetic glances and coy smiles, letting him know she was simply protecting him from his wife's wrath. In truth she was torturing him and I revelled almost as much as she did in his receiving a dose of his own medicine. When he moved nearer to her she whirled away from him, caught up in the dance or in desperate need of a drink. The more she ran, the more he pined, though there was nothing he could do about it with Risha there.

Venutius was happy to the point of giddiness. By the time we retired to bed, he was too overcome with alcohol to do more than fall heavily asleep, his face buried in the warm furs that muffled his snores. I undressed him and wrapped the covers around us, listening to the sounds from the guests that were still drinking and having fun. As far as it was possible for me to feel happy and at peace, I did that night. Even in the happiness of my new relationship with Venutius, whom I did love, I had worries about his family and their plans, about Antikia's game-playing with Tyrius, but mostly about the bigger issues I faced in helping my father keep our tribe and territory safe.

"Let the best man win, I say," said Venutius, banging his mug down and splashing the contents over the rim. "Caratacus deserves the victory if Verica can't defend himself!"

"It's not that simple," I insisted, "The Catuvellauni are becoming too powerful and that's a threat to us. Can you understand that? Any tribe amassing that amount of land is a threat."

"Or an ally."

"Unlikely," I replied, "Caratacus and Togodumnus have no interest in allies. They've invaded the lands of all their neighbours and taken whatever they wanted. The pair of them will never be satisfied."

"And where's the harm in that? They're making their own tribe stronger and more successful. Isn't that an example we should be following?" Venutius was getting cross with me, like he always did when he couldn't force me to agree with him.

"Are you suggesting I attack the Parisi? We could force them out to the sea, they're only a small tribe; it would be easy! Or maybe the Deceangli, we could send gangs of your Carvettii creeping down the coast to infiltrate their borders!" My sarcasm fell on deaf ears.

"Expansion of the tribe means increased security, so yes, maybe we should be thinking about increasing our land."

"We?" I yelled, "This is nothing to do with you, especially since you can't even grasp the sense in what I'm telling you. I already have a vast amount of land, more than any other tribe. Power doesn't come from the amount of land you have, it comes from developing mutual respect with your neighbours so you can profit from them and not be at constant war with them. The Parisi have excellent trading links, we need them, and they need us to sell their goods to. The Deceangli are the gateway to the

Druids – anyone who messes with them opens themselves up to a world of pain. We have peace here, and that is so important and precious. I can't believe you would jeopardise that for some short-lived battle glory."

Venutius was silent for a moment or two, brooding and frowning. I felt bad about pointing out that he was not my equal, but it needed saying if I was to keep his lust for power in check.

"You were the one talking about putting a stop to the Catuvellauni. So you started the war talk, Cartimandua."

"It wasn't war talk. I just think it could be a problem if Caratacus takes total control from Verica. Where will he go next? If we're lucky he'll turn his attention to the West, but if he moves against the Corieltauvi, what then? Next thing you know, they'll be back-tracking over our borders with the Catuvellauni on their heels."

"It's all a big guessing game. What's the point in worrying about it until you know for definite that it's a threat?"

I shrugged and sighed, too tired to argue any more. He nodded, as if somehow he had won, and headed outside. In future, I decided, I shouldn't start conversations like that with Venutius. He couldn't just discuss the possibilities; he only dealt in facts and in action. Even worse, he admired the Catuvellauni brothers' bloodthirsty nature and seemed to turn his nose up at the political approach my father and I took to keeping control of our tribe. Why couldn't he just be satisfied with what we had? Brigantia was the biggest tribe of them all and we had everything we needed. Keeping it safe was all we should be concerned with. I just wished Venutius and I could see eye to eye, rather than arguing all the time.

WINTER AD42
TO SPRING AD43

Caratacus was invincible. He moved through the Atrebates like a wildfire, driving Verica out, with assistance from his brother, Togodumnus. They were on the move constantly, controlling their ever-growing lands from all their grand centres – Camulodumnum (a large settlement that shared a name with our own strange southern hill-fort), Verulamium, Durovernum and now Calleva.

I travelled to the south, assessing and readying our own armies. We had talks with the Corieltauvi for the first time in many years. Dumnocoveros, one of their leaders, was busy on his own southern borders, but he sent the man who ruled jointly with him. Their system of leadership was unusual but effective. It relied on joint power between two or more magistrates and gave a great deal more security to a small tribe placed uncomfortably in the middle of several larger ones. Perhaps it was only a more overt example of the system of sub-tribes and council authority that we had, but the magistrates of the Corieltauvi were not necessarily blood relatives and yet restrained themselves from wresting absolute power from each other. By sharing the leadership, they could protect their tribe far more efficiently, as demonstrated by the fact that Dumnocoveros was manning one border while Senovellaus was meeting with me. I wished I had enough faith in Venutius to share power with him properly, but I feared that left to his own devices he would start a hundred little disputes and problems that I would then have to clear up. He had accompanied me on my trip – my father was in control at our homestead and Tyrius was travelling the northern regions, assessing our army numbers and weapon supplies.

Senovellaus was calm and quite measured in our talks. He agreed with Venutius that seeking Caratacus as an ally was their preferred approach as they did not have the might to fight him. We'd heard so many scare stories about Caratacus and his brother from the travellers and traders making their way through our land, that it was surprising to hear that Senovellaus thought he could reason with them. I was reassured by that, but less so by the other news that the Corieltauvi were able to pass on.

"Verica has appealed to Claudius for help," he said, "and we have heard that the emperor may respond."

"In what way? Men, weapons?" I asked.

"Possibly. He might arm Verica and send him back, but that is not really the Roman way. Their empire grows stronger every year. They have conquered places we cannot even imagine. The Cassiterides may not seem as mysterious and frightening to them as they once did." He used the Roman name for our lands with some disdain.

"You think they'll invade?" I was horrified and sickened. This was what we had feared for a long time but we all convinced ourselves it wouldn't happen, at least not in our lifetimes.

"Maybe. You see, last time they had to fight on land they did not know, against tribes that were mostly united in throwing them back into the sea. Now they have so much information on us and they know how divided the tribes are. For all we know, the Atrebates will stand side by side with the Romans, and who knows, the Trinovantes and Cantiaci might creep out from under the Catuvellauni chains and fight with them as well. Not to mention the fact that Adminius is in Rome and has appealed for help also. It won't be the straightforward resistance they met before if the Romans land with members of our own tribes."

"And so much of the southern coast is now in the hands of Caratacus and Togodumnus, how can they hope to defend it all if the Romans try to land?"

"Exactly. The Catuvellauni brothers rule too large an area in too strategic a place. They would have to divert all their attention to the beaches if the Romans come, but that leaves a risk that the populations of people they have subdued will rebel and hit them right in the flank."

The smugness I felt at having been proved right in my reasoning against Venutius was entirely quashed by the despair that was flooding over me as I considered this new situation.

"Our only hope is that Rome sees fit not to bother with us." I said.

"Or that we can use this as a bargaining point with the Catuvellauni and try to create an alliance to really hold the Romans back."

"This is why you're not so worried about Caratacus invading," I said, now I saw the whole scenario.

"The man must surely see sense in light of this new development. He and his brother hate Rome more than they hate their neighbours."

"And yet their actions are bringing Rome right to us," I said and Senovellaus nodded grimly.

I took the news back home, to the council who my father had gathered together. I shared all of Senovellaus's observations, grateful to my core that he had decided to pass on all that information.

"They value our friendship," I said, "and I think they would hope for our assistance if agreement is reached with the Catuvellauni."

"And once the Romans have gone, what happens then?" That was Baranak, my father's cousin, who was against any such alliance. Between him and his son, there was more short-sightedness than from a one-eyed owl in daylight.

"Once the Romans have gone, we should be thanking the sun, the moon and all her stars, cousin," said my father. "Then we can worry about what the Catuvellauni might or might not do next."

"What is the situation with weapons? Do we have enough?"

asked Fistoc, jovial at the prospect of some kind of fight.

"We have many more people working on making more shields and arrows, Jacavin is supervising the production of more weapons and a much larger proportion of our hides and leathers will be traded for swords and spears to add to the pile," my father answered. "We are in a good position, as good as we could be."

"Should we send a party to engage in talks directly with the Catuvellauni?" Venutius asked, unexpectedly.

"I think we should let the Corieltauvi handle that," I answered, after a moment of consideration. "They have more experience with the tribe than we do and should be more successful."

"And what if they get it wrong? The Corieltauvi are a small tribe and lack the aggression that Caratacus and Togodumnus understand. If they misjudge these negotiations, what then?" Venutius was insistent and I wondered if he might be right. Perhaps we were better off handling this more directly, since the repercussions could be so enormous. But I wasn't persuaded enough to change my mind and I guessed he was only pushing the point because he wanted to meet the Catuvellauni men who fascinated him so.

Let's give them some time," I suggested, "wait for word from the Corieltauvi magistrates. If they fail, we should step in then."

It was agreed, but Venutius was not comfortable. He insisted that this was too important an issue to trust another tribe with. Sometimes Venutius was blunt and crude in his understanding of difficult situations. But I would come to realise that often he was entirely correct.

We waited for news. The cold white days of winter, when breath bloomed from people's mouths and the trees drew a prickly silhouette on the skyline, faded into the green, watery weather of spring. Trade picked up a little. As my father had anticipated we were able to increase our weapon stocks by trading some of the cattle and also some of the dogs that our breeder families had trained. I had a fearsome new spear, light but sharp, which I could wield reasonably, if not exactly with grace. As I practised, a new fear gripped me. I began to suspect that I was not at heart a warrior. I had never killed anyone and had no real desire to do so. I watched others, like Fistoc, who revelled in the dangers of training and real fighting, seeming not to care about physical pain, and felt ashamed of the terror that sprang into my chest at the thought of a sword piercing my flesh.

Eventually a message came from the Corieltauvi. They had tried and failed to create an alliance. The Catuvellauni wouldn't take them seriously and were frantically busy making their own preparations for war. Venutius buttoned his lip and tried very hard to be magnanimous.

"You were right," I groaned, "What do we do now?"

He put an arm round me, pleased that I had asked him, and repeated his original suggestion about us negotiating directly with Togodumnus or Caratacus.

"We can try but I think we're too late." I said, shaking my head. "I don't believe they'll listen."

We didn't have the chance to attempt such talks anyway. A few days later, men came riding hard over the hills as if bloodthirsty wolfhounds were at their heels, to bring the most terrible news. The Romans had landed and were fighting against the Catuvellauni brothers.

AUTUMN AD43

Forty thousand Romans came. Forty thousand! All equipped and ready to do battle in the name of their emperor Claudius. Oh how proud he must have been, that man who had been called a half-wit and a simpleton, to be the one to finally stamp the Roman footprint into the soil of our lands. This was no ill-fated expedition like the one Caesar had commanded, but a ruthless and carefully planned invasion. They reached our shores in three different places, stretching Togodumnus and Caratacus to their limits. The brothers fell back and gathered their forces by a river where they battled hard but had to run once more. Finally, at the largest river in their territory, they set up a last defence, relying on the strategic foothold to help them hold off the superior forces advancing upon them.

Perhaps the Roman leader, Plautius, got lucky, or perhaps he had realised that the Catuvellauni forces would scatter at the death of their leaders and planned it with precision. Either way, one of his skirmishing parties got close enough to Togodumnus to wound him fatally, whereupon Caratacus and all his warriors, or at least all that was left of them, fell back to the great settlement of Camulodumun, Verulamium having already been taken.

When we heard what was happening, Venutius and some others were all for going to the assistance of the southerners. Others, like Baranack and his son, lived in the fantasy that Rome would subdue the Catuvellauni and a few more tribes then head off on their merry way, leaving us alone. My father knew the Romans would come to us, but he put a stop to all plans of going south to fight.

"We must stay on our land now," he said, "the war is already raging and we can't form a proper allied force in the middle of battle. If we go south, we'll die and leave our lands defenceless, as well as making our tribe an enemy of Rome. No Venutius, we're staying put and when the Romans come to us, we'll be in a position to make a deal."

"They'll slaughter us!" Venutius had shouted, "They'll chain us up like thieves and ship us off to slave for rich, fat Romans!"

My father laughed at that.

"You sound like a child telling horrible stories. Rome may be a power to be reckoned with but it needs support in the land it conquers. They'll seek the easy road when they can, especially from a tribe with such a large and difficult terrain as ours. All is not lost. We just have to wait now."

Venutius was not good at waiting. He chaffed at the familial bonds that stopped him disobeying my father and I think, had we not been joined already, he might have run away to fight alongside Caratacus. Little good that would have done! I agreed with my father and distasteful as it might be, I was beginning to realise that it would be better to play host to Rome than to be trampled underfoot. A snickering, cruel voice in my head whispered that I was just afraid of fighting, of dying, but I smothered the whisper with my father's good sense.

Our informants passed on word that Plautius had halted his offensive and requested Emperor Claudius to travel to the scene of the grand victory - the planned invasion of Camulodunum. In our lands, stockpiling of weapons continued and we worked hard to set up more lines of communication over our territory. Whereas before news travelled sporadically, we now had more of a system for different sub-tribes to pass messages quickly to us, and us to them. Instead of nameless men I couldn't recognise, I now knew by sight a large number of people from all over our land. It was my idea, probably the first I'd had that wasn't suggested in some way by my father. Venutius helped, begrudgingly. He was angry and upset that Caratacus was on the verge of defeat, even more so by the death of Togodumnus. I had to remind him that the Catuvellauni brothers were not our friends and had always been a threat to us. It confused me that he felt so sympathetic to Caratacus, but I suspected it was because he so admired the skill and cunning that Cunobelinus's youngest son had become famous for. Venutius was at heart a warrior, stunted by politics and strategy. He wanted to fight and the more we held him back, the more he identified with Caratacus.

The leaves were lying thick, red and dirty on the ground, when we heard that Claudius had arrived and the assault on Camulodunum had begun. We had all anticipated the end result, but it was still with mixed feelings that I heard the news that the settlement had fallen and Caratacus had fled to the west, seeking sanctuary in the forbidding hills of the Silures. Claudius was now accepting the surrender of tribal leaders in the south and parading the might of his political domination for all to see. His Praetorian Guard had accompanied him, along with many senators who were probably curious for a look at the long-romanticised, mysterious Albion.

The Corieltauvi sent messengers to relay much of this information, and the latest one now stood before us to request that my father and I meet with Senovellaus at their place by the pools. She said that Dumnocoveros, the other magistrate, was at Camulodunum, assuring Claudius of their own tribal allegiance to Rome, and suggested that we do the same, giving us a promise of safe passage through Corieltauvi lands. It was a great deal to take in, as we stood there with the Corieltauvi woman who had spoken the news.

"We must meet with Senovellaus immediately," my father said to me, brooking no discussion with the council. Then to the woman, "I know the place by the pools and could find it myself, but we'll travel back with you. Get some food and rest while we pack."

I retired with my father into our roundhouse, where we sent out orders as fast as we could – who was to come, what we would need, what messages to send out around our tribe. We settled on taking Tantoban, Presivin and Venutius, with a retinue of several attendants to serve us. Antikia and Tyrius would remain behind in the royal settlement. Mandulay packed my things – ceremonial clothes and armour as well as my jewellery and weapons. Within a short space of time we were ready to go and we headed out on our horses.

Our journey to the Corieltauvi's sacred place took several days. The nights were bitterly cold so we took a route that would lead us past homesteads that we could stay inside. Even so, we had little sleep and not much time for eating. It was a blur of hooves and trees and landscape that was new to me as we left the glory of the high hills behind. When we came at last to Lindon, the place by the pools, I dismounted in absolute relief. Senovellaus was already there, which saved messengers having to be sent to their tribal settlement just to the south.

"Kesaven, these are testing times in which to meet again," he said, gripping my father's arm solidly and nodding a hello to me. "I was glad to meet your daughter last winter."

"It's good to see you again Senovellaus, though I don't think we'll have much time for catching up with each other."

"Too true! I must ride south myself, to meet Claudius in person before he returns to Rome and I suggest that you do the same. They have a system of rule they are trying to impose – they call it being a client of Rome – and if we accept their terms we can continue to live much as before, without further violence. We are in a more vulnerable position than Brigantia and we have no choice, unless we want to go the way of Caratacus and lose everything. Even so, I'd suggest that you surrender to Claudius also, since they plan to conquer the whole of what they are calling Britannia anyway."

"And you don't want them tramping over your tribal lands to get to us, eh?" said my father.

"I want the best deal for all of us," Senovellaus assured. "But it's your choice."

"Not much of one!"

"No."

The two men sighed and clasped arms again.

"I've waited only to hear that Dumnocoveros has been peacefully received. Now I have to go also. I've made my offerings to the gods and goddesses here and you are free to do the same if you wish. Then you may spend the night in our settlement – Sitensa will take you there. Perhaps I will see you soon in Camulodunum."

"It's a fair assumption," said my father as they released each other's arms.

"Claudius won't stay long. Don't leave it too late," said Senovellaus as he mounted his horse and kicked it into a canter.

"I don't like all this," said Venutius, coming to where we stood but speaking loudly enough for Sitensa and several of her people to hear. "Why are we taking advice from the Corieltauvi, when they completely failed to engage with Caratacus after promising to?"

"Enough," said my father, "I want no more interference from you since you clearly don't understand the sensitivity of the situation. Senovellaus has shown himself to be a friend and he has spoken sense. There is no real choice here. We will travel south and we will make our deal with Claudius and hopefully we'll keep the Romans off our lands for a very long time. None of us like it, but that's just how it is."

I winced for Venutius, who fumed silently but pulled his wits together and maintained a dignified bearing.

"You are right. I'm sorry Kesaven, to have spoken my heart's fears without fully considering our position."

"Right." Kesaven gave him a quick grasp of the shoulder. "Let's make our offerings and beg the blessings of the ancestors."

The pools were beautiful, spilling from the river and catching what little light was left in the day. In the shallows, the occasional glint of metal shone up through the water though the deeper parts must have contained the most precious offerings. I took a dagger that Mandulay had thoughtfully packed for me, knowing we were coming to this sacred place. It was silver and delicate, though slightly damaged. We were cautious to appease the gods, but we weren't fools enough to throw away good weaponry. My usual dagger sat pressed against my outer thigh in a leather holder but this was one that Shamatin, the man learning his metal-working skill from our old Jacavin, had made a tiny fault on. I kissed it and whispered words of invocation to the moon goddess who already shone in crescent form in the dusk sky, before throwing the blade into the water.

We spent that night, or what was left of it by the time we arrived, at the settlement Senovellaus had told us of. It was similar to our own, though with more roundhouses. We ate, we slept and then we set out again, on the track to Camulodunum. My legs ached from the arduous travelling we had already undertaken, but after half a day, the pain eased off. I wondered if I would even be able to stand when I met Claudius as I knew it would catch up with me. We'd left the hills well behind us now and the ground became easier to ride over, the tracks wider and straighter. This was a popular trade route and it covered more open terrain, past flat marshes and fields and great tracts of land recently cultivated, with the criss-cross pattern of iron-sleeved scratch ploughs carved into them. We were entering old Catuvellauni territory now and when we passed small settlements, the people looked bitter and afraid. This corner of our world had suffered more instability than others in recent times and now they were entering a new era of subjugation. We had an uneasy night in a roundhouse that was loaned to us begrudgingly, but we were glad of the shelter because we knew that the following day we would come face to face with Claudius.

In the morning, I put on all my gold armlets, a necklace of intricately worked jet beads that had been a gift from the Gabrantovices and an iron breastplate that sat tight around my dress. I added black lines to my eyes with the powder Mandulay made, and highlighted my cheekbones with the blue. One of the women who had come with us to serve – was she called Beltia? I can hardly remember – combed my hair into a tight braid, held in place by bone combs and tied off with string laced with feathers. My father was equally attired, in his battle clothes with all his weapons upon him. Despite all my finery my father was firmly in charge on this occasion and secretly I was very relieved. I had all the confidence of youth, but only a smidgen of the diplomatic experience of my father and as we came within sight of the huge Roman standards set around Camulodunum's defences, I was very daunted. The feeling wasn't helped by the new decorations that Camulodunum had acquired. At regular intervals, sharpened sticks held the flattened, putrescent heads of Catuvellauni warriors and it took a great deal of will not to look directly at the distorted faces. We'd had only a short way to travel, which was just as well, because it's not easy to ride when wearing all your best ceremonial equipment and I felt hot, dishevelled and slightly sick as I dropped down from my horse to enter the newly created gates to the town.

The whole place was a hive of activity, with Roman soldiers everywhere and building work already being carried out. It had been known as a large, important centre before, but now, stone was being stockpiled to create walls and houses of Roman design and new ditches were being dug to change the boundaries and defensive works. A stone hall had already been erected and stood proudly at the furthest end of the town. I assumed Claudius was in residence there, and I was gazing at the building when Roman officers surrounded us and demanded to know who we were.

"I'm Kesaven, Chief of the Brigantes tribe," my father answered, "This is my daughter and these are members of our council. We are here to meet Claudius."

"Right," said one of the officers. "Put your horses over there and go wait inside that roundhouse. Someone will be along to see you soon."

He stalked off, back to the little hut by the gate, and we continued through, tying the horses up where he had pointed, by a trough of water. Four of his colleagues followed us, watching as we stood and took in the sights of Camulodunum. After a few moments, they grew impatient, and we stepped inside the roundhouse as we had been instructed. The four men moved closer, guarding the entrance and giving us the uncomfortable sense of being detained. We didn't speak while we waited but I'm sure we were all unnerved. After some time, another officer arrived.

"Out you come," he called from outside, and we dutifully trooped back into the daylight. "Follow me. Plautius wishes to see you first, to determine whether you'll be granted an audience with the Emperor."

As we bristled, the officer didn't notice, but turned around and set off towards the large stone hall. He took us first to a smaller stone building and stopped us at the doorway.

"You must remove all your weapons," he ordered.

"Will you be removing yours?" asked my father, pointedly.

"No, of course not. You cannot see Plautius or the Emperor unless you remove all weapons and hand them over now."

We did as he asked, following my father's lead, and the officer watched us pile up our various equipment on the ground. He motioned another soldier and instructed him to guard the weapons until we returned for them. It was an uncomfortable beginning, to have to remove essential parts of our ceremonial dress before even seeing the man we had come to meet, but in that atmosphere, we all saw that there was no point in refusing. We'd just have been kicked out or more likely, strung up. When the officer was satisfied that none of us had any serious weapons left on, he took us inside the small building.

"You are the Brigantian king?"

"I am Kesaven, chieftain of the Brigantes."

"I am Aulus Plautius," The man before us replied and listed a number of battles that presumably he had won. We stared, a little bewildered. "I serve the great Emperor Claudius who has arrived to claim Britannia as his own land."

"We hear you have Caratacus on the run. The Catuvellauni would appear to be defeated," acknowledged my father.

"There was never any doubt that they would be." Plautius had cold eyes, murky green under his thin eyebrows and heavily lined forehead. He stood with total confidence, erect and square, unflinching in the face of our wary group. "We have four legions working their way into your country," said Plautius, making us jump until we realised he meant the southern lands, not Brigantia. "We have subdued a number of tribes and we anticipate further success. But we are not monsters. Rome does not engage in murder. We can bring great benefits to you and your people. There is no alternative, so you would be well-advised to work with us, not against us as your foolish friends here in the south have attempted."

"The tribes in the south are not our friends." said my father carefully, "We do have some allies in our neighbouring people, but the Catuvellauni and the tribes they have previously invaded have never been our allies."

Plautius nodded, gratified if not completely convinced.

"You have a large amount of land, Kesaven." Plautius phrased it as a statement but I heard a tiny hint of a question in his tone and I thought, ah, he knows only a little about us.

"Large enough. We do all right for ourselves. We have no wars or disputes with our neighbours and Brigantia consists of many different tribes, who all regard me and my family as their leaders."

"A complicated territory," admitted Plautius, "You must work hard to maintain such a diverse tribe."

"I know my people. I know the land," said my father with a

nod of his head.

"And that is very important to us," said Plautius, studying us with his impassive, lined face. "In the south of this island, all the warring has made the tribal leaderships untenable and we have had little choice but to suppress the fighting and remove the men behind the trouble. Togodumnus is dead, his little brother has run away and the tribes that the Catuvellauni had under their grip are in disarray. Much of our work at present will be on quelling the rebellions and in-fighting and consolidating our position on these shores. Brigantia seems to be a place of peace and stability and that is something we would wish to continue. Rome will support you as a client king, if you will agree to be loyal and unswerving in your support for Rome and the emperor Claudius."

Plautius paused, letting us all consider his words.

"I have never been to Rome and I do not yet know Claudius," answered my father, "so it would be hard to swear such support to people and a place I have no understanding of."

"Naturally, there will be time to discuss arrangements and formalise the situation, but this is the only way forward and one that Claudius will expect you to agree to when you have your audience with him."

"I look forward to meeting the emperor. Can you tell me, though, when you have made client kingships previously, what is the general way of things? What do you require of us?" Kesaven was polite but he was going to demand answers. We might have little choice, but we needed to know what we were getting into. Plautius gave a small sigh.

"Rome will provide military support when necessary to protect your leadership and territory, so long as this is viable. In return, Rome expects you to do your duty in supplying goods that are native to your lands. We will especially want produce from your lead mines and any other mining you do. We understand you are known for the quality of your beef, hides and leather goods. We'll expect a large number of cattle. A certain number of slaves might be necessary also. We will take more from the south, as a result of the battles we engage in, but Rome always needs more people to work hard and advance the great civilisation we are building."

"Our lands are large, but the numbers of people are modest in Brigantia. Providing slaves as well as producing goods to export to Rome might be difficult."

"These are details we can work out. We are not unreasonable and once we have surveyed your land, we'll have a good idea of what we can expect." Plautius was upbeat, his negotiations, if they could be termed such, nearly at an end.

"Slavery is not a large part of our way of life," my father warned him. "Criminals, people who are destitute and people with some form of debt are often used as chained slaves, but we do not run a trade in people and we do not generally own slaves."

"The type of people you describe, if they exist in reasonable numbers, might suffice for our needs. Like I said, a survey of your territory will tell us more."

"Very well. It would appear that the type of client king or queen-ship you have described is indeed the way forward."

"Excellent." Plautius hesitated. "Queenship?"

"Of course. After all, my daughter is of an age to take full control upon my death and I would expect her, as the tribal chieftain, to be recognised by Rome as the client queen of this tribe."

Plautius looked from my father to me and back again.

"Is she married?" He asked. My father did not respond. There was an awkward pause as Plautius unwillingly turned his gaze back to me. From the other side of my father, Venutius crossed him arms and stared angrily at me also.

"What is your name?" He managed to sound respectful, but only just.

"I am Cartimandua." I kept my eyes fixed on his and he looked away first.

"A client queenship should not be a problem, particularly if Cartimandua is willing to keep to the same terms you agree to," he said to my father.

"Then I think we are finished," Kesaven replied and took Plautius in a parting arm grip before the other could object. Plautius followed his lead, a little surprised at the abrupt ending and possibly mildly annoyed that Kesaven had been the one to draw the discussion to a close. We were shown back outside and told to wait there until Claudius was ready for us in his hall. Venutius was quiet and moody, angry that he had not been introduced to Plautius.

"When he asked if you were married, why not just tell him?" he hissed. "They might be more confident knowing I could take control." He knew instantly that he had said the wrong thing and I felt a painful pressure in my chest knowing how eager he was for the power that I held. He muttered an apology which I accepted and then we waited in silence. What else could either of us say? He wouldn't openly admit to the yearning he felt for the status of being the Brigantian chieftain and I didn't dare force him into such an admission since it would split us apart. I tried not to think about it. There was so much else at stake. That small piece of the conversation with Plautius had revealed to me how dangerous and tenuous my position was. From the look on Plautius's face and the dismissive expressions of his counterparts, I could see that Rome did not value women, at least not as equals to men and while it was something I had suspected, it was still a shock to see how they regarded me with little more than contempt. In our tribe, people simply worked as hard as they could, did what they and their families had always done, and it didn't usually matter whether someone was male or female.

The matter of slaves was also weighing on my mind, though not as greatly. I added up in my head the numbers of slaves I knew about, tried to extrapolate a figure across Brigantia and wondered if it would be enough. Did Plautius want a single shipment of slaves, I thought, or might Rome require a certain amount each year? How would we choose the people to be sent? Perhaps, I considered, we would have to sacrifice some of the smaller tribes on our territory – people who would not have the resources to rebel and cause problems. I shuddered. It was not pleasant to think about trading our own people to foreign soil, to be subjected to who knew what kinds of atrocities, but what choice would we have? The only interruption to my gloomy thoughts came from an unearthly screeching noise, something between a growl and a cry, that came from the direction of the hall. We all jumped as we first heard it, not knowing whether it was man or beast making the sound and in our anxious conversations, we wondered if Claudius had brought some monstrous creature with him or was torturing prisoners so gruesomely that the sound was actually human. The misery of our position settled over me through that wait as I contemplated what we had lost and how our world would change now the Romans had finally arrived. My main hope was that the survey of our land would be delayed by fighting in the south and the work involved in setting up permanent Roman posts. For once I hoped Caratacus, still protected by the blue hills to the west, would cause as much trouble as possible and keep the Romans busy.

When at last we were summoned, and led around quite a number of roundhouses until we had a direct view of the grand new hall, we saw what had been making that terrible, raging howl. Stationed at either side of the high entrance to the building were a pair of huge animals, the colour of rain clouds. They had tough hides and legs like tree trunks, with great ears, but most peculiar of all was the long snout that dropped down from each of their faces towards the floor, flanked by a great white tusk on either side. Despite our pride, we froze and stared. In fact we may even have back-tracked a little. The soldiers escorting us sniggered, but even that didn't jolt us into bravado.

"What in the name of the goddess are those?" breathed Presivin.

"Elephants," answered one of the soldiers. "When you enter the hall, stay right in the middle of the path, otherwise they'll eat you." He barely got to the end of the sentence before he burst into laughter. They'd obviously had a lot of fun with this. As we watched, someone left the hall and the elephants didn't pay any attention. I saw that they were shackled by their ankles and I guessed they were of little threat, despite their terrifying appearance. I broke our reverie by walking forwards, my father quickly following.

Above the doorway hung great golden curtains and the smell of incense wafted out towards us as we walked carefully between the big grey beasts. The soldiers stayed behind us and, having shunted us into the entrance, retreated. We continued on into the hall, which seemed ablaze in gold. Ornaments and decorations filled the chasm of the hall, vases and statues lined the walls and beautiful tapestries draped down the stone. In and amongst the riches, people sat or stood. Some, like us, were natives there to meet the Emperor, others were from his own retinue, conducting the business of empire. My eyes were trying to register sights that were beyond my understanding – senators in white togas, a type of clothing I had never seen before and that looked wholly unsuited to our climate, furniture of a sophistication beyond anything we had in Brigantia, riches that made my own gold armlets and unassuming jet beads look positively mean. Beneath my overwhelmed senses, my gut was telling me to ignore it all. This magnificent scene was designed to intimidate and overawe, but the only thing that mattered was to make a deal with Claudius that would protect our future. I looked for him as we walked down the central aisle of the hall, my gaze settling on the raised platform at the far end.

On it stood a grand table, covered in a multi-coloured feast of weird foodstuffs and behind the table were a selection of men. I found Plautius immediately, his cool, green-eyed face in profile to me as he leaned in close, speaking to a man of unprepossessing demeanour. He had obviously hastened to the hall to pass on news of his conversation with my father. I scanned the others seated at the table, but found none that I could take to be Claudius. As we approached the platform, we attracted their attention and Plautius whispered something more to the man he was with who nodded and straightened up as he turned in his chair to face us. So this was Claudius, I realised. At the centre of all this pomp and ceremony, he was surprisingly slight with a tilt of his head that gave him an almost humble appearance.

For the past days since Camulodunum had fallen to his army, Claudius had paraded his wealth around and spent his time condescending to supposed leaders who were often puppets newly created by the Roman army - defeated people of high rank who would subjugate themselves to Rome for a chance to retain power and wealth. This method of creating client kings was not so important in the south, since the army was having success in stretching their iron-like grip over much of the area, but some clients were appointed, probably to create goodwill and ease the way for Roman progress. Nevertheless, we were perhaps unusual, being the long-standing ruling elite of a large tribal territory that would significantly increase Rome's claim to ownership of Britannia, without vicious fighting. Claudius stood up.

"I am Claudius, Emperor of Rome," he said.

"I am Kesaven, Chief of Brigantia," said my father. "This is my daughter, Cartimandua and these are members of our high council."

Claudius nodded.

"Join us for something to eat while we talk," he instructed and Plautius, who was already on his feet and approaching us, motioned for us ascend the steps to the platform. We all started forward but Presivin, Venutius and Tantoban were led away to a lower table. I watched with some misgivings as they took their seats, but followed my father towards Claudius, watching the two of them greet each other. When Kesaven stepped aside, Claudius studied me.

"Cartimandua," he enunciated, "Sleek pony. I understand you use small ponies a great deal in your hilly lands?"

"Yes, they cope better with some of our steeper terrain," I replied, "Although we use horses as well." I had expected to struggle to keep the contempt from my expression, to see only the man who had invaded our world. I never thought the man responsible for that would be a quiet, pensive leader with such a deliberate and inquisitive manner. Instead of contempt, I felt curious. But there was no time to talk further. I was ushered out of the way and Kesaven resumed his position at Claudius' side, taking the seat Plautius had previously occupied as Claudius also sat down

A Roman attendant propelled me a few seats away, where I took a chair and surveyed the food in front of me. As I considered what to eat, Plautius sat himself down on my far side.

"What must you make of all this?" he patronised. leaning forward to pick up some small pieces of fruit. "I expect you've never seen anything like it."

"Are you talking about the food?" I asked and he laughed, although I hadn't intended to be witty.

"I would say the signs are that Claudius is pleased so far. He and your father are certainly getting on well." We both looked sideways to where Kesaven and Claudius were apparently chatting easily. "How do you find Claudius?"

Plautius's question was blunt and I spent only a second deciding that answering quickly and truthfully was safer than trying to concoct the answer he might wish to hear.

"He seems a very intelligent man. Quite personable."

"Not quite the magnificent warrior you expected?"

"Not a warrior at all," I said, "but no doubt a very good leader."

"Ah yes, an excellent leader. Do you know, people used to make fun of Claudius? They said he was weak, feeble, a simpleton even - some still do - but for a simpleton he has made great gains for Rome."

I didn't speak. I wondered where Plautius was going with this conversation,.

"Don't be fooled by the exterior, Cartimandua. Claudius hasn't got where he is by being personable and clever, though perhaps he would have preferred that route. He is as vicious as any when he needs to be, he just gets others to commit the violence for him. But none of this need worry you. After all, your father is agreeing to the client-kingship and Claudius will agree that you and your heirs will also rule in his name in time, so long as you are all loyal and faithful to him. I'm sure Rome can trust you." His voice was low, threatening

"You can trust me to be loyal to the agreements my father makes. I hope we can trust you to be loyal to the agreements your emperor makes." Despite the cool air that circulated in the high building, I felt hot and itchy. My underarms were damp. Plautius was too close, full of menace.

"I am glad to hear that." He leaned back. "Would you like a drink?" He motioned to a boy carrying a large amphorae of wine and as the red liquid was being poured, excused himself from me, stepping down from the platform and threading his way past a group of dancers who had filed in and were beginning a bizarre series of movements to a faint melody played by a tall man on a stringed instrument.

It was a relief to watch Plautius's stocky body strutting away, so I could take a drink of my wine in peace. With those cold, fish-like eyes upon me, I felt clumsy and exposed and the underlying threat in his words left me feeling nauseous, the same way as when I had seen all those heads on spikes. It was a little like waking to find a rat on your bed – a vile interloper that makes familiar territory seem foreign and dangerous. I was sitting, sipping, watching the dancers and thinking when my father called my name so, keeping hold of my goblet, I rose and made my way back to where he and Claudius still sat. When I made to sit next to my father, Claudius held up a hand and asked would I sit next to him. I nodded, with a small smile and, being careful not to spill my drink, took the chair on his other side.

"It's stronger than your ale," Claudius murmured, "Don't drink it too fast."

"Thank you, I've drunk wine before. Do you like our ale?"

"Its heartening, a refreshing drink," he nodded.

We sat for a while watching the dark-skinned dancers in their colourful costumes.

"Do you understand that your father is now a client-king to Rome?"

"Yes, I do. Although I must admit to some uncertainty as to what that actually means," I confessed. There was something about the man, with his mild manner and his calm, slow way of talking that encouraged you to speak plainly.

"It means he is loyal to Rome and to all our endeavours. He will provide what he can for our causes and we will support him in ruling this new part of our Roman world." Claudius sipped his drink and replaced it carefully on the table.

"And when the trouble in the south is over, what then?"

"The same applies. Naturally, the legions will move north, taking more territory. We may require increased help from Brigantia, new forts at which to station our men, supplies for the soldiers, that kind of thing." He shrugged as he spoke. I didn't like the vagueness, it reminded me of Plautius, but I knew I wasn't going to get more detail out of him. They were the conquerors, we were the subdued tribe. They didn't need to be specific about the arrangements – we couldn't object even if they were.

"There are a couple of other points to note," he said. "I understand you will follow your father as leader of Brigantia. You should know I have agreed to this and therefore, you will be a client-queen. That is why it is so important for you to understand your responsibilities to Rome." He paused. "And also, I have imposed another condition, something to secure the bonds of friendship and loyalty between our people. Your father will provide Plautius with one hundred of his best trained young noble men. Plautius will treat these men as officers and they will be deployed within our operational legions for a period of five years. After that time, they will return home."

I sat back in my chair. One hundred young men did not sound too onerous, but one hundred noble youths was a different matter. Claudius was removing the very generation of people who should be succeeding to the various tribal councils and learning the ways of their people – or at least the male half of that generation. I considered my words carefully as I replied.

"I see. It will be like... five years of training for them? They can learn your ways and bring them back to Brigantia."

"Exactly, Cartimandua! You are thinking like a client-queen already, my dear. These men will return home ready to serve you with all their new-found skills at your disposal. In serving you, they will of course be serving Rome. It makes a great deal of sense."

"We'll need some men left to support Brigantia's affairs, though."

"Of course, I understand that and we won't take all your advisers. Your father can specify who he supplies to our army."

"So these youths won't be hostages then?" I took a sip of my own drink, in the nonchalant way Claudius had earlier, trying to balance the accusation in my voice with a relaxed countenance.

"Let me make it clear, this condition is agreed. There is no refusing it and these men will be expected to remain in service to Rome for the full five years. Deserting before this period has elapsed will incur the highest military penalty." He looked at me, his forehead pressed into a frown. It didn't have the menace of Plautius but the petulance of someone forced to confront an unpleasant self-image reflected in the eyes of another.

"My father has agreed to this and I fully respect his decision," I said, with the small fake smile I had been using all day. "When will the men leave?"

"Your father must choose the remaining men first and they may have to travel from very far north of here, so I have generously given fourteen days before they will be collected."

"Who is chosen already?" I asked, leaning forward over the table as I looked at him so I could see Kesaven on his far side.

"I made the first choice myself," said Claudius, "I hope you will forgive me but I must take Venutius, who I understand is the highest ranking young man in your tribe."

My breath caught in my chest and I put a hand to my throat. Of course he would take Venutius. Poor Venutius, to be a hostage to the Roman invaders.

"He will be well cared for. Your husband will return to you a changed man, but changed for the better – a man Rome can rely upon to support its client-queen."

"Indeed." I no longer felt like playing politics with Claudius. "It is simply a shock. Would you mind if I went to him now? It seems I must make the most of my time with him."

"Of course. It has been most interesting talking with you. I hope we will be good friends to one another."

"Yes, yes, you have my loyalty and service always..." I was already moving away from the table to join Venutius, scarcely thinking about whether Claudius would be offended. I could see Venutius with the others around the table they had been sent to and I hurried down the steps and across to him, bumping into several people on the way.

"Had a nice time up there?" he enquired as I arrived. A tiny bit of my anxiety crystallised into anger.

"I'd hardly call it that. Venutius, we must talk. My father is making arrangements with Claudius."

"So we've seen. They look to be getting on well."

"They are. The client-ship is agreed, but with conditions."

"No surprise there."

"Let's just wait for Kesaven to return and then discuss all this later," said Presivin, wary of all the ears that surrounded us. "Look, they seem to be finished."

I turned to see my father kneeling, Claudius holding out a bejewelled hand for him to kiss. We were all silenced by the peculiarity of the sight. Then Kesaven rose and made his way towards us.

"What conditions?" Venutius asked me, his curiosity aroused, but my father was joining us and motioning for us to stand and leave.

"What a magnificent place and such a wise emperor," he was saying as we made our way out, clearly speaking for the benefit of all the men hovering, listening and reporting back. "We shall have to travel home immediately to fulfil the initial terms of our client-ship."

We came out past the huge elephants, along the track that brought us back to where we had left all our weapons. The guard stationed by them gave us leave to retrieve them and once re-equipped we were free to leave. We found our horses and without any preamble, got out of the gates of Camulodunum as fast as decently possible.

"I should have been consulted. If you want to trade me for your precious client-king status, the least you could do is have some respect for me. You didn't even introduce me to Claudius!" Venutius paced around before my father, his wide hands planted on his hips and two spots of deep red growing on his cheeks.

"I did what I had to do. I'm sorry to have to send you away," said Kesaven.

"It's not the going away that's the problem – it's that you never include me properly in anything. You took Cartimandua up there to meet everyone, but left me sitting like a fool with them." He gestured unthinkingly at Tantoban and Presivin who were standing awkwardly nearby.

"Cartimandua will be the tribal chief. I can't risk them thinking otherwise. It's not that I'm excluding you, rather that I'm protecting my daughter's interests. You have no idea how these Romans think. Women to them are just goods to be owned. They have no real respect for our women and with you about to leave, they must be made to see at every opportunity that she is the highest authority in Brigantia."

"Oh, no one's in any doubt about that," Venutius scoffed.

"It concerns me that you have so little regard for her," my father observed. "You two should speak alone. This is a shock for you both." He left us, taking Presivin and Tantoban away and leaving us by our horses. We had stopped midway between Camulodunum and Lindon, on the road home. I sat down heavily on a patch of grass and wiped the corner of my eye with my cloak.

"Don't tell me you're upset. I expected you to be glad to be rid of me," he said, still standing.

"Why would you say that?"

"Oh don't pretend. It will be easier for you to run things without me getting in the way. You never take my suggestions anyway. You try as hard as you can to hide the fact that we're married. We don't even have any fruit for our efforts!" He motioned at my stomach as he said this and I gasped in fury.

"How dare-" I stopped myself. The servants who hovered too close to us were all ears. I stood up facing him and spoke more softly.

"I lead as I see fit because I am to be head of this tribe, not you. But I always value the help you give me; I want you to be more involved. It's just that sometimes I disagree with you and when that happens, it has to be my decision. As for the... personal side of it, I've loved you and I thought you loved me. I never thought you could be such a nasty lump of shit! Perhaps it is best that you do leave, since you despise me so much. But never think that I wanted you to go or that I would have chosen for you to be exposed to such danger."

He scowled and I knew I wouldn't get an apology. Even if he regretted what he'd said, he still felt angry at the position I held over him. There was nothing I could do about that.

The event of his leaving was a quiet affair. Tyrius and Risha watched with obvious pride but some frustration as he rode away amongst the Romans, attired like one of them but mounted upon his own horse. Plautius had sent a detachment to escort our chosen hundred back into the south where they would be assigned their military postings either in Britannia or overseas. We had taken men from across Brigantia - Latenses, Gabrantovices, Setantii, Tectoverdi, Carvettii and other, smaller clans too - so the impact did not feel too great. Even so, a handful of promising young warriors from the Brigantian heartland had to go and Vellocatus too was doomed to travel with his master. With Venutius gone, his parents' hopes for tribal dominance would have to simmer slowly for another five years and this must have been a blow to Risha's ambitions after the achievement of seeing us married at last.

I sent him off with a stilted embrace, both of us aware that something had changed between us. I hoped he would stay safe and that the military training and inevitable fighting would not be too arduous - for all his troublesome bickering, I did still care about him. At least he had Vellocatus by his side, to make sure his temper didn't lead him into difficulties. I couldn't say how Venutius really felt about me. Perhaps he was relieved to put some distance between us.

With Venutius gone, there was no reason for Tyrius to linger with us and he left with Risha for the Carvettii territory. My father and I said our goodbyes to them, knowing that we wouldn't see them for some considerable time and I felt a twinge of sadness that the dependable Tyrius would no longer be around. He made a useful counterpart to my father, especially now the latter was increasingly withdrawn and ambivalent. My aunt's reaction was different.

"Thank the goddess for that," she said when he had gone, "Another moment of his moping after me and I would have gone insane."

"If you dislike him that much, why not end it?" I asked.

"Oh, he's not so bad. I just like him in small doses. And you still need that man on your side. Better for you if I keep some sway over him."

"Does Risha have any idea about the two of you?"

"I'm not sure." She paused, gazing past me. "She knows that he's messing with someone, but I don't think she knows that it's me."

"I'm glad she's gone then, before she learned the truth. She's a dangerous woman."

"Ah, but so am I," smiled Antikia, showing her sharp little teeth.

WINTER AD46

Without Venutius or Tyrius to lend any support, I worked endlessly with my father to learn every little thing I could about our land and people. Aware that time was running out, I wanted to scrape up all his knowledge, ready for when he wouldn't be around to share it. The seasons passed, winter into spring, then summer, but it wasn't until the leaves were crisping into golden-brown flakes that I had news of Venutius – he was doing well and so was Vellocatus. The message was brief but he sent word that he was learning new skills and battle tactics and had already been involved in some aggressive manoeuvres in which he had impressed his commanding officer. I sent a rider north to take the message to his parents, who I was sure would be more excited than I was. I wondered which tribe had suffered in these "aggressive manoeuvres', if indeed Venutius was even on our soil – the Romans could easily move him across the water, to one of their other campaigns. Two more winters passed and as I arrived at the third, I barely thought of my husband.

Age had crept up on me while I was living a strange half-life – married but not with my mate, leading a tribe but not officially. White hairs had begun to sneak through my dark locks and my body, once soft and slim, was beginning to develop a plump, yet muscular appearance. I had seen twenty five turns of all seasons and I was ready for some kind of change.

Nothing much had in fact changed for any of us yet, despite the arrival of the Romans. They had set up campaign camps which encroached onto our territory, and had already begun establishing quarries and ruthlessly extracting stone which they transported south for their new roads, but our land was so vast we hardly noticed them. Sometimes officials visited me and my father and we entertained them graciously so that they went away again comforted by our loyalty. Plautius came a few times to solidify our tentative contractual arrangements, though his presence could barely be spared from the immense activity in the south. He didn't try to intimidate me again and with that aspect out of the way, proved to be a reasonable man to deal with. I didn't trust him as far as I could throw him, but we could share a meal well enough. There was no talk of the survey of our land they had promised. To keep it from happening as long as possible, I was careful to always provide supplies to Plautius when I could, sending gifts for Claudius also. I gathered some of the slaves from our people to the north east, and although they were angry about it, I told myself that deep down they surely understood the necessity. I told them slaves were being taken from across our land, though this was not actually true. But it kept them calm. And it was only a temporary lie - I knew I would have to dispatch all our slaves in the end, what few we had of them. It made life difficult for those who were using thieves and murderers to work their land and care for their animals, and it was those for whom I felt pity, not the slaves themselves who had done terrible wrongs in their time. I avoided thinking about the dark times ahead when I may have to send ordinary people away in chains.

Although I sent batches of mutton and spelt wheat to Plautius, along with some leathers and furs and a good number of cattle, I never sent anywhere near the full amount we could have spared. That way, if they increased their demands, I would still be able to satisfy them, at least up to a point. I received some gifts also, little tokens to keep me happy, I suppose. Claudius had ten plum trees sent to me and we planted them in a sheltered spot on good soil, with fencing around them. None of us had seen a plum tree before, though we had eaten the fruit in syrup several times. I have to admit I was a little excited by them - it was the first positive thing to come out of our arrangement with the Romans and even if it was symbolic rather than materially significant, at least it gave some optimism.

So now, the winter was upon us again, and here I was, just

waiting for something to happen. I rose one morning, the fire hot and crackling in our snug home. Outside, my breath was like a mist on the freezing air and I only stayed out there long enough to do the necessary. Once relieved, I went back inside to eat. Antikia sat warming her toes by the flames and talking to Tantoban. I could hear Mandulay still snoring in her bed. Fistoc, who generally attended me, particularly since two of my guards had been sent off to fight for Rome, sat whittling away at a piece of wood with his large hunting knife.

"No sign of my father?" I asked, glancing round them all.

"Still sleeping," said Antikia.

I wandered to the far end of the roundhouse, where the heavy leather drapes curtained my father's bed from view. Listening for a moment, I heard nothing. No breath, no movement. My skin prickled. I took hold of the leather and moved it to one side.

"He's not sleeping," I said, as I took in his pale, still face, "He's dead."

There were gasps from behind me and Antikia came over. She felt his forehead, which I knew would be cold as the air outside.

"Died in his sleep," she murmured, "not a bad way to go." But her voice shook and I couldn't look at her for fear I would break down. I dropped the leather, which fell into place with a whack, shielding him once more.

"Tantoban, Fistoc, send our riders out with the news, but ask them to be discreet. I want half our fighting people here within a day. By the time Plautius hears about this, we'll have an army here mourning my father and confirming that I am the leader of this tribe."

They nodded. Fistoc ducked out to make preparations but Tantoban hesitated and came slowly to my side.

"This is a dangerous time for you and you have to concentrate on taking control of Brigantia," he said, very quietly, "but it's a sad time too and you will need to mourn. If you need me, I'm here. Since your husband is not." He held me very briefly, and his ageing warrior's body was warm and welcome against me. He took my hand and kissed it as I nodded my understanding.

"We should send our own message to Plautius, not let him hear of it second-hand," said Antikia, as Tantoban followed Fistoc outside.

"I agree. We'll send a rider tomorrow when I can be sure our own people are on their way."

Mandulay was stirring so I left Antikia and went to tell her the news. It was on her shoulder I cried, since I could not go to Tantoban until nightfall and there was no one else to whom I would let down my guard.

An army of Brigantians saw my father into the other world, and though I had organised it as a show of strength should the Romans question my authority with him gone, still it seemed a fitting tribute. Antikia mourned deeply for her elder brother, the man she had always revered above all others. I grieved also, but that was tempered by the knowledge that he was with my mother and that the dark moods of his recent years were over. He had lived a long and fruitful life and died a peaceful, comfortable death. I couldn't ask much more, however much the loss of his constant companionship and support pained me.

Tyrius and Risha both came, though Venutius was by all reports overseas and unable to return. I didn't search for more information, from his parents or anyone else, but sadly accepted his absence. Risha made a little joke, something about weddings and funerals being the only time we met. I looked at her oddly and for once, she seemed unsure of herself.

"Cartimandua, you have my complete loyalty and devotion," she simpered.

"As I expect," I answered, unable to raise any warmth towards the woman who was my mother by marriage. Her dull grey eyes and fat face twitched with the connivances of her calculating little mind. I don't think I spoke to her again on that occasion.

Plautius didn't come. He sent his sincere condolences and said that he would pass the news to Claudius. He also said that I was now recognised as the client queen, with all the responsibilities that the role possessed. I heaved a sigh of relief. I had wondered whether Plautius might turn on me when my father died and I always remained suspicious that it was mainly the fighting with the tribes to our south west that stopped him seizing the chance to try and remove me. What a triumph that would have been to him, to take all my land under direct Roman rule – a gateway to the north and a hammer pressing down on the south! But they were overstretched. Three legions were spread over the entire south, fighting countless battles with all the small tribes. The tribes were falling, one by one, but it took time and effort and this was all in my favour. More importantly, Plautius was like a starving wolf in his quest to hunt down Caratacus, who was still protected within the blue mountains and their vicious people. The Silures and the Ordovices had taken him in like one of their own, not caring that he was Catuvellauni, only concerned with using any means at their disposal to fight their new enemy. I admired their clear purpose – if only the Catuvellauni themselves had allied with their neighbours, perhaps it wouldn't have come to this. Even so, Plautius faced an almost insurmountable task and it was by no means certain that the Romans could penetrate the high hills and mountains that defended Caratacus now. As I had hoped, Caratacus was making life difficult for Plautius and that was directly beneficial to me. Other tribes might look to Brigantia with envy and anger at our privileged client status but they didn't understand that we were balanced on the knife edge, in almost as much danger as they were.

Parts of Brigantia had more exposure to this threat than my own circle of people. We were relatively cushioned, being deep inside our territory to the north, but those on the south west borders, who had maintained good relations with the Deceangli, watched in horror as the Romans used their land to camp on whilst preparing attacks against these neighbours. This happened soon after Kesaven's death and I guessed that Plautius had chosen his time wisely, seeking to avoid conflict with my father and confident that I would relinquish my interest in the Deceangli as a show of goodwill to protect my own position.

"We can't let this happen," voices muttered and then shouted, when the council met. "The Deceangli rely on us!"

"We can't put the whole of Brigantia at risk for one small tribe," I sighed. "Plautius needs a route through to Caratacus and the Deceangli are in the way. If anything, the Ordovices should be supporting them, since the Deceangli are their own front line."

I was right, I knew I was and so did they, but the impotent anger on their faces worried me. I saw how it would all unfold – the Romans crushing everyone until only the client-tribes had survived. We might still be intact at the end of it all, but how would my own people feel about me, knowing the sacrifices that had been made? I had to cling to the hope and belief that Rome could offer something in return that would make it all worthwhile – progress, development, prosperity. I thought of my little plum orchard and wondered how I could show my Brigantes how they might benefit from our new alliance, distasteful as it might at present be. I didn't feel happy about the attack on the Deceangli though, and it rolled over again and again in my mind as the first betrayal I had been forced to commit.

I rode fast in the dying sunlight, knowing I had to get there that night. Tantoban and Fistoc were with me, and a few other men, but not my usual travelling companions. We made for the ridge of hills and moor that split the southern part of Brigantia in two. My cloak, a dark, mud-splattered one, was fastened around me and I wore no jewellery or anything that would mark me out.

"This is it," I yelled, and we drew the horses to a stop at a place I had been several times with my father. "This path leads down through the valley and we can approach through the woodlands there." I pointed in the gloom and Fistoc followed with his eyes.

"What then?"

"Lets see what we find when we get there." I gave my horse a kick and he set off again. In truth I had no idea what to do, I just knew I had to do something. It didn't surprise me that of all Brigantia, it would be this place that would lead a rebellion. Though our tribe had a reputation for being warlike and violent, most of the families living in Brigantia were so isolated they had little chance to make war with anyone. There might be some little communities emerging here and there, but it was rare to see more than two or three roundhouses standing near each other. In some areas, though, and particularly near the borders, clusters of families did draw nearer together, taking protection in numbers. Our Camulodunum was a little different, in that it was well within our territory, but I suppose it was an unofficial centre for the southern part of our land. The tribal centre was wherever my family based itself and that had traditionally been further north. Below us, Brigantia stretched into an arrowhead – the Deceangli on the the western edge, the Corieltauvi on the east and the Cornovii at the southern tip. In the middle of this southern arrowhead of land, the hill known to us as Camulodunun stood high and distinct in the midst of low valleys and steep surrounding moors. It was a strange place, a perfect defensive position, and yet not occupied. Instead, the summit of the hill was used for gatherings – trading, sports like dog fighting, rituals and the like. A large part of the flattened hilltop was just right for events like these, but the north corner still bore remnants of a large wooden building, sitting charred and broken within deep earthworks. No one remembered what it was for or who had lived there, but everyone believed a fire had destroyed the home that had once been there and the locals said the cause was a furious dragon who once lived in the hill and was angry at the settlers who had built their home upon it. Perhaps that was why none of them would actually live on the mount.

I steered my horse down the valley side and into the woods below. The geography of our southern regions had been explained to me by my father, and he'd told about the abandoned homestead at Camulodunum and how no one would use the site as a permanent settlement because it was cursed. We had ridden past it that time when he had shown me round all our southern borders, back when I had found the coin in the marsh. I remembered him telling me how spirited and aggressive the locals were, and how he wouldn't take me there that night. When I was older, we visited properly one midsummer and were the guests of honour at a fist-fighting competition on the summit. My father and mother led me up the hillside, followed by drinking, singing men and women, and they watched my surprise at the beauty of the old earthwork defences and the way that as you ascended the hill, the whole world seemed to spread out below like a patchwork of greens. The people were wild, and they fought like animals - even the ones who were not competing - but they sang and danced as the sun finally went down and my mother, who was from near that part of our world originally, pulled my laughing father up to dance with her too.

As we cantered our horses out from the thickest part of the woods, Tantoban saw a plume of smoke rising from beyond a low ridge of land and we continued in that direction. Our pace had slowed to a trot. The air was cold and still and only the thinnest sliver of light from the dying sun illuminated the evening. I heard movement in the thicket to my left and pulled my horse to a halt. The others drew up behind me and as they did so, a great whooping set off behind us and a band of men surrounded us with rough spears and dirty looking knives.

"Get down off the horses!" shouted one and I felt a hand grab my ankle. Behind me, Tantoban drew his sword, and but for me fetching a hard kick to the insolent man below me, he would have had his hand severed from his arm. Instead, Tantoban's blade stroked through thin air. I drew my own sword from its leather sheath and levelled it towards the man now rubbing his jaw.

"Name!" I barked, "Before I chop that head clean off."

"Give us yours first," he spat, his eyes taking in the quality of the workmanship on my weapon. The others seemed to have fallen back a little. I wondered if they were a gang of thugs out to mug unsuspecting travellers. If so they wouldn't be used to people as well armed as us.

"Cartimandua," I said and I dismounted, to Tantoban's obvious annoyance and concern. "I think you will want to tell me yours now." He looked to his friends, who were whispering to one another and made a timely decision to cooperate.

"I'm Ostet. I live just nearby. We were just keeping an eye on the paths, you know, like a patrol."

I re-sheathed my sword slowly.

"And why would you feel the need to do that, Ostet?"

"You can never be too careful, what with these Romans and all..." His voice tailed off and there was some coughing and shuffling of feet behind me. Oh dear goddess, I though, is this the nature of the rebellion - embarrassed, shambling ruffians without even proper weapons? I gathered the group together, six of them in all, each one a good deal younger than myself and looking increasingly unsure of themselves. Ostet explained that his home was the one behind the ridge whose smoke plume we had seen and that his father had known my father and would welcome us.

Once the horses were tied up outside, he took me in, along with my men and one of his, who turned out to be his younger brother. Inside, an older man jumped to his feet as Ostet whispered in his ear.

"I remember you, Cartimandua and I knew your father too. I'm Ostet's father, Hubek. We met a long time ago, when you visited us at midsummer."

"A messenger came to me yesterday with a tale of a rebellion," I said, taking his arm in greeting, "I'm hoping to get a true version of it from someone."

"Ah." He looked uncomfortable and motioned us to sit. There were others in the house; his wife, a man who could have been his brother and some younger children.

"It's in your interests to be honest with me." I kept my voice neutral and waited while he tried to organise his thoughts. I could practically hear them - is she a true pro-Roman, will she slaughter us for what we've done or is she sick of them too and will she support us? Eventually he started to describe events that had been unfolding to the south west.

"And you see, they're camping on our land, great big groups of them in their fancy get-up with their silly stone houses. All along the borders, so you can hardly cross the line, but you've got to stay on one side or the other of it or risk being cut down. Well it's not that simple, is it? I mean there's families what come from both sides and live on the border, they've all been moved out of the way. And there's them that rely on trading in that area and they can't go where they used to any more and they're losing business because of it."

"So it's a trade problem?" I asked.

"Partly, I mean you can't trade with the Romans, they take what they want for free, and if they did pay, it'd be with them silly coins that's no use to man nor beast. But trade can move. Families have resettled; some of them have come up as far as here, wanting to be well away from it all. But the real thing is, them Romans are killing people. Not our people," he added as he saw my face, "but they're really fighting the Deceangli now, and when some of them get through, onto our land, the

Romans are hunting them down and stopping us from taking them in. Well, it isn't right, not when they've been there for so long and it's their land and what right do the Romans have anyway...' He ran out of breath and stopped.

"So what is this rebellion I've heard of? How big is it?"

"Oh, it's big," he said proudly. "Every one south of here, well they're bound to be in on it. They all hate it you see, what the Romans are doing, and everyone says it'll be us next, no matter what they say about Rome protecting us. So we've been collecting all the weapons up ready and we've got gangs out watching for Roman movements and trying to pick up any Deceangli that make it through because they'll want to fight as well. All the young ones are ready for it, just show them a Roman and they'd chop him right down to size!"

"And all this is being organised from here? Who's in charge?"

"Well, no one especially. There's a group of us, you know, running messages back and forth so we know what's going on. Its easier from here, the Romans would be watching them like hawks nearer the borders."

"Do you think they suspect anything yet?" My heart was starting to beat a little harder in my chest.

"Oh no, they're too busy trying to sort their camps out and do the fighting and everything. They say the Roman and Gaulish auxiliaries are always cold you know, not used to it here and they're miserable having to be here at all." He managed to sound pleased and offended at the same time.

"And what is the plan? Do you even have a plan?" I had to admit, Hubek did not seen especially bright.

"When we've got enough people and weapons, we'll attack them, from behind. They won't be expecting that."

"And when will that be?"

Hubek shrugged and looked unsure. Some of the bravado slipped away from him as I looked him hard in the eye.

"This is a very dangerous time for Brigantia." I said, "You

are talking about drawing us into a war that would destroy the agreement we have with Rome."

"That was an agreement your father made. Perhaps you don't entirely agree with it?" Hubek tried, hopefully.

"Don't fool yourself that there was any choice in the matter. Can't you see how powerful they are? If you put a dent in the army on our border, Plautius will simply send more men. He has legions stationed in the south and the east." I stopped as Tantoban leaned close to me.

"Why are you bothering to discuss this with the man?" He whispered. "He obviously doesn't know much."

I looked at the floor and tried to gather my thoughts, but all I could see was my father, dancing with my mother at the midsummer celebration but the pretty twirls of my memories had become confused because my sister was there dancing too. I had no idea what I was doing. I persuaded myself I was being very clever, trying to undermine Rome in secret, but I look back now and realise that I was grieving hard and I was out of my mind.

"I want to speak with some of these rebels, the ones who are really behind this," I said to Hubek. Tantoban sighed and shook his head but I ignored him. "Get them here tonight, I'll wait for them on the hill."

They were a mixed band of men – a couple of young warriors and a handful of older ones. I knew a few of them, by reputation only, though one remembered me from when I was a child. It was full dark but about to make the slow turn to dawn when they came and Fistoc had lit a fire that burned while we got some sleep before they arrived. Ostet and his friends were guarding the entrances at the foot of the hill, making sure no one else decided to come up and investigate.

"I know about your plans," I said, without preamble, "and I understand why you want to take this kind of action. I can't support you openly. If I do, the agreement Brigantia has with Rome will crumble and Claudius will send more legions to crush us. There is only one way this can possibly work."

They watched me with suspicion and I felt a stinging pity for them. They would most likely die but I knew I could not stop them if they were determined. I could only advise them.

"Keep collecting weapons, but hide them very well. You will need to wait for the right moment to attack. That moment will be when Plautius is busy elsewhere and the army on our border is heavily engaged with the Deceangli."

"The Deceangli will all be dead if we wait much longer," said one of the older men.

"No, they won't. Their land is very hard to attack. The Romans are struggling to gain a foothold and they're taking their time to get it right. Plautius won't let his men all rush in and be killed. Neither will I. You must wait, possibly another winter. I don't need to tell you how to fight and you've shown that you can organise yourselves. Now you need to hold your nerve and wait until the time is just right."

They agreed, eventually. Then one of the men asked whether I could get them more men and weapons from the north.

"I can't do that," I said, shaking my head, "There is too much risk that Plautius will get wind of what I am doing. Your best chance of success is if I am not involved at all."

"And what if he gets wind of what we are doing?" asked another.

"That's the risk you are all taking. I have an agreement with Claudius that keeps our tribe safe from persecution. That agreement protects you too, until you step outside of it by attacking the Romans. I can't put all our people in danger to support your rebellion, which only has a small chance of success. Do you understand the difficult position I am in?" I knew I sounded helpless, but I wanted to be honest with them.

"We understand," said a large man with a huge beard

that covered most of his face, and he looked to the others. "Cartimandua is right; this will work better if she's got nothing to do with it."

"And if it fails," I added, "then I may not be able to do anything to save you."

"Yes, we understand that." The bearded man kept his voice level, but there was an edge to him. They were all disappointed in me. Despite my explanations, they couldn't really see why I wouldn't raise the whole tribe up to fight against the Roman army. It was pointless continuing. All I could hope was that they had heeded my advice about picking the right time to attack.

"Good luck. If I hear anything that will help you, I'll send a message through Hubek."

They accepted my well wishes begrudgingly and left, picking their way carefully down the hillside in the dark and I sat for a while longer with my gang of attendants. Fistoc was uncomfortable and went for a wander by himself. I watched him kicking at clumps of grass and the ancient stumps of blackened wood that poked from the ground. He was too far away for me to read his expression, but his body language said it all – he was embarrassed and dejected.

"Fistoc is an idiot." Tantoban had been quiet until now, not speaking at all while the rebels were there. "He's as bad as they are – eager for a fight without even thinking where it will get them all."

I blew a long, heavy breath out and tipped my head back to look at the charcoal grey sky which was covered in thick, slow moving clouds.

"They didn't understand at all, did they?"

"Why was it that important to you that they should?"

"I suppose part of me feels I've done the wrong thing. I'm the chieftain of this tribe, but I've given them nothing at all – no help, no weapons, just a wish of good luck. I should be fighting all this."

"You can't fight against the tide," said Tantoban, resting a hand on my shoulder. "Your father knew it too. We could all go out of this screaming and dying or we can come through the other side of it, different but still alive and happy. If you asked people in Brigantia what they wanted, I know what most would choose."

"Really? I've wondered whether it's just in our nature to want to fight. Peace doesn't appeal to everyone."

"Not everyone, no," Tantoban shot a look over at Fistoc who was a blurry shadow on the edge of the hill. "There are people like him and me who've lived for the fight, who can take pleasure in slicing an enemy down and not fear the same in return, but most people, just getting along with their lives and raising families, don't want war in their fields and hills. They don't like the Romans but they've heard about what the legions can do and they know we have no choice."

"We have the choice to die fighting."

"And those that want it can go and join Hubek's friends. But it's not their decision whether Brigantia fights Rome, it's yours. You've done what you felt you had to do – more than you had to do. You've spoken to these men at your own risk, you've promised them information. But don't put all our safety at risk just because a little gang of thugs have made you feel guilty. There's no more you can do."

I knew he was right, but it didn't make it any easier. I hated the way those men had looked at me and I felt crushed inside that they thought I was a coward. And yet, something deep within me said that if I let the views of lesser men, such as they were, get to me, then my leadership of the tribe was doomed. I had to be above all that. I had to believe in every decision I made and I had to disregard the negative opinions people might have of me. If some people didn't like me, then so be it. I wish someone had been there to tell me that before I went chasing off on that fool's errand, but the only person who would have spoken such sense to me and to whom I would have listened was my father and he was gone.

My parents, my guiding stars, were dead and gone. My aunt was grieving for her brother. My husband, or what passed for one, was far away in more than one sense of the word. People within my own inner circle were uncomfortable with the pro-roman choices I was being forced to make. On top of my natural grief at my father's death, I was questioning all my decisions and starting to feel the dangerous hesitation that can lead to prevarication and topple a leader. I returned home with a sense that nothing was stable and with a desperate need to reconnect with something bigger than myself. I turned to the solace that Tantoban had offered, and that he had provided to me once before. Losing myself in the oblivion of sex with the ever-faithful warrior who had served my family across two generations and believed in me even though he'd witnessed my insecurities was the tonic I needed.

SPRING AD48

Tantoban was a risk. I knew that and so did he. I wielded a lot of power and could do more or less as I pleased, but even so, it was bad form to bind oneself to the leader of another tribe, then bed down with a lesser man in his absence. So we kept our liaisons highly secret. It was surprisingly easy to do, since we had known each other for so many years and simply continued to act very naturally with one another. There was such an age difference, no one would have suspected anything anyway. Although I appreciated the need for caution, I felt no guilt over our relationship, given the state of my marriage. I needed Tantoban in those years. He was the calming, reassuring presence who echoed the wisdom he had heard from my father and helped me believe in the decisions I had to make. The only other person I trusted as much was Antikia, but I could never be quite as honest with her about my occasional self-doubts. Anyway, in reality, Tantoban and I only coupled perhaps once a month or thereabouts so perhaps "relationship' is too strong a word.

Antikia seemed to have a succession of male friends, none of them very serious, and when anyone mentioned marriage to her she would visibly shudder. Tyrius occasionally visited, usually on the pretext of escorting goods down from the Carvettii to be traded on or passed to the Romans. Sometimes he brought word of Venutius and sometimes I would pass on news I had heard, but I wouldn't need all my fingers to count the number of times this happened. Tyrius was proud of his son, but I could see the worry in his eyes, that perhaps Venutius had forgotten about us all, forgotten his heritage, or worse, that something might have happened to him. I often said that perhaps it was just his way of dealing with his new situation - sending messages home all the time would surely only have increased any home-sickness he felt. Perhaps he was even prevented from contacting us regularly.

The selfless, sisterly part of me that still cared for him hoped that Venutius was well and that he was having a good time rampaging with the Roman army.

Tyrius had another reason for visiting and that was to grasp rare, short snatches of time with Antikia. She entertained him happily enough, like a familiar blanket that she could cosy up to, but she didn't love him and she was as happy when he left as when he arrived. I felt a little sorry for him as his infatuation seemed to grow, not diminish, with the passing years.

One big event had occurred since I met the rebel leaders at the hill named Camulodunum. The last autumn, a full year after they had agreed to hold off their offensive until an appropriate time, the governor Plautius left our lands and returned to Rome. I heard of his leaving only a short while in advance as they kept it very quiet, knowing a change of leadership would give rise to a possible period of instability. I immediately sent word to Hubek, the man who had told me of the rebellion, but the message was delayed because of horrendous weather and by the time he let all the others know, it was too late to take the initiative and anyway, the legion on our border was holed up for the early winter and attacking would have been too difficult. It was a shame because the new governor, Ostorius, was as iron-willed as his predecessor and barely missed a step as he moved into Plautius's role.

We were lucky once again that the Romans were too heavily occupied in the south and the west to worry much about Brigantia, but disturbing news filtered through that Ostorius had ordered all the tribes to be disarmed.

"Surely this doesn't apply to us?" people asked at the council meeting I held. Baranak had passed away, but his son, Davit, was wild-eyed and furious at the suggestion that we might have to surrender our weapons. Even the more moderate advisers, like Antikia and quiet, elderly Binto, were very concerned. I sent a message to Ostorius, full of support and offering our hospitality any time he should like to visit. The reply I received was courteous and clear. He thanked me for my offer, promised to take me up on it, but requested that in the meantime our tribe remain loyal and vigilant for any defiance towards the Roman empire. It wasn't a threat, at least not the veiled style of warning that Plautius would have sent. In fact, it was a good indication that Ostorius did not mean to strip our tribe of its weapons, so long as we used those weapons on the side of Rome. Once again, the size of our territory probably helped us, because the Romans just didn't have the time or energy to strip us of our arms. Even so, we discreetly passed word around that any excess weapons should be hidden and that people should be ready to conceal their most valued pieces if the army moved into our territory – the ones that had been handed down through generations. Ostorius could easily change his mind.

I felt uneasy all winter about the situation in the south of Brigantia – so much so that I confided in Antikia about the involvement I had with the rebels. I told her how we had met, how I had explained that I could not support them but that I would pass on information.

"Phew, its not too bad then," she said, once she knew I hadn't made promises to arm them or fight with them, but she was shaking her head at me. "What were you thinking?"

"I didn't know Ostorius was coming, let alone that he would start confiscating weapons!"

"But you suspected it might happen? You warned the rebels to hide their weapons, didn't you?"

"It seemed like the right thing to do. It was a difficult time," I said. I wished that I could take back the whole thing, and that I'd never gone down there to meet them. It hadn't won me any friends and all it had achieved was to put me in danger - me and our whole alliance with Rome.

"We need to stop this whole thing from happening," Antikia said, conscious, even if I wasn't then, that my judgement must have been heavily impaired from losing my father. "I have no idea how we do it, unless we warn Ostorius before they act?"

"Be traitors to our own people? Invite the Romans onto our land to impose their justice?" I was horrified at the prospect.

"You could round up these trouble-makers yourself."

"No, Antikia. I just can't do it. I can't face them all again. I'll warn them not to act, I'll say it's too dangerous."

"Do you think they'll listen? Anyway, you're not sending them any more little messages. Each one is a link back to you, and if the Romans ever investigate properly they could easily find out you've been involved. No, what you should do is issue a command to the whole tribe that we are fully in support of the Roman legions who need our loyalty and assistance and that anyone who transgresses this order will be severely punished. Ostorius will be pleased and the rebels will know that it's a warning directed at them. Whether they choose to heed it or not is their decision. We just have to hope they don't try and drag you down with them."

"I wish I'd talked to you in the first place," I whispered, "It just seemed wrong what Plautius was doing to the Deceangli and I was worried people would think-"

"-that you were weak for not fighting? Only an idiot would think that. Come on Cartimandua, you are doing what your father wanted and no one thought he was weak."

If I needed more proof that rebellion was a bad idea, it came right on the heels of that conversation. Presivin, who had been away trading a batch of trained dogs, came back with news about the Iceni.

"Who?" I asked, "Oh, you mean the rich horse people. Aren't they a client-tribe too?"

"They've revolted! They hid a huge load of their swords and bows and then after the supposed disarming, they attacked the Romans."

My stomach did a small flip.

"But they were too small in numbers, the Romans have flattened them. They killed all the men involved, and all their families too."

"A foolish move by the Iceni, then," said my aunt, shooting a glance at me.

"But brave." said Presivin, "They just couldn't stand being made to hand over all their weapons. The Romans have no idea what that really means - giving up swords and bows that have been handed down through families, arms that really mean something to their owners. Or maybe they do know, and they set these conditions on purpose, to break their enemies completely."

"Is there any other news? What will the Romans do now?" I was impatient for the facts.

"The Romans are satisfied that they've weeded out all the conspirators and so they've chosen a replacement Iceni leader."

"They've removed the previous one, then?"

"Yes, Antedios or something? He's been executed and so have a couple of the high-ups who rebelled with him. The Romans have picked out someone completely unconnected. Prasta... Prasuta... oh some name I can't remember, but he's going to be the client king and they'll all have to remain unarmed."

"Is that all of it?"

"Yes, that's as much as I heard. Although people are saying that Antedios thought he could take advantage of Plautius leaving and the Romans being unsettled. By the gods, they thought he was bad, but this Ostorius sounds even worse!"

Presivin rushed off to share his gossip with anyone who would listen and Antikia gave me a nudge.

"Better issue that warning straight away," she said, "I think we should keep on Ostorius's good side. If he has one."

I had a nightmare, just before the Brigante rebels made their move. In it, I was in the woods, but as I sat there, the trees began falling, until there was no forest and I seemed to be floating in the dark. I saw Venutius but he didn't even recognise me. When I awoke I was clammy and my fist was gripping the fur that covered me. We were into spring and it was over two years since I had met the men who were so intent on attacking the legion based to our south. They mustn't have been able to hold themselves back any longer and had finally broken out in full revolt. When I heard that they were fighting, directing their offensive at the Romans on their border, I acted instinctively to protect my family and the majority of our tribe.

I sent a message to Ostorius, who was already travelling up around the blue mountains to get to us and was apparently furious that his campaign to find Caratacus had been disrupted. I said I would meet him and support whatever actions he took. I arranged a large army of my own – carefully selected sections of the war host – to move south with me and we arrived before the governor, in time to take up a position just back from the Roman campaign camp on the border from where we could provide Ostorius with the requisite help and also discourage any attempts by this new governor to push further into Brigantia. The Romans had taken some losses from the unexpected rebellion, but had abandoned the push into Deceangli territory and entirely regrouped on our land to counter this new threat so most were at the campaign camp anyway.

If I was in any doubt about the seriousness of our position, a walk through the improvised Roman military base provided all the horrific evidence I needed. In some of the strange stone buildings they had erected, they'd crammed Brigantian prisoners. Round the back, attracting flies and rats, was a huge mound of dead people. This grotesque pile of mashed and sliced bodies, with limbs and heads sticking out at sickening angles had been heaped efficiently out of sight. I didn't know why they'd been brought here and not left where they fell. Perhaps it was to frighten the survivors or to intimidate the locals. Perhaps it was to intimidate me.

I hardened myself against all that, even though it was like nothing I'd ever seen before - it was worse, even, than the spiked heads at Camulodunum - and I knew my future dreams would be pitted with the evil of that sight. The only thing that mattered there and then was securing our tribe's position with Ostorius. I met with the captain of the legion who was initially hostile but soon warmed up. He was a man living on foreign soil, battling the weather as well as the Deceangli and now rebel Brigantes. He had clearly decided he needed all the help he could get, and fortunately my reputation was, so far, intact.

"Do you have enough help for your wounded?" I asked him.

"We might use some assistance," he admitted, "Supplies are running low and if you have bandages, medicines, anything of that nature, we have need of it."

"Our medicines might be a little different to yours," I said, "But I'll send some people along to help. What about food, firewood...?"

"The rebels set one of our food stores on fire. We can manage, but...'

"I've brought sacks of grain, cured meat and other food. From our own stores," I added and he nodded gratefully.

"The... army you've brought, can you be sure of their loyalty?" He looked doubtfully at the varied mix of men and women who were setting up temporary roundhouses and leather tents and getting fires going as the sun was dipping down on the horizon.

"Absolutely," I said, "they are entirely at our command." I put a hand on his arm. He gave an awkward smile and escorted me towards his own quarters.

"I expect you find our buildings as strange as we find yours," he said, as we approached the greyish, stone box with its square holes for windows and a narrow wooden doorway.

"I'm sure they're fine in Rome, but in all truthfulness they don't seem very suited to Brigantia."

He motioned me inside. There was a woven rug on the floor, a fancy-looking table that held papers and books and alongside it stood a few chairs. The building was separated into two rooms and I assumed he slept in the other one. I took a seat. We waited for Ostorius. Someone came in after a while and lit a fire in the corner. The captain arranged two candles. I felt cold, despite the fire. Draughts were leaking in everywhere. He talked to me, just a little at first, but opening up more as we waited, about his life here and how he had worked his way up through the ranks of the army. He even mentioned something about a wife back home, though he changed the direction of conversation as he veered too close to the thorny issue of Venutius and his enforced absence from my life.

Eventually we heard the noise of Ostorius approaching. Much as I had disliked Plautius, he had at least become a known quantity to me. This was to be my first meeting with Ostorius and I had no idea how he would regard me. His few messages had been diplomatically polite but his actions towards the Iceni pointed to a disdain for even those tribes that had accepted the client status. For all I knew, he might believe I had been involved in the rebellion and have me removed, installing someone else as leader of the Brigantes, someone in whom he could place more trust. I thought of my secret meeting at Camulodunum and though I had not, strictly speaking, condoned the rebellion, my chest tightened and my breathing grew shallow. It was these fearful thoughts that kept me fastened like stone to my chair while the Captain went out to meet the Governor.

"Ah, Cartimandua?"

I rose and turned to face him. He towered above me, broad-shouldered and with a nose that looked like it might once have been broken. He was dirty, with traces of muck on his face and arms, and stains on his clothing. In the dying light and the shadows cast by the candles and the fire, he seemed twice the size of a normal man and I had to fight the instinctive reaction of being over-awed.

"And you must be Ostorius." I greeted him as warmly as I dared, taking his arm and to my relief he responded.

"Forgive me, I need to sit down. It's been a hard journey." He pulled a chair towards him and I sat back down also. "Get someone to fetch me a drink and some food, will you?" He asked the Captain who was standing behind him.

"They'll have hot food ready in our camp by now. Get my man outside to bring it," I said, and the Captain disappeared for a few moments. The man outside was in fact Tantoban who had stayed close but discreet ever since we arrived.

"The captain tells me you've brought your own army to help out? That bodes well. I hope you're going to give me your full support in dealing with this so-called rebellion." Ostorius didn't have Plautius's iron gaze or threatening tone, but I kept in mind that Plautius had not stripped tribes of their weapons nor culled hundreds of disarmed rebels. Ostorius was friendly, warm even, but he was clearly not worried about taking bloody action.

"Of course, it goes without saying. However, from what I can gather, this is a very disorganized action by a tiny minority of Brigantians."

"They've managed to do quite a lot of damage." Ostorius was rubbing his calloused hands in the heat of the fire.

"And that is very unfortunate. What are your plans now? I understand the prisoners are all being held nearby." I thought of Hubek and Ostet. I hoped they were not there.

"So the Captain tells me. I shall give it some thought. Execution, perhaps. Or maybe enslavement. And we must ensure that we have the ringleaders so there will be some further investigations." He was matter-of-fact, probably only concerned with getting back to the real battle further south.

"Can I make a suggestion?" My voice was tilting a note too high, nearly giving away my nervousness. "My tribe have been very welcoming towards the Roman... occupation, and it is only a small group of troublemakers who have agitated the minds of normal, hard-working people. If you exact a harsh punishment, it may only serve to give these southern Brigantians the false belief that Rome is merciless, cruel and unjust. With more moderate action, it would be far easier for us to quell any bad-feeling that has arisen."

"Moderate action?" He laughed and looked hungrily to the large wooden bowl of hot stewed meat and barley that Tantoban had just brought in. There was one for me as well and we began to eat. My stomach growled. I had not realised how famished I was. Tantoban handed the food over and stepped back outside. If anything, he was becoming too careful around me these days, growing wary that he would overstep some appropriate boundary and betray the arrangement between us.

"Moderate might be the wrong word," I said, striving for an amiable tone to my voice and wishing Tantoban had stayed in the room. "What I mean is, harsh action, but only against the main troublemakers. Let all the poor fools who don't know any better go free. Then they'll remember how fair and forgiving Rome was."

"That is one tactic, yes, but I'd feel a lot easier knowing the whole lot of them were out of the way." He slurped his stew. "This is good stuff."

"It's just that with us being such a large tribe, if bad feeling spreads, it will be much harder to manage than, say, it was with the Iceni." I held my breath, hoping I had not gone too far.

"True," he pondered. "I can't be turning round to face Brigantia all the time when we're busy trying to get to that bastard Caratacus." We ate for a little while in silence. The Captain was waiting silently near the fire.

"I'll tell you what," Ostorius said at last, "Since you have shown such willingness to help and I have no cause to believe you are in any way involved in this sorry mess, then perhaps on this occasion I might take your advice. If you had been involved, it would be a very different matter!"

"The thought is appalling to me, I am loyal to Claudius," I answered, without any hesitation.

"The Captain and I need to discuss details now." he said, "you should return to your own camp and organize the supplies and assistance you have promised. Tomorrow we'll see if we can sort the wheat from the chaff. I'm sure the Captain has some methods for rooting out the leaders of this rebellion."

I nodded and wished him a restful night before leaving the draughty little building. Fistoc had joined Tantoban and the pair of them were waiting outside.

"Did you hear any of that?" I asked them as we walked away.

"Only bits," Fistoc answered, under his breath. "This is a mess. They should have picked a better time."

"It would never have worked. There are just too many Romans to fight against. I know it's hard, but we're on the brink of a war here, no matter how nicely Ostorius is acting. All we can do now is to limit the damage."

Fistoc nodded reluctantly and Tantoban hummed in agreement.

"If we can give Ostorius the main rebels, or at least men who will claim to be the leaders, then he might not start executing everyone. If he is given cause to investigate further, his army will find hundreds of Brigantians who hate Rome and will be put to death for it. They might come in force to disarm us all."

"I'll do what I can," said Fistoc, "From what I've heard, they have some of the men who arranged this attack. They might be persuaded to confess if it means the others can escape and maybe rise again some day."

It seemed a foolish dream to me and perhaps to Fistoc also, but he needed something to believe in and so did the men who would have to lay down their lives.

I slept reasonably well that night. My main fear now was that one of the rebels would tell Ostorius that I had met them and sent messages to them. But I had faith that Fistoc would protect me, by getting them to see the greater good they would do if they just ended this now. I myself would have had no chance of appealing to them, both because I could not reach them unseen and they would probably deride my efforts even if I could, but Fistoc truly understood their single-minded passion for the fight and they would listen to him, I was sure. Looking back, the alternative was probably too frightening for me to contemplate, since I had no doubt that Ostorius would execute me for my involvement, as easily as he had shared a meal with me.

In the morning a small group of our council met - Antikia, Presivin, Tantoban, old Gorlensa and a few others, chosen specifically for their moderate attitudes. Davit and some of the more troublesome high-ranking people were under orders to remain at our home to the north, taking care of matters there. As soon as we'd heard of the uprising I had demanded that we establish the location of Venutius and send him word of the situation. He was nearing the end of his five year commission with the Roman legion and I was sure they would relieve him, particularly since, if he was truly converted, he would be a good man for Ostorius to have present. I felt I needed his support and I was sure he would come, once he knew the predicament I was in, though I had no idea how long it would take him to travel from whatever place, near or far, he may be.

I presented myself and the other council members to Ostorius at mid-morning and we had a short discussion. He wanted to assess the situation by himself first and I began to feel a little uneasy. Despite his assurance that he trusted me, I knew that now, in the cold light of day, he was treading warily.

"I plan to interrogate the prisoners and send out small detachments of soldiers to visit and question local homesteads," he told me, without preamble.

"I'm sure you'll find the locals willing to help. I have personally requested that all my tribe demonstrate their loyalty to Rome. If you find any places where this is not the case, I would like to be informed," I replied, though his muffled grunt in return hardly constituted a proper answer.

A vast line of armed men had been arranged during the night, north of our position, to block any unauthorised movement north or south. A number of Roman auxiliaries appeared to have been stationed to keep track of our movements. I wasn't especially surprised by these developments. It made sense and was more in keeping with what I had been led to expect of Ostorius. He was a nice enough man in person, but he was no idiot. All we could do was continue to be pleasant and hospitable, as if we really were the hosts, and they were welcome guests. For their part, Ostorius, the Captain and their troops played along, eager to still have our cooperation when it came to food and other supplies. The people I had brought with me worked alongside the Roman soldiers who were in charge of food preparation and our herbalists and wise men and women helped the Roman experts in healing. Watching all these people work, it was odd to see their increasing friendliness and then see the suspicion and distrust on the faces of the more hardened soldiers who were keeping their eyes on us. Of course, many of the so-called Roman soldiers were really Celts and Gauls, first or second generations of conquered tribes from the land mass across the south eastern sea. They had more in common with us than they did with the natives of the country they served, so the ease with which working relationships developed was not quite so surprising.

The situation continued for quite a few days, although I ate with Ostorius each night and he conveyed to me some of the progress they were making. It was a delicate and uncomfortable time and I felt increasingly alone and vulnerable. The camp gave me none of the guarded privacy of my homestead and Tantoban's own careful hesitation had made me more inhibited around him. Antikia was my most useful companion, but there is something about having a strong man by your side and in your bed that makes the world more bearable and I missed that comfort. I wondered if Venutius had been found. Maybe he was dead after all, as we had sometimes feared. As days passed, I began to believe he would never come. Then, finally, a group of riders came into camp. They were Romans, but they came directly to me and one of them slid straight from his horse and approached, tall and menacing in his Roman dress and headgear. I looked past him to the rest of the group, who were dismounting, but saw no sign of Venutius and my heart sank.

"Cartimandua, it's me," said the man in front of me, and I saw at last that it was Vellocatus, my childhood friend and Venutius's closest companion. The years away had changed him immeasurably. He looked so much older, with creases around his eyes and mouth and his hair was cut differently. In his Roman outfit, he passed easily for a simple Roman soldier, but when I focussed on the colour of his eyes and the shape of his cheekbones, it was the same old Vellocatus there in front of me. I embraced him tightly, so thankful to see a man I could trust and with whom I would not have to watch my words so carefully. He hugged me back and his breath was warm against my ear as he let out a deep sigh.

"Come inside, have something to eat," I said and we entered the roundhouse that had become my home over the previous days.

"It's good to see you looking so well," he said, "I was so worried about you when we heard the news and I came as soon as they let me."

"Are you here for good, or do you have to go back?" I asked.

"No, they've discharged me. Venutius offered to remain in his position and send me to your aid."

"He's not coming?" I gasped. "Does he know how serious the situation is?"

Vellocatus hesitated, his brow deepening into a frown. Then he said, carefully, "I think that's why he's not coming."

We sat down and I pulled a fur around my legs which had been aching during the long cold days of organising my encampment and tip-toeing around Ostorius. Vellocatus stared in concern and I wondered if I looked old and haggard to him, after his five years away.

"He's afraid of being dragged down with me if everything goes badly. He thinks if I am executed, he can slip into the saddle and become the new Brigantian chief," I guessed, sparing Vellocatus from having to explain further. He gave a single nod.

"Coward!" I spat, biting my bottom lip and imagining Venutius with his new Roman friends, no doubt distancing himself from me, perhaps dripping poisonous comments, when all along he was the one who wanted to fight against Rome, not I.

"I'm sorry-" Vellocatus began, but I cut him off.

"I should have anticipated this," I said. "It isn't a real surprise. I'm glad he sent you, Vellocatus, although perhaps that says something of his feelings about you too."

"That I'm expendable? You're probably right." He laughed, a short bitter sound, and then turned grave. "So are things really that bad. Was Venutius right to stay away?"

"I don't know. Ostorius is a difficult man to understand. We have a kind of friendship and I've supported all his actions. We're supplying food and medicinal help and for his part, Ostorius has taken some of my advice. I think he is beginning to accept that executing large numbers of Brigantians will just store up further trouble. He's a man who adapts quickly and he knows that what worked with the Iceni won't work here."

"Ah, I heard about the Iceni trouble," said Vellocatus.

"And what did Venutius think of that?" I asked, curious about my husband's shifting allegiances.

"He was shocked, I think, and angry. But he kept it well

hidden."

"He's not a true Roman yet, then?"

"Oh no, Venutius is a Carvettiian to the bone, but he's playing a careful game."

"As am I. Ostorius seems to trust me now and Venutius will be most disappointed to learn that I am unlikely to die horribly in the near future." I tried to sound light-hearted but the years of our childhood together and the sacred vows we made when we were joined together throbbed through my mind in painful reminder of what we had lost.

"What can I do, now I'm here?" Vellocatus asked after we had been silent for a while.

I detailed for him how the camp was working, what reserves we had and how we were rationing them. I told him as much as I could of Ostorius and said he could accompany me when I met with the Governor, to represent Venutius and act as a reminder of my husband's faithful service to Rome. Venutius could at least be of some distant help in that respect.

From that morning, Vellocatus subtly took control of running the camp, encouraging me to stay inside as much as possible. He made a good impression on Ostorius and at dinner told stories of the campaigns he had been involved in during his time serving Rome. Ostorius was pleased with the loyalty Vellocatus displayed and his increasing ease with us was complimented by the lack of success his army was having in finding any grand Brigantian plot to overthrow the occupation.

"My men have made final reports to me today," he said one evening, wiping food from the corner of his mouth. "We've covered the area as planned and found no evidence of a large-scale threat. Your people have been relatively forthcoming, Cartimandua, and apart from a few little incidents, I have to conclude there is nothing much to worry me here."

The little incidents were unpleasant - families who had been openly hostile when the Romans came searching and interrogating had found themselves thrown in with the prisoners already awaiting a grim fate for their role in the rebellion. But the warning I had sent out before the rebels attacked had prepared many people to be, at the very least, coldly civil towards the invading army.

"Brigantia is loyal to Rome. Your findings are no surprise to me, of course, but I am relieved and happy that your operation here has been successful." I raised my goblet of ale and took a gulp, trying to hide the immensity of my relief.

"There is still the problem of all the prisoners. My captain tells me we have four hundred and twenty men and women locked up now."

"Are the leaders of the rebellion amongst them?" Vellocatus asked.

"Apparently four men have admitted under questioning that they organised the attack. They claim two other men involved were killed in the fighting."

"So you have succeeded in rounding up all the leaders?" Vellocatus kept just the right level of praise in his voice, without sounding overly obsequious.

"So it seems. They will be executed. But that leaves me with a lot of others to deal with." Ostorius was waiting, testing us.

"Well you could execute them as well," I pondered aloud, "or perhaps send them as slaves."

"Two options, yes," agreed Ostorius.

"Or perhaps some of them could be used in your own army – the ones who regret their actions, at least. I'm sure you could use men who know the land and understand the people?" Vellocatus paused. "It would help us to increase the goodwill towards Rome amongst our tribe if you avoided executing all four hundred and twenty people."

"Yes, I believe Cartimandua pointed that out to me when we first met." Ostorius had the smug look of someone who has already made their decision and Vellocatus nodded graciously and fell quiet.

"I'll tell you what! I'll release the women. My men aren't happy killing the fairer sex anyway." He put an emphasis on the word "fairer", as if he didn't believe Brigantian women were particularly fair. "And we'll identify some of the younger men who are willing to join our army, say for twenty years of service. The rest, we'll execute, along with their leaders. Does that sound reasonable?"

It wasn't a question. It was a challenge. Part of me was curious as to what Ostorius would do if I argued. After all, he had no evidence against me and I had been forthcoming with aid and support since the rebellion had occurred, not to mention all the produce Brigantia had been supplying to the Roman effort beforehand. Mind you, I suspected that he hadn't needed evidence to execute all those Iceni nobles and he was watching me in a manner that suggested he was interested in what would happen if I argued too. Ostorius was a man who built strategic alliances but he wasn't a man who made friends. All our shared evening meals in the previous days counted for nothing now.

"I believe that is a fair and just solution. May I be present when you identify the recruits? Some of them are just hot-blooded fools, no doubt, and a calming word from their queen might just help them see that their cause is pointless and a soldier's life far preferable to the alternative." Vellocatus had glanced at me when I used the word 'queen'. It was a term that the Romans understood better than 'chief' and although it tasted sour in my mouth, I had learned to speak with a Roman tongue when I needed to.

"Absolutely, the more good soldiers we have, the better." Ostorius nodded at me with a satisfied smile. "Let's get on with it tomorrow."

We ate the rest of our meal quietly. Business was concluded and I had done the best I could.

In the morning, the sun shone through the trees casting long spidery shadows over the ground outside my hut. When I stepped out, the warmth of the rays fell on my arms and I guessed summer would come early this year. I made my way to meet Ostorius, with Vellocatus, Tantoban, Fistoc and Gorlensa alongside me. Antikia had travelled north to check on our homestead. The Captain was waiting outside his odd little house and he waved me over.

"The Governor is tending to a few other matters this morning. He asks us to go ahead and pick out the recruits."

"Let's get on with it then," I nodded, eager for the whole evil day to be over.

He took me to the larger of two buildings where the prisoners had been housed. A vague rotten stench drifted in the air, even though the bodies of the fallen rebels had all been cleared away and burned. The Captain yelled a few orders to the soldiers waiting nearby and within minutes, the dishevelled people within the building, and those in another compound further away, were assembled in the dusty clearing in front of us. I scanned hastily for faces I might recognise, and picked out a few. There was an older man who I remembered watching in the fist-fight competition all those years ago. There was one of the boys who had been with Ostet the night I had travelled to the hill. There was a woman whose face I remembered and whose roundhouse I had stopped at with my father on one of our travels.

"We've separated the main trouble-causers to avoid any flare-ups," the Captain said to me. "Most of these are just idiots."

I bit my tongue. Gorlensa strolled to the Captain's other side.

"I believe the women are to be pardoned," she stated, in her grainy old voice.

He took a step forward, ostensibly to shout to his men again, but more likely to position himself away from the gnarled woman whose long grey hair floated in the faint breeze like mist over a forgotten valley.

"Women, over here," he commanded, pointing his arm away to the left of us.

There was a shuffling as some of the females followed his orders, but quite a few stayed put. The Captain yelled again.

"What's the matter with them," he asked impatiently. "Don't they understand?"

"They're staying with their families," I explained, feeling sick. I looked out at the stubborn faces of at least a dozen women who had not moved, some with blood dried around grazes and wounds, all dirty and tired. Beyond the shuffling crowd, I saw Roman soldiers dragging some bodies out of the building where the Brigantians had been held. I tried not to think about what it must have been like in there, these past days, waiting to be executed or worse, with the smell of death all around.

He tutted and shook his head as if the whole situation was ridiculous, then he began to explain, very slowly as if they were all stupid, that the women were to be pardoned and the men offered the chance to fight in the Roman army. Eventually, following embraces and quickly spoken words, most of the women moved away, grouping together where the Captain had directed.

"Do you want to speak to them now?"

I had asked for this, I'd told the Governor they might listen to me, but I felt an awful sense of futility as I looked out into their unyielding faces.

"I cannot force you to take the Captain's offer," I said, "but you must see how pointless further rebellion would be. The Romans are our friends and we must find a way to live together in peace." There was an outbreak of muttering and I heard curses being spat into the ground.

"You can take the offer of a military career, learning how to fight like the Romans do and travelling to all kinds of new places, or you can die here today. I am telling you this as your chief, and as a leader who is answerable to the Emperor. You can help to keep our tribe strong and safe, or die for the sake of another tribe who will be crushed anyway. The fight is not ours, we have a pact with Rome and we must uphold it." I was pleading but I didn't care if they saw my desperation. Maybe, if they did, they would see how I had no choice but to ask them to take this offer. I racked my brains for more words that would convince them, but as I stood there at a loss, Vellocatus came forwards.

"Cartimandua speaks what you already know in your hearts," he called out, "and I know how you may feel about serving those whom you have called your enemy, since I myself have been in service to Rome for the past five years – as indeed has Venutius, the great son of the Carvettii. But Rome is a strong and noble empire that will help those that fight in its cause. You have the chance of a glorious future and so do your families, if Brigantia remains loyal to Rome and stays within the Emperor's favour. A soldier's life is hard, but you'll have the chance to travel, to fight, to learn. It is your choice, die for a cause which no one else in Brigantia supports or make a new life for yourselves."

"Think about it," shouted the Captain. "Soldiers over there, dead men stay where you are!"

Vellocatus turned away from the crowd.

"Thank-you," I breathed.

"Lies, lies," he whispered back, "They'll die in some foreign place, worked to exhaustion, more slaves than soldiers." His face was lined with bitterness.

"But what choice is there? We've done what we had to do." Now that I had to console someone else in the position I had been in for years, I knew it to be true.

The small crowd was beginning to separate out. I saw doubt on the faces of all those who had decided to take the offer but I hardened myself against any guilt. We waited a few moments, and then the Captain strode over to examine the band of men who waited uncertainly to our right.

"Too old, too old," he said pointing his finger at about five or six men in turn.

"We took that deal in good faith!" blurted out one of the men, eyes full of fear of execution.

"You lot, get over there with the women. Pardoned on grounds of remorse and infirmity." The Captain gestured, and one of his soldiers shoved the bewildered old men in the direction of the women. "The rest of you can get to work cleaning that building out. You've left it a stinking mess. Consider this the start of your army training."

They trooped away, glancing back uncomfortably at those who remained, resolute, in the middle of the clearing. Some of them were looking towards their women, probably understanding that they would never see them again. One woman wailed and would have run towards her man, but the group around her held her back. The remaining men stood before us.

"All of you, back in the furthest barracks until after noon. The Governor wants to be back for that part," the Captain added to me.

I was turning to leave when a voice rang out.

"Dirty whore!"

The shout was shocking and brutal in the solemn atmosphere and I turned, gasping, to see a man lurching forward from the condemned group, his arm outstretched and ending in a fist that pointed straight at me. Vellocatus stepped sideways in front of me, though the man was too far away to be any real threat.

"Roman bitch!" A different man, but both had the same look of disgust in their eyes. Then the soldiers who were all around us swarmed forward with their weapons raised and forced all the men back and towards their gaol.

"Looks like we're doing you a favour by killing them," observed the Captain. "They don't like you, do they?"

He moved away and we were left in the clearing – me and my

three trusted aides and a gang of women and old men who were eyeing me with an unpleasant fascination. Fistoc and Tantoban took charge of these pardoned Brigantians, taking them back to camp for food and help with their injuries. Gorlensa and Vellocatus waited while I stood in the morning sun, still with the scent of death all around me.

It must seem odd that although we were by nature an aggressive tribe, I so disliked bloodshed and death. It was simply not in my nature and although I could hunt and kill animals without any difficulty, I felt my stomach rise up like a swollen river if I had to look directly on the torture or death of another person. Fortunately, with the exception of one or two bad incidents, my early years had been relatively peaceful, given that the efforts of my father and grandfather meant that the Brigantes were largely united despite consisting of smaller groups with their own little identities. As I went to the place that had been cleared for the execution of the rebels, I had the sinking, suffocating feeling that such peace was at an end and I would have to witness more of this kind of violence, if not worse.

Ostorius was a practical man. For him, there were two main purposes of the event; to get rid of the troublesome rebels and to send out a message of deterrence to others. He also knew he had to temper his message of deterrence with some indication that Rome was merciful. Brutal slaughter had worked with the smaller tribe of the Iceni, but here, in the vast hills and valleys, news of malicious Roman vengeance would simply inflame opposition and Ostorius did not have the resources to monitor and suppress every uprising that might occur. He settled on a coldly simple plan. The remaining rebels would be executed by crucifixion. His men had orders to allow a few hours to pass, and then start breaking legs to speed death on.

I had heard tales of Roman crucifixion – how sometimes they would nail up hundreds or thousands of people, leaving them hanging on big sticks of wood until their bodies just gave up. Compared to some of our own methods, it didn't seem too bad, but then any enforced death is gruesome, for the person suffering it.

I waited with Vellocatus until Ostorius called for us and then we joined him on the short walk, where I felt that dizzy, sickened feeling come over me. In front of us, on a shallow hillside, the soldiers were finishing off their business of tying men onto stakes of roughly-cut wood that had been planted into the ground like ugly, barren saplings.

"I heard you used nails," I murmured, my eyes wandering over the scene of misery.

"Sometimes, sometimes not. It's easier to string them up, rather than wasting nails and struggling to hammer the things in." Ostorius was distant, only partly interested. He was eager to be off, to get back to the real fight with the tribes beyond the blue hills to the west.

There were moans rising from the eerie living trees in front of us. I tried not to look at faces, not to stare into the eyes of all those men who blamed me more or less entirely for their demise.

"Is that a woman?" Ostorius pointed in disbelief at a figure in the distance. "I thought we let all the women go!" He shouted the last bit and a few of the soldiers nearest to him pretended not to hear.

"Yes, I saw her this morning," I said. "She didn't leave the group of rebels bound for execution."

"Foolish barbarian," muttered Ostorius. "Sigustus, get over there and break her legs now. If we have to suffer the bitch's screaming, let's get it over with."

He turned to me.

"You might wish to leave now, Cartimandua."

"I'll go in my own time," I answered. I watched the stout man named Sigustus take some kind of club from another man.

He made his way, reluctantly I thought, towards the woman, who spat at him as he approached. Then with a great swing, he brought the heavy weapon round in an arc and smashed it into her pale, dirty legs. There was a bone-crunching noise, followed by a low, unearthly howl that grew for a few moments till I thought I would spill the contents of my stomach onto the floor. Then the howl descended into a moan of agony. Her legs were bloodied and shattered. A crucified man a little way apart from her began shouting a torrent of abuse at all of us, his curses mixed with screams and cries.

"Husband?" Ostorius enquired, his voice tinged with the barest hint of discomfort.

"Or brother, maybe. I don't know." I kept my attention on the woman. Her body, strained from being hung up, and bleeding from her broken legs was now making jittery movements, like a half-dead animal.

"It's quicker this way. Nasty, but effective. It's worse when they're left for days, trust me."

I shrugged. He was probably correct and it was no more brutal than the things my own tribe might do to each other, or to outside enemies. Knowing this didn't make it any easier for me to witness.

The moaning from the woman had all but stopped. Her head hung to one side, as though there was no will left in her to keep it upright any longer.

"That's it for a while," said Ostorius, "My men have orders to break all their legs by dusk. Tomorrow we'll be moving on and I trust we can rely on you and your council to keep order here and continue to supply us with the necessary taxes?"

"Yes. I wish you well, Ostorius." I felt numb to this powerful Governor now. As my natural enemy, I detested the level of subordination he had brought to my tribe. Yet if he had been a Brigantian man, I would have probably liked and admired him. What I wanted most was for him to be well away from me, so that I did not have to play with my words any more and maintain this difficult balance of diplomacy.

"I'm going back to camp now, to start packing up," I said and he nodded and took my arm in the parting grip.

"The emperor was worried about the Brigantes, but he will be pleased to know that you have supported us in this matter."

Vellocatus put an arm around my waist once we were out of the governor's sight and I leaned on him as he guided me away. I saw Tantoban watching us though I barely registered it at the time. But afterwards, I remembered the curious, almost hurt expression on the old warrior's face.

AUTUMN AD48

As the forest that bordered the royal settlement began to turn a thousand shades of red and orange and the nights drew in closer and colder, I received a message from Venutius to say he would soon be returning. The tone surprised me, for it was full of warmth and, apparently, desire. He said he was longing to return to our home and my arms and had been preoccupied all the long days with my safety and security. I found the message more unsettling than if he had simply said he'd be back soon.

Since Ostorius left our land and we were able to withdraw back to our base in the north of Brigantia, I had felt much more confident and comfortable. I had nagging doubts about the well-being of our borderlands in the south, which would still be ridden over by Roman troops in need of camp and supplies, but it was easier to distance myself emotionally when I was also at a distance geographically. Perhaps it helped that Brigantia was never so much one tribe as a collection of smaller tribes, allied together. In my head, I had sacrificed that small, strange corner of our land and people, to preserve the majority, even if my heart still sickened with the memory of what they had suffered. They distrusted me anyway and I could do little to help them. In the north, I was still the venerated Cartimandua, daughter of Kesaven and I could breathe easily, at least for a while.

With help from Vellocatus and Tantoban, I set about expanding our small collection of roundhouses into a grander enclosure with larger huts and a garden area around where I had planted the plum trees Claudius had sent me. I think Tantoban found it all rather foolish, but Vellocatus understood my need to throw myself into an activity that was domestic and homely. Antikia thought we should build up our defences around the site and I let her take control of that. She was a harder woman to know these days. Her face gave away little of what she was thinking and I doubt that she confided in anyone. The more

135

optimistic among our family and council still wondered if she would find a man to settle down with, but I believed the time for that had passed. Antikia would no more chain herself to a man now than roll in the dung heap for fun. In fact, she seemed to regard it as highly unfortunate that I was chained to Venutius and did not hide her feelings when I relayed his message to her.

"Ah, sweetening you up before he returns." she grimaced, "That man has no shame, after abandoning you to the Governor like that. You want to watch him, Cartimandua, he is playing games as usual."

"Maybe," I agreed. I partly hoped it was all a game for appearances sake because I could not imagine how it would be to genuinely receive this near-stranger back into my bed and my heart.

He arrived on a still, misty day, cantering in like a returning hero with a big smile on his face. Vellocatus rushed out to greet and assist him and I was reminded of the hierarchical relationship that existed between the two men who had once been such friends. It jarred with my own friendship with Vellocatus, which had always carried a casual equality and mutual respect. But when Venutius swung down from his horse, the signs of age on his face blurred by his movement, he looked so much like the easy-going boy who had been like my brother that I softened a little and returned his smile.

He approached and embraced me and I saw a scar along his neck and another that ran over his left cheek to his jaw line. I touched it instinctively.

"Old wounds," he whispered, "Nothing to worry about."

"And you are well?" I asked, striving for some formality.

"I am that. And you? I thought of you often, especially when I heard of the rebellion and all that you had to deal with. I hope Vellocatus served you well in my absence?"

I nodded, biting back the harsh words, the questions

about why he had not come himself, questions he had deftly side-stepped with his ready choice of words. We went inside the new roundhouse I'd had built for us and Venutius admired its size and the beautiful leathers and woollen cloths I'd arranged as partitions and decoration.

"You must have a great many stories to tell," I said, going to the fire and settling myself down on a soft bed of rugs. None of the others had followed us inside, so it was just Venutius and I.

"Mostly stories I'd rather forget," he answered and a shadow passed over his face. He rubbed at his cheek and then turned on his bright smile again. "But I have done what the Romans asked of me and that is all over now."

"You seem glad to be away from them. I thought you would enjoy the opportunity to fight and to learn all the new skills they have to teach."

"At first, maybe I did." He sat down heavily across from me. "But fighting against people who have no chance to win is not so much fun. And as for what they could teach me, well perhaps I understand more about battle tactics and troop formations now. But they couldn't teach me to handle a weapon or to kill a man any better than I already could."

It might have sounded like arrogance to anyone else's ears, but I knew Venutius and I could hear the disillusion in his voice. He'd had five hard years of gruelling work with foreign invaders who assumed they were superior to him. No wonder he was all smiles to be home. I felt cruel to be asking him questions about it. I overlooked that he had chosen to stay with them rather than return to me when I needed him and Ostorius would surely have allowed it. What did I really know of what he had suffered or what circumstances prevented his return to me? A part of me niggled, "why don't you ask him?" but the larger part told me to leave it alone. Handing him a big jug of ale, I asked if he would be travelling north to see his family.

"My family is here," he said. "My family is you." And he

moved round next to me and kissed me.

Vellocatus became quieter and more reserved with Venutius back home. We no longer shared long conversations or went for walks together and it made me feel that perhaps I had acted inappropriately throughout the summer. I dismissed those worries whenever they popped into my head. Such ideas about propriety and hierarchy were more Roman than Brigantian. I'm chief of this tribe, I instructed myself, and I talk with and walk with whomever I like. Yet I did not seek Vellocatus out and he kept a distance from me.

I was preoccupied with rediscovering the stranger who was my husband and I did not miss the company of Vellocatus, or indeed Tantoban who had shifted completely into the background of my life. Since the rebellion, Tantoban had resumed his stoic, supportive position as one of my trusted friends and advisers and never assumed any over-familiarity beyond this. If on some nights I missed the sturdy presence of his reliable arms around me, I dismissed the longing easily. If he had any serious yearning for me then he hid it absolutely. I found that I missed more the gentle conversation and advice that Vellocatus had begun to routinely provide, but I did not allow myself to dwell on this.

Venutius became my constant companion, showing interest in the garden I was building and giving advice to Antikia on construction of walls to line the boundary of our homestead. She wasn't altogether keen on using the stone he recommended, but her curiosity about Roman building techniques outweighed her cynicism and I was pleased to see the two of them getting on together as they arranged for increased defences to be built around the rich, well-watered pasture-land that was home to our precious livestock. When we received an order in the winter for supplies of grain, meat, leather and slaves to be sent south to Ostorius even that did not entirely spoil our mood. Venutius and I sat down with the council and worked out exactly where to take these supplies from. Venutius suggested by how much we could reduce the amount we actually dispatched.

"They always ask for more than they think a tribe can provide," he insisted, "but they always have a figure in mind, below which they will not accept."

The slaves were becoming a difficult issue. We were running out of our own slaves and criminals and dipping into the resources of smaller sub-tribes was giving us home-grown enemies that we did not need.

"What happens to the slaves we send?" I asked Venutius, one evening. He had become my unofficial source of Roman information and enjoyed being the one to reveal all the secrets of our occupiers to me.

"They go where they are needed," he said. "Some back to Rome where they always need fresh blood and some into the army. Rome has soldiers in far away places we've never even heard of, where there are animals you couldn't imagine and where the sun shines so hot it burns the skin of people not born there."

"You make it sound like an adventure," I laughed.

"I doubt it's that. They're bound for a short, hard life when they're shipped off."

"Do they get worked to death?" I asked questions of Venutius like a child, which probably goes to show how relaxed I had become with him. I knew the answers really, or could imagine them, but I liked just to hear him talk.

"Sometimes they do. It depends where they go and who buys them. A hard-working slave with a good owner can sometimes work their way into freedom. They buy themselves back you see. But a more unlucky slave might be beaten, raped, for punishment or just for fun."

I hadn't seen any of the men and women we had sent. I had them rounded up and sent in chains without ever needing to go anywhere near them. They didn't really exist to me.

"I could deal with all the demands that Ostorius makes, if you like," Venutius suggested. "I know what he wants and it would save the council a lot of time if I was in charge of checking the orders and organising the dispatch of supplies in future."

I considered this.

"It needs to go through the council," I decided, "but you must always be there for such discussions, since you know better than we do what we can get away with."

He smiled, but I thought he looked a little disappointed.

Another season passed, and another. I hid in the comforts of my newly designed home, which was looking more like a village now. Following all the excitement and horror of the rebellion, our tribe had gone quietly to ground, slumbering like an ancient dragon and pretending to ignore the invaders at our heels. I had my mind on other matters too. With every cycle of the moon, I was reminded that I had no children and sometimes, the nasty words Venutius spoke so long ago came back to haunt me. I wondered if I was barren, like he had said, or if our union was cursed. Venutius was ever active in bed, so it wasn't a lack of intimacy that was the problem. He didn't bring it up and neither did I but I assumed he was as disappointed as I was each time my bleeding came.

While the rest of us almost forgot about Rome and about Governor Ostorius fighting his ongoing battle with the Ordovices, Venutius brought them into conversation whenever he could, usually to point out how complacent we were being.

"They'll turn on us in time," he would warn, like a gloomy doom-sayer predicting carnage from a bundle of dried bones. "They're busy now, but when they conquer the Ordovices, they'll head north."

"I'm a client-queen," I kept reminding him. "They have no need to turn on us, not while I support Rome."

But Venutius itched with the worry that our time of peace

would come to an end. He wanted to stockpile weapons and even asked if he could organise a great army to defend us if necessary.

"You can't do all that without Ostorius knowing and then he'll simply sweep in and take whatever you've created." But Venutius still burned under the yoke of my leadership and yearned to build something of his own. Through his eyes I saw a vision of Brigantia completely unified with a massive and organised resistance that even Ostorius could not break, but I did not believe that Venutius could really achieve this. More likely, he would get us all crucified for treachery and that was a fate I did not want to come close to for a second time. When he brought it up, again and again at council meetings, he received similar replies and only Davit came near to supporting his ideas.

"If they knew how you really felt about them, how surprised the Romans would be!" I said to Venutius one night.

"If they had treated me correctly, as befits my status, then they would not have had to worry," he retorted and I could almost see his old pride, like a noxious vapour, seeping back into his heart.

SUMMER AD50

It was over a year since Venutius had returned, nearly two since our tribe's rebellion had dragged the Governor away from his fight in the west. We'd heard that Ostorius's health was suffering from the constant, terrible fighting and it felt as though the war would go on forever. Tantoban happened to be travelling in the south-east when finally there was decisive news.

"The Deceangli have fallen completely and the Ordovices and Silures are fighting under direct command from Caratacus," Tantoban informed me on his return. "Ostorius is breaking through at last."

"He is taking a long time to do it."

"They say it could go on a lot longer, with Ostorius chasing Caratacus round the hills, but the Governor is getting closer."

"This news will get Venutius worked up again," I sighed and Tantoban gave a sympathetic smile.

Sure enough, all Venutius could talk of for days was how this might be our one last chance to join with the great Caratacus and overthrow the Romans once and for all. As far as I could see, Caratacus was more lucky than great, and had spent years hiding out in the impenetrable hills while the Deceangli were gradually crushed. Granted, it had given him time to gather his strength and put together an admirable alliance between the formidable Ordovices and Silures, but he was still racing around like a cornered rabbit, holding off forces far larger than his own.

"We could attack from the rear; crush the Roman army between us, the mountains, and Caratacus's force."

"Like the rebels tried to do while you were away?" I asked. "Look where it got them!"

"With a proper leader, things would be different," he answered. Did I hear accusation in his voice? I hoped not and pretended to ignore it.

"We don't have enough people or enough food to fight this

battle. We're a client-tribe, not an enemy of Rome. Let's just see how this war between Caratacus and Ostorius turns out."

"Oh yes, sit and wait. That's always your answer!" He flounced out of our home for the first time since he had returned to me.

I was so thrown by his behaviour that I went out myself, in search of Antikia with whom I could talk the issue through more sensibly. At first I couldn't find her. It was just after midday and she wasn't in the main enclosure. I walked the path that led to several more roundhouses and as I passed the metal-work hut, I heard Shamatin's voice like a steady hum from within. Shamatin had been apprenticed to Jacavin and since the elder had died the year before, he had finally become the most senior of our skilled craftspeople producing weapons and ornaments that Jacavin himself would have been proud of. He was older than me, but a little younger than Antikia with plain brown hair and matching non-descript eyes but set in a beautifully shaped face that bowed out at his cheekbones and then sculpted back in to make a pointed chin. I stepped closer to the doorway and saw him leaning over his solid wooden work bench while he talked. Close to his side stood Antikia.

"Can you see the bloom?" he was saying, "Now that the iron is cooling, the impurities sink to the bottom and the iron rises up, like bright clouds."

Using his tongs, he lifted the soft, spongy iron out of the bowl furnace and dropped it on the black wooden surface.

"Now I have to beat it with this," he said, yanking up his huge sledgehammer from the floor and proceeding to pound the innocent metal with such vigour that Antikia flinched back, even though his blows were expertly precise, governed by his bulging upper arm muscles. "Can you see the impurities still coming out?"

"How long do you beat it for?" She asked and I heard honest curiosity in her voice as she dared to move a little closer again.

"As long as it takes till it's clean, then it's ready for forging," he answered, between blows. He happened to glance up as he spoke and caught sight of me by the doorway. He threw me a grin and gave a jerk of his head in my direction. "Someone wants you."

Antikia glided out, with only a slight flush on her cheeks.

"Got a sudden interest in metal working?" I enquired but she politely ignored me as we wandered from the hut. "Venutius has just stormed off in a temper. He thinks we should ally ourselves with Caratacus and attack Ostorius from the rear."

"Ha, is there anyone left around here who hasn't heard him going on about that?"

"What do you think?"

"I think you have everything to lose and he has everything to gain."

"How so?"

"You're still the chief, and you have all the power and a good relationship with Ostorius and therefore with Rome. Venutius is your husband and that is all, and even though he fought for Rome for so long, they still don't acknowledge him. Or at least that is how he sees it."

"But this is stupid, it's just like before he ever went away!"

"Ah well, men never really change you know. He's still the same man, just older and more dangerous. I warned you, when he returned, that he was playing games."

I rubbed my head in frustration, hurt that I had thought we were getting somewhere when really nothing had changed.

"Come back inside and see how he forges that iron," Antikia said, "It's like magic watching him work metal."

"Some other time," I said. "Are you sure it's the metal you're interested in?" But she just laughed as she walked away.

SPRING AD52

On a warm day when the buds on the trees were starting to unfurl and the birdsong rang out high and clear, I took a walk into the woods to leave an offering for the spirits of my father and mother. In amongst the dappled light and the ferns I was at my most peaceful and could almost pretend I was a child again, without all the weight of the tribe on my shoulders. The days of studying my father and learning how to command such a large territory seemed at once terribly distant and just like yesterday.

I reached a big old oak tree, off the path that ran alongside the stream and unstrapped a leather pouch from my waist. In it I had two beaded, leather necklaces and I hung them both on branches of the tree with a murmured remembrance of my parents. I stood and listened to the strange, twittered conversation of the birds high in the canopy above me and considered that I may have no children to remember me once I was gone. I touched my stomach and felt numb. I no longer had a pressing desire for children or for the kind of immortality they offer. I would have settled for a happy marriage with Venutius, but it seemed that was not on offer either. We would always be up and down, I realised now. It was just the way we were meant to be.

There was a crackling behind me and I went for the dagger strapped to my arm, turning with the blade ready in my hand.

"Whoa! Just me," said Vellocatus, stepping backwards. "Sorry, I didn't want to interrupt." He had his bow slung over his shoulder with a bag of arrows and his legs were wet to his thighs from wading across the stream. I sheathed my weapon and motioned for him to come closer.

"You've been out hunting?"

"Just a bit of target practice," he said.

We stood in silence for a few moments. Then he said he would walk back with me if I liked, so we set off at a strolling pace.

"Does Venutius ever talk to you about me?" I asked, eventually.

"Not really. Passing comments, you know."

"Like what?"

"He hates it when you override him, especially in front of the council." Vellocatus shrugged. "You know how proud he is."

"Always his pride!" I spat into the undergrowth. We continued walking for a few minutes.

"I didn't expect you to answer my question. I thought you'd keep his confidence," I said.

"I'm his armour bearer, his closest servant, but you are the chief of this tribe. I answer to you above anyone else." He swung one arm as he walked, the other holding the long bow on his shoulder. His easy gait made me think that this reasoning was something he had arrived at a long time before. Perhaps he had wrestled with the divided loyalty, perhaps not, but either way he was my man.

"If Venutius could accept my authority with as little fuss, life would be much simpler."

"There's nothing you can do about how Venutius feels," he replied. "He'll never be completely happy unless you bow down before him."

"Would any man?" I sighed.

"I would."

We had come out into the meadow, in sight of the enclosure of roundhouses that now looked far grander than in my father's day. I glanced sideways at Vellocatus, the spring sunshine catching his dark gold hair and lighting up the side of his face. As I opened my mouth to reply, he pointed into the distance.

"Riders, coming over the hill," he said.

I followed his outstretched arm and saw tiny figures on horses, galloping at a fast pace.

"Trouble," I said and we headed with speed to the enclosure.

He was dark and lean with the dirt and blood of battle still upon him. He wore his hair scraped back so that the skin of his face stretched over his cheekbones and when he smiled, he bared his teeth like a wolf. I took his arm in greeting.

"I am glad to be on your soil, Cartimandua," he said, "If you will have me, that is."

"Caratacus, it is high time we met. If only you had come to us when Plautius first arrived!" I could not keep the disparaging tone from my voice. Here was the Catuvellauni leader, who thought himself so high and mighty that he needed no assistance from us or the Corieltauvi when the Romans invaded his lands. Here was one of the three famous sons of Cunobelinus, who between them thought they could take over all the lands and tribes that surrounded them. This man and his family before him were once a distant, potential enemy and now he came to me for refuge. I was not going to give him an easy time.

"Ah, who could know what was to come? And it was too late to form an alliance by then, Cartimandua. We were already in the thick of the fighting."

"And yet, thankfully, you allied with the Silures... Are there any left? Do you have a fighting force of any kind?"

"All dead or captured. I come to you in a sorry state in the hope that you will accommodate me at least for a short while."

"Do you have any wounds?"

"Nothing serious," he motioned towards his leg where dried blood had caked around a strip of cloth tied to his calf.

"Mandulay, can you fetch some ointment and something to dress this with? And for his men, if they are hurt?"

She nodded, and shuffled her ageing frame off towards the hut we used for storage, where she kept her herbs and strange brews. She kept looking back as she went, fascinated to finally see the legendary Caratacus, whose fighting in the hills had kept everyone enthralled for so long. Looking at the faces of those hovering nearby, I saw the dangerous mix of awe and respect in their eyes.

"We need to speak privately," I said. "Will you come inside?"

He followed me, along with Vellocatus who had no intention of leaving me alone with the man.

"So the battle was lost?" I asked. "Ostorius won?"

"It pains me to say it, but yes that much is true." He settled back and raised his leg up with a slight wince. "We picked a site along the river, good and high, and built a great rampart so we'd have the advantage. They could only come at us across the water, soaked through and heading uphill. It should have worked, we should have crushed them. But they crossed the water without effort - the level was lower than we hoped for - and then they lifted their shields up over their heads all at once," he raised his arms, lost in his story-telling, "and made one great big shield that we could not break through. They came so slowly! Like a drunk beetle swaying up the banks, through the marshes. We threw all we had at them - our best bow-men rained arrows down, we sent spears, and we even hurled heavy rocks to try and break their shell, but still they kept coming. Worse still, they brought tools with them - pick axes and shovels - and while we battered them with useless sticks and stones, they dug our defences out from underneath us. When the rampart gave way, they flooded in and of course, all the men at the back, who simply had to walk with their shields up, were ready and willing for the fight. All of our people were exhausted from their futile efforts. You cannot imagine how it destroys your spirit to see an army advance on you like that, with no way of stopping it, no exposed flank or throat to rip into."

He paused and took a swig of the drink I held out to him. The scene he had conjured was vivid and depressing. I wondered how I would feel if, like Caratacus, I had lost all my lands, wealth and army. I could not fail to be impressed by his resilience, by his ability to tell such a miserable tale without being overwhelmed by the dire nature of his situation.

"And so they set upon us and tore us apart. I'd be surprised if they did capture anyone in the end - more likely they cut them down on the spot. The Silurian leaders might have got away. If they headed south or east, they'll be hunted down easily. To go north would mean passing through Deceangli territory and the Romans are all over that now. But they might have made it through."

"Well you did," I pointed out, interested that he did not ascribe his own level of cunning to his counterparts.

"Yes I did, but it wasn't easy. The Roman presence around your borders is quite extensive."

"Brigantia is a client-tribe. What did you expect?"

"I expect you have no choice, and that you are playing this game the only way you can," he cajoled, "when all the while you wish them dead and gone, just as I do."

"Are you asking now for the alliance that you refused once before?"

"I have little to offer besides my skill, but if you are willing...' He opened his hands towards me and his face took on the beguiling expression of someone used to persuading people against their better judgement.

Mandulay came in carrying a bundle.

"Better get this leg sorted out," she said. "Oh and Venutius has just arrived back with Antikia. They're coming now."

"I think you may have to retell your battle tale a few more times," I said to Caratacus, who was peeling away the crusty length of fabric from his injured leg. "I'm sure people will be eager to hear it."

I introduced my excited husband and my aunt to the war-leader and sat back as Venutius ingratiated himself with the fallen hero. A few more people had entered - Fistoc, Davit and some of those who held a deep-down wish that we had fought the Romans, no matter the cost. I let the crowd swell, to halt the conversation between myself and Caratacus. I could let him continue to hope for my help, while I worked out what to do.

He stayed with us for some weeks, re-cooperating while the gash on his leg healed. Mandulay insisted that he rest it, to avoid it turning bad, since it was quite deep and ragged. During most of that time, Venutius kept him company. The two of them discussed Roman military tactics, since both had experienced them, albeit from different sides. Caratacus spoke about his father and brothers, but only a little, since he was not a man to live in the past. Instead he was looking to the future all the time, calculating his next move and dropping tantalising hints that we might join in his inevitable glory.

"How does he stay so optimistic when he has nothing left?" asked Antikia, when we sat alone one night.

"Oh not you too' I moaned.

"What?"

"Everyone is too taken with him - the great leader who never stops fighting! It's easy to stay optimistic when you are using other tribes to do the work for you. He's got the Deceangli subdued, the Silures defeated, the Ordovices in pieces. If he gets his way, Brigantia will be next. The man is clever and he can fight, I'll give you that, but he's made some very big mistakes. If he wasn't so keen on his own advancement, he'd have made better alliances at the start of all this and perhaps he'd have had a chance against Rome."

"He has made alliances," Antikia persisted, "He got the Silures and Ordovices together and he's avoided Ostorius for ages now." But she knew she was on losing ground. We had offered the tentative hand of friendship to him through the Corieltauvi at the start of it all and he had turned us down. And now here he was practically begging for help, though his arrogance helped disguise his desperation.

Everyone was captivated by Caratacus, but I never heard anyone say outright that Brigantia should follow his call into battle. People expected him to get well and then leave again, keeping out of sight of Ostorius as he had done before. No one really believed he could win against Rome now. No one except perhaps Venutius, whose boyish dreams of glory and power were ignited once more by the presence of the war leader he had admired for so long. I itched with impatience when I saw how eagerly he followed Caratacus's tales and how he nodded in agreement at most of the latter's pronouncements about how a decisive victory could be achieved. My next move would hit Venutius hard and I was not sure our relationship could withstand it. But my hand was forced. Caratacus was a fool. He should never have come to me.

"They've got the chains on," said Tantoban, coming towards me and wiping a hand across his damp forehead. "That man fights like a beast."

"'You wouldn't think it, from the scrawny look of him," I answered, thinking how muscular Tantoban still was and how his eyes shone like dark amber when he was roused. "Is he under control now?"

"Oh yes, a few cracks to the head and he went down."

"Have him brought to me here."

Tantoban turned on his heel and strode back in the direction he had come from.

"Do you trust that they'll keep him and not just set him free to run?" Gorlensa was with me. Antikia had distracted Venutius, taking him out on a trip to inspect supplies arriving from one of our north-eastern sub-tribes.

"I'm not sure about Fistoc, but Tantoban would never disobey my orders."

We stood a while longer.

"This is the right thing to do," she whispered, barely moving her lips. "No matter what he says, whether he pleads or curses, this is the only thing you can do."

I gave a single nod of my head. It was good to hear her words, but I already knew it. Gone were the days of indecision, when I wished to fight Rome, but didn't dare come out into the open to do it. Now I knew that there was only one way forward and that was to keep Rome on my side.

They brought Caratacus to me, pulling on a length of chain that was secured to two heavy metal links on his wrists. Taking no chances, they had bound his ankles too, so that he walked slowly with small steps. Strands of his hair had come loose during his fight with my men, and they whipped about as he came forward, like thin snakes coiling round his pinched and angry face. Tantoban pushed him down onto his knees in front of me.

"Caratacus, son of Cunobelinus, leader of the Catuvellauni who have been no friends of ours, I am duty-bound to hand you over to Emperor Claudius. You will be imprisoned until Governor Ostorius arrives to take you away."

"You're no chieftain! You're just a tame dog that Rome holds on a lead. You're in more chains than I am!"

"Look around you, Caratacus. This is my land, full of my people who do as I ask. Where are your lands? Where are your people? My alliance is with Rome, a land across the water who can provide us with trade and progress. I have no interest in allying myself with a man whose family's sole aim was to strip other tribes of their land and wealth."

"Those days are gone, we have a common enemy now," he tried.

"Rome is my friend, Caratacus. My lands and position are secure. Brigantia has no wish to join your foolish efforts at war with Ostorius." I gestured to Tantoban that I was finished and turned away. I heard Caratacus spit in my direction, and then the muted sound of a foot connecting hard with some part of his body that made him grunt in pain. I didn't look back as they dragged him up onto a horse and then rode away to the place I had instructed. My dealings with Caratacus were over. My message was on its way to Ostorius and I knew he would come as soon as possible. I just hoped my men could hold the cunning Caratacus until then.

Venutius paced the floor with his hands fastened to his hips and a groove across his forehead that grew as he paced.

"I cannot understand why you did this," he yelled yet again. "Why not just let the man go? Why do we have to be the ones to do this? You don't have to fight with him, but neither should you be handing him over. It's just not right!"

"He knew the risks when he entered my territory. If I let him go, how would that look to Ostorius?"

"He'd never even know Caratacus was here," fumed Venutius.

"Don't be so stupid. Of course he would know. News travels and it was only a matter of time before Ostorius came looking here anyway. This way, we avoid any blame and instead we get to prove our loyalty to Rome. This act will go a long way in securing the future of this tribe. You know I'm right."

"No I don't! This man is one of us, fighting against Rome just as we should be!"

"He's not one of us, he's a Catuvellauni. Or have you forgotten? Have his clever words blinded you so much?" I was shouting at him, furious at his naivety.

"The Catuvellauni never threatened us. They never came to steal away Carvettii lands!" Venutius looked me in the eye as he said this, a direct reference to the control that my family held over his sub-tribe which in times past had been free of Brigantian involvement.

"I'm not going through this with you any more," I said, tired by all his petty grievances. "If you have that much against me then why are you even with me?" I left the hut, not caring about his answer and he didn't follow. Probably, he was shocked that I had raised the question that each of us had avoided for so long. I was no longer scared of the answer. In fact, I had started to wonder whether it would be easier on both of us if our relationship came to an end. From Brigantia's point of view, I could call on Roman help if the Carvettii ever decided to cause me real problems, so my marriage to Venutius was no longer that necessary. From a personal point of view, Venutius made me miserable. I had loved him as a brother and then as a lover but he had made it impossible for me to go on loving him. Perhaps he felt exactly the same.

When Fistoc and the other men returned, they reported to me that they had handed over Caratacus directly to Ostorius, who had immediately rewarded them personally and sent his sincere gratitude to me.

"Where is Tantoban?" I asked, having expected him, as my senior warrior, to relay the news.

"Tantoban is dead," said Fistoc. "We have his body outside."

"How?" I cried out. "Tell me what happened?"

"Caratacus got hold of a dagger. It was Faruwan's. He must have got too close and Caratacus swiped it and kept it hidden. Then he got difficult and when Tantoban grabbed him, the little shit stabbed him in the side. He'd got one of his wrists free of the chains and he got the knife round to Tantoban's throat. He was threatening to kill him unless we let him go but Tantoban forced him off, even though it cut his own throat to do it, and he knocked the runt out. But then he bled and there was nothing we could do to stop it."

"Where's Faruwan?" I asked, my body prickling with hot anger.

"On his own. He feels terrible but even Tantoban would have said it wasn't his fault." Fistoc looked alarmed.

"No? No. You're right. This is Caratacus all over. The sneaky little..." My voice trailed into a grunt of fury. I wished I had had the man put to death here, in my settlement, and sent the mutilated body to Ostorius. "I hope they torture him before they execute him."

Fistoc nodded uncertainly, perhaps surprised by the depth of my feeling for Tantoban who, after all, was not family to me.

"Tantoban was my father's warrior," I said, in explanation. "I had known him all my life."

"He was a good man, always loyal to you," agreed Fistoc. A few moments passed and then he quietly led his men back outside. I stayed inside. I had no wish to see the dead and damaged body I had so admired for its vitality just days before. I sat with Antikia, who rubbed my back and shed her own tears, while I nursed my newest grief.

SUMMER AD54

"More jewels?" asked Antikia as she walked past my chair looking for her hairpins.

"An amber necklace from Claudius." I held it up to catch the light and the burnt orange beads twinkled as they twisted slowly on the gold chain. "He sends his appreciation of our prompt payment of the taxes and a personal note of thanks for the gifts I sent him." I tossed the thin wooden tablet with its spidery writing onto a large wooden casket by my side.

"Ah ha!" My aunt waved her found hairpins at me and started to twist her hair up at the sides. She kept it long, but the dark colour of her youth was being overtaken by white. Age was turning her sharp beauty into a haughty attractiveness, rather like a torch flame, alluring but harsh, burning all approaching moths. She had very few wrinkles and kept extremely active. Though she was in her mid forties, she had the stature and demeanour of a younger woman, probably because she had not endured the hard experiences of childbirth and rearing. There were also the benefits of being in the highest class, of course, since we had a much better diet and lifestyle than most.

"Where have you put the face cream?" she asked. I rolled my eyes then pointed to the little pot of Mandulay's special preparation. She used honey and milk but I had no idea what else went into it. I reminded myself to make sure Amelan found out since she was taking over most of old Mandulay's work.

"Is he worth all this effort?" I scoffed. Tyrius was going to be arriving any time within the next few days and she was clearly making ready for him. I had learned some time ago that Venutius knew about the pair. He admitted to me that he'd always had an idea they had an intimate relationship.

"I just thought it was normal," he'd shrugged when we spoke of it, "that he had my mother up north as his wife and Antikia here, sort of like a second wife to care for him while he was away from home."

Venutius was so young when he first came to us and he had accepted the situation with relative ease as it became apparent to him, but he didn't know, or care to know, the ins and outs of their relationship. He assumed Antikia was in love with his father. He knew she had other men when Tyrius was not around but he thought they were surrogates, there to pass the time while she waited for his father. I suppose because he hero-worshipped his father, he believed that she did too. Then again, she gave every indication to them that she truly did.

"Worth the effort? No, not really. But I am." She took a pot of blue dye, dipped a little wooden spatula in and then ran it through the grooves of her eyelids. "What do you think?" She feigned a pose.

"Oh yes, the men will be swarming over you like flies on shit," I answered, "now be quiet so I can get some sleep."

"Sleep? What about the meeting with the south nab lot?"

"Oh, let Venutius deal with that. It'll please him no end."

Antikia nodded but shot me a look of uncertainty as she left. I closed my eyes pretending not to notice. It was true, I had been leaving more of my work to others, spending more time bathing in my new wooden tub sent by Ostorius as part of a joke we had shared, or trying on new clothes I'd had made, or pruning and watering my little orchard of exotic trees. It's part of being the leader, I told myself, to delegate to others and have some time for myself now and then.

A fly landed on my forehead and I batted it away. Venutius could handle our neighbours well enough. They were from a fort just to our south and they had been trying to cultivate new tracts of land for grain production. We didn't have the soil or the weather for it in most of our territory, but previously we had always been able to supply ourselves with the amounts we needed, especially as we mostly ate a diet based on what our herds of livestock could provide. However, now that we were supplying the occupying Roman force with grain as well, it was more of a struggle. I had checked on our own grain storage pits a few days before and they were one quarter full, plenty to see us through the few moons until the next harvest, but I knew parts of Brigantia faced a dangerously lean time.

I shifted in my seat, decided I couldn't get comfortable and flopped onto a leather cushion stuffed with straw that lay on the floor. The amber necklace lay cold against the hollow of my throat and I started thinking of the journey the little stones had been on. Had Claudius himself wrapped it in the soft cloth it came in? How many days had it tossed and turned on the open sea? Rome was such a part of our lives now and yet I had only other people's descriptions to know it by. I doubted I would ever go there – I couldn't imagine being in a place where I was the subject, instead of the leader. But sometimes I wondered what it would be like to live in a place so warm that togas were always worn and grapes grew and plum trees didn't have to be so very carefully tended. I imagined the furniture they might have and what a city full of buildings might look like and how exciting it would be to sit at a meeting of the senate. I wondered if Claudius's own position was still precarious or if his stranglehold on Britannia had secured him as emperor.

He must have felt reasonably confident since he had allowed Caratacus to live. I was horribly galled by that. When the arrogant Catuvellauni leader arrived in Rome, he completely charmed Claudius with his vivid tales, warrior ethic and supposedly dignified bearing. Or so certain Roman administrators told me (I suspect they were as distressed as I was, since they expended enormous effort chasing the man down – the goddess only knows what Ostorius made of it, I never dared to ask him and now he was dead of exhaustion and illness, his remains somewhere in the blue mountains he had fought for). Why did everyone fall in love with Caratacus? He caused so many thousands of deaths, to no good end, apart from distracting Plautius and Ostorius from us in the north for a while. I had earned a very large credit of gratitude from Claudius when I handed him over, so he was of some worth in that respect but it caused me terrible pain to know that Tantoban had died in the service of myself and Rome and yet Caratacus was over there living if not a great life then at least a comfortable one. The rebel fighter who caused Plautius and Ostorius such problems was living well while the tribes who had agreed treaties with Rome struggled under the burden of taxation and occupation.

Eleven years had now passed since the Romans arrived on the southern shores. Six of them I had spent with my husband, drifting along relatively comfortably as we (leaders at least) reaped the rewards of client-tribe status. In the two years since I had washed my hands of Caratacus, Rome had favoured me and all the pent-up fear and tension, that had gnawed on my innards since the rebellion, melted away. Once my grief over Tantoban had subsided, I felt able to relax at last. Why couldn't Venutius just sit back and enjoy our life together? He would sulk with me over trivial matters, like the time I burned the hem of his cloak as I carried it past the fire; or he would fume and shout at me over tribal issues. The more I tried to include him the more he took the opportunity to challenge my decisions and belittle my reasoning.

"Do you hope to wear me down?" I asked him one night. "Do you think that by going on and on and on at me I will suddenly say, 'oh all right Venutius, you take over'?" I had drained my cup of wine and stared into his dark, complicated eyes under their brooding brow.

"I don't know what I hope," he had declared and whatever paltry subject we were fighting about had disintegrated as we faced the painful truth about the state of our marriage. It had silenced us both, that miserable evening. There was no answer or solution to the problem that had plagued us from the very start. My sadness outweighed my frustration then, because Venutius could no more help his problem with my authority, than I could help my natural-born duty to be chief of Brigantia. The situation was never going to change but in all the preceding years we had never found a way to deal with it.

Shortly after that night, he stopped sleeping with me. It was not so obvious at first, since we were both busy and often had to travel, but gradually I realised that he had not lain with me for a long time and that neither had I sought him out. This was a bad sign. The relationship we'd had as siblings was long gone and we had ceased being friends over the years, but at least the passionate night-time intimacy we'd retained went some way towards healing the rift between us. Without even that, we had nothing. We were two leaders of two tribes circling each other and finding no common ground.

He barged in to see me after he'd spoken with the people from the south nab, disturbing my thoughts of Rome, Claudius, Tantoban and Caratacus.

"You couldn't even be bothered, could you?" he sneered, waving an arm contemptuously in my direction. "Too busy lying around, resting, reading your precious letters." He hated my correspondence with the Roman administrators and with Claudius, limited and basic though it was. They never addressed him alone, never acknowledged him as more than my consort. Perhaps he would have felt appeased if he had ever considered that Rome was more than happy to leave an apparently barren woman in charge of Brigantia, knowing that they could swoop in and claim all the land after my death and that maybe the lack of acknowledgement for his position was more to do with the threat he would pose if he did away with me and pupped some other woman. Then again, the thought didn't really occur to me either until much later, when events in another tribe gave me pause for thought about Rome's ultimate intentions with regard to our lands.

"Oh go away," I sighed, "I really don't want to speak to you."

He gave a bitter laugh.

"You speak to me the same way you speak to the servants. Aren't you interested in what we discussed?"

"I'm sure you handled everything very well. Why are you so angry? You want me to leave business in your hands, then you complain when I do!"

"I don't need you to throw me crumbs," he retorted. "Why don't you get up off your backside and do some work you fat, old cow." He stormed out again before I could do more than gasp.

I sat still for a few moments after he left, then picked up a looking glass and poked at my face. At thirty three, I thought I looked well enough. My cheeks were plumper than they used to be and I'd always had the kind of face that was considered good looking rather than beautiful, but when you hold an exalted position, you rarely hear bad things directly. Sometimes I felt old, felt ugly too, but you don't dwell on that when people are bowing down to you and presenting you with gifts and compliments. Now Venutius had struck at my hidden insecurities and his attack was all the more stinging as it was so spontaneous. Is that why he won't sleep with me any more, I wondered? I pinched at the fat on my waist and hips, then blew out a sigh of irritation. I was letting him get to me. I stood up, brushed my dress down and smoothed back the strands of hair that had worked their way loose from the gold pins fixed against my scalp.

Outside, it was warm, but with a breeze and I wandered out into my enclosure to get some air, careful to maintain a bland smile. If anyone had heard our little exchange, they weren't going to see that it had unsettled me. Mandulay was sat bent over, weaving a small basket and looked up briefly with a smile as I passed. A little further away Presivin was talking with a few other men, a cluster of dogs at his heels. He was still breeding and training them and we had in fact traded some to Didius Gallus, the new Roman governor. I say traded, but of course, we had handed them over as part of our taxation, though it was dressed up as a goods-for-protection agreement. Over towards the woods, a heat shimmer had settled across the meadow, blurring my view of a gang of men who were carrying great bundles of branches from their coppicing work. All the spindly, flexible pieces would go for woven wares, like the basket Mandulay was working on. Larger pieces, for firewood and simple tools. When a tree was felled, the wood could be used for bulkier items - bowls, clubs, stools. I watched them walk through the meadow where once Venutius, Vellocatus and I played, sunbathed and talked. It seemed a long time since I had lived so simply. As I ambled towards the gate, footsteps fell behind me.

"Cartimandua. Can we walk?"

I turned to smile at Vellocatus, whose calming presence was always welcome, especially when I was feeling down. We still usually kept a distance from one another, but occasionally allowed ourselves a few moments alone. It was a careful avoidance that we never actually discussed.

"Of course. Isn't the weather perfect? I was just watching those men." I gestured off into the distance where the group with the coppice bundles were disappearing. He glanced in their direction, nodding vaguely.

"How are you, Vellocatus?" I asked, knowing he wanted to talk to me about something but was unsure how to begin.

"I'm well, very well." His stride had lengthened as we left the enclosure of grand roundhouses and I found myself being escorted towards the woods at a fair pace.

"Are you in a hurry?"

"What? Oh, no, sorry." He slowed up and we ambled along the dirt path.

"You can talk to me. You know you can." I kept my gaze fixed ahead, didn't want to embarrass him.

"It's Venutius. He just came to see you didn't he?"

"Yes, he did." I was guarded, not wanting to tell Vellocatus, of all people, what my husband had called me.

"He's really angry. Even the people we met with today could sense it. When they asked to speak with you, he was, well, almost sarcastic about why you weren't there."

"Was he, now." I bit the inside of my cheek, furious at Venutius for betraying the situation between us to people outside our immediate circle.

"Why weren't you there?" Vellocatus asked, with sudden bluntness.

I started to answer, and then paused. Did I even have a reasonable answer? Our neighbours had come to us about the grain shortage, a direct consequence of our tribal allegiance to Rome, and I had not met them in person to discuss it. I supposed it didn't look good.

"I had a letter from Claudius to read," I answered, defensively.

"Mmm." He was non-committal, dubious, and it annoyed me.

"Do you have a problem with me too?" I demanded. He went quiet. I sucked my bottom lip in between my teeth and shook my head. "You, of all people," I muttered.

"Yes, I think there is a problem," he said at last. "I don't understand why you're letting Venutius handle matters that you should be dealing with, especially when you know he is disrespectful about you. It seems like you're hiding inside all the time, pretending you have other matters to deal with, when all I see is you sitting around, not doing much of anything."

The words stung worse than those Venutius threw at me - probably because Vellocatus was right.

"I do a great deal." I was defiant, but sounded more like a petty child than leader of our tribe. He was quiet. He always knew when to be quiet. Perhaps that's why I found him so much easier than Venutius to be around.

"I know how it looks," I said, eventually. "Maybe I have

become too relaxed. But we went through some very difficult times, you know how hard it was for me back then." He stayed silent, but I knew he was picturing those dying rebels as clearly as I was. "It's not an excuse but...oh maybe it is, I don't know." I threw my hands up. "What am I doing Vellocatus? My husband hardly talks to me, people in my lands are going hungry while I receive gifts from the man who owns us all and I'm lazing around when I should be doing something. But what is it that I should be doing? I can't make any difference to anything. Client-queenship is meaningless."

"I know the position you are in, but there's always something you can do, even if it's just a case of bartering for a better deal. The people we saw today are furious that the legions are letting grain spoil by keeping it above ground when everyone knows it keeps better in the underground pits. They keep doing that and we have to keep replacing it. Maybe you can talk to the governor about it, to stop all the waste? And don't forget, Claudius respects you, that counts for something. I know how hard it was for you with Ostorius and the executions, but you can't let men like him and Gallus force you into seclusion. Roman women might sit back and laze around, but not Brigantian women, and especially not you."

"You have quite a high opinion of me. I'm not sure it's justified," I said in a flat voice, thinking of the amber beads I still wore at my throat.

"I know you, I always have." His voice caught and I turned, a little too sharply, because he looked away. "You're not on your own," he added quietly, studying the ground, "if it helps."

"It does help, yes."

We were under cover of the trees now, the air cooler and damper beneath the green canopy, and we continued to walk, following the stream. It was my habit to follow this route and it calmed me to see how it never really changed. All across Brigantia the landscape was changing as the Romans moved in and set up their camps and brought their strange ways and ideas into our midst. We hadn't anything like the Colonia that were being built in the south, but our settlements were getting larger, families grouping together more for protection and building villages in the process. Roman roads were snaking ever closer, threatening to increase the ability of the occupying force to traverse our territory with greater speed. But here, in my woods, the stream flowed as it always had, past trees that had stood for centuries, into a valley that had held my ancestors in its cosy grip for generations.

"I know what some people say about me," I whispered, "I know what they call me. How many of them think like that?"

"Is that why you're so remote?" He asked me, "You think your people hate you so you're hiding from them?"

I didn't answer.

"Okay, some of them, especially in the south, harbour a grudge about what happened with Ostorius, but not up here! These people trust you. They loved your father."

"But they don't love me."

"Every leader has to prove themselves before the people will love them."

"But how can I prove myself when I'm not a real leader any more, when I have no real power?" I shouted in despair. This is what it came down to, why I had become so passive. Everything felt so futile.

"You still lead this tribe, Cartimandua," Vellocatus patiently insisted. "Claudius may set the terms to an extent, but you manage our tribal affairs, trade negotiations, disputes, everything. Don't let your despondency ruin what you still have, or the people really will turn against you."

We had come to a stop by the small waterfall that splashed over a smooth grey rock. I breathed in the fragrance of fresh water and wild flowers and felt a lightness in my chest where for ages it seemed I had been nursing a heavy weight.

"Do you remember when we were young and we played up here? Venutius was always jumping around and you had to keep your eyes on him all the time."

Vellocatus smiled.

"He always came first with you then. What went wrong with you two?"

Vellocatus rubbed the back of his neck. He seemed to consider the question for a while. I saw that his arms were still covered in fine golden hairs, although his skin was much rougher than it had been.

"I've always tried to do the right thing, by him and by you, no matter how I felt. I could claim a noble purpose but honestly, I just didn't want to lose my position. Because that's what would have happened, if I'd acted on how I felt. Maybe Risha guessed that, because she never liked me. As soon as you left for the north, she started to set Venutius against me, pointing out the ways in which she thought I was overstepping my status and implying that I was too close to you."

"Your face when we returned-"

"He picked a fight, eventually. Picked at me until I realised he needed to satisfy his mother with some kind of big display. So I mouthed off at him a bit, swung a fake punch and let him floor me." He gave a humourless laugh. "We acted it out, but that black eye was real. It changed things, even though Venutius tried sometimes to make a joke of it. I took his punch, a hard one, because in my heart, I had been disloyal to him and perhaps for that I deserved it even though I would never have acted on the way I felt. But he threw it because his mother had made him uncertain about our friendship. I knew after that, that he could rely on me because I had sworn to myself that I would always protect him, but I would never be able to rely on him because he felt no such allegiance to me. We couldn't be friends after that. But then, maybe we should never have been friends to begin with. I was always his servant after all."

"You never felt like a servant to me," I said, honestly. "You've always been a friend."

"Ah, people who are secure in their own authority don't need the subjugation of others to stay powerful."

"Secure? That's something I don't feel very often."

"You know what I mean. Deep down, you know you're the rightful leader of this tribe, and whatever happens you'll have that always. Venutius doesn't have that – at least not until he takes the reins of the Carvettii clan."

I exhaled loudly.

"I can't win with him. The more I've tried to pacify him, the worse he's got. I don't know what's going to happen between us." The water from the stream splashed and flowed as we stood, droplets of spray landing on my skirt and feet. The things Vellocatus had said earlier replayed in my head. "What feeling did you have, that was so dangerous to your position? How had you betrayed him, in your heart?"

He didn't answer, perhaps it was still too difficult for him to voice the emotion that ran so contrary with his duty to my husband. I moved closer to him, took his hand, felt a shudder run through him.

"All this time?" I asked, genuinely curious, for I had never believed he thought of me in that way, and his hand, vulnerable somehow, squeezed mine as he dared at last to put his other arm round me and lay his head against my shoulder.

Tyrius arrived a few days later. He was looking old now. His dark hair had turned to grey and I had barely noticed. That's how age creeps up; slowly, while nobody is paying attention. In fact, I don't believe he had noticed either. He still acted like an arrogant, playful young man.

"How is Risha?" I asked him, as usual.

"Oh, the same as ever," he laughed back, "probably got her spies following me," and he tipped me a wink.

"And Iticus?" I didn't like to get caught up in his conspiratorial banter.

"Getting married! We finally found him a mate. That's the news I came to pass on. She's a beautiful girl, going to give him some fine children, I'll bet!" He seemed pleased with himself, then abruptly coloured and looked uncomfortable when he remembered that I didn't have any. It was not a subject he dared discuss with me directly, but I could be sure he had badgered his son about it.

"How wonderful for Iticus," I said, "He must bring her to visit us."

We had seen Iticus sporadically over the years and he had matured from the tiny fish-eyed toddler gawping at his impressive older brother into a quietly intelligent, slim-built man with the same dark hair as Venutius, though a more gaunt face and his mother's grey doe-eyes. I liked him on a personal level but had to be wary of the boy. He had been under his mother's influence his whole life and I had no idea if she'd primed him to undermine Venutius and take over the Carvettii leadership or whether on the few occasions he visited, he was acting as a spy for her, though what she might gain by spying on me I was never quite sure.

Tyrius didn't waste much more time with me but went in search of Antikia. He didn't have far to go as she was fanning herself in the sun, drinking ale and pretending to be nonchalant. I watched him with her, fawning over her and stroking her hair and for the first time, thought him quite ridiculous. He was an old man and had not treated her well. Did he really believe he was her true love?

Even Mandulay mentioned how infatuated he appeared, when she sat with me that afternoon. She was tired and uncomfortable but when I asked her if she ailed, she brushed away my concern and turned the conversation away from herself.

"Do you think your aunt is happy?" I would have liked to see that girl settle down properly. It's a shame she never did."

"She seems happier than most," I said.

"Happier than you, you mean! Ha, you've got your hands full with Venutius, there's no doubt about that."

"I think my mother had a point when she objected to our union," I grumbled.

"Maybe. But she loved Venutius after he came to live here. He's like family to us all now even if he's a difficult boy at times."

We were all just boys and girls to Mandulay. Speaking to her, I could forget for a while that we were the ruling elite of Brigantia and think of us all as just like any other family.

At the evening meal that night, Venutius sat with me, probably so Tyrius would not notice the growing separation between us. He chewed his meat with grim, slow determination and spat gristle onto the floor near us, as if trying to provoke me with his bad manners. I fixed a smile on my face and tried not to feel the churning turmoil in my chest as the ambivalence I felt for him swelled and surged. I loved him. I hated him. He was my brother, my husband, my rival, my enemy.

"Your father says Iticus is to be married," I said, intent on maintaining civility.

"So it seems." He gnawed on a piece of pork.

"Maybe Iticus will visit us?"

"Maybe," he said, then after a moment he gave a grunt of dissatisfaction in my direction.

"What?"

"Why don't you talk about something important, instead of wittering on like this?"

"Why? What do you want to talk about?" I spat back.

"Don't you care at all what is happening to our neighbours? The Deceangli are under attack now, the tribes south of them are already ripped to shreds. They'll turn on us next and you're just sitting here waiting for it to happen."

A few heads had turned in our direction.

"Not again, Venutius," I ordered. "You know our position. If you want war with Rome, go back to your Carvettii and fight from there, but Brigantia will have no part in it."

He sat staring at his food, fire raging in his eyes as he considered what I had just said. It was the first time either of us had alluded to a proper separation. It was also another stab by me at his inferior position in the hierarchy of my tribe. Vellocatus was watching from close-by and when Venutius got up and strode off, he did not follow, but joined me.

"How can this continue?" He asked, full of fear for me. "You've all but told him to go. His pride will not allow him to stay here, but if he leaves-"

"-then we are at war with each other. I know." My eyes filled with tears. Antikia, quick-witted as ever, was entertaining everyone with some old story and I blessed her silently. I waited a while, and then rose to leave the group. Tyrius looked over, worried, and mouthed a concerned query. I managed a bright smile and motioned at my ale cup as if I'd had too much to drink. He nodded, not entirely convinced and turned back to Antikia while I made my exit. I was not alone, because after this marital fight, Vellocatus followed me.

The night was balmy, birds twittering an evening song and we walked out into the meadow where the wild flowers waved tall and pretty in the fading light. A moth fluttered past my temple, its feathery brown body making me jump as it caught against my skin. Vellocatus took hold of me and let me sob as he guided me away, over to the west side of the meadow and out of view of our home. I don't recall much, if any conversation. What was there to discuss, when the situation was so messy and inevitable? When we lay down together, I let go of Venutius. I cried for him that first time I was with Vellocatus, but I promised myself that I would never cry for him again. He had given me up. He had been cruel to me for a long time. When I needed him so desperately, when Ostorius might have had me executed, he had deliberately stayed away. When I had tried to share power with him, he had goaded me, argued with me, criticised me. If he was a council member, I would have ousted him. Now was the time to let him go. After years of patiently waiting, another man had finally taken his place.

Since I was the head of my tribe, answerable to no one (apart from Rome, I suppose, but I tried to ignore that when possible) I didn't hide my feelings for Vellocatus. I didn't flaunt it, but we stayed close together and he shared my bed from the following evening onwards. I had joined with Venutius, but our type of marriage was not like yours. Our gods and goddesses might frown upon us stepping outside of a bond, particularly if we had invoked their blessing on the union, but it was their wrath that a separating couple faced, not an earthly court. That's not to say that people would be happy about it, though. I knew there would be ramifications to my actions. Tyrius would be confused and angry, the council would be worried and disappointed. At least we had no children to face.

The day after my argument with Venutius and my night in the fields with Vellocatus, Antikia came to me.

"How serious was the argument?" She asked.

"The argument doesn't matter. Venutius and I are finished," I told her as I ate my first meal of the day. Mandulay, tutting over my situation, had brought me a barley milk porridge with honey that she knew I loved and I was eating slowly as I pondered my next move.

"Finished?" She sat down heavily, causing the small stool to grate the rush matting against the hard earth floor. "Sweet goddess."

"You're not really surprised are you? You know how things have been between us."

"Yes, I know. But even so... this is big, Cartimandua. I hope you have a plan. Have you told him it's over?"

"Not in so many words. He'll know it soon enough. Vellocatus and I are together now."

"For Brigantia's pissing sake, you don't waste time! How long has this been going on?" She had leapt back up from her chair and was staring down at me, hands on her hips.

"Just since last night. But it's serious, not a fling, and I do have a plan. Are you with me?"

"What? Of course I am."

"No lingering attachment to Tyrius?" I eye-balled her hard.

"No. He's just a diversion when I'm bored. You know that."

"Good, then I need your help. When all this breaks out, you have to convince Tyrius you're horrified by my behaviour. Even if it means leaving here with him, though more likely he'll want you to stay behind since he can't exactly take you up home to his wife. Then you have to give him the idea that he should have a small group of warriors he can really trust travel here secretly and murder me along with any of the council they can get their hands on." She nodded uncertainly and I went on. "If it hasn't already occurred to him, suggest Iticus does it, and some of the other noble warriors of the Carvettii - an elite group, led by his very own son. Suggest Venutius will never beat me in a pitched battle since I have enormous weapons stores and the support of my tribe, not to mention Rome. Tell him Venutius is best not knowing any of this, since he might baulk at murdering me. Then, when Tyrius makes arrangements, find out what they are and let me know. That last bit is crucial," I added with a raised eyebrow, "or I might find a northern axe through my skull."

"Anything else?" She whispered, her forehead set into age lines I'd never noticed before.

"No. Can you really do this for me?" I asked, my chest tight with the fear that I had asked too much of her.

"For you, anything." She rubbed her temples and relaxed her

172

face into a mask of composure. "You are just like your father. He'd be proud of you, although probably a little disappointed that his match-making didn't work. While we're making our plans here, you should know that Tyrius thinks Risha has sent spies with him on this trip. She suspects, at long last, that he is having a serious affair with someone." Antikia couldn't keep the smirk off her face. "So we should probably both try and work out who the spies are. It could be useful to know."

She gave me a nod and squeezed my shoulder then as she made to leave, suddenly turned on her heel and bent down to give me a proper hug. A strand of her hair swept across my porridge and I used my finger and thumb to remove the sticky residue from her long locks.

"I'll have to be cool towards you from now on, for your plan to work. Don't ever doubt me. I love you," she said and left.

If there was one thing I would go back and do differently, it would be to announce my separation from Venutius to the tribal council. I never did that, you see, and I think it made a difference to the tone of the following events. Instead I rather arrogantly assumed I could act on my own prerogative, as chief and client-queen. Rome, for all its insistence on pomp and ceremony, couldn't have cared less about my marital situation (not until it started costing them time and attention), but my own tribe with their wild and individualistic attitudes apparently were a little more shocked than I had anticipated when word spread that Vellocatus was sharing my bed. Not to put the chariot before the horse though – the first terrible event was Venutius realising what I had done.

Two nights after the heated exchange with Venutius, I shared a meal with Vellocatus. We were alone. My hair was ruffled from his caresses. I had lips stained with the dark grape wine, the empty amphorae kicked to one side. It sounds bad, put into words like that. It sounds tawdry, base. It didn't feel that way. I remember the surge of freedom that had unleashed itself within me, the way I felt invincible now that I had released the part of me that had been striving to make my husband respect me. I hadn't known until then that his constant dissatisfaction and my inability to appease him had weighed down on me like so many tanned hides on a trader's horse. And now I had bucked and thrown them all off, and in so doing happened to find a man I could love and who loved me, honestly and without expectation.

Of course, what Venutius saw when he entered my great roundhouse and threw back the drapes to my private area, was his wife cradled in the arms of another man as she ate her evening meal. He'd kept away from me after the argument, probably deciding what to do – maybe struggling to find a way to repair the damage though it pains me to think that. People had gone to him on that day with their little pointed comments – "Don't you think Vellocatus is getting a bit too involved?" "Isn't Vellocatus your man?" His disbelief must have grown into horrified realisation as he searched the settlement that night for Vellocatus and then found him with me.

"You have to go." I whispered, sick to my stomach, as the two men froze. Vellocatus gazed up at his erstwhile charge defiantly. Venutius curled his lip in fury and balled a fist.

"You have to go, Venutius." I repeated, in a louder voice. "It's over. We can't go on any longer. Go home to the Carvettii." I shut my mouth then, not wanting to ramble on. I had so many things I wanted to say to him – all the conversations we should have had over the years; why he never came at the time of the rebellion, how he really felt about us not having children, why he felt so emasculated when I had tried so hard to share my power with him. It was too late to speak of any of that now, so I shut my mouth. Still, "go home" seemed like such an insufficient proclamation of the end of our union.

He gave a slight retch and I thought for a horrible moment he might vomit over us, but then his face hardened to a murderous mask and he wrenched the drapes down and kicked our platters of food over. Then he spat, a full and foul load, over the skirt of my dress.

"Roman whore, with your little pet servant. I'll take everything you have, you stunted bitch."

Vellocatus was on his feet and unsheathing his long dagger, but I threw myself between the men and gave Venutius a hard shove that sent him backwards into the gathering crowd of onlookers.

"You won't take anything from me, not my land, not my people, and if you think you can then you really are the idiot I suspected," I said, my voice like ice. "I've ordered you to go, now go." I reached for my long war spear which I had purposefully kept close. Vellocatus put it in my hand. Venutius's eyes flicked to him, then to me.

"You'd make my slave into your chief?" He mocked.

"No man is my chief," I bit back, levelling the spear at his throat. "Vellocatus will be my husband in truth, something you never were. Now get out before I slice open your throat."

Now it was his turn to shut his mouth, not that he really believed I would kill him. I could see in his eyes the contempt he had for me. But neither was he ready to kill me, so he left, shaking with unspoken anger.

"No turning back now," I said to Vellocatus. But I wasn't afraid and neither did I regret the end of my union with Venutius.

It would have been so nice to revel in my new-found romance, but there wasn't time for that. I had perhaps underestimated how much trouble Venutius was capable of causing me, but at least I had the beginnings of a plan. I had seen Antikia and Tyrius in the background during that final confrontation with my husband and I hoped she was playing her part well. There was a great commotion at dawn the next day as Venutius and those of Carvettii origin packed up and left. Tyrius went also, taking Antikia with him, so I was wrong in my guess he would leave her behind. I didn't object when Venutius had his servants pack up some grain and dried meat. They loaded the food along with Venutius's chests of belongings onto a travelling cart. Venutius and his father were out of sight. It turned out that they had taken their best horses and headed away before sunrise. Perhaps they feared my threat with the spear after all.

Later that same morning, I saw an oddity on the outskirts of the settlement. Two Carvettii men, both of whom I believed had travelled with Tyrius on his latest visit to us, were saddling up their horses and slinging travelling packs across the rumps of the animals. It was strange that they were so late in leaving and I had my men bring them to me.

"Why are you still here? Aren't you eager to head off like the others?" I enquired. One man kept his head low, his fingers tapping on his thighs. The other eyed me gormlessly and replied.

"Just leaving now, packing up some things for the trip south. You let all the others go, why you stopping us?"

South? The Carvettii territory was far north-west of us. Why would Venutius be taking his party south? Their retinue had headed north from us, giving the impression they were heading home. If they were really going south, they would have to circle round. I would send trackers to check for them. The quiet man had stopped tapping. He waited for my response.

"It seems odd that you would linger." I decided to stall them a little. I wondered if they were spying for Venutius, but that didn't make sense since they had been far too obvious. "Weren't you afraid that with Venutius gone you would have little protection?" I motioned to my men behind them, and they moved forward with weapons ready. The gormless Carvettii swung his head round, saw blades and started talking.

"Look, it's not what you're thinking."

"Shush, you fool," hissed the quiet one.

"We're not going with them, we're going north to Risha. We

were just looking out for Tyrius for her, that's all."

"Ah," I breathed, "Just looking out for him, so you could report back to her all about his affair?"

The gormless one nodded, blushing while the quiet man looked furious with his partner. These, then, were the spies Antikia had warned me about. And while Venutius was heading south for whatever reason, they were going north to tell Risha that it was Antikia her husband was bedding. But why was Venutius south-bound?

"And you'll no doubt pass on all the recent developments too?" They stayed mute. "How will you explain Tyrius going south instead of home to her?"

The man who had stayed quiet must have decided that he couldn't lose much now by being honest, since his thick-headed friend had already said so much.

"Venutius is going to rally support from the people there, the ones who rebelled when he was away. Tyrius has gone to help him. Your Antikia has gone too, you can't trust her any more. We stayed back so Tyrius would not notice us heading back to Risha." He spoke earnestly and I understood that he was trying to trade this information for his own release. I began to see a way I could use this pair of idiots.

"Oh Antikia, why did you do this to me?" I called, as if in pain and I brought my fist down into the palm of my other hand. "You know she and Tyrius plan to marry? Oh yes, they think they can marry and then use Venutius as a puppet to rule - Carvettii and Brigantia allied once more! And poor Risha, she thinks her problem is his affair? More likely a knife in her back while she sleeps! They'll want rid of her, just you watch." I rubbed at imaginary pain in my temples as they glanced at each other, ashen-faced.

"You two can go," I said, waving my arms at them, "I have bigger problems than you today. Let them out, make sure they get on their way quickly," I motioned to the men around the spies and they lowered their spears and swords. The two men scampered back to their horses, looking full of anxious excitement.

As they left camp, I arranged a small party of trackers. Two of my men would track them all the way into Carvettii territory, making sure they arrived to give Risha my story. Four others would take the Western path alongside the hill ridge and lie in wait for Venutius and his party, to check that they were indeed doubling back on themselves and going south.

When the trackers had left, I called an emergency council meeting. The summons went round like a wildfire and everyone from the settlement along with many who had already been travelling to us, crammed into the big central roundhouse or hovered outside. I looked around them all, counting faces and noticed only one obvious absence.

"Where's Fistoc?" I asked Vellocatus.

"He's gone."

"Not with Venutius?" I felt a chill on the back of my neck. Fistoc was vicious and mean but totally loyal to me. I trusted him, valued his connections with the south of our tribe and respected his fighting ability.

"Yes, he's gone," Vellocatus said again. "He's a man out for himself."

"Oh no," I cried, "Even when Ostorius had the rebels executed, Fistoc stayed with me. He wanted to fight with them, but he didn't. He stayed with me."

"What's wrong with you?" Vellocatus asked, his voice tinged with impatience. "He's just one man, and a nasty one at that."

"It's just, well I thought he was loyal to me, that's all." I looked away, embarrassed that he might see my eyes shining with tears. How many other people I trusted might turn away from me now? Did Fistoc think I was weak-willed? Did he resent me for never fighting the Romans? How many others thought like that?

I bit the inside of my cheek, pinched the back of my hand and shoved the clamouring, negative voices out of my head. If I lost myself in front of this big gathering, I may as well go and hand my weapons and treasures over to Venutius right now.

"Silence!" I yelled at the council and all the hangers-on, picking my way over cross-legged people to the centre of the hut. They simmered down and I ploughed in hard and fast with our strategy.

"Venutius has gone south to raise support. We should anticipate hostile action." There was a chorus of noise. People exclaimed in shock and anger. "I expect vigilance from all of you, everyone to be armed and ready. However, if any small parties of Carvettii are seen travelling towards us, they are to be left to pass as if they have not been spotted and the information relayed to me. Davit, you must organise patrols to the north west – be subtle, low key. Presivin, you can cover the south west. But I'm stressing again to both of you, no killing unless it's absolutely unavoidable. Let small groups pass and send messages to me immediately. If Venutius raises some kind of army then that's different, but we'll no doubt have some warning of that before they attack. We have more loyalty in the south than Venutius realises." I hoped that was true. I felt better saying it, tried not to picture the families of the people I'd had executed or pressed into Roman service after they rebelled.

"Maybe we should contact Gallus. He could send troops to us," Vellocatus said. There were a few tuts and derisory comments from those who still hated the Roman presence on our land and in our affairs. It didn't help that some people in the meeting evidently didn't want to take any advice from a servant-turned-consort. I blushed despite myself, wishing he hadn't spoken up.

"Not unless we have to," I considered, "it really shouldn't come to that."

"Who knows what it will come to?" growled Gorlensa, her hoary voice making my spine creep. "Venutius is angry and shamed. He has friends, family, a whole tribe, small though they may be, behind him. This is no simple matter, Cartimandua. What you have done will put us all in danger."

I blanched, pale as spelt flour I am sure, because I felt all the blood rush away and noise filled my head as my brain clamoured to make sense of this direct attack. Even Vellocatus flinched, shifted in his seat. I looked down, blinking to clear my eyes, trying not to feel Vellocatus's discomfort, after his earlier optimism, as a form of betrayal. I swayed, perhaps visibly, feeling my whole life was on a sword edge. My unchallenged position as chief, in which I'd been so secure, suddenly as slippery as a river trout, flashing its rainbow beauty at me before disappearing downstream.

Hold on. My mind spoke in my father's voice. Grasp the nettle. Hold on.

"It is Venutius who puts us in danger," I thundered back at her, masking my distress with a cloak of anger. "Have you forgotten his constant desire for power, trying to undermine me at every turn, pushing for war with Rome when we stand not a chance of winning? Have you forgotten how he courted Caratacus, even when that foolish man had cost thousands of lives, lost his own tribe and come begging to us with nothing but his name and a promise? I tried, the goddess knows I tried for years to keep Venutius happy and give him the power he craved, but nothing was ever good enough for him. He could never accept me as his leader. It is not me who has acted rashly, nor put you all in danger as you say, but Venutius with his selfish aspirations!" I licked my lips. My throat felt dry and my heart was thudding as I looked around at the silent gathering. I let my eyes find Gorlensa again, daring her to speak out of turn once more. She held my stare, her features impassive, and then shrugged. Cold settled on me, dusting my shoulders with icy, feathery wings even though the hut was warm and people were sweating. Gorlensa's pupils seemed like tiny pinpricks in the yellowy-brown gauze of her irises. There was no hostility, but no friendliness either. Age had rendered her impervious to the whims of the present, including any pretence at social niceties (though it hurt me a little that she had no deeper bond with me, given all the years she had advised my family). She saw far back into the past, lived there, but seemed to know the future too, so though she did not speak another word to me that day, I knew that what she had said, she meant. We were all in danger. What I had done, and she was correct that it was me who ripped that final thread holding Venutius and I together, had broken the solidarity of Brigantia.

When I received word that a small band of Carvettii warriors had been accosted travelling covertly through thick forest to our north, I commanded a horse and rode up to see them for myself. Taking no chances, I went in a large party of riders, equipped with chains and a slave cart - a rough, enclosed vehicle of the type we had been using to transport Rome's quota of slaves southwards. The weather had taken a cold turn, unusual for the time of year, and I was robed in a fur cloak for the ride. I wore imported leather boots, gold bracelets and torcs and carved bone combs in my hair which was twisted into vicious plaits that pulled my face gaunt. One of the women who attended me had painted my face with blue woad and a sooty black mixture, making me look feral and cruel. As my sleek fur cloak streamed behind me on the ride, a thrill coursed through my veins. What a fool Venutius was! I had outwitted him at the first move.

Pleased though I was, the sight of the seven Carvettii men, in their ripped and bloodied attire, held at spear-point by my loyal scouts, reminded me of the perilous path to violence we had ventured upon. I stayed on my horse and cantered up close to the clustered assassins, enjoying the intimidation in their eyes. One of them kept his face a little averted from me.

"You," I said. "Look at me." He turned his face slowly and I leaned forward with a cold smile.

"Iticus, It's so nice to see you once again. Perhaps you would accompany me home so we can talk properly." I motioned for one of my men, a muscular warrior named Lerica who bore a huge jagged scar down his left cheek, to bring the slave cart near and load them on. As Iticus was shoved onto the splintered wooden wagon, he shook his head slightly, perhaps in embarrassment. He wouldn't meet my eye, whether because of the indignity of being caught or the shame of having threatened my life I was unsure.

"I want them alive, for now," I told Lerica. "Don't let them die until we know exactly who each of them is."

The sun, pale and distant that day, was sinking far on the horizon, blinking out slowly like a bored deity. I took off on my horse, wanting to be back home. There was some exhilaration in capturing my enemies, who had obviously been travelling to murder me, but a deep hurt inside me that my father by marriage had most likely arranged it and my erstwhile husband may have known of it. I was worried, too, about Antikia. She had not sent any word to me warning of the assassination party nor letting me know her situation and for all I knew, Tyrius had suspected her secret loyalties and would hold her hostage to me. Even the sight of Iticus bumping away down the track like a common criminal had discomforted me. He had visited me as a brother, as a little boy and again as a young man. Here he was, this child I had known, come to kill me and now imprisoned by me. I kicked my horse harder in the flanks, needing the rushing breeze to fill my head and take away the confusion of feelings that threatened to engulf my reason.

"They're in the old fodder pit," Lerica told me the next morning. The hole was outside of my immediate enclosure and was one of several where we stored feed for the livestock. When the barley had been parched, all the husks were thrown in there for the animals, along with anything else we could use as fodder but that particular pit was currently empty. Lerica had thrown the men some scraps of food but kept them in the grain pit with a grid of birch branches fastened over the top, hammered down with big, sharp iron nails. "Do you want me to leave them there?"

I considered. Lerica asked the question with no emotion, his darkly scarred face impassive and blunt. He was not a cruel man, but he would keep his charges in the most horribly deprived circumstances without flinching if I asked him to. It was summer, but a cool one, and the men in that pit would have to shit and piss where they sat, unless Lerica passed buckets down. They would be cramped, cold and shamed.

"Get Iticus out, he's the one I spoke to on the road. We'll talk and if he tells me what I want to know, perhaps we'll house them somewhere a bit more pleasant."

When Lerica brought Venutius's brother to me, he looked tired but reasonably well and I wondered if I should have left him to stew for a bit longer. It was not in my nature to make people suffer, but these were dangerous times and I had to think with my head, not my heart. I asked him to take a seat and he lowered himself gingerly into a chair, his care betraying the bruises from his cart journey the previous night.

"These are unhappy times we find ourselves in. I know why you were travelling here, Iticus. I know what you intended to do."

"I was travelling to meet my brother," he answered, "I was not aware that Carvettii access across Brigantia had been restricted." His voice held a tone of injustice.

"Oh, don't even try to lie; you're very bad at it. You were coming here to kill me after getting a message from your father and Venutius. I know this. You won't make your case any worse by admitting it, but you will infuriate me if you persist in playing stupid. Now I want to know exactly who I have in that pit." I stood over him, feeling like a parent to a naughty child. He was a grown man, but I still saw the gangly youth within him and suspected that he had the same distaste for all the bad blood as I did. I waited a while but he stayed silent.

"Ansuvan!" I yelled, and a man appeared at the entrance to my hut immediately. "Go to Lerica, tell him to chop the head off one of the men in that pit. Any man, it doesn't matter which." Ansuvan nodded and turned away.

"No, wait!" Iticus held up a hand, pleading. Ansuvan looked to me and I motioned for him to wait where he stood.

Iticus took a breath.

"What are you offering me, Cartimandua? I won't speak without some security for those men."

"Won't you now?" I smiled. "You know, I remember you as a child, Iticus. Small and wondering, gazing up at your big brother, idolizing your father. You were a sweet boy. I always liked you." I sat down with a sigh and threw my arms out despairingly. "All this hostility is awful. I have no desire to hurt or kill anyone, but what your brother is doing threatens our whole land. If he makes war with me, Rome will step in and if they do that, they may decide that client status is not working here in Brigantia and strip all our power from us. You'd have Romans storming all the way up to your corner of Brigantia if that happened. So I think you need to consider the security of all your people, up there in the north and not just the few sitting in that pit right now. Having said that, I can promise you that if you give me all the names and ranks of your men and all details that you know concerning the plans and movements of all the members of your family, then I will house you and your friends and keep you safe from harm."

"Prisoners? Hostages?" He scowled.

"I don't intend to use you to get more than is my due, Iticus. All I want is to stop Venutius raising a war that will divide our whole tribe. He can return to his homeland and rule there for all I care, but he will not cause the Romans to swarm onto our land, not while I am alive."

"Will you make an oath of that?" He asked, "That you'll leave the Carvettii alone, including all my family, if Venutius promises peace?"

"I will," I nodded. And I did, there and then, calling in three witnesses - a man, a woman and a child, and by dripping my blood onto a sharp willow stick that was notched, marked with my name and wrapped in leather tied with twine. I gave Iticus the parcel, which was my word, and which the witnesses would attest to and begin to spread as soon as they left my hut. There would be no gainsaying it. Everyone would know what I had promised. When we were alone again, he spoke.

"Venutius is in the far south of our lands, below Camulodunum, trying to raise a war band against you. He has some support, but not as much as he really needs and the line of forts Gallus has had built is making things difficult. His blood lust is rising though. Whatever you did to him has made him lose his senses." He paused, but I didn't respond, sick to my stomach with regrets, anger and impatience. He spoke carefully as he continued. "It was decided that you should be killed and on advice from my father, my mother sent me. She wouldn't trust anyone else to do it anyway, although others thought it would look bad, our family having a direct hand in your murder. It doesn't surprise me that we were caught. It was a fool's errand, trying to sneak through the heartlands of Brigantia and into your very home. Two of the men with me are my cousins, one of whom is the head of our war council in the absence of Tyrius."

He gave me the names. He drew a map of where he believed Venutius was based though it was rough and uncertain. He told me his mother was pacing her roundhouse crazed with ambition and anger and that he did not share his family's eagerness for tribal control, even if he was insulted by the treatment his brother had received at my hands. He spoke probably more than he had intended, flopping back in his chair exhausted and defeated at the end, but his honesty had softened me and given me hope that a peaceful resolution could be found. When he rose to leave my roundhouse, Ansuvan escorted him to a small hut, infinitely more comfortable than the grain pit, where he found his weary, defeated friends waiting silently inside for him.

"They've got her, they've got Risha!" One of my women, a niece of Mandulay, came running in to tell me.

"No!" I exclaimed, despite myself. She had truly come south, I couldn't believe it. "Where, do you know?"

"Somewhere south of us. She nearly got past us but we got the old sow," Amelan giggled.

"We need somewhere to keep her, somewhere decent," I said, sternly. "Get Mandulay to organise it."

"She's not well. I can do it."

"Fine. Sort something out and then go tend to your aunt. Make sure you get her anything she needs."

She slipped back out again, a little more sober, to sort out a hut. My enclosure had grown steadily over the years, added to bit by bit as our community grew and as our people began to huddle together under the threat of Roman occupation and the pressure of Roman taxes. We had several big roundhouses, one of which was my practically rebuilt home, the place that had been the heart of our tribe for several generations now. There were smaller huts, storage huts, underground grain storage pits, stone querns for grinding grain into flour, shelters for horses and ponies and for our livestock. I had my orchard and there were little gardens that Mandulay had designed, containing herbs and plants that she once used for her cooking and curing, and also the specimens that we occasionally received from Rome. Our governors overseas were presumably keen to test what plants would thrive or die in our strange and hostile environment. We had become an almost bustling hub, but still nothing like the towns and colonia springing up in the south. We didn't have roundhouses to spare, and Risha would probably have to share with one of the high ranking families – perhaps that of Presivin.

When she came, she was silent, her dopey grey eyes blank and wide just as they always were, belying the cunning, unpleasant mind behind them. Her forehead was pinched in lines and her lips drooped at the corners, rivulets running deep in her cheeks around them. I made no wonder Tyrius preferred my handsome aunt to this miserable hag of a wife.

I had her brought in to me. I had no sympathy for her. A part of me blamed her entirely for the sorry mess we had found ourselves in. If I lifted the veil of the past to find a single point where maybe everything could be changed, it would be the time I travelled away to the north and left her with Venutius and Vellocatus; the time she convinced her son to challenge his best friend and loyal servant. They had never recovered their easy friendship. Venutius had changed after that. She had set him on a path of ambition and blood lust that he may otherwise not have chosen. His years of enforced service to Rome had not helped, but by the time he left to serve in their army, he was already bitter and angry with his lot. I felt more anger to the woman before me than to the killing party I had already apprehended.

She stood prim and straight, her hands folded in front of her and gazed through me dispassionately. For a woman with an errant husband and one son revolting while another sat imprisoned, she looked remarkably calm. Either she had no fear or she was so convinced of her own importance that she could envisage no harm befalling her.

"So you heard about my aunt and your husband? Is that why you were slinking across my land trying to get to him?"

She didn't answer, just kept staring.

"I've given my oath that if Venutius promises peace and retreats to the Carvettii, I'll take no further action. If your husband and son give up and go home, you'll be safe. Otherwise..." I let the word dangle and turned away from her to pick up my drink which I sipped. She still kept quiet.

"Why did you travel south, Risha?" I wondered aloud. "Did you think Tyrius would abandon you for his love of my aunt? Or were you just eager to be at the centre of the action?"

"Tyrius would never abandon me," she answered, surprising me, "But men need proper guidance from their women. Something you have been sorely unable to provide for my son. They both need me now, whether they know it or not."

"Well it's a terrible shame you won't be there for them."

Her face sharpened, pupils like tiny dots in a grey storm cloud, mouth pursed. I resisted the urge to speak at length, to accuse her of turning Venutius against me, because I knew I would sound like a ranting fool if I started. Instead I kept my taunts brief.

"Perhaps when they learn you are here, they will consider their position more carefully." I said.

She braced herself, folding her skinny arms across her stomach and pinching her lips harder so the wrinkles around her mouth were white lines puckering inwards.

"And maybe," she said after a moment's thought, "they will reconsider your beloved aunt's position more carefully, when they learn I am here."

I forced myself to laugh nonchalantly and motioned for two ladies and the man set to guard her to lead her out of my presence, shaking my head slightly as if she were a foolish woman whom I humoured, although in fact she was anything but and had just reminded me of the danger Antikia was in. Even if she had kept Tyrius persuaded of her loyalty all this time, maybe once he heard his wife was held captive, he would see the benefit of using Antikia as a hostage also. He would know that even if I believed she had betrayed me, I would hate the idea of her being harmed. Even if he did not want his wife back, Antikia's value as a hostage must still occur to him. I moaned as

I rubbed my aching forehead and Amelan came back in to me with medicine – a drink that should sooth the tension in my head. She was a good girl really; Mandulay had taught her all the herbal remedies she knew, anticipating that her own days were numbered.

"How is Mandulay?" I asked her.

"Not very well. We think this might be the end."

"Oh." I felt winded. "I'll come over now."

Mandulay used to live in with us, but she had moved out a few years previous, when her brother's daughter, Amelan came to our settlement with her younger brother. The three of them had a small hut within our central enclosure. As I stepped inside it, Mandulay gave a little cough as she tried to sit up.

"No, lay back down," I insisted. "Amelan told me you were very ill."

She just sighed and I took her hand.

"Go back to your work," she whispered. "Important."

"I will. Amelan will look after you but send for me if you need me. Everything else can wait if it has to."

"Antikia..." Her face crumpled in distress.

"No, no, she's fine," I said, "Only the high council knows, but she hasn't betrayed me. She's working for me."

"Ah." Mandulay relaxed again. "Secret safe with me." Her breathing was heavy the conversation tiring her out.

"Get some rest now. I'll come by again later," I said and dropped a kiss on her hand.

Later, Vellocatus and I sat with the most senior council members and appraised our situation in hushed tones. Around me were Gorlensa, increasingly less of this world as the days passed, Presivin who was quiet and reassuring as always, Davit, calmer now he was older and less inclined to loss of temper, Alabas, a cousin of my mother who had moved his family closer to ours several years before, Namandea who was Gorlensa's niece and Shamatin, our metal worker who also had a good head for tactical matters. We talked of Antikia and the danger she could be in.

"We have to get her back," Davit insisted. "She's done what you sent her to do – thanks to her, we have half of the top Carvettii family and Venutius will probably crumple and go home. But he might just take his anger out on Antikia before he does."

"Surely not," countered Namandea, "They were close before all this. I can't believe he would hurt her."

Eyes turned to us, and I realised they were waiting to see what Vellocatus and I, who had known Venutius best, would expect of him. I shrugged hopelessly. I had no idea what he was capable of, which spoke volumes about my marriage.

"He'll do whatever he thinks is most advantageous to him at the time," answered Vellocatus, with a surety I had never had in my husband's character. I turned to him with curiosity.

"Well, didn't you all expect that?" He asked us in confusion. "I mean, after he wouldn't come to Camulodunum when the rebels were to be executed? He left Cartimandua to face that alone. He half-hoped she would be put down with the rebel leaders and that he could return, the consort-turned-client-king, since he had long served Rome and believed they would support him."

I closed my eyes for a few seconds. It was hard to hear, despite the passing of time and recent events, that the husband I had still loved had been so unmoved by the danger and horror I was in at that time. We were all quiet for a time, then Davit spoke up again.

"Can I go south, take a small party and try to get her back?"

"And get caught by them, just like Iticus was captured by us?" Presivin was cautious.

"This is still our land. We have more support than Venutius," said Shamatin, in a voice shaking with emotion. He had always had a soft spot for my aunt and was probably one of the men she had taken in the times when Tyrius was not with her.

"Make no deals for us, if we are captured. We know the risk we're taking. You must let us go," insisted Davit.

"So be it," I answered. "But take people you trust, and none of the other council members. You can leave as soon as you are ready." Shamatin didn't argue with me, but I saw his frustration and I heard his quiet, desperate entreaty to Davit to find her and bring her back safe.

Three days later, Davit and his three chosen men returned, grey-faced with hunger and lack of sleep. His foray into the far southern tip of Brigantia had been more fraught with peril than he had expected and the support for Venutius there had taken him by surprise. Even so, on a horse at his side was Antikia. I ran to her and helped her down, sending Davit's wife, Essalea, running off inside to prepare a bed and a hot drink because honestly, Antikia looked terrible. Her summer gown was dirty and torn down one side and her hair looked dishevelled and wiry. She was filthy, but carried no bruises as far as I could see. She fell against me as she dismounted and murmured a greeting that sounded vague and hollow.

Inside my roundhouse, we bundled her onto a bed of stuffed furs and blankets and Essalea wiped her face. Amelan hadn't appeared all day and I had left her alone to tend to her aunt, so instead I asked Essalea to sit by Antikia and feed her. Shamatin came rushing in and sat there also, holding her hand, and then taking over the task of spooning stew into her mouth, but I kept everyone else away, anxious that the council did not descend on her with questions and queries while she was so enfeebled. I had a quiet word with Davit as he discarded his heavy weaponry outside.

"We got as close as we could to the camp – it's bigger than we expected – but she'd gone by the time we got there. We heard rumours about it. Apparently she got out even before they heard Iticus had been captured. She knew which way the wind was blowing - that Tyrius was suspicious after she had tried to send a message north to us, even though she explained it away as a plea for you to surrender and not drag us into war. When we discovered she had left them, we scouted round, back-tracking, and found her holed up in the hills, in an abandoned hut on some awful moorland. I don't think she'd eaten for a few days and I think she might actually have fought her way out of camp. I'm guessing she was going to get her strength back then travel back to us. She mustn't have trusted anyone enough even to venture out for food or a horse. That tells you something about the way people down there feel. It's not that they hate you, or like Venutius even. Just that they hate all the Romans on their borders and Venutius is promising a war that will get rid of them for good."

"What a fool. And what fools they all are," I sighed, rubbing the back of my neck wearily. "Still, he must be having second thoughts, now he knows we have his family."

Davit paused, hands on his hips and gaze on the floor, and then he raised his tired eyes to mine.

"No. He isn't."

"What do you mean? What do you know?" I asked, feeling my stomach turning over and sinking. Essalea came out from my roundhouse and joined her husband. I glanced back inside and saw Shamatin holding Antikia upright with one strong arm and feeding her with the other.

"He's amassing an army, Cartimandua. Worst of all, we've heard that Claudius is dead and the word is spreading like wildfire. They all think it's a perfect time to act, while the change in emperors occurs and Gallus is distracted. Venutius is going to attack as soon as he can, regardless of what promises or threats you make. He wants you, your family, and the council dead. He would have killed your aunt if she hadn't run when she saw the

192

chance. We're at war, Cartimandua. Call a war council and start planning how we fight him, because he's coming for us."

Davit, the man who used to infuriate me but who had just saved my aunt and who remained loyal to me even though he hated Rome as much as Venutius did, gripped my arm for a second, as if to impress on my flesh the reality of what we were facing, and then he gathered up his long bow and his sword and turned away with his arm around his wife, towards the roundhouse where their children anxiously waited.

AUTUMN AD54

I sat on the news for a night, tossing and turning and hoping that Davit was simply being dramatic, but his weary face had told me all I needed to know. None of us wanted war, even the men and women who several years earlier had been ready to fight the Romans. Most of them were settled now, with children and a tolerance for Roman rule – Davit himself was the perfect example. The younger men had grown up only knowing client status and didn't fully appreciate the freedoms they had lost. I had no idea how they would react to the uprising by Venutius and his family; my fear was that it might spark some buried impulse to fight our foreign oppressors and that my tribe would drift towards my husband and his foolish promises. Even if they stayed loyal to me, I had to lead them in aggression against the man I had shared a childhood with, the man who had shared my confidence and my bed for over ten years. I was not a violent person, I told myself. How could I fight him? And, worse to contemplate, how could he fight me, knowing he would have to kill me in the end?

Vellocatus felt me shifting at his side and laid an arm over me to stay me. I remembered that when Venutius used to do that, I felt it almost as a yoke, pressing me down and binding me to him. With Vellocatus, I felt I had found a solid branch to grasp in the treacherous waters that had flooded my life. He didn't ask me what was wrong, didn't really need to. I think most of the people who had witnessed Antikia's return appreciated how bad things had got.

I woke at dawn. The grey filmy start to the late summer's day did nothing to lift my spirits and I rose with heaviness in my chest and an ache in my head. Mandulay had died the day before, hours before Antikia had returned, though I didn't learn it until well into the evening. She never fully comprehended the danger my aunt had been in. Amelan had sat with her all through the

194

morning, her brother Strisen joining her after he had done his jobs, and the pair of them were both there for her as she died. So I had that to be thankful for. I dressed and left the enclosure without waking anyone. I wanted to take a walk and clear my head before I had to speak to them all. I crunched through the spiky grass, dried out through weeks of sunshine, out through the meadow and beyond. Following the path, down past the woods, over the brow of the hill I came to the point where I had a good view of the valley to the north-west. I should post someone here permanently, I decided, wondering that I hadn't done it already. What was I thinking? We were in such danger and I was walking around in some kind of dream. I stomped on, angry at myself, shooting venomous glances into the far distance where I imagined the Carvettii council sitting around plotting my doom. For the first time, fury that they actually planned to overthrow me, their chief and queen, outweighed the terror I had of battle gore and death. I welcomed that rush of pride and purpose. I needed it, I realised, to get me through. When my mother died, I had travelled north to repel possible invaders on our lands and I had been ready for the fight even though it hadn't come to that. I'd had a singular purpose then – to establish myself as my father's natural successor, and I'd painted my face with woad and slipped on a mantle of leadership as though it was an unquestionable right. I had become chief because I believed I was. Now I would defeat Venutius because I believed I could.

Over in the valley, I saw wood smoke rising and recognised with some satisfaction a Brigantian patrol, vigilant on this quiet morning for any threat to our royal heartland. I decided I would set up a ring of patrols all around us. Venutius and his family knew our land as if it were their own and could attack from any direction, sneaking over hills or through quiet valleys, since we had such a low population compared to our vast land mass. I guessed he might try another assassination attempt, since he probably did not have sufficient numbers for all-out war. Once we had established a military presence around our already secure territory, we would march south and force the idiot to surrender. He couldn't go any further south than he already was or he would be fleeing into Roman-ruled lands and they would easily accost him on my orders.

I almost skipped back home, eager to set plans into motion, but as I approached, Vellocatus ran towards me, half-kitted for battle. I came to a halt and waited for him to speak, his breathless voice seeming to come from a world away.

"Venutius is on his way, less than half a day away by all accounts."

"Why did no one warn us?" I shouted, hands on my hips like a disobeyed mother. Behind him I could see Davit arranging weapons into heaps, Antikia swaying in the doorway of the roundhouse and Gorlensa sitting peacefully on the huge tree stump that had been there since I was a child. They made an odd scene. Gorlensa caught my eye and with a peculiar little smile, beckoned me over. I stepped past Vellocatus, patting his arm as I did and he followed me towards her, still talking, his words passing around me like a cool breeze.

"You'd better rein them in, Cartimandua, or they'll run around like children with spears and fall on their own faces." Gorlensa smiled again and I wondered if she was going mad, like old women sometimes do.

"There's no time," I breathed, conscious of others around us who might overhear. "How can I get our defences here before he comes?"

"I think you'll find you're more prepared than you realise," she said, and motioned towards Davit, who was talking with messengers on horseback and sending boys and girls running back and forth with arrows and shields and the goddess only knows what else. Beyond him, Presivin was holding packs of braying dogs on leads and yelling orders at his children and several of his cousins. "Do you remember who we are?" She asked suddenly, a bit of spittle in the corner of her mouth and eyes blazing. "Do you even remember who you are?"

I looked back to her, thinking she was raving, and then saw a deeper truth in what she was saying.

"I remember," I whispered. I saw horses in my mind, flying hooves and slicing swords, spears jabbing down. My older sister, wielding a sword high over her head, with a scream that pitched above the sound of fighting. A scream of glee, not terror.

"Cartimandua, you have to come. Now." Vellocatus was panicked but I quietened him with a hand on his chest.

"It's fine, Vellocatus. You go on and help Davit. I'll be there soon."

He gaped at me but I ignored him and sat down next to the old woman. Eventually he turned and made his way over to where the others were gathering, aiming quizzical glances my way, but caught up in their own excitement.

"He's a good man, I suppose," Gorlensa muttered, twisting a twig this way and that between her fingers until it snapped, leaving two short pieces with sharp, tapered ends. She stuck one into her mouth, working it between her few remaining teeth. I didn't reply. She wasn't going to apologise for her previous harsh words about our union but this comment indicated we had moved on.

"Do you recall Hesavea?" She asked matter-of-factly, spitting into a clump of long grass.

"Sometimes. Only a little." I answered. In truth, I hadn't thought of her for years and never spoke of her - a habit I suppose I picked up from my parents.

"You were only young," she conceded, "and she was much older than you."

Older, prettier, stronger. Her brilliant hazel eyes, stark in a pale face and framed with thick, light brown hair, flashed through my mind.

"I think I remember... you know, the end." I couldn't find

the words. She nodded curtly.

"You were there. It was an ambush. Your mother kept you well back, with the other little ones. Your sister, well she was of an age to fight, even if your mother didn't think so."

"Who... I've never been sure what-" Even now, I couldn't get my words out.

"Northern tribe, I forget which. Your father had travelled up with all of you – he used to do that more, back then. It was a vicious attack, not expected at all or he wouldn't have had you there. They came at dawn, a large group of them, half-naked and waving huge spears. One man had a skull rammed on the shaft of his weapon. Some of them had painted themselves up with red ochre so they looked fierce and bloody. They were a sight, I can tell you. Lesser men would have run away, but they underestimated your father. And your sister. Oh, she was on fire! Knew how to handle a spear and a sword, never much of a shot with a bow, but then she liked to be up close for the kill. So young and yet so brutal. And there's you, hates the killing and no stomach for death. How strange that she should die and you be left to lead us."

Her words hit like a punch to the stomach.

"You think she would have made a better leader than me?" I asked, wounded.

"No, I don't. The times call for a different type of chief. Hesavea would have torn Plautius limb from limb if she'd had chance, or murdered Ostorius who came after him, but where would we be now? Flattened like the Iceni. Wiped out like the Catuvellauni. You've done all right, my girl, so far. But now you're going to have to dig deep and find that hot blood that's pooled somewhere inside you. Stop caring so much about what other people think, or about the pain you are going to inflict on them and raise up your sword." She sighed and shrugged her shoulders abruptly, dispassionately concise in her old age.

I had three memories of Hesavea, tucked away somewhere

dark and undisturbed, and I flicked through them now, sitting next to Gorlensa whilst my council prepared for war against my husband. The first was of her feeding me, tearing up some pieces of bread for me to dunk in a meat stew. I remembered her hands, which were ruddy from outdoor work and play, breaking the hard, flat loaf into small chunks that I could grasp with my hands, tiny in comparison to hers. The second was of her punching my arm, making my eyes water, after I broke something of hers. I remembered calling to my mother and being scooped up in her arms, Hesavea sent outside, her face red and angry from the stern shouting-at she had received. The third memory was of the day she died, a mingling of visions of her playing with me, humouring my childish games, and then her hair flying out behind her as she charged into those painted nightmare men, a grin on her face as she met her match. She must have killed a handful of those warriors before one of them sliced her down. I saw some of it, not all; not the very end.

Oh Hesavea, how I longed to be like you when I was a child, and then how quickly I forgot you and buried my pain at your loss. My parents missed you so much, though they would never speak of you. I wonder if they compared you and I, and found me wanting through the years.

Enough of that. In desolate moments, I have drifted over that question and quickly decided each time that Gorlensa was right in what she said that day, sitting on the old tree trunk. Hesavea and I were very different, but I was no less a strong woman just because I took no pleasure in violence. In fact, I don't think my father ever particularly enjoyed killing. He, like me, just did what was necessary and if that included cutting down other living beings, then so be it. Yes, I made my peace with it later on, but at that point, having just had my head spun back to one of my earliest and most traumatic memories, I still had to prove to myself that I could fight, could kill, when circumstances demanded it; that I wasn't the weak-hearted fake that Venutius had often implied.

I said thank-you to Gorlensa and stood up, with my heart pounding. I marvelled for a moment at how so many people were busy organising our defence and as I felt a note of redundancy sound in my soul, humming that I wasn't needed, I reminded myself that the very reason these people were part of my council and community was because they were intelligent, fierce and self-motivated. Their industrious activity was a reflection on my careful leadership.

"Davit, tell me what you know," I ordered as I approached him where he stood with Vellocatus, Presivin and Namandea.

"A patrol below the South Nab spotted some front runners scouting the territory so they travelled in a circle around them and found Venutius camped with a huge retinue, sheltered in forest and avoiding the settlements in that area. There's no question about it. They're ready for battle."

"He doesn't care that we have his brother, his mother and several of his war council," I mused, incredulously. "He obviously doesn't think I'd dare do anything to them, despite my threats."

"Or, like you said, he just doesn't care," remarked Vellocatus.

"How did they come so far north without us knowing?" I directed this to Presivin, who had most knowledge of our patrols and scouts in the south.

"He has more support than we realised, for a start," Presivin admitted, "but also, he has Fistoc who apparently has been travelling around stirring up unrest and converting people to Venutius's cause. They're making it into a pro- and anti-Rome dispute, rather than a simple tribal take-over, and that has won a lot of people round. I'd guess they got the bulk of their army in the south, perhaps even from the neighbouring tribes who are faring worse than us under Roman rule, and then Fistoc arranged safe passage north. He would have gone from roundhouse to roundhouse along the route, twisting their minds against you."

I shook my head in disbelief. This was the man who had stood shoulder to shoulder with me as we dealt with Ostorius. But then I remembered Fistoc at Camulodunum, standing on the south-west peak in the darkness, the hunch of his shoulders displaying his frustration and anger that we couldn't support the rebels. His problem then was that he knew those rebels were doomed to failure. With Venutius he must think he had a real chance at overthrowing Roman rule. I shook thoughts of him away with sadness.

"So our status now is...?"

"War bands are coming from the north and north east. Some also from the north west - neighbours of the Carvettii who don't want to be ruled by them," Davit answered. "Lerica has gone to organise a meeting point, just north of us."

"We're gathering in all the stores of weapons," Namandea added. "There's a good amount of arrows, bows and daggers, especially as everyone has been hoarding them since the Iceni were stripped of all theirs. Shamatin is checking all the metal work and strapping on the chariots and Alabas is preparing the horses and ponies."

Looking past her I could see Shamatin examining one of my own chariots, running his hand around one of the smooth ash wheels checking the iron tyre that bound it and fingering the oak spokes that ran in to a central hub of birch. He passed his hand over it quickly, moving on to the next within seconds. I brought my attention back to the group around me.

"What about Venutius? Do we know what his plan is?"

"There's a route that runs to the west and then north-east which, from his position, would most easily bring him towards us," said Vellocatus, who'd had time to consider this while I'd been talking with Gorlensa. "Whether he's planning a pitched battle, or to attack us here, I can't say, but I'd guess the former."

"And he's half a day away?" I checked again. Davit nodded.

"We won't have enough people to fight." I said. No one

disagreed. "I'm sending messengers to Didius Gallus. This is the kind of threat that our Roman allegiance is supposed to protect us against, so they can get their fat backsides north and fight for us for once. Davit, tell Lerica to send everyone east of here. That's our best guess for Venutius's approach and I want to meet him head-on."

"We're going in half-ready," Vellocatus shook his head.

"That maybe so, but it's unavoidable. What we have to do is hold him off and limit the damage until Gallus gets reinforcements here. He should be able to send men from the frontier of forts he's been building on our border so they're not too far away."

"He might not even help," pointed out Davit, still suspicious of our foreign overlords.

"I'm betting he doesn't want to have a northern rebellion on his hands when he's still so busy everywhere else. At least, that's what I'm counting on."

Truthfully I wasn't at all sure. After all, Venutius had fought in the Roman army for five long years. They may not even have realised his about-face or might think that if he did overthrow me, he could be converted to their cause. I had a cold fear that secretly Gallus and his kind would prefer to deal with even a troublesome client king instead of struggling constantly to fit a female leader into their patriarchal view of the world. Would they leave me high and dry? I had to hope not, since they were all I had to rely on.

I rode out later that day on my finest horse, a huge creature with broad flanks that quivered with the wild urge to ram forward. A caravan of people, weaponry, chariots and supplies followed as we made our way to a place I knew would give us some advantage. As the pathway breasted a hill, we looked down onto a gently sloping plain, craggy in parts and leading down to a stream that cut the wide valley in two. We stopped there, at the top of the plain, hoping that Venutius would approach from the bottom, and be forced to cross the stream and attack uphill. It's a common tactic, one that Shamatin was very much in favour of, but it doesn't guarantee victory. The principle is sound, as long as your enemy doesn't mount a surprise attack in your flank or rear. I was counting on Venutius not having enough support for such a devious plan and pleaded with my goddess to send him the way we expected, up through this broad valley and onto our spears.

We camped out there, roasting meats on open fires so the delicious smell would dispirit the opposition who had trudged northwards for several days and so our bellies would be full for the fight. There was a plentiful supply of ale. I discovered that by drinking a good amount, my usual fear of pain and injury was supplanted by an aggressive self-confidence that seemed to rally and inspire my fighters. Even Antikia, who had roused herself to come with us, came fully to her senses and joined me in loudly condemning and ridiculing my husband and his father. There was a celebratory atmosphere with only a slight edge of tension and we worked ourselves up into a state where we almost believed the upstart Venutius would not dare challenge us at all, but would go skulking off to his homelands in the knowledge of certain defeat.

"Standards!" yelled a voice, "Down there!"

"Venutius is here!" The call went up, and my army was suddenly on its feet, clamouring for shields and swords, swearing and yelling all kinds of foul language. People stampeded past me, diving for travelling packs full of bows, arrows, pieces of rough and ready armour.

I ran for my chariot, which Alabas was bringing out to our front-line, and threw on my battle armour – leather jerkin with an outer skin of thinly pressed metal pieces and an enormous woven shield that weighed heavily on my arm as I grappled for the reins and brandished my sword, which Shamatin had thrust to me. We coalesced into a heaving, bloodthirsty mass and I was eager, in that moment, for the blood-letting to start, to make my way to my husband and slice open his traitorous throat. Vellocatus had given me a clumsy hug and a warm, hurried kiss before I mounted the chariot, and now he rode astride his own chariot. Other council members and long established families fielded their chariots, many of which were adapted carts, whilst the large majority were on foot, with some few on horseback. I would like to be able to say we had an organised front-line - bowmen at the fore maybe, flanks of warriors positioned to swoop as we drew the opposition in perhaps, any such tactic really. But in actuality, we were a rabble of angry people. That's how our wars were fought, two sides rampaging against each other with the single, simple aim of slaughter. Caratacus had told me how the Romans had employed the devastating method of creeping forwards under a shell of shields while his own force hammered useless blows on the giant beetle's back. It had made me consider the possibilities for more sophisticated warfare (partly because anything that reduced the risk of a sword in my back or belly was a welcome thing) but now, in the face of a real and present threat, I fell back on my instinctive, tribal memories and found that the potential for fearless, mindless violence lurked in my blood. I think it hides in everyone, and I wondered then as now that the Romans could be so organised and reserved in their approach to killing when all-consuming rage seems so necessary.

I gave a sharp jerk on the reins of my two war ponies, small, sure-footed beasts that would manoeuvre deftly in battle, and drove the chariot out to the front of my army. As I passed Antikia, who was grimly hefting her shield onto her upper arm, she grabbed the back of the vehicle and leapt on. Positioned behind me, we could fight back-to-back. It was a small chariot but extremely manoeuvrable. I had another, my father's beautiful vehicle that was more for show than for fighting, but I had told

Shamatin to leave the big, ornate carriage behind. I couldn't handle that one as well as I would have liked and for battle, I felt more confident with this well-crafted and swift machine. I drew us to a halt facing south, downhill, and we stood looking down the shelving slope at the dark, swarming shape of Venutius's invasion force. I could see him; not his face, not at that distance, but I knew from the defiant stride and shape of his body that I had so often held close to me that it was him.

I thought about shouting some rousing words to my warriors, but they were making such a commotion I could not have been heard anyway. After I had held position for a while, staring silent and still down at my enemy, I settled instead for galloping my chariot back and forth a couple of times, raising a ground-shaking roar from my army that would show Venutius we were intent on crushing him. Perhaps he had thought until that point that I would be a push-over. It would explain his confidence about attacking me, uphill on my own territory.

There was a lot of growling and posturing from both sides, but eventually Venutius began to lead his force forward. I yanked my great spear out of its bracket in my chariot and held it aloft on one arm, sword high in the other. My meaning, thankfully, was plain enough to all behind me - do not move until I tell you. The last thing I wanted was for everyone to scatter downhill and impale themselves on a row of upcoming spears and swords. Let the rebels wear themselves out cresting this hill, and then we would flood over them. My arms ached within seconds. After minutes I wanted to cry out, so taut were the muscles in my arms from supporting both weapons, but I couldn't drop them, not until the time was exactly right. A few arrows had started to fall around us, shots from the long bows with the deepest penetration. I waited as long as I could, until the possibility of my being hit became too great, then I screamed as deep and loud as I could and brought both arms down. On both sides, men and women bolted past me, while I held my position. No one expected me to charge directly in – all would be in vain if I was cut down now – but my fists were balled around my weapons, reins tied loosely to my waist so I was free to fight. The pony would know what to do once I steered him forwards. My heart was thudding with the desire to lunge into the fray, and my arms twitched as the muscles in them strove to put the sword and spear to use. Still we remained, a rear-guard of higher-ranking people whose lives could only be risked if truly necessary, and watched as a wave of Brigantians clashed with crunching, slicing horror into the roaring pretenders stomping up our land.

"Is that Alabas?" shouted Antikia, as she squinted past me into the red and black clamour. I spotted his distinctive chariot with its red and yellow leather fringe. He was driving his sword down again and again, but had attracted quite a cluster of opponents.

"He can't hold them off," I observed.

"Why is he out there?" Antikia was angry, disbelieving.

"He wants to fight," I observed. "Look at him! He may as well, he's getting old anyway."

We followed his progress as he cut a swathe into the enemy, blood and spit flying from his blade, until he disappeared into the thick of it, from where we knew he would not emerge.

"That boy fighting there, who is that?"

Antikia looked to where I was pointing, at the boy of perhaps twelve at most, who was slashing and diving like a fish between the scram of adult bodies. He was doing a lot of damage, but I winced as I saw how close he came to being chopped down.

"It looks like Strisen,, Amelan's little brother, but surely not? He's still a child."

"He doesn't fight like one," I said, proud of Mandulay's little servant nephew, who had just earned himself a much higher position if he survived the battle.

Some of Venutius's fighters were scrambling past the main fray, making their way towards where we waited. I saw with pleasure that they couldn't make it through in large enough numbers to be any real danger to us and though I could have stayed still and watched others finish them, I was determined to take part in this battle. Vellocatus had already driven forward and was fighting for all he was worth. I checked the reins about my waist and gave a short sharp tug to spur the war ponies forwards. I had my sword firmly grasped in my right hand, the spear tucked away for now into its holding place in the chariot. My heavy shield was strapped to my left arm, my left fist gripping hard to the hand-hold along its edge. Armoured up in this way, I had to use my hips to tug at the reins, but the fierce little animals didn't need much help to find their footing. They ploughed us into the oncoming gang, manoeuvring slightly to the left of them, so I could slice along their flank with my blade, and then they pulled away left, turning in a tight circle so we spun round to re-attack, this time with my shield arm facing the enemy, to block their blades as Antikia swung herself about on the back of the chariot, swiping and smashing with her blade. Again, the ponies pulled us away. The whole point of being on a chariot was about remaining mobile. If you stayed still, the mob would cut down your animal or wreck the vehicle, forcing you to dismount. As we drew away, I slid my sword into its metal-tipped leather sheath, the tangy smell of fresh blood mixing with the earthy scent of dry leather. My sword arm and hand were covered in spatters of red, some wet, some sickeningly clumpy. I rubbed it on my skirt, to keep my hand from becoming slippery, then hoisted my spear up. It was an ornate weapon, the shaft made of carved and decorated ash so it was strong but light enough to handle and flexible enough to stand a crushing blow into a human body and not splinter with the force of impact. The metal head was smooth and long, shaped into a perfect point which would draw blood if it was gently stroked across the skin. It was designed to penetrate then withdraw with ease, so you could use it to kill again and again, whilst on the move and not suddenly find it yanked from your grasp as your chariot moved on but your spear wedged in some unfortunate person's chest.

We had turned and were facing them again. Most had fallen, dead or dying, with opened necks or bellies, one with a mostly severed arm, I noticed. But more were joining them. I glanced to the main throng, a mess of moving limbs and whistling swords, cutting through the air that was fast becoming dank and foetid with the stench of killing. It was impossible to tell how we were doing. I jerked my hips back and the ponies bolted again, ramming us into men and women with snarling lips and painted faces, the whites of their eyes brilliant against the dusty blue-black hollows of their cheeks and eye sockets, and their blood and mud slicked hair. They were a vision from a nightmare, I thought; then remembered, so am I. I jammed my spear hard into a chest, an eye socket, a thigh. Unplanned, disorganised, just murdering them as fast as I could. Behind me, Antikia screeched with effort as she wielded her own sword, heavier than mine, taking off heads and arms with wild abandon.

I never would have thought killing could be so much fun. I began to understand why Venutius had so longed in the past to fight our Roman occupiers. He had tasted battle on a grand scale in their service, had killed countless times in the course of being my husband and helping keep order in our tribe. He knew the feeling of freedom and power that came with the cutting down of an enemy. He knew it was the perfect antidote to the emasculation he felt as my husband and Rome's servant. He needed the release of it, but for all these years I had held him back. No wonder he was so wild and angry. Not that I was allowing him any sympathy. I didn't care about him. I was too busy marvelling at my own blood-lust.

Is it a shock to hear me say I liked the killing? Well, the times called for it so I had no choice. I wasn't some weak-willed woman trying to run a peaceful little community. I was a tribal chief of disparate groups, with an authority based on my cunning and intelligence but also brute force. Other people had carried out most of the violence for me in the past, but it didn't hurt for me to discover my own potential at this stage. In fact, I was fairly sure, my performance on that day would go a long way to securing my position.

So the battle continued. We all fought like wild cats and eventually, Venutius had to retreat. We had the better position, being uphill and he couldn't quite overcome that, although it was close. As they backed off, we retreated too, moving up towards the huge caravan of carts, animals and of course all the non-fighters and children who were watching from a distance. The crowd had grown, more people arriving during battle and I was heartened to know we should have warriors arriving to replace those we had undoubtedly lost; there were bodies and body parts slumped across the hillside.

The camp fires were burning, pots of broth and stew waiting for all of us weakened by the hours of hard fighting. Everyone was tired, muscle-weary and strained - the excitement fading and the memory of horror and death rushing in to fill the void now the lust for killing was over.

I sat with the council. Vellocatus sat by me. Antikia, Shamatin, Namandea, Gorlensa, Presivin, Davit but no Alabas. He had perished as I knew he would, and though I missed his familiar, benevolent presence, I was happy for him to have died a worthy death. His woman might not have agreed, for I had seen her, sobbing and distressed earlier. There were weeping people dotted in and amongst the crowds, others looking stunned and shaken. It's the way things are after a battle. Some are still riding high on the back of their battlefield prowess and others have been thrust into misery by their loss. I kept my mind focused on the bigger worry - when and where we would fight next. I had no time to consider the petty losses. Except one. I had searched out that boy, Strisen, which wasn't hard because he had joined a rough group of men nearby and was being loudly praised and fed lots of ale. Reassured that he was still alive, I took him aside and told him he should train as a warrior. I also whispered how sorry I was about Mandulay, which he acknowledged with a silent little nod and a terribly sad frown. Then I pulled him away from the men he had joined and sent him to spend the night near Davit, who could keep an eye on him.

We all ate and slept, exhausted and spent and knowing our enemy were doing the same. I had guards patrolling anyway in case some lone warrior tried to sneak through with a blade for me and a death wish for himself. I fell into a sound, dreamless sleep that lasted clear through to the following morning when my stomach rumbled and hunger finally woke me. Amelan was on hand to fetch me some food and she brought a rubbing ointment too, that she massaged into my shoulders, arms and back.

"It'll take the burn out," she explained. "Otherwise by tomorrow you won't move for aching." I sat with my eyes closed while her hard little hands pressed the knots out of my body. When she had done, I swallowed some ale and ate a bowl full of barley porridge. The thrill of the previous day seemed far away as I considered the logistics of what would happen next.

"He'll move west," I insisted to the council, which by now included heads of families and clans that had arrived from across the northern swathe of our lands. "He's got the far south, the Carvettii in the north-west and I'd guess he thinks he can get some support from the Setantii in the far west, since they're getting trodden on heavily by the Romans. That's where he'll go and we have to follow him."

"Maybe we should retreat," argued Presivin. "We could build our strength from a secure position and then attack him."

"No, we have to keep at him. I can't let him win any more followers. I can't let people think I'm not fighting him. We let him get a day or two ahead, then follow and hope we've got a larger army to balance the fact that this time, the terrain won't be in our favour."

There was grudging acceptance and so that's what we did. We passed an uneventful day recuperating, another night's sleep under roughly pitched tents or stars and then began the slow scramble to load up and move on. Scouts went ahead to ascertain the lay of the land and the state of Venutius's war party and we followed on behind. I longed for my home as we travelled – the comfort of my bed with its straw-stuffed mattress and exotic imported furs along with home-woven woollens, the sounds of my enclosure filled with peaceful activity rather than battle preparations, the view from my royal enclosure out towards the meadow and the forest. No matter how protected I had been, and would be on the battlefield, there was always the possibility that I would never enjoy those homely pleasures again. I had a fleeting thought that no one would care for my little plum tree orchard, then berated myself for being so petty and ridiculous at such a critical time. I suppose the mind finds escape in the little worries when life and death problems are crowding in.

Venutius had indeed picked a second site that suited him much better than the first. This time he was uphill, but only slightly. His main advantage was to be sited on the edge of woodland, with a craggy outcrop to his left. Scattered boulders would slow our attack and provide shelter for his bowmen. It was no worse than we had anticipated. We camped. We waited. More of our reinforcements arrived – families from far to the north whose allegiance was normally patchy except in times of serious threat such as this. People had raced and scrambled to be there, crossing land in several days that would normally have been covered at a safer, slower speed. I was humbled by the great caravans of fierce men and women and their laughing, excited children who were facing great danger with such good humour.

On the second day, Venutius lined up his fighting force and they sneered across at us, waving their spears and gesticulating obscenely. We responded, furious and indignant. I heard personal slurs yelled against me which were so outlandish I almost laughed, but my tribe took them to heart and shrieked venomously against Venutius and his family, including some rather nasty suggestions as to what had happened to his mother and brother. I wondered if Venutius and Tyrius heard and how they felt about that. In truth, Risha and Iticus were safe and I had no immediate plans to harm them since it would apparently bring me no advantage with Venutius. However, they weren't to know that, and it was unsettling to me that my husband and his father had not even tried to negotiate any terms for the release of their kin. War and ambition had evidently turned their heads.

In this battle, Venutius waited. I saw him again, and Tyrius also, charging about on their chariots, inciting hatred in their warriors. I kept to the rear as our people set off towards them with teeth bared and blades aloft. This time, I wouldn't fight unless the situation got desperate. I had shown the iron in my backbone last time so no symbolic displays were necessary. I am sure Venutius was similarly cautious, though Tyrius went in with his sword flashing. I saw him hack heads off my loyal supporters and struggled to remember him as the good-natured man who had met with my father to discuss my betrothal when I was just an infant.

After only a short while, I could see we were in trouble. They had more warriors than we realised, hidden back in their encampments in the trees, and bowmen perched up high were taking out large numbers of our side. I squinted and realised with horror that most of these tree-dwelling assassins were little more than children getting lucky with copious numbers of arrows. I desperately tried to get our fighters to pull the battle in our direction, by appearing to fall back a little, so that our long bows wouldn't have to start picking off the foolish boys and girls raining their points down on us. I cursed Venutius for exploiting my weakness. He knew I would not see young ones slaughtered if I could help it. Although having said that, I couldn't help it completely, since the fury of a war party won't be contained even by the barked orders of its chief. Children did fall from those trees, hit by fatal arrows.

My heart was therefore taking as much of a beating as our fighters, when from our rear came the pounding of hooves and the blaring of horns. Warriors slowed their attack, dared to turn mid-fight and gradually the chaos of battle simmered down as the might of two cohorts from one of the huge resident Roman legions galloped over the plains behind us throwing up mud and dust and scattering the hangers-on and families who had lingered to watch the fighting. They rode in formation and in full armour, bearing their peculiar rectangular shields and efficient, cruel javelins and with a determination and discipline that was awesome to behold. In their wake marched the infantrymen, with their oval shields and short broad swords all held in exactly the same position, to a man. We may have looked barbaric, even frightening to them, painted as we were with our ceremonial colours so our faces were more monstrous than human and splattered as we were with the blood and guts of our enemy (I speak for my people here, since I had kept clean and safe in this fight though I had my war paints on) but they looked equally alien and terrifying to us, with their orderly precision and unstoppable course. Unless you have seen a Roman squadron ride down on you with standards held high and horses snorting steam and faces half-hidden behind helmets of metal, you really cannot know how intimidating they are. I was awed and I was also hugely victorious. I held an arm high and let out a loud screaming cheer and after a few seconds, so did all my warriors, and all the young and old people loitering nervously in our camp. Venutius's army held their ground for a fleeting moment, then turned tails and ran for their lives up into the woods, receding like rabbits on a field as a dog races in. We fell to the side, running to make way as the Romans charged through and beat down the ones who hadn't been fast enough to their

213

own camp and we watched, yelling our support as they halted, rounded and returned to our side. I rode my chariot to their head, feeling oddly childlike so low to the ground in my vehicle with its little pony when they seemed so high, mounted as they were. The man who led them cantered forward to greet me, and swung himself down confidently, removing the ornate headgear as he approached. It may have been my relief at being rescued in so timely a manner, but he seemed to me very handsome and strong, the most welcome of all the Roman men I had so far encountered.

"Septimus Avarasi," he announced by way of introduction. "You must be the famous Cartimandua."

"I am," I responded, grinning. "Thank you for your help."

"You're welcome." Our exchange was almost flirtatious and I realised Septimus was basking in the admiration and gratitude of my army - after all, it was probably a rare thing for a Roman army to experience here in the furthest corner of their realm where the inhabitants were usually either trying to kill them outright or pretending loyalty while they covertly caused trouble. I gathered my wits which had been scattered by the unexpected arrival.

"I have to admit, I don't think your arrival has solved the problem entirely. Venutius was unprepared for you, but he still has a large army and seems very determined to unseat me." We looked up towards the trees where a line of our enemy hovered, watching proceedings, probably taking in exactly how many Romans had arrived, what legion they were from and what preparations we appeared to be making. Septimus nodded and made a motion with his hand as an invitation to walk with him. I stepped down from my chariot.

"How many are you?" I asked, glancing behind us to the rows of identical soldiers with their matching uniforms.

"Three hundred," he answered, "Gallus only wanted to send just enough to contain the problem. You know how serious the demand for military support is everywhere."

I nodded. Gallus was being squeezed on all sides, just as Ostorius and Plautius had been before him. But whilst those Governors wanted to push the boundaries of Rome further and further across our soil, Gallus seemed content to fight fires, maintaining his gains rather than thrusting forward into untamed territory. The problem was, I needed enough soldiers to defeat Venutius, but not so many that I risked being ousted by Rome instead, whilst they had sufficient arms on my land to do it. I sighed. As always, it was a balancing game.

"You'll be all right," reassured Septimus, mistaking my weary sigh for one of anxiety, "with these two cohorts we can easily send Venutius packing."

I smiled wanly at this optimistic Centurion, who had no idea of the complicated hostilities he had waded into.

"What was your next move?" He enquired, eager now to plan our offensive.

"I didn't have one," I answered honestly. "other than to survive to fight another day. I was hoping Gallus would help out and here you are. Let's sit down with my council and work out where we go from here."

He nodded, looking slightly rebuffed as I put an end to our private discussion and we rejoined my people. I stared at him for a moment, unsure I had interpreted the look in his eyes correctly. My stomach gave a sickly involuntary heave. So that was what he expected. A promiscuous queen who would be grateful for his help and who might just possibly fall into his arms. He expected to take me for a short walk, perhaps be invited somewhere more private and reap some kind of intimate reward. A sit-down meeting with my tribal council was not what he had been looking forward to. I shuddered inwardly. I had not expected that my fall-out with Venutius would be so readily interpreted by other men as a sign that I was openly available, that my reputation in Roman circles would become that of whore overnight. I had a fleeting, gripping impulse to order the arrogant Septimus off my land, but quashed it immediately. Not only did I no longer have any rights to order any Roman soldiers from my lands, but I did actually need this particular one. Without him and his cohorts I was probably doomed, so I bit my tongue, and feigned the friendliness I had earlier given honestly, as I introduced him to my war council who had gathered around us. Septimus, to his credit I suppose, began to observe me in a more careful and respectful manner - perhaps realising my earlier enthusiasm for his arrival was solely due to the military advantage it gave us. He began to tell us that a new emperor, Nero, now ruled and that rumour held that Claudius had been murdered by his wife.

I stayed close to Vellocatus, no doubt confirming the rumours Septimus had already heard, of how I had joined with my husband's armour bearer. I saw the rapt attention he had for my lover, and it dawned on me that the scandal I had created would fascinate people across these besieged islands. Tribes up and down the land would have heard stories of my illicit behaviour by now, stories that were probably wildly inaccurate and did my character no favours at all. Too late, I started to ask myself if I could have handled everything better - a drily amusing question, since my handling of Venutius had landed our entire tribe in deadly warfare which could surely only end when either myself or my husband was killed.

We decamped again. The ground we left behind us was dank with patches of blood from the fighting. We had burned the dead, bandaged the wounded and retreated. Venutius had headed north to regroup.

"I'm so tired," I admitted to Vellocatus, laying my head on his shoulder in a quiet, private moment. "I wish none of this was happening. Do you remember how we all played together?" My voice caught; I pressed my face into his arm trying not to let tears come. I could almost smell the summer grass and hear the voices of two boys who had been my friends.

He didn't answer me, just held me a bit tighter, but I sensed in the rigid unease of his body the inner turmoil he was experiencing. I saw that same turmoil on the faces of all those who had once been close to Venutius, who had known him as an infant. But none felt it as sorely as Vellocatus and I.

Septimus had no time for sentimentalism and was keen to bear down hard on the Carvettian uprising, as he referred to it, so he could be on his way again, ready to deal with any number of more serious pursuits on the Western fronts. We had settled on a strategy of multiple skirmishes and ambushes that should grind Venutius down, using the superior horse power of the Roman cohorts to surround and subdue the surprisingly large enemy we were faced with. One thought that sustained me was that surely Venutius could be expecting no more reinforcements. He seemed already to have harnessed the whole youth of his home tribe, not to mention swathes of the southern Brigantian population. We probably had greater numbers, but Venutius had self-righteous anger, ambition and stamina on his side. I didn't dare underestimate him, but it appeared in subsequent days that Septimus had.

The skirmishes he believed would bite away at the fringes of Venutius's army served only to relieve him of his own men. When we fronted up once more for a pitched battle, I was alarmed to see that not only were we evenly matched, but Venutius's side looked as confident and aggressive as before. I had hoped the knowledge that Rome had reinforced us would have cowed them.

So, for the third time, fighting ensued; the smash of metal and bone, the shouts, roars and screams of warriors, the pounding and skidding of horses hooves and chariot wheels. The arrangement was ungainly – Septimus commanding our side but with only limited control over an army he barely understood. While they flung themselves into the fight, Septimus used his own men to drive a jagged edge into the opposition. I watched his technique with interest and I noted that Venutius had tried to counteract it, instructing his army to find the weak points in the Roman armour and try to infiltrate the onslaught of tightly packed soldiers. For a while it seemed he was making progress and I had the grip of fear in my stomach, especially when Septimus seemed to change his approach and began roaring orders and commands that I couldn't understand. But then we started to really push through. The unceasing tide of the Roman front was battering down the Carvettii fighters and as it did so, my own men and women were flocking around and cutting down the tired enemy. I watched from a distance. Septimus had been keen that I keep far enough away to be safe. I'm guessing he did not want the responsibility for my death on his hands since his paymaster Gallus would not have appreciated the headache that appointing a new client leader would cause.

There isn't a point in a battle where someone simply announces "we've won" and everyone packs up and heads off knowing where they stand. Rather, we continued hacking people down until there was no one left. And then we trawled the battlefield, slicing open anyone that looked remotely alive. And then the energetic and enterprising amongst our side went scouring the bodies for jewellery, good quality weapons and useful armour while others searched for loved ones. We removed our warriors from the field – too many of them – and later, people from Venutius's side came and took their dead away and we left them to get on with it. No one wanted a stinking pile of corpses rotting in the late summer heat.

"I almost feel sorry for him," I commented, as we all took a meal together – the council, Septimus and several of his best men. The centurion just shook his head at me in disbelief, but for my council, it was a muted celebration as we all knew the problem of Venutius wouldn't just disappear and we all had complicated feelings about the man who had been friend and family to us for so long.

"He'll approach us for terms now, I would think," said Septimus, draining a cup of ale. "Have you considered what you'll grant him?"

I hadn't, mainly because I expected him to be dead. Surely the only way to be sure of my safety was to remove my husband once and for all? I said as much.

"Ideally yes," Septimus replied, "but we don't have the resources to track him down and even if we did, won't the Carvettii people continue to attack you? Better to call a truce under strict terms."

"Let me think about it then," I said, feeling very unsettled. Was I going to have to live with Venutius on my borders indefinitely?

Later, when Septimus had discreetly retired, we clustered around.

"Will he really seek terms, do you think?" I asked.

"He has to." Davit gave me his opinion. "He hasn't got enough people to attack again and up in his homeland they're probably getting cold feet about this whole escapade. They've just lost a whole generation of warriors so Venutius's popularity may be on the wane. And they probably want Risha and Iticus back."

"I agree. He's failed, he's got no choice but to slink off home," said Namandea. "What are you going to do with the mother and brother though?"

"I haven't decided yet." In fact, the question had been burning in my mind ever since Venutius refused to capitulate after I took them hostage. Should I kill them, free them or keep them imprisoned. I blew out a mouthful of air through pursed lips, drumming the fingers of one hand on my cheek pensively. "If I kill them, what do I gain?" I wondered aloud.

"They can't cause more trouble if they're dead," pointed out Davit.

"They can't exactly cause trouble while they're held in my homestead."

"They're eating our food and taking up space," he huffed.

"It would stop Iticus joining with his brother to command a future army against us," Namandea suggested.

"So would holding him hostage," I answered.

"It might break him further, if you killed his mother and brother." Vellocatus spoke without conviction and I shook my head.

"I think it would anger him more, send him into a rage. No, I can't see any real benefit in killing them and to be honest, I don't really want to anyway. I knew Iticus as a tiny boy. I dislike the mother, but I do respect her. They're dangerous though. Iticus is bright, probably more intelligent than Venutius, and Risha is the most ruthlessly ambitious woman I've ever known. I think I'll have to keep them with us, at least for a while."

"Why don't you trade one of them?" Presivin asked. "Make a deal that Venutius goes home and keeps his Carvettii in line and one of his family stays with us, under threat of execution if Venutius steps out of line."

"That threat didn't work before," I reminded him.

"Yes but now he's had a taste of defeat. He's watched all those men and women fall under his command and he's been brought low by his wife. I should imagine in his current state of mind, he might not want to be responsible for the painful death of his mother or brother. It can't hurt to include it as part of the terms."

"I suppose not," I agreed. "But I just can't imagine Venutius ruling his tribe and me ruling mine right next to him without constant friction. I'd like a peaceful solution, but do you all think Venutius could really live with that?"

Vellocatus, the man who had been Venutius's friend for so long, spoke up.

"Venutius could go either way. He's like two men crammed

into one body. Part of him will want to fight on, to throw everything he's got at us, but part of him will be tired and miserable and ready to go home. He's lost so much – he's lost you, Cartimandua, and even though he pushed you away, he loved you and he'll be missing you. He's lost the authority he had as your husband over all of Brigantia. He's lost some credibility now he's failed to overthrow you. I think we just have to hope he's miserable and sensible enough to realise that he should go home and salvage what's left of his tribe. Anything else is suicide on his part. But you're right to be worried about the future. Venutius is the kind of man who doesn't sit still for long. We'll have to be watching him constantly."

I couldn't speak for a moment. My mind had hitched itself to the sentence about Venutius loving and missing me. It made no sense that I had pity and pain for a man who had been trying that very day to take away everything I held dear, but I did. I hurt for him. I called a halt to our meeting, told everyone to get a good night's sleep, but after what Vellocatus had said, I spent most of my night staring into the dark.

I never expected to see Venutius face to face so soon after our fighting, but he came with a heavily armed guard and two members of his war council under a promise that he would not be harmed or captured. Septimus had arranged it, eager to sort out a deal and be gone, and he stood between us with a nervous smile as his own men formed a thick barrier between our talks and my army. I bit my lip as I took in Venutius's appearance. He looked more rugged from his time living in basic conditions and the stress of recent times had sent the hair at his temples paling into grey but his eyes were fiery and alive, which heartened me. It's ridiculous, but I couldn't bear him to be completely downcast and defeated.

"Can we talk alone?" I asked him directly. I knew he would be pleased at the submissive tone of my question. I could have ordered it and he'd have had no choice but I wanted a deal that would hold and antagonising him was not the way to get that. He inclined his head in assent, then asked his council and guard to step back, out of earshot. Likewise, my council moved back, including Vellocatus. The two men had been staring at each other with a blunt kind of dislike but as we found ourselves alone, Venutius looked properly at me.

"You did well, I heard you fought," he said, plainly.

I ignored the compliment. I couldn't let myself be unbalanced by his familiar tone.

"I have terms for you. You can return north and rule the Carvettii, if they'll have you. Any signs of trouble and you'll have war on your hands again. Gallus has promised reinforcements any time I need them and if you do try and attack me again, there will be no meeting to discuss terms, believe me. I'll release Iticus; he's a calm man who knows that war is in none of our interests. But Risha will stay with us. If you invade again or cause any other problems, I'll have her killed. Do you accept?"

"Did you take any scars from the fighting?" he asked, as though I hadn't spoken.

"Why, are you concerned for me?" I sneered.

"No, I guessed that you probably stayed safely at the rear, maybe just fought when it suited you and when you weren't likely to get your dress dirty." He smiled at the offended expression on my face. I shook my head, impatient with his foolishness.

"If you are trying to anger me there is really no point," I replied, keeping my annoyance in check. "Perhaps you could just answer the question.

"The answer is no, I'm not concerned for you."

"The terms, Venutius, answer whether you accept the terms!" I was beginning to feel like I was dealing with a petty child.

"You know I have to accept the terms," he said, all playfulness gone in an instant. "I'll return to the Carvettii and have as little

222

to do with you as I can. In return I would appreciate it if you didn't murder my mother." He stared past me, his face clouded and hard to read.

"I have no intention of hurting your mother unless you force my hand," I said.

He nodded, looked back to me.

"Is that it?"

"Yes, Septimus will just want to confirm that we're agreed. When I release Iticus, he'll be given detailed instructions to relay regarding the borderline that our tribes must both observe."

"Right." He started to move away from me.

"Venutius," I tried, "I never wanted it to come to this. We were so close once. But this is not all my doing. You've pushed me away again and again all because of your own jealousy. It's not my fault I couldn't make you happy."

"Make me happy?" he mocked, "You never even tried. What could I be to you? Vellocatus might be content to be your servant, but I never was and I'm not going to apologise for that. You might think you love him now, but how long can you love a man who crawls at your feet? One day you'll look north to my tribe, where I rule, and wonder why you threw away the man who could have made Brigantia stronger than ever. One day when you've got past the limited attractions of my armour bearer."

"Servant he might be, but he respects me as leader of Brigantia. You never did. You only resented me," I replied sadly. "There's no point in this. Let's go talk to Septimus."

We didn't speak to each other again, just made our blood-mark on the agreement that promised Venutius would rule the Carvettii and I would rule the Brigantes and that Risha would remain safe but as my hostage to Venutius's good behaviour. We were still married and in the interests of keeping the peace, I didn't query that status. It seemed important to the safety of our whole tribe, since without a commitment to that union,

223

Gallus might have considered the truce untenable. Who knows what that would have led to – more soldiers arriving, invasion by Rome into Carvettii territory, even replacing me as head of the tribe. So, since it seemed easiest, Venutius and I agreed to remain married, but separately govern our two homelands. Septimus was so relieved to have the whole situation sorted out that he overlooked the fragility of the solution and brought a hasty close to the negotiation.

We released Iticus a few days later. He was concerned about his mother, but I reassured him I would treat her well and bear no malice.

"Do you think your brother can really stand by this agreement?" I asked him, as Ansuvan readied horses for Iticus's journey home. The men who had travelled with him to murder me were being released also.

"He'll be in a foul mood about it, but yes, he'll stick to it. He doesn't have a choice." He observed me for a moment as if considering whether to speak, then decided he may as well. "He feels he's completely justified, you know. He won't accept any responsibility for this whole crisis between the two of you. He thinks he should have ruled Brigantia and that you should have accepted his superiority."

There was a tone to his voice that I didn't like.

"And what do you think, Iticus?" I could feel angry heat prickling the back of my neck.

"Well wouldn't it have been easier just to let him rule? We all know Kesaven meant you to be chief, but did it really matter that much?"

"Iticus," I growled, "I have a responsibility to this tribe. It's mine. I was never going to give it away, no matter what Venutius did. But don't you see, the very fact that he tried so many times to push me into it is what shows so clearly that he didn't deserve it. If he'd honoured me at all, we would have ruled this land together, but he threw that chance away." I realised I was balling my fists at my sides. How many times would I have to explain and justify?

Iticus inclined his head in something of an acknowledgement, although I knew deep down he was still thinking I should have just given Venutius what he wanted.

"My father and I may wish to visit my mother from time to time to check on her health," he said. "I doubt that Venutius himself will come."

"That's acceptable, but send word first so we can expect you. Would you like to see her before you leave?"

I walked with him to the roundhouse where Risha was constantly guarded and left him there, with Ansuvan supervising. I hardly knew how to speak to them any more. They had been my family. I had known them nearly all my life and now they all wanted me dead, or at least out of the way. How does it happen that the world turns upside down like that? I wanted them out of my home and out of my life and it galled me that Risha had to stay on my soil. I vowed never to go near her and to always be away when her thuggish husband or calculating younger son came to visit her.

SPRING AD55

We walked down to the orchard. The air was thin and clear, a light dew still evident on the grass and Vellocatus stroked the back of my hand with his thumb as he held it. After the turmoil of only two seasons ago, it felt oddly incorrect that we should be enjoying such a peaceful spring morning. I had gone from watching men and women dying under my command to gazing on a bright new morning – a morning that hundreds of people were not alive to see because of my actions. I shook away my brooding thoughts and instead picked up my pace as we neared the trees. Under their canopy, we paused and gazed back up towards the settlement walls. The modest enclosure of my father's era had become a much more imposing landmark during my years. I turned to say something to Vellocatus about the way things change over the years and found him twiddling a piece of apple blossom between his fingers, giving it far more studied attention than it deserved.

"Is something wrong?" I asked.

"No, no." He hesitated. "It's just, all those years with Venutius, did you take the herbs? I mean, the ones to stop children coming? Didn't you want babies?" It came out in a rush, as if he had wanted to ask for a long time but not found the right way to say it.

I raised my eyes up to the trees, where the tiny, white flowers clustered incongruously along gnarled, twisted branches and gave a sigh that sounded far more world-weary than I had intended.

"No, I didn't take any herbs." I looked back to him. He looked down at his feet.

"I just wondered–" He began, but I quietened him with a raised hand.

"I understand." Although actually, I never guessed people would think I had prevented a baby from coming and in all honesty I was pained by his question.

"It just never happened. Don't forget, he was away all those years as well. But even before then, it wasn't for lack of trying. It just never happened. Him or me, I don't know...I gave up on it." I shrugged, empty of words. What more could I say?

"So you could, I mean," He had twisted the little flower between his fingers into shreds, "you could still maybe have-"

"Oh! I don't think so now, Vellocatus. I'm too old for it." My chest constricted as I recognised the hope sparkling in his eyes.

"Your bleeding has ended?" He looked confused, he knew it hadn't, it was far too soon.

"No, not yet, but I just know my body is too old now. Some things aren't meant to be." I turned away from him, feeling my own eyes prickling now, but with threatened tears rather than hope. I didn't want to cry in front of him over this. I didn't even want to think about it. I had made my peace with my lack of children a long time ago, when it didn't seem quite so important. I realised I had folded my arms around myself and was shaking slightly.

"I'm sorry," he whispered. "I shouldn't have mentioned it. It doesn't matter anyway. I have all I want." He slipped his arms round me and hugged me tightly. If it had been Venutius, I would have doubted him, would have known he was masking a true desire for offspring. But with Vellocatus, I believed him when he reassured me. It crushed me that I couldn't bear a child for him but I knew I needn't fear his resentment because of it.

Since peace had returned to our beautiful fortress in the northern hills, I had begun to settle into a domestic life with Vellocatus that filled me with content. Simple pleasures that I'd never known with Venutius were a revelation. Vellocatus would wander with me to inspect my plum trees. He liked me to talk of the past - my meeting with Claudius, my thoughts on Plautius, Ostorius and Gallus, old anecdotes about my father and mother - and he was interested in my thoughts for the future -

how I intended to handle increasing Roman tax demands, how I thought we could further unite Brigantia, perhaps bring more of the border people into the governance of our tribe. It was easy to converse with him on matters of such importance when I knew he did not forever have an eye on his own role within them. Perversely, because he did not constantly demand respect, reassurance and inclusion in tribal affairs, I gave all three to him unreservedly.

We were not married – that is to say, my joining with him was not officially recognised by my tribe, family and ancestors – but in the sight of the gods and goddesses to which I bowed, I believed we had been well-received. After all, how could we be so happy if that were not the case? And informally, those around us were beginning to accept the union we were forging. Vellocatus was genuinely included in the council now, his loyalty to myself and our tribe beyond question. He didn't have the fiery enthusiasm Venutius had possessed but he showed a constant determination and quiet stamina and he was a calming, mediating influence on us all. I don't believe anyone thought of him as a servant any longer, if indeed they had for many years, since he had been proving his capability in our elite circle long before he raised his status by mating with me – proving it, in fact, ever since he beat the wolves away from Venutius.

Sometimes a worry would thud softly in my chest that this had all been too easy come by (three pitched battles not-withstanding) and that something must surely happen to ruin everything but as days went by I was starting to relax into my new-found homely bliss. When I woke on a morning, it was to see Vellocatus's locks of dark gold falling over his high cheekbone and to feel his arm thrown over my hips. I liked to watch him wash, throwing cold water over his lightly tanned body raising goosebumps on flesh that was just starting to show the sag of middle-age. He still had the golden hair over his arms that I had noticed when we were little more than children, though the hair on his legs was much darker. He had a crescent-shaped scar above his shoulder blade, and a dog-legged scar down the side of his thigh, both from his time serving in the Roman legion, but he never talked of those years. When he was sleeping I would sometimes run my fingertips over the marks and contours of his body, marvelling that I had known this man most of my life and yet not truly known him at all. It flattered me enormously that he had wanted me all of that time and the early passion of our relationship, which can hardly be sustained for long at the age we both were, was quickly replaced by a deep affection and trust that came from years of mutual dependence. It was comforting to think that he had always been watching out for me and always been loyal to me, even when I was not aware of it.

Despite the tranquillity that had settled in our stronghold, there existed one dark and lumpen reminder of the pain in the past and the constant threat in the present. Risha, with her drawn oval face and cloudy grey eyes, mooned about in miserable cloaks and shawls maintaining an ominous silence and yet managing to convey to everyone the level of contempt she had for them. She had her own roundhouse now, a small basic hut that had been erected as soon as it became clear her presence was permanent. She was still guarded of course, but more informally. At her age, it was unlikely she could make a run for it and she had no opportunity for access to a horse – everyone maintained vigilance over her. She received goods from her family in the north west, large bundles of pelts, gowns, jewellery and dried or cured foodstuffs and she had amassed plenty of items that she could use for trade if she wished. Still, presumably out of boredom, she spent hours twining spindly coppice wood into delicate and ornate baskets that she piled up in the corner of her hut. She had already given a pile of them to one of our traders who thought there might be some interest in them. I wondered whether this was more about the novelty of owning a basket made by the hostage Carvettii matriarch, than the skill and craft of her produce, but either way, at least she was being productive.

The conversation with Vellocatus about my lack of children had got me thinking about Risha and her peculiar predicament. Betrayed by her husband and sacrificed by her sons, she was a figure more of pity than of derision within our community and for the first time I really thought about how she must feel, cut off from the children she had birthed and raised and the man she had always supported. I started to nod a greeting to her more often, to her initial surprise and disdain. After a while, she began to raise a hand in reply. Her eyes, which had once seemed so full of animal cunning had taken on the pinched and weary glaze of a tired old woman and when one day she held up her latest woven intricacy when I called a hello, I walked over to examine the little basket in her hand.

"For you," she said.

"Me?" I was shocked.

"I never gave you a gift, did I? In all the years you were betrothed and married to my son, I never gave you anything personal from me at all." She said it plainly, without apology but with obvious regret. I took the basket from her outstretched hand.

"It's pretty. Thank you."

She inclined her head and shuffled back inside her hut. I was going to leave but she glanced back at me.

"Would you come in for a while?" Her face flickered with competing emotions - loneliness bitterness, anger, eagerness. She didn't wait for an answer, just continued on inside where she lowered herself onto a bench by the smouldering central fire. I followed, warily. I may have developed some empathy for her plight, but she had been no friend to me over the years and I could not afford to forget that she was my captive. Still, as she poured me a drink and offered me some salted fish and sorrel with herb-flavoured flat bread, I felt myself relaxing, curious to know what conversation she would instigate (for I was quite determined not to lose my poise and be the first to speak).

"I had a message from Tyrius. He plans to visit me within a moon's turn."

"That will be acceptable. I'll send a party to escort him when he crosses the border."

"I don't expect him to stay long."

"Oh?" I watched as her face twitched with the urge to say more.

"He hasn't been eager to visit before. I think this is just a cursory trip, out of obligation. He probably has more unfinished business with your aunt than he does with me."

"I don't believe he has any business at all with Antikia," I replied. She barked a laugh.

"That's not the tune you were singing before. As I recall, you implied he would leave me and make a pact with her."

I shrugged, unwilling to be drawn.

"I know they were together, probably for a long time. Did she love him? I have to know." Risha had a peculiar ability to sound imperious and demanding even when her words belied her pain and embarrassment. I relented. What harm could it do to tell her the truth?

"She loved him once, when she was younger and more foolish. She thought he would turn to her, but when you visited that first time, he ignored her, belittled her, treated her like a common woman. He took her love for granted, which was a dangerous mistake. When she saw that his ambition and status held him duty-bound to you, she kept his affection but held little for him in return."

"And then she took her revenge?"

"I'm not sure she ever intended revenge. When everything crumbled between myself and Venutius, she was quick to see the advantage of pretending loyalty to his father. She put herself in a great deal of danger to give me an extra tactical opportunity. It was strategy, not revenge."

Risha seemed to consider this and then gave a nod.

"That sounds like your aunt, from what I know of her." There was a lull.

"She escaped from their camp, you know. She believed he would have killed her if she hadn't. Do you think he would have?" It had plagued me, the idea that the man Antikia had once so loved could have mercilessly slain her.

"His pride must have been cut to the core," Risha said. "He has a temper, though it doesn't get the better of him often, but when it does, he rages like a bull. He would have smashed her skull in and grieved later. He loves like a child, full of selfish passion and greedy expectations."

"Do you love him?"

"Yes, I do. He's the father of my children, so of course I love him. I've known him a long time, much longer than your aunt has, and I understand him. He's a good man. And he loves me."

"Yet you say his visit to you is out of obligation?"

"He's angry, frustrated. He's lost a war, lost a younger, attractive woman he thought adored him and he's left with an imprisoned, ageing wife who got herself captured by acting against his instructions."

"Even so, if he loves you, surely he wants to come and see that you're well?"

"Like I said, he loves selfishly. One day he'll worry about me, but for now he just wants to lick his wounds."

We sat in silence. She prodded at the fire with a stick, rekindling the slumbering flames to combat the spring breeze that seeped into her hut. I could have left, but it felt oddly comfortable to be in her presence. I still had no idea why she was even talking to me - I didn't believe she simply wanted to find out about Tyrius and Antikia. She gave no indication that she wanted me to leave either so we nibbled on the food she had laid out and watched the flames lap around a bundle of dry, old birch wood. Outside, Ansuvan passed by and paused to peer in. Seeing me, he blinked, half-waved and then hurried on.

"They keep a good eye on me," Risha remarked. "Though how they expect an old woman like me to run off, I don't know."

"I'll tell them to stop doing that. They can show some proper respect." I was genuinely annoyed on her behalf. I hadn't expected that the servants would actually be staring inside the hut at her, like she was some form of entertainment for them.

"Respect? Is it respectful to keep me here, like this, away from my family?"

"I don't have a choice, Risha. How else am I to force your son to behave?"

"And my being here does that? He didn't care before, why should he care now?"

"Because those battles wore him down and the last thing he wants is your blood on his hands."

"But when he raises a new army, what then? Do you honestly think any feelings he has for me will stand in the way?"

"I hope they will. And anyway, if you were with him, I would count him an even greater force to be reckoned with."

She smiled a little at this, pleased at the compliment despite herself.

"Why are we talking like this, Risha," I asked at last, "when you never wished to when we were true family?"

She let out a sigh.

"Ask yourself that question also. You made it quite clear, with your haughty ways, how little you thought of me."

"Did I?" I was taken aback. "You were the one who came here all self-important, making jokes after my mother died."

"Perhaps I seemed insensitive to you. It's just my way. But you - you were the self-important one. So young and yet such a child. Never tested in battle, never tested in child-bearing. Running the biggest web of allied tribes these lands have ever known and with barely a kill to your name! How was I supposed to talk to you?" She threw her hands up in a brisk display of the impossibility of it.

"You were jealous," I asserted.

"I wouldn't say that. I was more-"

"-insulted? That I was so young and untested and you were expected to submit to me?"

"I suppose something like that," she admitted. "After all, I was much older than you with all the experience that comes with running a tribe - albeit a much smaller one - but I sensed you weren't much interested in hearing any advice I might have to give."

"Well you didn't exactly give me much chance to ask. But no, you're probably right. I wanted to do things my own way and I had my father after all."

"But a woman always needs another woman's guidance. You're lucky in a way that you never had children. You would have missed Metassia very much then."

We were quiet again, each pondering the admissions of the other.

"How long will you keep me here?" She asked eventually.

"I don't know. How can I let you go, knowing the Carvettii might strike back at me any time? How do I know that isn't, in fact, what you want? I know your own ambition lies at the heart of Venutius's bitterness. He has never yet gained the glory you craved for him."

"Do you think he cares that much for what I think? Venutius has his own mind."

"A boy never escapes the yearnings his mother has for him and for that matter neither does a husband escape the pressure his wife exerts. Those two men are good honest supporters of Brigantia who have had their minds twisted to greater fortune." Despite our earlier confidences, I couldn't help but present her with the angry truth that had frustrated me for so many years - that her ambitions had made monsters out of Venutius and

Tyrius. To my surprise, she laughed.

"Good honest supporters!" She shook her head, dispelling her mirth. "Do you know what Tyrius said to me after the first time he met you? He said you were a pretty little pup, ready to grow strong and give us a brood of Carvettii rulers. I won't deny, I sowed the seed of thought in his mind, that his son should mate with you, but that is neither here nor there. It would have been the son of one sub-tribe or another so why not ours? And who does not wish to see their grandchild rule vast lands? Such ambitions are normal, my girl, and all of your precariously-held little tribes nurture dreams and desires of overthrowing you and your family and rising to greatness themselves. It isn't normal to enjoy a life of subservience or to revel in the unchanging bondage that secures us to our post in life. Take Vellocatus, for instance. Do you think he would have been happy to always be a servant? That boy always wanted more, I could see it in his eyes. An accident of time and place and he finds himself in the bosom of his chief's family. How fantastic a prize for a little nobody! How could he help wanting more, once he saw what was possible. And now look what he has achieved! Union with the leader herself, his rightful ruler dispossessed."

"Vellocatus never wanted a thing except my safety and happiness." I retorted. "He came to my aid when I was in the greatest of peril, when your son wouldn't leave his station with the Roman army for fear he would be bound up in my downfall."

"Or else Vellocatus saw an opportunity to step in and gain your huge appreciation. They were both playing a game, Cartimandua. Venutius hoped to gain by staying away, Vellocatus by coming to your aid. In the end it worked out well for Vellocatus."

"He wasn't playing a game," I insisted, "he cared for me. I know it." I was calm because I knew it was true. I didn't doubt Vellocatus.

"Maybe. But bear in mind, Venutius cared for you too. He just had to balance that with the love he had for his people and his land. He wanted to emerge as leader rather than having both of you executed by Rome and leaving them to fill your positions with leaders of their choice, as they did with the Iceni."

"But not even a message? Not even a whispered word to Vellocatus that could be passed on to me to ease my burden?" My lingering pain over the whole rebellion incident must have shown. I hadn't meant for her to draw it out from me.

"You loved him then? My son?"

"Yes, of course I did," I snapped. "I did everything to try and make him happy and nothing worked."

"Interesting, since he says more or less the same thing."

"It's pointless talking about it. We always come to the same impasse."

"Life's like that. No two people see it the same way. What a mess you two have created though!" She laughed again, too old to really care any more about the consequences.

"Risha, I could let you go if I thought you would stay his sword, but everything you said before leads me to think you will encourage him to come against me. If ambition and desire is as important and natural as you say, how can you bear to limit him to your small corner of the world?"

"If his ambition and desire is strong enough, it won't matter what anyone else says or does, least of all me."

I left her a while after that, feeling stirred by our conversation. She was right about one thing, and that was the importance of having an older woman to talk to. She was very different from my own mother, who would have said love and loyalty were the strongest human forces, not personal desire and ambition, but she had spoken to me with a philosophical honesty that few around me ever had, at least since I lost my father. I found myself looking forward to visiting her again and therein was another reason not to release her back to her family.

Tyrius came as promised, accompanied by a small guard of his own men, and a large warrior band of mine, who had met him at the borders of our lands. It was a fuss and commotion that seemed ridiculous when I thought of the countless hundreds of times he had visited us, stayed and lived with us as a friend and member of our family. But then, of course, I reminded myself of those battles when he had stalked at the head of our opposing army and led an embittered and bloody assault on me. Days out of time, days of nightmare unreality.

He approached me gruffly, no polite enquiries, just a request to see his wife. I had him escorted to her roundhouse where she waited inside. I would have loved to see just what was said and done between the pair of them, but kept to my own roundhouse in a seemly fashion and had his men escorted away for a meal, whilst a small and trusted group of men, Lerica included, kept watch at a respectful distance on Risha's roundhouse.

Antikia hovered, like a moth to a flame, pacing around in my presence and generally annoying me.

"What do you think he's saying to her?" She kept asking. "Will she tell you afterwards, since you're so friendly now?"

"I have no idea," I kept replying, to both questions. She fidgeted and pulled at the gold bangles on her wrist until they left red welts.

When, finally, Lerica came in and broke the tension, it was a relief to us both.

"Is he finished?"

"Yes, he's just come out, but he wants to speak with Antikia." Lerica gestured towards my aunt with his hand. Antikia jumped back a step as if she had been burned.

"Absolutely not." I shook my head and turned away.

"He's quite insistent."

"I don't care-" But before I could finish, Antikia caught my arm.

"Perhaps I should speak to him."

"For what purpose? The man would have wrung your neck if he'd had chance. Do you want to give him further opportunity?"

"In your presence, then. He could come in here, with you and Lerica as witnesses. We do have unfinished business. I should speak to him."

"And tell him how you tricked him? Oh, if you desire it so much." I waved Lerica out to fetch Tyrius, curious and uneasy in equal measure. Why did we have to have all these dissections of past relationships? It tired everyone out and never, as I was beginning to realise, resolved anything. Still, he came in, followed immediately by Lerica who had his long dagger drawn and held ready.

"You can address Antikia," I said, stepping back away from the pair. He wasted no time. I could see that this was the real confrontation he had come for. Poor Risha had probably sensed all through their meeting how he itched to face his disloyal lover.

"Antikia, you found your way back here then, after running away from me. Had a change of heart, did you?"

"Don't pretend not to understand," she breathed, "You know what I did."

"Aye, that I do." He glowered and waited. Did he expect her to explain, apologise? I wasn't sure what he wanted but surely he knew he wasn't going to get it.

"Oh for the love of the goddess, Tyrius. What do you want of me? Were you so stupid as to think that I loved you so much I would betray my brother's daughter? Don't you, of all people, understand blood loyalty? You should have seen through me sooner, you fool, and sliced my throat open the second you suspected."

"You warned her about Iticus?"

"I planned the invasion by Iticus, can you not remember? I did that, convincing you it would work and that your youngest son should do the job himself and then I warned her – or would have done if you hadn't intercepted my messenger. The whole thing was a trap. But you and Venutius were ready to sacrifice our hostages anyway so what's the difference? It didn't stop the war and in the end you got your son back in one piece. Your wife's capture was her own fault. Why does it matter what I did?"

"How could you do that to me?" he raged, "after all we had together?"

"What did we have together?" She seethed. "You had a wife. You made quite clear what I was to you. I was just the woman you mated with every now and again."

"But you loved me."

"Did I? Yes, once, maybe, but not for a long time. At least, no more than you loved me."

"Evil, evil woman," he said, moving back from her.

"Oh stop it. Don't you have bigger things to worry about than an affair we once had?" She turned away from him as if he was ridiculous and he reddened in fury, looking much like his son when the latter found me with Vellocatus. I thought again how pointless this all was.

"You're two of a kind," he spluttered, forgetting himself and gesturing at me as he nursed his wounded pride.

"That's enough," I ordered, coming forth as Lerica positioned himself between us and Tyrius. "I haven't allowed you onto my land to hear insults against my family and I. You've satisfied yourself as to your wife's condition which is, I believe, the reason you came. This visit is over. You may come again, when I send word." He bowed his crimson face and I turned my back on him while Lerica escorted him outside.

"Satisfied now?" I asked Antikia, once Tyrius was safely away from my home. She was biting on the side of her thumb, a flush upon her sharp cheeks.

"He infuriates me," she said.

"I know that feeling," I answered, thinking of all the circular arguments and fruitless discussions I'd had with the man's son over the years. "It's the way Carvettii men are. You're well rid of him."

I had a sense of finality as I watched Tyrius and his entourage trundle away, up the track, over the meadow and out of sight. Antikia and Tyrius would never speak to each other again. Venutius and I were over. Our close affinity with the Carvettii had ended and I should have felt free but after so many years tied together, bound ever since I was a little child, I only felt a lonely chill and that my world had shrunk a little.

WINTER AD57

Sometimes I longed for the carefree days of my youth - never more so than as my bones began to creak and ache with the onset of freezing cold weather. Where once I could skip about in a short gown and deerskin waistcoat, balling up snow to throw about or smashing frozen puddles with my leather-clad heel, now I bundled myself up in long dresses, woollen cloaks and swaddling hoods about my head. Every minor infliction one suffers as a bairn seems to magnify with the travel through life, so that the ankle I once mildly twisted gave a dull throb on cold days, and the shoulder I pulled wielding my great spear on the battlefield pained me if I attempted to lift more than a moderate amount. How Gorlensa had survived to such a great age, I had no idea and I felt embarrassed by my own lack of fortitude at the relatively young age of thirty six when I saw her walking at a snail's pace with a large bundle of coppice as kindling for her fire balanced on her bent back (she brushed away assistance if anyone offered it). The Romans favoured their white togas as a form of dress for their conquered subjects but really such an item would have been completely ridiculous in our climate. I had several and wore them in summer, if I had a leaning to do so or if we had Roman visitors, but in winter they stayed packed away and I sheltered in my homespun woollens and the wonderful, soft leathers we were so famous for.

I had taken a few long trips around Brigantia since the fracture in my marriage, the purpose being to ensure the loyalty of my people and the security of my borders. It was a bland and somewhat unsatisfying experience, since everyone was compelled to be polite and confirm the sincerity of their love for me or face execution or slavery. Most, I suppose, were genuinely happy that I remained their tribal chief, but I always saw a flicker in their eyes when they saw Vellocatus or heard his name mentioned. It was as if they could not bear that a servant, one of their own, had somehow risen to be greater than them, to have power over them. It was a revelation to me that our tribe was indeed so split along the lines of ruler and ruled. I had, in the younger days I so yearned for, envisioned us as a giant family, bound together by our love of our land and freedom but I had been forced to recognise that the toil and suffering of the majority was what greased the wheels of my own comfortable lifestyle. We weren't as divided as some others – I knew that in the past the Catuvellauni leadership especially had stoked their success on the broken backs of the peasants, using their strong agriculture to create enough wealth to satisfy a violent and determined warrior class. At the top of their tribe, Cunobelinus and his sons had reaped the rich rewards of land, deference and luxuries while the vast majority worked themselves into the ground or died by the sword. That was never our way, since the high, desolate moorlands on which we lived supported only the disparate, loosely connected herding communities, reliant on their sheep and cattle for any kind of living. You couldn't control a land like that nearly so effectively. But it had been revealed to me that in fact I, and my father before me, had done our best to control it as much as possible. The Romans called it taxation and did it in a measured, indifferent manner, but we had been doing the same thing for much longer, taking food, goods and slaves and maintaining our position at the tip of the tree, so to speak. In such a setting, the way Vellocatus and I had bonded was resented rather than romanticised and for the ordinary person, I had fallen in estimation.

That's another annoying thing about age – the tendency to pontificate. Suffice to say, my trips around my territory only made me more conscious of the precarious nature of leadership and of the false love people profess when they really have no other choice.

In our own homestead, real love seemed to abound so I ought not to have been so gloomy. Antikia had cast off the shackles

242

that her years-long affair with Tyrius had laid on her, and now lived permanently with Shamatin, who openly adored her. She didn't speak to me much of their relationship, which is how I could tell it was the real thing. They even held hands sometimes although she got very impatient and annoyed when I giggled and drew attention to it. Vellocatus and I were, of course, still deeply content together. Even Lerica, that scarred and battle-embittered hard man of mine had found himself a mate recently. It was peacetime and everyone had relaxed.

Risha still occupied her private roundhouse within our tribal capital. She had gradually and reluctantly found herself on speaking terms with a number of different people so her life was not quite as lonely as it had been. In addition, people had stopped gawping at her and no longer peered into her home as they passed. I shared a meal with her once or twice a moon, though it still irritated Antikia that we had something of a friendship. As for her husband, Tyrius, he had not visited since that one time, though he occasionally sent messages from home for her, and once a whole barrel full of various salted fish that she said reminded her of home when she closed her eyes. To me, the smell bordered on unpleasant, but for her, it brought the scent of the sea to her land-locked prison.

With the return of a calm state of affairs, we held our usual, regular tribal council meetings to discuss all manner of matters. Whilst other tribes had been forced to hand over their internal governance to resident Roman authorities, we were still, of course, a client tribe, managing our own matters including justice, territory issues, food production and arms to name but a few. Not least of our concerns was the ever-present worry of maintaining good relations with the Roman governor. It was exhausting, keeping on top of that thorny problem and raising the necessary taxes when the time came, but it beat having troops of soldiers swarming over our land or trying to disarm us. Compared to many others, we had it good and we contented ourselves with the self-preserving arrangements we had in place. When we heard of the oppression of more and more small and large tribes in the West, we shuddered but didn't dwell on it. We swept it to the far reaches of our minds.

Then, mired in the banal arrangements of a life lived under the thumb of Rome, we heard that Suetonius Paulinus was marching up towards that dark little isle, the place of our terrifying but all-powerful priests, the blue island of Mona that I had once gazed upon with my father. The home of the Druids. The ancient and secret store of all the collected wisdom of our race and all the magic of the initiated few. The beating heart of our world. An attack on the Druids was unprecedented and unthinkable.

"They can't do it, they can't take Mona," Gorlensa was saying, raking sharp, gnarled fingers over her scalp. "How can they do this?"

"It was only a matter of time," said Davit, always the voice of gloomy pessimism, but usually accurate. "They think if they slice off the head, the body will fall."

"So it will, so it will," wailed Gorlensa. We were all disturbed to see her so unnerved and it lent a dark atmosphere to this particular council meeting, held on a strangely humid early winter day, when the sky hung heavy with fat rolling clouds and the leafless trees stood silently waiting for the rain to fall.

"They're not at Mona yet," I reminded everyone. "Veranius has a way to go and some fighting to do first."

"An attack on the Druids would be an attack on all of us, surely we have to act," replied Presivin.

"And risk our position for the sake of a privileged few?" asked Namandea.

Gorlensa waved a fist at her.

"You have no idea, you young people," she shouted, "and you, my own niece!"

"Veranius does seem determined," I interjected, keen to calm everyone down. "Although I expect the path of any governor would eventually wend the same way. After all, he was already pressing hard into the blue west. Mona was undoubtedly his end target."

And of course so it should be, for any Governor worth his salt. What else could we expect the Romans to do but to cut down the priest tribe who were so venerated across our foggy lands? For, on Mona, the men, women and children learned all the mysteries of existence. They passed down the tales and lessons of our most ancient ancestors, learning them by heart and even, so it was said, using a special written language to preserve them on thin plates of wood sliced from their copious oak groves. They lived only a short distance from the mainland, yet were rarely seen except as dark shadows moving, flitting, through the trees, or occasionally travelling through the mainland in aloof and intimidating fashion on whatever pressing mission demanded it. They saw emissaries of the tribes on Mona when circumstance dictated and if any law existed in our lands besides that which the chiefs arbitrarily handed down, then it came from the Druid priests, who decided the absolutes and boundaries of our lives. If they ordered one tribe not to attack another, then that tribe would abide by that order. If they insisted on a sacrifice, a trade, an execution, then that event or arrangement would happen, unquestioned. They never bothered themselves with the petty affairs and turned away individuals approaching them to help settle minor disputes. Their role was in the governance of our whole lands – no surprise then, that Paulinus and all the Governors before him should feel so personally challenged by the mysterious Druids – and they held us all in a web of their casting, which not only bound us, but protected us. We knew about them, we went to them if we had to, but mostly we kept a safe distance. They were not simply another tribe, they were a class of blood-letting, all-seeing, black-eyed wraiths.

When I first heard of Mona, travelling as I was with my father, I knew very little of them, and I am ashamed to say that I had not learned a great deal more by the time Paulinus was planning his assault. I had never had need for any dealings with them, nor them with me, probably because the affairs of my tribe had been so settled for so long. When Venutius and I separated they might have had something to say on the matter, but that was still an internal tribal situation, the Carvettii being under my control. It was true also that my alliance with Rome had in some intangible, unacknowledged way distanced me from their spidery grasp. All I knew of them came from folk tales - stories passed on by traders or itinerant craftsmen. Some of the people on our south western borders who had upped sticks and travelled further north as the Romans impinged on the fringes of our land, brought tales too, passed to them by the Deceangli, who had in turn heard through the Gangoni. With each telling, I am sure the content became a little more vivid and stomach-churning. Fistoc had always been an avid listener and teller of tales - I missed him still, despite his disloyalty - and he had on many evenings resorted to his ever-popular stock of Druid delicacies.

There was a tale, though I cannot account for its veracity, that stirred a fascination, morbid though it was, in all of us who listened. It had been passed down, through generations and was well-known through the Gangoni tribe, from whom Fistoc had first heard it. Long, long ago, the Druids had learned of a danger coming across the water. Their bones and blood that they cast in their shining bowls showed a man, coming in a ship. They knew that this man represented great danger and that they must repel him from the shores upon which he meant to land. They gathered all their strength, summoning a giant circle of their most skilled men and women who spread throughout the grove joining hand to tree to hand to tree, so that they formed an enormous band of human and dryad power. There they stayed for three days and nights, keening and howling so that the Gangoni tribe on the mainland who heard every wail, pressed the heels of their hands to their ears and stayed, white-faced and sickened, inside their homes. The Druid circle went without food or water during this time and as the third night ended, all had fallen, exhausted, to the floor of their oak canopied lands. All apart from one man, who remained standing. With his remaining strength, he walked to a big stone sacrifice table that stood within the circle. He took a bronze knife of horrifying sharpness from a leather hilt on his thigh and climbed onto the table top where he laid down and carefully sliced lengthways down each arm, laying the blade on his chest afterwards, the point deliberately directed to the south east, the direction from which the supposed danger was emerging. The Gangoni say that as the man's blood pulsed and ran down the stone columns of his deathbed, the oak trees themselves began to scream and a whipping wind flickered through the leaves, razing them from the branches and throwing them high into the air, to be spun around into a heaving black mass that rippled through the skies above Mona. This awful black entity drifted up high, until it could be mistaken for cloud and seeped away, causing the very day to turn sour and miserable, with wind and rain. It was this, claimed Fistoc triumphantly, that drove Caesar and his ships away the first time he tried to land.

There were other stories too, of blood sacrifice, of men, women, children, babies, animals, all going to their painful end on those stone-topped altars. I didn't like those stories. I hoped they weren't all true. If they were though, I believed as we all did, that those things were necessary. No one questioned the Druids and their power. Tribes were careful to seek from the Druids an attitude of indifference, and sent gifts regularly - another tax, but one which we were all happily accustomed to and which, we felt, was matched by the Druidic protection we received.

The idea of the Druids under threat was therefore shocking,

not only because of the potential loss of our other-worldly priest class, but because the possibility that they could even be under threat brought into question everything we had known or believed about them. There was also the issue of the ramifications of an attack on the ancient blood groves and their dangerous people. Would their wrath once unbounded, spill out on all of us? Would the Druids, for their ages of governance, require us to respond to some honour-bound call to arms? If we did not, would they have their revenge on us, whether they won or lost? I had to consider all of this, and to force my mind beyond its unwillingness to deal tangibly with a tribe whose very existence seemed not to be anchored in our reality.

"I'll write to Veranius," I said to the council, "and plead with him to reach a peaceful settlement with the Druids." As I said it I knew there was no hope. Even if Veranius was willing, the Druids would not be. They would not share or bind their ancient wisdom with anyone else, not in a hundred thousand winters.

Veranius never had time to reply to the message I sent, if indeed he ever received it at all, because as the darkest day of middle winter passed, he died abruptly. There was a lull across the land as the snow fell and the ground froze and the Roman presence hovered in anticipation, awaiting the next man who would lead their conquering efforts. Veranius had been sound in judgement and stubborn in nature and everyone had expected grand progress under his rule. With his untimely demise, we all, Briton and Roman alike, wondered if a new governor would unwittingly stall the creep of the Roman frontier across the West. The answer arrived in the form of the unremittingly hostile figure of Suetonius Paulinus. Fresh out of some campaign high in the hills of an exotic foreign realm, he swept into our world like a noxious breeze and picked up exactly where Veranius had left off, ramming all the force he could gather against the tribes still lingering in the West.

"He's a brute, this one," said Vellocatus, with a sadness that reflected my own premonition of doom for our weird Mona.

Gorlensa had given up speaking. She wandered about like a crazed mute, scratching at her scalp which, through lack of care, was infested with lice. I tried to have Amelan run a fine-toothed bone comb though it, but Gorlensa had smacked her away.

"Will you write to this Paulinus?" Davit asked me and I had to look away as I pondered my answer, which in fact I never gave him at the time. What held me back, when I had been so disposed to contact Veranius and plead for some kind of mercy towards our priests? Perhaps deep in my psyche I could sense the savage wounds that Paulinus was about to score across our people and that there was really no way to avert them.

I went to Risha. We conversed privately and I told her I wished greatly for some kind of alliance with the Carvettii, whether to protect Mona or to protect us from the aftermath, I did not know.

"Will he care about the Druids?" I asked her, unsure where the loyalties of Venutius would lie. Surely in his opposition to Rome, he would wish to fight for Mona?

"I think he underestimates their necessity," she said, picking through her words slowly.

"You mean, they're not worth the risk to him?"

"Something like that."

"And what do you think?"

"I think we ignore the Druids at our peril," she answered immediately. "Your old woman probably has the right idea."

She meant Gorlensa, whose continuing distress in turn unseated all of us.

"Without the Druids, what are we?" asked Risha. "Just a rabble of different people with no history and no future." She spoke simply without emphasis, as if it were indisputable fact.

"They're violent people. We don't know much about them. I've never had any real contact with them," I said.

"Even so, they know all about you, just as they know the business of every tribe in this land. They have a language of their own, you know, a written one that they carve into wood. And they pass their stories down properly. They don't forget like we all do."

"They give blood sacrifice. Some would say they murder innocents."

"Perhaps they do. Perhaps it works."

I had an ambivalence towards the odd tribe of Mona. I felt we ought to do something to protect them, but this was largely motivated by superstitious fear of the consequences if we did not. Then again, other tribes had been conquered and had emerged bowed but still largely intact, if under a Roman yoke, so was this such a terrible fate for the Druids? With mixed feelings I sent a deputation of our council to speak with Venutius and his Carvettii council about an appropriate course of action.

SPRING AD58

"There's a whole legion camped there. The Gangoni are pressed right up against the sea, so they say." Davit was jumping around full of morbid excitement at the latest turn of events, which had seen Suetonius Paulinus march with bloody determination up the abominable new Roman road that had cut a swathe through the hills and valleys. Davit had travelled south, to the far point of our territory, to survey the general situation. With so much military activity under the new governor, I was mostly staying put at home, concentrating on developing and strengthening our stronghold with new ditches and walls. It was partly to increase my physical security and partly to reinforce my authority, both to the Romans and to Brigantians themselves.

"How close did you get?" I asked.

"I stayed on our land, so not as close as I would have liked, but it's unpleasant down there. If you stray into the wrong bit of land, they grab you or cut you down without even checking who you are. I didn't want to take the risk, so I stayed inside Brigantia. Even then, the patrols down there, all the posts we have set up on the border, were really nervous. Some of their men and women have disappeared and they blame the legionaries who are wandering around looking for fun or a fight."

"That shouldn't be happening!" I said with indignation.

"What can we do about it? Half these Romans can't spot the difference between a Brigantian and a birch tree, and even if they do know who we are, they don't all seem to have the same level of respect for the client treaty."

"That's a dangerous development. Paulinus should be reminded that he has a contract of mutual protection with us."

"It may be best not to press that point, or we may find ourselves roped into supporting this war against our neighbours."

"Hmm. What about his stance on the Druids, did you hear any talk or rumours about his plans?"

"I certainly did. It's like we feared. He wants to crush them. The more anyone suggests that he should take a modest approach, the more he reacts against it. He's a real bull, this one, all for charging right in and flattening them."

"Why is that, do you think? Is he a very aggressive man or have the Druids in particular got his blood pulsing?"

Davit raised his palms in ignorance.

"Both?" He suggested. "Anyway, what's our plan? I don't think Paulinus will take kindly to any interference from us."

"I have a meeting with the Carvettii council and some heads of the other sub-tribes. Next full moon. We'll see what comes of that."

My own council were in doubt about the point of having such a meeting at all. Presivin and Namandea had travelled with a small escort to meet with Iticus and several of the Carvettii council, on my orders. The two sides agreed to call a gathering of the war host representatives since the issue was so enormous. Yet Presivin reported that the initial meeting was oddly flat. Venutius had given no sign at all through his brother that he had considered raising arms to protect the Druids, so no matter what the smaller members of our federation believed, we probably couldn't act. Even if we wanted to.

Around that time, I took delivery of a large amount of building materials, sent to me by Roman craftsmen in the south who had been instructed to commence work on a radically improved residence for the Brigantian royal family. There was stone that had been shaped, sculptured and polished, tiles, slate, pre-cut timbers and so on. I housed the supplies in one of our empty grain storage pits, pondering on the irony of Rome's stale gesture of comradeship sitting there in the hole that evidenced our sudden agricultural poverty at their hands. It was lowered in with the full expectation that within a few years, work would begin on a grand residence. A little orchard of plum trees was clearly no longer symbol enough of our partnership with Rome but I had some apprehension about the suitability of a Roman villa to our inhospitable climate.

"They'll adapt the design," predicted Vellocatus, not altogether optimistically. "The craftsmen will find ways to hold the weather out. And you'll have a bathhouse, imagine that – warm water to saturate yourself in whenever you want." His tone was derisive, good-humoured.

"I can't see myself in a bathhouse," I laughed, "and won't it take a huge amount of work and fuel to maintain?"

"Most definitely," said Vellocatus ominously, "Work by tiny children and fuel from our dwindling forests."

"Careful. You're starting to sound anti-roman, my love."

"I'm no rebel. I just object to some of the wasteful and inhuman things they do. Did you know they have children scrabbling around the flaming hypercausts under those great bathhouses of theirs? Grown slaves won't easily fit, you see."

"Ah." I sensed Vellocatus was launching into one of his occasional rants against inhumanity. "Would you rather I didn't have this villa built?"

"I'm not saying that," he answered, "just that it's all well and good keeping in with Rome, but it's another thing having their architectural brand seared into our landscape."

I agreed with him, but not building the thing would have looked petty and it would have been difficult to explain when the governor chose to come and stay – the principal reason, I'm sure, why they wanted me to build it. We weren't ready to start yet anyway, so the building materials slumbered in the pit, biding their time.

We chose a settlement on the northern fringes of Brigantia for the war council. It was an obvious decision since it would have been unwise to alert Paulinus to our discussions and any movements in the south were immediately noted by his spies and scouts (though officially, of course, he was not spying on us). I was concerned about leaving our flank unprotected, lest Venutius should attempt some underhanded manoeuvre into Brigantia, but his council had given their word against such action and in any case, I was leaving what you might call a rear-guard in place to the west of the great ridge of hills that ran through our land, just to hold the line in case the Carvettii broke their promise. I travelled north on horseback with nearly all the council apart from Vellocatus. He stayed behind to man the royal settlement partly because we feared his presence may have been inflammatory at what would be sensitive discussions. As my horse skirted the steep hillside paths and moor-top lanes I missed his companionship even as I accepted the wisdom in his remaining behind. Truthfully, he would have had little to add to the debate since he was not swayed either way. His only real concern was for my position and what we would endanger if we opposed Rome at this late stage. What I really wanted to know was how the sub-tribes felt about the Druids. It was a pressing point that if they believed in their hearts that I should act, and I did not, they may defect and join the Carvettii in overturning me. I couldn't ignore that risk and if the feeling of this war council was that the Druids were owed our protection then I would have to act, regardless of the risk of losing my client-status. Oh, it was all up in the air again, just waiting for which way the wind would blow.

Gorlensa was supposed to stay behind. We did not think her health could stand the journey, but she appeared on the road as we set out, travel pack tucked under her arm, and Davit lifted her up onto one of the carts with a sigh. She eyed me indifferently, the weeks of pulling her hair out and wailing seemingly having blunted her passion. Up ahead, Davit and Shamatin lead the way whilst Antikia rode just behind me, occasionally calling out bits of conversation when the terrain and weather allowed. It was getting towards summer, but a drizzle fell steadily and the wind came and went in unsettled gusts. Namandea, who rode at the back with another woman, was a blurry shape through the dank daylight.

Horse hooves fell heavily behind me and I turned in my saddle to see Lerica approaching at a pace. He was commanding my own personal guard of five who would protect me from such supposed threat as Venutius and his family were deemed to present.

"Large party of horses coming in from the west," he called. "Probably the Carvettii."

We thought with our early start we would beat them north and avoid this awkward encounter but they'd clearly had the same plan. I laughed.

"Better pick up our pace then," and I motioned for Lerica to ride ahead and tell the men up in front.

When we approached our meeting place, the Carvettii had fallen well behind, purposefully giving way to our entry so they wouldn't appear to be following immediately in our wake. We cantered in and a group of young boys and girls took our horses as we dismounted and led them over to a small paddock with a big trough of water. So far so good. One of the older locals hurried across to greet me as I stretched my limbs from the long ride. He led me over to a big, temporary structure that had been erected for us to sit beneath. A conical roof woven of thin branches and covered with hides sat on top of thick low posts so that we would have to stoop to enter but should be comfortable once in. A few people were hanging woollen blankets and more hides on one side of the roof, to give more protection from the wind and a big fire had been set in the centre to ensure we'd all be warm. It was a good effort and I felt slightly guilty that these northern parts had suffered more than their share in the grain and slave taxes that I'd been forced to impose.

We seated ourselves in a huddle at the warmer end of the

shelter and had a quick meal washed down with some wine that we'd brought. I was developing a fondness for this imported drink and our home-grown ale seemed to sit heavier on my stomach these days. Looking at the great flagons of the brown stuff set to one side, I was glad I had my alternative supply.

Venutius arrived shortly after, flinging himself down from his horse in an exaggeratedly energetic manner. I tried not to watch but found myself stealing glances as he greeted our hosts and organised his entourage. Was Tyrius there? I craned my neck and found him, dismounting and looking about him warily. That was interesting. They didn't seem overly comfortable here and that would suggest they hadn't built up any covert alliances that I should be aware of. I turned away from the scene and saw Antikia do the same. Both of us were watching the men that were once ours and were now such dangerous strangers. Shamatin had moved closer to her. Lerica had stationed himself near me and had set his chosen four in a wider circle around me. I could see that the openly accessible nature of the meeting hall had him on tenterhooks. Outside, the wind dipped, but the rain started in earnest, driving everyone outside in. The Carvettii ducked in silently, with half-nods and uncertain glances, until Venutius entered, straightened up and addressed me directly.

"Cartimandua. Good journey?"

"Venutius, yes, and you?"

He nodded, with a curt grimace that could have been an attempt at a smile and the conversation around us picked up to fill the awkward gulf between our two camps. I reached for my cup of wine and took a mouthful, studying the people present and watching others arriving outside. Presivin, mindless of the rain flattening his hair to his scalp, was chatting away to a local man with three huge dogs at his side – no doubt they were swapping breeding or training tips. Presivin was a quietly amiable man, private but with none of his late father Binto's misanthropy. He had brought his wife on this expedition too.

They were a solidly dependable pair.

Across the meeting shelter, Venutius and Tyrius had settled down in the midst of their people and were studiously not looking our way. A leather curtain to my rear flapped in the breeze, knocking languidly against one of the wooden posts. I let my attention drift until a man stepped into the centre, by the crackling fire, and called for quiet. His name was Grishtar and he had volunteered to manage the discussion and make sure everyone had the opportunity to voice their thoughts. He was younger than I, perhaps thirty winters or so and I hoped he was capable of the sensitive approach required. He looked about, gesturing again for everyone to be quiet and then clasped his hands in front of him with a nervous smile that raised his plump, bearded cheeks into two rosy apples.

"Thank you all for travelling here. We hope the arrangements are adequate," a quick glance at me and then at Venutius for our approval, which I gave with a nod and Venutius with an impatient incline of his head, "and so can we get started immediately? As far as we know, Paulinus is still making progress towards Mona and could attack very soon. Do we raise a war host and defend the Druids or do we abide by the terms of our client status and do nothing? They are strangers to us and yet their power holds us all under their spell. If we do nothing, we risk their wrath. If we act, Rome may turn upon us. Which is the worse fate? Which path should we follow, how should we-" I cleared my throat loudly as he flung out his arms to wrestle physically with his dramatic dilemma, and he dropped his outstretched limbs back to his sides. "Oh. Yes, so shall we start with our chief, Cartimandua?" He backed away gracefully enough, though looking slightly peeved to have been cut off in his prime. I rose to my feet, moving forward where the head height was greater.

"As Grishtar has so eloquently described, the Druids are now at risk of invasion by Paulinus's force, which has already driven most of the Gangoni aside. There is no point attempting to negotiate with Paulinus. He is determined to subdue Mona. The question we must face is whether to oppose him. You all know what that will mean; loss of client status, which means a loss of all the privileges we now enjoy. Paulinus will most likely turn his attention away from Mona and press into Brigantia, since his forces are at our borders anyway. Rome has no shortage of men to send, especially with all the soldiers from over the eastern sea that they are always shipping in. On the face of it, this is a battle we cannot win, which is why my father and I accepted the client status in the first place. However, we never expected in those early days of this new age that our highest priests, whose ways we have always revered, would be directly threatened. Perhaps our gods and goddesses will smile upon us if we act to protect the Druids – perhaps they will help us turn the tide of Rome away."

"These are all questions, but what is it that you believe?" Gorlensa's crackling voice was implacable and I looked up sharply, annoyed to have been challenged by one of my own in front of this gathering. I had to pause, consider how I would answer. It was the question I had been hoping to avoid, letting others have the argument while I sat back as the final arbiter, but Gorlensa was not going to let me get away with that.

"I am unsure," I admitted. "I want to understand how you all feel, because I'm not convinced we should risk everything for a tribe we hardly even know. I've never met a Druid, have any of you?" I looked around keenly, so they would know that I was not being rhetorical. Someone at the back raised a hand and then another closer to me.

"Would you both come and tell us what you think?" I motioned encouragingly to the floor and the woman at the back made her way through. She wore a long dress of finely woven deep blue wool that was still thick with damp at the hem around her worn leather sandals. Her hair was the pale gold of sunshine on an autumn day and she had pinkish skin with crows feet wrinkles around her cornflower eyes. A thin scar ran from the base of her throat across her collarbone to disappear under the neckline of her dress. She looked to me and I nodded and stepped back into my place, glad to be finished speaking. I shot a look at Grishtar to let him know he had control of the meeting once more.

"My mother was Deceangli, my father is a Brigantian trader," said the yellow-haired woman. "so I have lived and travelled in the blue mountains and beyond. When I was a child I visited Mona to help deliver goods. We weren't allowed to travel across the water, so I can't tell you anything about the groves, except what I could see from the shore, and that's just that they stretched as far as I could see, thick and dark and silent apart from birdsong of course. A man came across in a rowing boat and stood by while we loaded it for him. He was a Druid, but young. He wore a very dark cloak with a hood that dropped over his face so that at first we barely caught a glimpse apart from his mouth. He was silent and faced away from us, but I was young and you know what children are like. I pestered him with questions, about why he was wearing the hood and what his home was like and did he have a family. At first he didn't speak, but I must have amused him, because at last he gave in and answered me. He said he was in training, learning the Druid way of reading the trees and hearing the spirits. He said he spent a lot of his time in the woods, memorising stories and lessons and he told me that sometimes it was very difficult being a Druid. He asked about my life and I remember being surprised that he was interested, because he actually sat down next to me and listened quite seriously while I told him about my pet chicken and what it was like travelling around with my parents. You all want to know what these Druids are like, well that one was just like any one of us. Just a young man, struggling with his burdens the way we all do." She shrugged and looked about as if there was nothing more to say.

Grishtar came forward quickly.

"So you would say there was nothing other-worldly about him? Nothing that made you think he had powers above any other?"

"He scared me at first, in his hood, with his silence, but no. When he talked to me, I saw he was just like anyone else. Of course I can't speak of what the fully trained Druids are like. I never met one of those." She went to sit down, looking sadly at the ground. It was an odd fact that the more human they were, the less likely we would be obliged to act.

"What about you, would you come forward and tell us your story?" Grishtar gave a flourish with his arm and an oldish man, the second to put his hand up, raised himself begrudgingly to his feet. He had a mouth set in a permanent downward turn and hair the colour of thunderclouds. I learned later that he was from the Setantii.

"I met some proper ones and I've seen the groves too. You'd not want to go there, it's a dark piece of earth, with all kinds of strangeness lurking around. It weren't trade that took me there, just curiosity, and I wished I'd never gone, after. The women, they're fierce, all with long hair that flies around loose if they take down them hoods they all wear. The men, when they're proper priests, wear colours on their skin, like the old ones, like in the stories from ages ago. I think they paint blood on their skin too, their blood or that from others I don't know. It's true they sacrifice people and animals. I saw the big stone tables they use, although I didn't see them do it. I was lucky I didn't end up on one myself, when they caught me and my friend there. The Druid who found us, he said he'd kill us and take our skin off to decorate his roundhouse but maybe he was just trying to frighten us. He had another Druid carve some kind of spell on a thin bit of wood and bury it in the ground and he said if we ever so much as put a foot on Mona again, the ground would open like a giant mouth and the tree roots would drag us right in and swallow us up. He cut me and my friend too," he paused and showed us a small scar on the inside of his wrist, "and dropped our blood on that slice of wood before it went in the ground. He said it was so the land would taste who we were if we went back. I weren't going to put that to the test."

"You really believed the ground would eat you?" asked Grishtar.

"I believed I'd come to harm. That much I believed," answered the old man, nodding his head emphatically. "I never went back there. Never would. They're dangerous people and they don't live by any rules but their own. You can feel it in the air, like it's pressing on you harder because you don't belong there. When we were hiding in the woods there, I thought I was going to suffocate. I couldn't get a breath. And then they found us and made that spell about the ground." He shook his head in wonder. We waited a moment, but he didn't continue and seemed to have travelled off into his own world. Grishtar took his arm and led his back to his place.

"Perhaps we should ask," he said, returning to the fireside, "whether anyone here has particularly strong feelings either way. Cartimandua has made plain her position – that she will move against Paulinus if there is a strong Brigantian notion to do so. Have we anyone who feels that way inclined? Venutius?" He opened the discussion to the Carvettii, presumably supposing that because we had been so violently opposed in recent times, Venutius would take any stance that caused me trouble, especially if it put him also against Rome. If anyone else there thought this, they were about to be disappointed.

"The Carvettii will not support the defence of Mona," he announced, standing up. "We have not prevented the massacre of many other bordering tribes so see no reason why the Druids should be different. They're no better than us, no more powerful than any of us. Just because they commit their atrocious rituals and pretend to control the elements, we fear them. Too long we've submitted to their apparently superior judgement, letting them decide on the most important matters that affect our world, and yet as we've heard, only a few of us have ever even met one of them. We're never invited to Mona, they never talk with us on any matter, just make their pronouncements and threaten us if we don't comply. The presence of Rome's forces has stopped them interfering in Brigantian and Carvettiian issues and in all honesty, it's a relief. What do they know anyway, of our tribe? And ask yourselves this – why are they so quiet all of a sudden, if they are so mighty and powerful? They fear the legions just like anyone else. If they truly had the power they claim, they would have held Rome at bay, but they couldn't or they wouldn't. I say they don't deserve our protection and we should look after our own land."

There was a surprised silence. Many had expected, I think, that Venutius would welcome an opportunity for war against Paulinus and the forces of Rome. Some of his own party looked a little frustrated, but even they kept quiet and submitted to the inescapable tactical position. If we moved our armies to the south west, we would expose vast sections of our borders and Paulinus would storm all over Brigantia, ruining whatever bargaining power we currently held and removing any possibility for us to defend ourselves if at any future point the client-ship became untenable. This was my gut feeling now. If I am really honest, I will say that it took the confirmation by my estranged husband to settle me. He may have been my most dangerous enemy but he had been at my side advising me for many, many seasons and he was no fool. It wasn't the same listening to Vellocatus on this issue, not because I respected him less, but because the weight of leadership and personal responsibility was not there to fill his words with the same gravity. I found that now I was dealing with Venutius as the Chief of his tribe, I could balance his words more equally with mine than I had when we were bound together and I saw him only as my husband.

He had nothing more to say, so unequivocal was his position. I glanced round other faces from other subtribes. The Lepocares, the Tectoverdi, even the eastern Gabrantovices were there, the head of whom I had met only twice in my life. There was unease, but no will to argue. I was about to call the gathering to an unexpectedly early close when Gorlensa rose and moved forward.

"Did you wish to speak, old woman?" Grishtar asked, but she ignored him, raised her hands and hurled a handful of mistletoe sprigs onto the floor. Everyone stilled. Mistletoe was the plant of the Druids, with its smattering of tiny white orbs like sightless waxy eyes and to throw it amongst us was to draw the malevolent gaze of the bone goddess upon our proceedings.

"What are you saying, all you leaders of Brigantia?" She pointed at me, "You who cannot make up her mind and you," a crooked finger directed at Venutius, "who is so sure of his own authority? How dare you speak like this? There wouldn't even be a Brigantia if not for them. Cartimandua, your own grandfather went to the Druids when he began to bring all our tribes together, and they put their blessing on his actions and their power in his sword. Without them, your family would have been nothing! What rights do you have to overturn generations of obedience to the Druid priests?"

I was used to rantings like this but Venutius sat open-mouthed at the sight of the elderly woman casting her contempt upon him. The sun-haired woman caught it next.

"What would you know? Just a child when you met a single Druid. For all you know, he was not a Druid at all, but a servant, pretending as to be one. The only man here who's even been to Mona and felt the power and mercy of the Druids tells us of their skill and their strength and you all ignore it! You will only feel the true power of the Druids in their absence. You've lived with their protection all your lives, how would you know what it is to be without it? Well, you'll know soon enough if you let this foreign army destroy them. Who do you think is holding our ragged lands and tattered tribes together now? Who forces a cold wind and a driving rain across the hills each time the legions try to make progress? Who sends shadows and spirits into the woods and valleys to scare the Roman invaders away from our sanctuaries and sacred places? Who makes the water run wild and silver to hide the weapons we stow in our rivers and the precious offerings that rest there for the goddess? All these things you think are the natural way of the world, these things are the Druids. Without them, our world will fall apart and all chance of repelling Rome will be lost. Fight now or fight never. That is your real choice. Tactics, strategy, ha! It doesn't matter. If you fight now, the Druids will make sure you win. You must fight now. We all must. If we don't, it's all lost. I've seen what will happen, ah I've seen it." Her voice had been rising and now it broke into a shrill wail and she gasped past tears. I closed my eyes and felt my head begin to pound.

"What do you see, what will happen?" asked Grishtar, his cheery manner momentarily dispelled.

"War, I see war and death and everything lost. None of us left. Unless we fight now."

We all sat, frozen and quiet. The wind whipped the loose hide against the post, beating out time in the rhythm of my own heartbeat.

"Anyone else?" asked Grishtar, "Anyone in agreement with this old woman must declare it now."

"We would fight," said one of the Tectoverdians. She was Patissa and I knew her reasonably well. She led a family and tribe of moderate size that held a string of settlements on the far northern borders. I had travelled to her homelands after my mother had died, when I assumed partial control of the tribe from my father. In age she was somewhere between myself and Antikia. Her thinning brown hair was plaited tightly back against her skull so that scalp showed through. "With all respect to Venutius, we agree with Gorlensa."

"Anyone else?" asked Grishtar. And so it went on, with the smaller tribes taking sides and as many opinions now as there were talkers. I listened to it all, the same arguments over and over and outside the rain splashed steadily into the the mud, large drops of mournful water hitting the leather curtains at our backs and rolling down like tears. In a nearby hut, someone was cooking a big pot full of mutton, roots and herbs so that the breeze was full of the smell of stew and after a time, everyone was restless to eat. Grishtar called us to a halt and we disbanded, some out into the rain, some merely shifting in their places, stretching their legs and yawning. I had brought Ansuvan along to serve me and he went off to fetch me some stew while I stayed at the side of the fire and contemplated the discussions. I drank more wine. It soothed me and helped me see clearer what I had to do.

Venutius, seeing that I was remaining in the big shelter, took his Carvettiians away and camped under a makeshift shelter his servants had assembled earlier. None of the Brigantians in my party spoke to the Carvettiians. The world was moving on, true enough, but much blood had been spilled and not enough time had passed to leave all that suffering behind. One thing was clear though - in the main, the Carvettiians agreed with the majority of my Brigantians that defending Mona was not feasible. Without the weight of mine and Venutius's orders, Brigantia would not go to war. Gorlensa had spoken movingly and I could see many had been shaken by her doom-laden prophecies but her heartfelt words were still a form of superstition and mystery - the very thing that many of us felt was unjustifiably shielding the Druids from our scrutiny. No. I had stirrings of unease in my breast about it, but my mind was made up. A second day of talks would be unnecessary. When we rejoined after our meal, I would give them my decision.

"Vellocatus, where are you?" I called, walking round our home and into the pretty garden I had created behind it. I was sure he would have heard our approach, but there was no sign of him as I had dismounted and now I was desperate to see him. I needed his arms round me to relieve the gnawing sense of anxiety that bowed my shoulders. I shielded my eyes from the evening sun that rippled deep and brilliant towards me from the horizon. Scanning the low wall that banked my horticultural creation, I spotted him, laying inert in a patch of grass, between the scented herbs and a border of heather. I ran to him, but still he didn't move.

"Is this what you've been doing while I've been away, lazing around in the garden?" I mocked and gave his thigh a gentle nudge with my foot. He groaned and rolled over from his side onto his back, screwing up his eyes as he came to. For a second, a grimace flickered over his features and I checked, stricken with worry.

"What's wrong? Are you ill?" I dropped to his side and stroked his face.

"No, not ill. Just a few old aches and pains. It's good to see you." He reached up and pulled my face down to his, kissing me softly. "How did it go?"

He sat up and brushed himself down, looking at me expectantly.

"There was hardly any resistance at all," I said. "Brigantia won't step in."

He nodded and we watched the golden sun basking on the hilltops. In the meadow, grasses swayed carrying early flower heads dancing on the surface of their wispy sea, the beautiful colours forced into grey silhouette against the vivid skyline. Voices carried on the warm currents of air, those returning from the Brigantian war council and those welcoming them home and, crowning them all, the chirruping singsong of the birds, basking high in the trees.

"Venutius was adamant he wouldn't act. Some of the others were surprised. They thought he'd take an anti-roman stance at any opportunity. Patissa was ready to fight. A few more, but not enough and the passion soon left them when they realised how few they were."

"Even Gorlensa?"

"Ah no, she's still railing at the madness of our decision. We lost her somewhere on the way back. She took a fork in the road to go and consult the spirits at a bend in the river." I rolled my eyes. My patience with the old crone had worn out.

"Maybe you should send someone back for her?" Vellocatus suggested.

"Namandea's taking care of that. Even she's sick of her aunt's wailing and moaning."

"Hmm." His head was turned from me and he watched the sunset, the groove between his nostril and the corner of his mouth deepening as I studied his profile.

"What?"

"No, nothing," he said.

"There's something bothering you."

"It's just, I don't know, I don't like what's happening."

"None of us do," I said, a touch defensively.

"Aren't you frightened?" He said, then shook his head to take the question back. "No, let's not talk about it. The decision is made."

"Do you think I should be frightened?" I asked, with a snake of unease uncurling in my belly.

"Who knows? Mona, Rome, who knows where the greater danger comes from?" He sighed. "You've done all you can, as you always do. It's out of your hands now."

"Were you stricken before, when I found you?" I asked, my biggest fear finding its way into words at last.

"Sometimes it comes over me. I need to rest and then it passes. It's just a bit of pain," he said, staring carefully into the distance.

We sat in the open evening as the twilight set in and faded to dusk, silencing the avian world overhead and blacking out the view. When the stars twinkled high and bright we went to bed, neither of us wanting to eat.

SUMMER AD60

In the tepid warmth of the late afternoon, I received riders from the south, three men on horseback who were part of the wide net of eyes I had cast over my region to keep myself apprised of significant events.

"What news?" I was terse. We had been apprehensive for many a moon, since that dismal spring gathering where we sealed the fate of the Druids.

"It's the Iceni," they began and I frowned in confusion.

"What about them? Come, sit and Amelan will bring ale." I snapped my fingers to her and led the men to my garden where I liked to sit whenever possible. I had cherry trees now, as well as plum, and we were trying grapes, although they hadn't done well at all. Vellocatus walked beside me and Namandea, Antikia and Davit, who came when they heard the horses also followed to hear the news. One of the riders, a pale-faced man with close eyes that slanted slightly and arms covered in black hair, resumed his delivery.

"The Iceni leader died a short while since. He left instruction that half the tribal wealth, land and leadership were to pass to his children. Two girls, not yet of age. Procurator Catus has taken offence and insisted that the Iceni are now to be entirely subjugated to Roman control, without a noble class at all."

"Ah." I considered this, as the messenger's narrow eyes burned with the implications. His hairy skin seemed to bristle with agitation.

"There is more. The mother, she confronted Catus and said this was not what they had been promised, so," he swallowed and bowed his head as if in apology for the dire news he was about to impart, "he tied her up and flogged her and then he had her daughters forcibly mated many times with his soldiers. The girls and their mother are alive, but barely. It was very brutal."

"Great goddess," I breathed. Namandea gave an involuntary

269

moan. Davit began to pace, clenching and unclenching his fists. He had a daughter himself, a little girl of perhaps four years.

"Not of age?" I murmured, then shook my head temporarily free of the horror. "Is that everything?"

"For now, but a fire has been lit in the bellies of the Iceni. It's easier to travel into that area, with the Roman armies concentrated in the west, so we're listening closely for more news. We knew you would want to hear this quickly. People will no doubt be worried what this means for our future."

I didn't respond to that comment. People would be worried? I was worried, never mind the people. But then, I calmed myself, the Iceni situation was very different to ours. Their relationship with Rome had been far more turbulent and the whole leading clan was born of controversy.

Several years after Claudius added our distant Cassiterides to his collection of overseas triumphs, the Iceni tribe had rebelled. I told you of it much earlier, how they were stripped of their weaponry and how the ruling clan were entirely removed and replaced with a new home-grown leader chosen by the Roman governor of the day. That leader was Prasutagus, some Icenian warrior who had seized the opportunity offered by an occupying force that did not have the resources necessary to overturn the client-ship already in place. Prasutagus was bound to a chestnut-haired woman whom I had never heard of, who bore him two daughters. They were a new ruling family, but their recent ascension did not matter to the Iceni, just as it would not have really mattered in Brigantia. It was true that the authority often flowed down the family line, but these descents were interrupted and scattered by wars, deaths and all manner of occurrence and new ruling elites sprang up all the time. So Prasutagus and his wife and their two daughters headed the Iceni tribe for a respectable amount of time until Prasutagus died. He had unwittingly left his small south-eastern hump of land in reach of the grasping hands of Decianus Catus, a man I had not met but who was the latest in a line of procurators, charged with raking in the taxes due to the emperor. Catus was contemptuous of client arrangements – a greedy reed of a man who sheltered in his villas and let fighting men like Paulinus quash the opposition while he sucked the lifeblood from the land and its people. Now, faced with a widow and her two children, he had apparently been unconcerned at violating them so horribly and completely overriding the agreement that previous governors had secured. There had been war in the Cassiterides for a very long time now. Whole tribes had been crushed, scattered and torn apart by the Roman war machine. But never had there been such a callous and personal attack on an elite tribal family. Even the infamous enemy of Rome, Caratacus, had been treated with immense respect given his insubordination – himself and his family given a comfortable life in that foreign land he had claimed to detest. How this poor woman of the Iceni could have deserved such a reaction, I could not imagine. Our Roman owners must have gone mad. Worried? We should all be terrified.

The Iceni situation had us all drawn tense with concern, like hides hooked out in the sun, as we waited to hear what, if anything, that long-suffering tribe would do. It was a storm of a different nature that broke first, however, when finally Paulinus sated his angry appetite for Druid blood.

I can tell you what happened but of course I wasn't there. It was a long time after our war council of Brigantian tribes decided not to intervene, that Paulinus positioned himself on the mainland opposite Mona and sent his soldiers over the water in a fleet of purpose-built flat-bottomed boats at a shallow tide to roust the Druids from their oak-shrouded homes. The water was mostly low enough for horses to pass, so his cavalry splashed their way across too, man and horse swimming through deeper parts where necessary. A summer dawn, silent and pink, was spoiled by a foreign army cutting a swathe through the forbidden sea channel. The Druids met them in force on the shores of their sacred little island and sang out a curse in their horrible screeching voices, waving their spears and knives and casting bloodied offerings into the water before them. As the auxilliaries rowed their boats through entrails and ripped mammalian bodies, they must have blanched and thought to turn back, but Paulinus was at their heels and they had been promised for many moons that the slaughter of the barbaric fake priest tribe would bring the glory of Rome and the favours of all those foreign gods upon them. So they jumped from their boats into the already bloodied shallows and pressed into the outraged bodies of the Druid men and women, who tore fiercely at their aggressors but were hopelessly outnumbered. The Druids were driven back into their secret groves and executed on and near their own stone tables and ancient trees. Their sacrificial temples became unwilling hosts to the Roman deities. Not one Druid was left alive. The men of Paulinus decorated the trees of Mona with the bodies of its people then burned them all, oak and human alike, until the secret island was flattened and black and stinking of charred flesh.

"Where do you think Gorlensa is now?" Vellocatus asked me one day soon after the massacre had happened. I wished he would not bring it up. He seemed to pick at her absence like you would scratch at a scab. It troubled him, the way she had wandered from my entourage on the return home and never rejoined us.

"Maybe she travelled there, to Mona," he said, when I did not answer. "Or perhaps she is living in a cave somewhere, an old crone casting her spells."

We were sitting to eat, but now I lost my appetite, and almost my temper.

"Please, not this again," I commanded coolly. He looked

snubbed for a moment.

"Namandea must find it hard."

"Enough." I slammed a hand on my thigh and finally he went silent. We resumed eating. I had learned this of Vellocatus - that sometimes his wandering mind or need for conversation would override his usually intuitive tact. It was a childish trait, innocent but aggravating, and I often brought him up sharply because he had touched a sore point. Sometimes he talked nostalgically about my mother or father and I had to stop him because his vivid recollections caused a physical pain of loss within me.

"Have you seen Risha lately?" He asked. He couldn't bear to let a hostile silence linger between us. I gave in.

"I haven't talked to her for a while."

"She wants to go home. She tells whoever will listen that she thinks she's dying and she wants to go back to her own home. Will you let her go?"

"Are you asking out of interest or on her behalf?" I countered, part-mocking since he still bore a certain amount of enmity towards her, born of the way she had treated him so long ago, so he would never advocate for her.

"Neither. I'm just raising the question because soon enough she'll force you to answer it herself."

"Well then I have some time to decide," I replied.

The Druids had been crushed, the ancient oak trees burned to shrivelled husks and yet the sky had not fallen in, the ground had not opened to eat us and we were not plagued by thunderous storms of revenge. They had not, in their spirit form, turned on us to exact a revenge for the abuses they had suffered at Roman hands, but as the blackened flakes of their mortal remains still floated in the Prittain winds and their aggressor drew his soldier hounds from the hunting grounds of the groves, there came news from the south, news so urgent that the rarely-used bonfires were lit up in a string, carrying the signal all along the great hills into the north that something of momentous importance was happening. When we saw the fires, not used for so long that we had hardly remembered that people out there still tended their upkeep, I called the council together and drew in my army. I had a personal guard now of many people - perhaps four hundred - who would come when called to encircle my great enclosure. They were no match for any serious invasion force but they gave me an immediate protection and visible presence of force that was needed in those swiftly changing times. I considered riding south myself, to meet the news head on and perhaps gain time for whatever action or decision-making was needed, but I was quickly persuaded against it. Best to stay in my fortified northern homestead than ride out looking for trouble.

Trouble, when it finally came to us, staggered in on a horse. The wolf-like man with the narrow eyes, who was my messenger, this time brought with him a companion who was unknown to me and clad in red and brown leathers with some kind of gilt edging and a blood tattoo of a bird on his shoulder. The stranger burned with excitement as he was brought before me to give the incredible news. The tortured widow of the Iceni had turned war leader. Her people called her the Boudicca. She had drawn the greatest war host in the history of our fragmented world and she and her furious daughters were razing the south to the ground.

"They're doing what?" I asked stupidly. "You mean she is actually gaining ground?"

"Boudicca has taken the advantage while Paulinus is in the west. She has destroyed Verulamium and Londinium. The temple of Claudius stands in ruins. The murder of the Druids may be the undoing of Paulinus." The tattooed man smiled slyly, unable to hide his pride in the cunning of his small tribe, for it turned out he was, in fact, an Icenian. His name was Usonagus.

"Thank you for bringing us this news," I said, preparing to

dispense with the man and discuss the emerging situation with my council, but he took a step towards me and lifted his hands in supplication. Vellocatus moved closer to my side.

"Boudicca asks you to join the war host. Others, like myself, are travelling further afield to gather the support of more tribes. This fight is in the interests of us all."

"Not quite. Brigantia still has a client arrangement with Rome," I reminded him coolly. "In fact, you take a risk coming to me at all."

"Ah, I hope you will consider me a friend and messenger. I am no Caratacus." Again, that sly smile which I did not like. It seemed to say, we are on a level, you and I.

"I can see that you are not."

"Can you also see that what has happened to the Iceni could easily happen to your tribe? Paulinus, Catus, these men do not honour the agreements their predecessors made. They do not act with the civility they claim to represent. Paulinus has even in this past half-moon, slaughtered all our Druid priests. You know what Catus did to the Boudicca and her daughters. Who is to say they will not decide one day that your status is untenable because you are female? They may remove you and replace you with Venutius, or just remove the pair of you and govern Brigantia directly, as they proposed to do with the Iceni. Your arrangement with Rome is like breath on the wind, words spoken and forgotten a long time ago. There is no safety in allying yourself with them. Join our war host and fight with us. We can defeat them. Before, as separate tribes, we had no chance. Together we outnumber them at last."

He came to the end of his unexpected speech, which I had permitted as a courtesy because he had travelled a long way to speak to me. His words had taken me back to the time when we had tried for an alliance with the Catuvellauni and they had refused. Cynically, I considered whether the once rich and prosperous Iceni would ever have allied themselves with a

Brigantian war host, particularly if they held a protective client agreement with Rome. Definitely not, I told myself. The tribes of our water-locked world had spent an eternity fighting each other before Plautius marched into our midst with the first of the Roman legions and such a history did not lend itself to any kind of inter-tribal solidarity. The Iceni had been outraged in a terrible manner, there was no question about that, but they were following a personal grudge and drawing to their side the other local tribes who had been offended and subjected to effective slavery by the Roman occupiers. My instinct was to have no part in it. I had much experience and knowledge of the Roman war machine now and I truly believed that if Caratacus, with all the naturally fortified benefit of the western hills and their ferocious tribes, could not defeat it, then nothing would. Boudicca's apparent victories were surprising and and gave me a passing moment of envy, but I knew in my gut that once Paulinus reached her, he would find a way to pierce through her hastily established war host. Of course, there was a chance I was wrong. I proceeded cautiously.

"Usonagus, you have given us a great deal to think about. Would you take a meal and a rest and leave us to discuss these developments." I smiled, but taking my tone as a hint, Davit had taken the man's arm and was drawing him companionably but firmly away. Usonagus glanced uncertainly towards me then let himself be conducted out of sight. I turned to the council who had stood alongside me to hear the Icenian's news.

"We're not getting involved in this," I said. "It's not our fight and I know almost nothing about this Boudicca. If we can't step in for the Druids, we can't step in for the Iceni."

"But what if this is it – our last chance to stop the Romans?" Namandea was flushed, unusually anxious. I remembered what Vellocatus had said about her concern for her elderly aunt and hoped she was not challenging me because she held me somehow to blame. Perhaps she was wrestling with her own need to make recompense, since she too had opposed Gorlensa.

"There's no chance," I sighed, "Once Paulinus returns, it will all be over."

"But you heard what Usonagus said about the war host. With sufficient numbers, surely it's possible?" She wasn't giving up.

"Perhaps. But remember the stories Caratacus told? How they felt themselves so secure, couldn't possibly lose and then the Romans came burrowing up underneath them, wearing a shell of shields so that even though they were a smaller force, they routed Caratacus's whole army?"

"That was different."

"It doesn't matter," I said, shaking my head. "The point is that they always find a way. When they're out there fighting, they don't rush about killing and maiming. They move as one unit, protecting each other, working to the same plan. Boudicca has to either massively outnumber them or else fight a very strategic battle. From what we've heard, there doesn't seem to be much strategy in her approach. She's just flattening everything in her way. She's an angry woman, rightfully so, but however justified her retaliation is, passion alone won't win this war. Not to mention that we don't have any kind of relationship with the Iceni or the tribes that are supporting them. How can we plan a real tactical assault against the legions when we'd be fighting with an enormous angry mob who'd likely have no interest in listening to us. We're out of this. We'll send Usonagus on his way."

Towards the end of that summer, Antikia and Shamatin held a binding ceremony at last. Despite their age – she had seen her fiftieth year and he was only a few years younger – the event was welcomed by all of us. The years of Tyrius's dominance of her affections had stunted Antikia and rendered her a peculiarity; an attractive, intelligent and healthy woman reduced, in surface appearances at least, to a plaything. When finally he was out of her life, she regained something vital that none of us had even realised was missing.

We held the celebrations in a new structure that had been built in the lower half of the meadow. I suppose you could call it a form of temple - it was a high and hugely wide roundhouse, but with just one room, several entrances and an ornamental bank and ditch that ran around it. I'd had the idea for it after we held the war council meeting in the far north, within that cold, half-finished hut that was barely serviceable. The number of our roundhouses had increased greatly since my youth, but they were all of a similar design and I had realised I needed somewhere to convene more formal meetings, particularly for receiving Roman guests, at least until my villa was built. For Antikia and Shamatin, pretty garlands were hung round all the posts, the scent of sweet meadow flowers filling the air. A feast was laid out inside on a long wooden table and musicians played cheerful tunes through the whole afternoon and evening. It was a happy but wistful affair, inevitably, given that we were all advancing in years.

"Will you speak?" asked Shamatin, as he took a pause from dancing, his heart-shaped face flushed and emotional.

"What do you want me to say?" I laughed.

"Something memorable," he replied, teasing.

The music stopped and I stepped onto a low bench and clapped my hands a few times to gain attention. When all heads had turned I started a speech, about the qualities of my paternal aunt and how she had always been to me more of an older sister, advising and guiding me. I added, of course, how happy I was that she had found her equal at long last in our unsuspecting metal-worker. I'm not sure I said anything memorable at all. Someone called out that maybe I should follow their example and I allowed a small smile and continued with my vague and well-meant words.

Vellocatus came over when I had done. He was wearing the

dreamy, benevolent smile that characterized his ageing features these days.

"Will you have some more food?" He asked, and took my arm as we walked to where the feast was laid. We had plates of oysters and mussels, sent fresh from the coast along with whole, salted fish that had been skewered and crisped to golden over the fire, pieces of slow-cooked beef that flaked apart in the salty gravy and the most succulent roasted joints of pork, with crackling fat falling deliciously from the tender meat. There was a plum sauce, made from my own little harvest of the fruit in my garden and a warming pudding of barley and honey. We had dishes of greens too, fresh leaves, some from imported seeds, like the vibrant coriander, and some of our local favourites like sorrel and dandelion, all flavoured with imported oil and sprinklings of sea salt. The first of the apples had been picked and there were thin slices of the crunchy fruit in the salad leaves. There were piles of stone-baked flat breads, that served as trenchers when the supply of wooden bowls and leather platters ran out. There were other delicacies too, I forget them now.

We took our food and sat at chairs reserved for us at one side of the temple house. I was tucking in hungrily to the pork - ah, I can taste it even now! - when I heard a crackling noise, just faintly, in the background.

"It's been a good day," Vellocatus was saying, as I strained my ears and tried to distinguish the snapping, popping sound that was on the periphery of my hearing. "Antikia looks so happy."

I cast a distracted glance in my aunt's direction. She did look happy - flushed, like Shamatin and with a plumper, rosier face than usual. She had put on weight in these last months.

"Healthy too," I commented. Still that bristling sound, except now it was edging into all our hearing and there were some shouts outside.

"There's a fire," I realised, speaking to no one in particular, and I placed my food down on the chair and hurried outside with Vellocatus following.

It was late into the evening and the horizon was just barely tinged with a blue glow that merged into starry blackness, but there was a half-moon and the silvery light threw our settlement into silhouette. To the north of our largest huts, thankfully well away from mine, was a great orange beacon reaching burning tendrils into the night.

"Water, fetch water!"

"Is anyone inside?"

"Whose hut is that?"

The crowd of well-wishers had pushed outside and were surging up to the central enclosure in disarray, calling out their panicked questions. I did likewise, moving almost at a run up the path that lead from the bottom of the meadow in through the western gap in our banked walls.

"It's Risha's hut," I panted to Vellocatus. "Pray to the goddess she's all right, for if she's harmed, we'll answer to the Carvettii."

Some of the crowd had veered off towards the well to grab buckets and limit the damage. Fortunately there was no wind that night and the hut was a comfortable distance from any others so the fire couldn't spread. I went straight towards the flames, looking for my hostage. All I could see were people throwing water at the flickering fire, which hissed and flared in response. Children stood and marvelled at the brilliant tongues of sunset colours.

"Is she in there?" I yelled. "Does anyone know where she is?" But people shrugged and I feared the worst. How would I explain this to Venutius? It would look like revenge. He would think I had murdered her. How could he know we had become something like friends? Oh, how awful that she might be in there burned to death, in slow, roasting agony! That frail old body, with its desperate need to get back to Carvettii before the time came. And now the time had come and instead of fresh sea air and family, it was scorching hot and smelled of ash .

"Cartimandua! Over here." A man's voice rang out from a roundhouse entrance - Lerica's old place, a smaller hut which he once shared with other single menfolk before moving out and building a new one for himself and his wife. I stumbled on the rough ground, tears in my eyes.

"What happened–" I started, distressed.

"I put her in here," Lerica said, grimly, his lower jaw set and his lips pressed together, making the scar on his cheek stand out in its jagged little line.

"Oh thank you, thank you." My heart hammered inside me. I gulped in some air and steadied myself with my hands on my hips, leaning forwards as the stitch in my side from the run up the hill caught up with me. I straightened and made to go inside.

"Wait!" He yanked me away from the entrance and spoke low. "She did this herself. She set fire to the hut and blocked her doorway so we had to fight to get her out. Two of us had to hold her in here just to stop her running back into that blaze." He jerked an accusing finger at the evidence of her vandalism, the ball of flame that was now abating slightly as it ran out of material to consume.

"Why would she do that?" I shouted, relief turning into angry confusion, "And tonight, of all nights."

"She's going on about Antikia stealing her husband and her being left all alone," Lerica grunted. "Silly old mare."

There was a crash behind us as the bare, blackened structure of Risha's hut crumpled to the ground, sending a cloud of burned flakes sailing into the air like dark butterflies. The onlookers moved back, coughing and covering their faces. I stepped into Lerica's old roundhouse, balling my fists. The hut was sparse, with a dusty earthen floor and small, curtained sleeping areas. All the utensils for daily living were piled to one side, bowls unwashed and gathering mould, dirty blankets awaiting washing and airing - a typically male place. On a shallow box densely packed with straw that presumably served as a bed, sat Risha.

She was scrunched up, knees almost to her chest and bony hands clasped round the sides of her head, face down. Her body shook as she cried to herself.

"This is a far remove from the Risha I know," I said, speaking as I found, since I was otherwise at a loss for words. She didn't answer.

"If you were trying to kill yourself, couldn't you have found an easier way, maybe one that didn't ruin a good hut?" Still no response. She had sooty marks on her arms, mixed with red bruises where the men had restrained her. The marks circled her thin arms like manacles. I exhaled heavily and left Lerica's hut. As I stepped outside, her reedy voice rippled out after me.

"Send me home or kill me. I've had enough of this, send me home, Cartimandua. They don't care that I'm here anyway." Her words were shrill to my ears in the smoky night air, but the crowds of people had already begun to drift away from the flattened, smouldering hut back down the meadow to continue their drinking and dancing, so no one else heard but me and Lerica, who stood nearby, chewing on a piece of willow bark.

"Can you find somewhere for her to stay?" I asked him.

"Amelan can make space for her," he stated. I paused, then nodded. Prior to that night, I wouldn't have installed her with servants, but she had burned down the home I had provided for her and I didn't care to spend my resources pandering to her insubordination. I saw Vellocatus steering the last few people away from the scene of the fire and went to him.

"She's not hurt," I told him, "but she won't speak to me. She did this herself. She wants to go home or die." I shuddered. Now the fire was dampened, I felt cold.

"Will you return her?" he asked me.

"I can't, not while the Iceni lead this rebellion. It's unlikely, but Venutius may attempt to invade again while Paulinus is busy in the south."

"You really think he cares enough about her to hold off an

invasion on her account?"

"Not really, but if I send her back, it may just embolden them, give them the impetus they need to rise up again. And with the Roman legions under such pressure, I don't want to do anything to prompt that kind of threat."

We returned to the party. My plate of food was still where I had left it. People were dancing to the music which had started up again. I watched them spin and laugh and wondered if Risha would try to kill herself again and when, if ever, it would be safe to return her.

At the foot of the country, the Romans had taken a great beating. I rode to one of my southern forts, on the border with what had been the Corieltauvi, a newish settlement adapted by Gaulish auxiliaries who occupied it as and when they needed to. They had extended the ditch arrangement and built walls to form the place into a squarish shape, quintessentially Roman but presently quietly inhabited by the native families who now earned a living working for and with our Roman rulers. I had travelled there to learn the latest about the rampages of the wild Boudicca, as well as to ascertain that our border protection was sufficient, should she actually succeed in defeating Paulinus and choose to manoeuvre her forces north to gain more territory while she was so blessed by the war goddess.

I sat and chatted with a woman called Mesuvian. She was Brigantian, but happily paired with a Roman soldier. I met few people in this type of circumstance in my northern territories, but down here on the borders it was obviously more common. Her man was relatively important, insofar as I understood the hierarchy of the Roman army, and so she held some status in the settlement. She was a heavy-hipped woman, with slim shoulders and wide eyes. She laughed and talked easily, sewing through tough leather and squirrel fur to make a pair of winter boots while we conversed.

"You heard about the temple massacre?" she asked and was surprised to hear that I had not heard the details, though I knew the Boudicca had all but levelled Camulodunum and gone on to do perhaps worse to the far southern trading place known as Londinium. She explained eagerly. "You know the temple they built, the Romans that is, the temple for Claudius? That's where all the people in Camulodunum went to hide when she came charging in. They thought she'd leave them alone in there, be frightened of the Roman gods or some such thing. But the Boudicca isn't frightened of anything. She doesn't care who she kills, or who comes after her. She burned them all – Romans and tribes people alike. People like us, who live with the Romans, you know? She hates them too. Don't get me wrong, what that Catus did was terrible. It was a bad thing. But killing for killings sake, that's wrong too, especially when it's people who have nothing to do with it."

"I heard she'd moved on now, that she's getting ready to fight Paulinus himself."

"So they say," said Mesuvian. "What will Rome do, if she wins?" She gazed at me expectantly. People often thought I held all the secrets of our distant rulers, that I was in their confidence and received detailed information of their intentions. When Claudius was emperor, perhaps I did have something approaching that status, but now, with Nero at the helm, I had fallen out of obvious favour. Men's memories are short and fickle and probably no one over the seas even cared that I had once, not so long ago, handed over their most wanted man. That man, incidentally, was still living a charmed life at the hub of the empire. No, to Rome I was not a glamourous, loyal queen. I was just a barbarian leader who owed them taxes.

"They'll regroup and invade in larger numbers," I told her. "Unless trouble elsewhere in the empire draws them away. But no doubt your husband has more idea than I do of Roman intention."

She smiled, biting her bottom lip to prevent her mouth spreading into anything resembling smugness.

"He's not that important," she insisted.

Later she and her brother, along with several other men and women from the camp, rode out with us. We followed the border that ran towards the south-west before sharply turning back up towards the north-west, forming a pointed tip to the southern edge of our land. I had ridden parts of the area when I was little more than a child, at my father's side, and even though I had of course returned for various reasons over the years, it was memories of the early trip with Kesaven that filled my mind. It wasn't just the nostalgic sentimentalism of middling years that caused me to dwell on those remembrances, but the disconcerting contrast between the land and people I had observed then, and what I witnessed now. In my father's time we had intermittent signal fires along the border and a couple of outposts for keeping an eye on the trade routes in and out of Brigantia. Now there were regular patrol stations, scores of roundhouses, legionary camps and the makings of many new tracks and roads. The increase in activity was due in part to direct use of our land by the Roman forces but also the result of a Brigantian response to increased opportunities for all kinds of relationships with the legions, from trade to personal. I was glad to see evidence of such mutually-beneficial interactions but it had scarred the landscape and changed the people. As the Roman influence crept throughout Brigantia, would we lose our heritage and become completely Romanised, I wondered, and fingered the amber beads at my throat pensively.

Suffice to say, there was no shortage of people on the border and I was confident any challenge to our territory would be relayed to me immediately. We weren't properly armed though - no doubt due to some complacency given the extensive Roman presence and even some attempts by the Romans to actively disarm us, though this wasn't an official policy - and

I ordered extra weapons to be brought south and deposited in stockpiles along the border. In other times, the Romans might have objected to this but now they were struggling against the might of the wronged Boudicca, they were in no position to argue.

While we were there in the south, we heard that the Boudicca and Paulinus were finally about to come face-to-face on the battlefield. I stayed there at Mesuvian's settlement, keeping my entourage with me. That included Davit, Presivin, Namandea and Vellocatus. For once I did not have my aunt at my side. Antikia and Shamatin were holding the fort at home. Though I had ventured south, I was prepared for a hasty retreat home, depending on the outcome of this anticipated battle. The buffer zone of the Corieltauvi still existed between Brigantia and the old Catuvellauni hunting grounds, on the fringes of which lay the Iceni lands. I reasoned I had plenty of time to retreat and gather my army if the Boudicca did triumph and head north. Standing on the battlements of one of the border patrol stations, I gazed to the far southern horizon, at the overlapping curves of tree and field and the dips of the valleys and imagined the flame-haired Boudicca meeting her craven-faced Roman governor. Paulinus, I knew, would show no mercy after what she had done.

I hear she set fire in the bellies of the men and women she led, screaming a tirade of abuse against Roman dictatorship and uttering obscene curses in retribution for the violation she and her daughters had suffered. Of course, that could just be glorification of the dead, for she did die and so did most of her war horde. It became a famous story, retold across the lands. They probably even told it in Rome; they liked a good, tragic story, especially with a heroine fighting dictatorship, even if she was against Rome. I think a lot of the common people in Rome resented the power held by the emperor and liked tales where the downtrodden masses rose against a minority, elite power. Also, for them it was a nice, safe story, because the tragic heroine was of course defeated and Rome preserved.

Paulinus had a smaller force, but as I had predicted (and I take no pleasure in being correct) his army was organised to perfection and sliced the Icenian rebellion apart. The version of events we heard reminded me so much of the vision Caratacus had once given me; the unstoppable, incisive, impenetrable onslaught of a pure fighting machine. Paulinus employed a jagged edge approach, by which I mean his front line was organised into sharp points of shielded, heavily armed men plunging into the soft underbelly of a disorganised native rush; spears, arrows, axes, knives, swords, rendered useless by the superior tactics of the enemy. Those jagged points of men cut deep into their opposition, sucking warriors into their jaws and closing upon them. To make matters worse, the Roman line pushed forward until it had pierced the ragged, home-grown army against its own caravan of carts, wagons, chariots and animals. A fast retreat was impossible and Paulinus ignored any decent convention of allowing surrender. There's a word for what happened, though we didn't have it then. I think you call it genocide.

The irony for me was that even though Boudicca no longer presented a vengeful threat to me, a greater danger suddenly loomed dark before us – that of Paulinus, his honour and position momentarily threatened and now hugely expanded to match his fury. We went north. We burrowed in to our fortified homestead, with our guard of four hundred stationed around us and our wider forces alerted to the danger, and we waited for the irate governor to unleash his wrath.

287

WINTER AD61
TO SPRING AD62

Paulinus wasted little time. Spurred on by the rapacious malevolence of Decianus Catus, he sent tax collectors north to discuss with me our meagre offerings. I cursed Boudicca that she had not slaughtered Catus along with all the Colonial residents she had strung up through Camulodunum, Verulamium and Londinium. Fine for her, now she was dead and gone, but the rest of us were at the mercy of the victors whose burning humiliation and determination to regain lost ground made them even more fearful adversaries than before. The tax collectors who arrived came in an escort of heavily armed militia led by a tribune with a reputation for indiscriminate violence. As he saluted me in a impersonal, almost disrespectful manner, I considered that he may have been present at, or even part of the assault on the Boudicca and her daughters. The man gave me shivers and I tolerated his presence at the ensuing discussions only because the less offensive-looking administrators insisted on it. I didn't want to get off to a bad start.

As it was, they didn't like my newly constructed meeting hall, with its great fire and seats that ringed the warmth. They coughed and wafted the air in front of their faces as if it were distasteful to them, which I could not understand since the hint of smouldering birch was sweet to me and there was hardly any smoke given the funnelled hole in the roof directly above. Surely a roundhouse like this was better in a Brigantian winter than one of their cold, stone built oddities would have been? Nevertheless, they set about their spiteful business with single-minded directness.

"May we discuss your most recent payment? I have the details here." The man's question clearly did not require an answer and I waited patiently as he unrolled a scroll on which someone had inked the amounts of livestock, hides, slaves, grains, mined minerals and other trivial commodities we had provided shortly before Boudicca's rampage began.

"I see the grain allotment was smaller than required?" This question, framed with a raised eyebrow and straight gaze, did require an answer.

"Grain, as you will be aware, is a resource we struggle to produce on our land. We aim always to make up the shortfall with our other produce but it is not always possible."

"You struggle to produce it, with territory as expansive as you have?" asked another of the men, his thin, level eyes tightening dubiously. I sighed.

"Our land may be expansive, but it is largely moorland, rocky hillside, boggy marshland and dense forest. It's very difficult to grow crops on land like ours. In the south, the land is completely different – flatter, clearer – so crops can more easily be grown."

"But you must grow grain for your own consumption," asserted the first speaker, a man whose light hair was close cropped and whose lips seemed too fat for his oval face.

"We do – some anyway. But not much. The diet of most Brigantians is mainly meat and milk. The people live off their herds, and the herds live off the hard land. It's the only way to exist in a place like Brigantia."

"Hmm." The fat-lipped man was not satisfied but had no return argument. His colleague made a disbelieving, puffing sound. "But herds do well, that must mean you could provide more beef, more mutton, more hides?"

"As I said, we do try to give the most we can."

"That may not be enough," he intoned. I waited.

"Slaves, then. Always so few! We get more from the tribes with a quarter of your land in the south-west."

"Brigantia is sparsely populated. I should have thought that was evident from the explanations I have already given. We have much more land, but far fewer people." At my side, Vellocatus shifted forward to reach for his drink.

"Let's be absolutely clear about this," said the thin-eyed man. "You can't grow grain, you can't spare more hides and meat and you don't have enough people to meet your slave quotas. Is that what you would like us to report back to Governor Paulinus and Procurator Catus?"

"I can only tell you the truth," I said. My council, sitting there beside us, were deathly silent as they had been from the start. Vellocatus drank his ale and beckoned for a new jug to be provided for our guests. They looked irritated at his companionable manner.

"I'll put it this way," said the fat-lipped one, "there is no excuse for unfilled slave quotas, not until the last person has left your land. There is no excuse for unfilled hide quotas unless not one of your precious herds remain. And if you struggle to grow crops, perhaps you should cultivate your land to make it possible."

There were frustrated gasps at this ludicrous suggestion, that we should somehow turn nature on its head, but the two Roman administrators sat coolly insistent, with their scrolls of figures and smug little faces. They hadn't come to discuss or even negotiate, but to admonish. Their questions were minor arrow shots before the main event. I had no patience for their patronising games.

"Perhaps you could leave precise new instructions with us and we will endeavour to see they are followed?" I said.

"We have here," said the fat-lipped one loudly, as if I had not spoken, "a new list of taxes, to be provided by the time spring arrives. Next year, your contributions are expected to double, and then again the year after. And you are expected to divulge the whereabouts of any mines or areas of metal collection, especially gold, silver and tin. Nero cannot afford to have ignorant client-rulers taking advantage of his good nature and it seems to us that that is what you have been doing."

He finished on a proud little vocal flourish and as he placed his white, writer's hands together on his rotund stomach, I rose very suddenly and crossed the room till I was a few paces from him. The tribune had started, his little dagger drawn as he stepped in the circle to face me. I don't know why they bothered to equip men with that paltry little blade. It looked more ornament than weapon. The fat-lipped man was cowering backwards in his seat, his arms raised as if to fend me off. It was an unpleasantly ridiculous sight and caused me to smile.

"May I have the list?" I said and took another step to rip it from the thin-eyed man's hand. The tribune lunged towards me and grasped my wrist. His fingers bit in to my bones but I kept hold of the vellum scroll I had grasped. In the seconds that had passed, Vellocatus, Davit and Presivin had all risen and formed a half-moon behind me.

"Remove your hand," I said to the tribune and he did, slowly. I addressed the tax collectors again. "You've said your piece and I have your instructions. You may now leave. But before you go, remember that I have long been loyal to Rome, ever since I gave my allegiance to Claudius. You may have been burned by the Iceni, who have given you an appetite for vengeance, but it does you no favours to inflame the anger of my people or insult the woman who alone governs the vast hills of the north. Tell Catus I will endeavour to meet any reasonable taxes imposed by Rome. Tell Paulinus I continue to govern Brigantia in the name of Nero. Now get out!" The deep howl of my voice echoed in the high meeting hall and none of the Roman party found a tone to match it, for they rose wordless, sneering contemptuously and departed, swaddling their foreign bodies in heavy cloaks against the bitter cold outside. The tribune's men escorted the collectors out. He paused a moment, alone in front of the council and I.

"I'll pass your words to Paulinus. He will be pleased to hear of your compliance." Then he nodded a goodbye and exited.

"Davit, go outside and see they leave immediately, will you?" As he turned to carry out my order, I stomped back to my seat and threw myself down.

"I thought we were going to play it calmly," said Vellocatus, resuming his own seat.

"I was. But I won't be condescended to by a fat little nobody such as that," I retorted. My breathing was still heavy from my outburst and Vellocatus handed me a goblet of wine, which I drank down.

"There was a time when we would have put to death anyone who spoke to our chief the way they did," observed Presivin.

"Different times," said Namandea. "Different rules. Taxes are the new sword to slay us with, and they who bear the orders carry as much weight as a warrior these days."

"Nasty little men," I muttered. "I hate having to deal with them."

"It's better than if Paulinus himself had turned up," laughed Vellocatus. "I doubt you'd have been able to order him away so easily.

"No, but I might at least have had a conversation with an equal."

"Don't mislead yourself. Paulinus has as little respect for native rulers as his servants do and he wouldn't be scared to venture into our rocky northern world either – the man's used to dealing with hill tribes, they say, and he's massacred his fair share of them. Better that he let Catus send those underlings." Vellocatus had an easy manner about him, but there were red spots high on his cheeks that belied an inner, impotent fury.

"It upset you, when that tribune took my wrist," I realised.

"Of course it did. But what should I do, cut him down? No, I swallowed it, because that's what we all have to do." He stood and paced about. "We can't let them provoke us. We must just hope that they are too busy regaining ground in the south to seriously press for these latest taxes from us. Hopefully we will find that sending those men to insult us was just a way for Catus and Paulinus to let off some steam."

Davit re-entered.

"They've left the boundary of the settlement by the south-east road. I had some food passed to them for the journey. They were most surprised, but I explained we are not as barbaric as they expect and we treat our Roman siblings fondly." He seemed to take great humour from this.

"I would perhaps rather they had starved," I said sourly, but when Davit looked concerned I shook my head. "No, no, you did exactly the right thing, which is just as well because I couldn't have brought myself to do it."

The list of taxes was a joke. There was no possible way we could provide what they asked for and it was evident that this had been their intention. The increases planned for the next two years were simply a way to intimidate and subdue us, force us to our knees begging for some alleviation from the burden. Or perhaps Catus had done the sums, purposefully asked for far too much, in the hope that when we failed, he could encourage Paulinus to march upon us. I had no idea what level of evil alliance existed between the two men, so it was all a guessing game. The depths of winter arrived and passed, long dark nights stretching between each of the crystalline days, days during which activity was at a minimum whilst we existed on our stores and huddled by our fires. It was a harsh winter - little snow, but a persistent hard frost that clenched an icy grip over the land every evening and seemed hardly to let go while the weak sun was up. I ached in the cold weather and Vellocatus suffered more than in previous years also, despite our roaring fires and carefully maintained roundhouses. The younger folk wandered around, tending to the livestock, attending to the general outdoors work and not, by the looks of it, feeling the cold at all. Perhaps the days were not colder than they had been in the past. Perhaps I was just more weary.

Much as I hated the strain the winter placed on my daily life, I couldn't wish it away because it was the only barrier between us and the tax demands. I was not sure what we were going to do when spring arrived, nor what the Roman response would be. Sporadic information reached us, detailing troop movements south of our border. The Roman army had pulled back, regrouping in the old Catuvellauni lands to stamp down any residue of the rebellion. Londinium was being rebuilt, repairs were underway at Camulodunum and Verulamium. The stain of Boudicca was being gradually wiped away from the Romanised face of the south, and with it all hope of the end of Roman rule. Paulinus was desperate to put his stranglehold back on the Prittain territory – I'm sure he was terrified of going down in history as the governor to lose the Cassiterides. Even though he was so preoccupied far away from us, I feared the worst. When he heard we could not fulfil our tax obligations, he would have the excuse he needed to depose a woman leader, of whom he disapproved, and gain the biggest tribal region in all of Albion.

Then, as spring began to break and the first, miserly flowers pushed gingerly out of the earth, a reprieve arrived. I could not take it in when I first heard it. The messenger handed me a slice of wood, scratched with the bare message. Catus had gone and a man named Classicanus had taken his place as procurator.

"Who is Classicanus? What are his intentions?" I demanded of the party who brought the news.

He's far more moderate than Catus. Rome sent him to calm things down, by all accounts. They say he's going to investigate what Catus did."

It was music to my ears. With the perverse Catus removed, the tax burden imposed on us would hopefully be forgotten. We entered spring with a new-found spirit of optimism and I even felt gratitude towards Rome for the reparation they were attempting. Nero and his senate must have seen that they could not retain such a distant place if they alienated all the inhabitants and made them bear the brunt of their frustrations. Classicanus set about his internal investigations and then one day, Paulinus discreetly disappeared from our shores, despatched far away from the scene of his brutal conquests. It was more than I had dared hope for. Boudicca's rebellion had been, on the face of it, a failure, and yet we were reaping benefits now that had surely arisen directly because of it. Her legacy, it seemed, was not to rid our lands of the Romans, but to remind them of their paternal responsibilities to the civilisation they were trying to absorb into their empire. Her success was to force them to return to fairer, more manageable policies of taxation and territorial control. Her downfall was my gain. I entered into a relatively friendly correspondence with Classicanus and the new governor, Turpilianus, agreeing terms for our contributions for the next few years. I was under no illusions – the army was still staffed by hard-hearted, antagonistic killers like the tribune who had bruised my wrist – but toleration and mutual respect were the new order of the day and we could rest easier than we had for some time. It seemed we were forever taking three steps towards danger and then two steps back. This overall trend was ominous but for the meantime, it felt like we had been dragged well back from the precipice.

I planted new herbs in my garden, strange smelling little plants brought by Italian traders to our country and transported from Londinium to various places by native traders. I liked to study them, see how they took to our soil and whether they would cope in their new conditions. Amelan, who was even looking more like Mandulay these days, experimented with their flavours in her cooking and one or two even came with instructions for medicinal purposes. In days gone by, I would have spent my spring and summertime riding out, close to home and further afield, to make my presence felt and govern over any matters arising, but this year I was more inclined to stay within the settlement. Life had tired me and I felt my age. Besides, I had no need to make my presence felt within my wide assortment of allied tribes. I was infamous. I was the only client queen remaining and had dodged every sharpened spear that had come our way for decades. The people had, so I thought, settled down to trust and respect me.

Our council meetings had returned to the simple affairs that once dominated our lives - punishing wrongdoers, settling boundary disputes and managing trade. I had one clear issue, though, that had haunted me since the night of Antikia's joining ceremony - Risha, and her desperate longing to return home.

"We should keep her here," argued Davit, a lone voice in a gathering that was generally disposed towards benevolence. "She's a hostage to the agreement we have with Venutius and, in that respect, nothing has changed. The Carvettii still present a threat to us."

"Surely not now, after all this time?" Antikia's new domestic arrangements had softened her outlook, but also she would be glad to have the final reminder of Tyrius removed from her homestead.

"Whether they are hostile to us or not, what good is a hostage with no value? Tyrius and Venutius couldn't care less about her safety. They've never even visited her, except when Tyrius came that one time," Presivin concluded.

"Isn't it more dangerous to keep her here anyway? If she kills herself as she intends, the Carvettii could use that as a justifiable reason to disregard our peace treaty. Or she might burn down another roundhouse, maybe killing someone next time," added Shamatin.

"All right, I've decided," I said, quietening them all. "She goes home as soon as possible. We'll present her to Venutius as a gesture of goodwill. I agree that it's going to do more harm than good keeping her here."

I went to her that same night, to tell her what we had

decided. She was lodging in with a family on the outskirts of our settlement, a personal servant with her to assist her, but also to guard her. She was never alone, for fear she might start further mischief, though I suspected that the fight in her had burned out the same night her hut did. She fretted when she saw me, in the trivial and pathetic way old people do, fussing over nothing, fiddling with her hands. It pained me to see her so reduced and further confirmed to me that I had made the right decision.

"Risha, I'm sending you home," I said, gently. "You can leave in a few days."

Her creased face sagged and there was a tremble of her lip.

"Thank you," she whispered. "It's been long enough coming."

"I know," I said. "What will you do, will you go back to Tyrius?"

"What else would I do?" She looked confused and I decided not to question her further about her plans. Ours had been an awkward little friendship, punctuated by moments of true affection but coloured by the enmity of our history. When she left our dun, she would leave the vestiges of any bond with me behind and I would have no further responsibility towards her. Even so, I worried about what situation she was returning to. She was old and frail now, not the woman Tyrius had known, and even if he was equally as decrepit, I had my fears that she would not be entirely welcome in her old home. At least Iticus would look after her, though I suspected Venutius might be indifferent.

"I'm sorry I burned down your hut," she said. "It was a foolish thing to do."

"It doesn't matter now. I wish you well, Risha, I really do."

"Thank you. And I wish you well in return. Don't forget, you still bear a responsibility to the Carvettii. You must find a way to reconcile these two halves of Brigantia. I will encourage Venutius to do the same."

"Oh, please, don't worry about that. We have an agreement

already that seems to be working." I was horrified at the thought of her interfering. Venutius wouldn't appreciate it and she could do us both more harm than good. "I'm going to send word ahead to the Carvettii council that you'll be returning. Would you like me to include any personal message or any instructions?"

"No, no - no need for that. They'll know how to prepare for my return."

Already, she seemed to be filling up with that old confidence I had always associated with her; that dangerous arrogance was still there, faded but lurking. I took my leave. It was time for her to re-assume her mantle as matriarch of her tribe, and that was a Risha I had no fond memories of at all.

SUMMER AD65

After Risha had gone, the atmosphere of our settlement took a turn towards the nostalgic. With the occupying Romans so busy rebuilding in the south, we had less contact than in previous years and sometimes, if it were not for the still onerous taxes, the people in the central parts of our territory could almost have forgotten about them altogether. We were isolated, up here in our mountainous country, with its high hills and swampy valleys. The fearsome roads which had begun to snake out of Londinium and Camulodunum still did not make much headway into our territory. They were mostly old tracks anyway, those roads, that the Romans then built upon in their own style. I dreaded to think of them trying to impose their straight, flat style of track upon our old criss-crossing traders routes, just as I dreaded to think of the villas that would spring up once the Roman influence fully permeated Brigantia. I still had my store of building materials for the villa Paulinus had insisted I needed, but they remained in the disused quern until such a time as I might be forced to use them. In any case, the Roman craftsmen who I would have needed to perform the work were all greatly needed in Camulodunum, which had been ruined by the rebellion. Even four years later, they were still undoing the damage she had wrought.

So in our peaceful dun, we relaxed. I took long walks in the meadows and woods of my youth, which had stood all around me since, but which I had rarely had time to appreciate. I hunted sometimes, with my old bow, and took my horse riding around our perimeters, checking on our modern defences. The stone walls which Antikia and Venutius had spent so much time planning and building stood firm around the southern ramparts, and great ditches encircled the northern face. Vellocatus usually rode with me when I went out further, but the need for any big protective entourage had receded.

299

Venutius had, as far as I knew, welcomed his mother back into the fold. I received a curt message of acknowledgement, barely bordering on gratitude, but that was unsurprising since my actions in capturing and holding his mother had been a source of embarrassment and annoyance to him. Iticus had met Risha on the border with some ceremonial fuss, as I heard from Presivin and Namandea who had escorted the old woman home. She had appeared pleased, but apparently distracted. Perhaps she had hoped that her eldest son or husband would come to greet her. Or maybe she was overcome with emotion at being home. She never corresponded with me and I had not expected her to. The Carvettii had gone quiet, save for the mechanical delivery of taxes which came silently in response to every request. There was never any border trouble, partly because the border was so blurred in that region. There were no clear lines between Carvettii people and surrounding tribes because for many generations, these tribes had intermingled – a result of our Brigantian wartime federation. So when I say we returned to a nostalgic past, we did so in respect of the Carvettii too- they had gone back to being just another sub-tribe, beholden to and managed by the Brigantian chieftain. I hoped Venutius had found happiness – that he was calming down into a peaceful old age, as I was.

The danger, of course, in revelling in nostalgia and growing old, is that one forgets the importance of young people, particularly when one has not had children. Our royal settlement had become a staid place, headed by those of middling years. There was Vellocatus and I, childless, Antikia and Shamatin, childless, and Namandea, also childless and without a mind to couple. Presivin and Davit had families and to my shame I had not previously taken much interest. One of Davit's reedy sons came to my roundhouse one day with some message or other and his naive, innocent bearing caught my eye for once. I saw how green he was, like some tended sapling, unaware and falsely brave.

"How old are you now?" I asked him.

"Fifteen turns."

"And do you hunt?"

"Yes, very well. I brought home a boar last full moon."

"A boar! Well done. That's a challenge indeed."

"I have its teeth. See." He reached into his tunic and pulled out a leather thong on which hung two sharpened fangs. He dangled them in front of me, eagerly then dropped them back into place, trying to conceal his display of boyishness.

"Your father must be very proud," I said. He gave a half-nod.

"You have a brother, don't you?"

"Yes, younger than me by three years. And a sister, but she's just a bairn."

"Ah, I see. So you're the eldest boy. And you look after your mother, when your father is away?"

"I do. I look after the animals for her and see to the fire and all that. She says she'd never cope without me." Again, the boyish pride. It reminded me of Venutius from long ago, like a mild stab to my chest.

"Well I should like you to hunt with me sometime and perhaps we can catch another boar for your mother, what do you think?"

"I'd very much like to," he answered.

His name was Estoroc and I resolved to meet his siblings.

"I met Davit's eldest today," I said to Vellocatus later. "A nice boy, well-mannered and knows his way with a bow and a spear. He killed a boar last moon."

"Oh yes, I remember the quarters being shared out. He's a good boy, though Davit has his hands full with him. You know what they're like at that age."

"I don't really."

"Don't you remember? When you think you know everything and you argue with your parents all the time."

"I didn't really do that," I said, trying hard to remember if I was difficult at that age.

"Ah, it was different for you. You concentrated very hard on learning from Kesaven. Most children flout everything their father says and find their own way. Davit says Estoroc disappears off on his own all the time and it makes him furious. He wants to teach the boy all the skills he needs, but Estoroc would rather learn by himself."

"He struck me as being quite independent. Surely that's a good thing?"

"Maybe. But when you're a parent, I suppose it's hard to let go."

"How would you know?" I sounded snappy though I hadn't meant to be.

"I'm guessing really. I mean, imagine having a baby and it's so defenceless. You have to hold it and feed it and do everything for it and then it grows up and suddenly doesn't need you any more. I think it would be hard to let go after all that, especially when you know your child isn't as clever as he thinks he is."

"Everyone has to make mistakes," I mused.

"But a mistake on a hunt could be very dangerous."

"I suppose so. You think I'm cold, don't you?"

"Not at all. You just haven't had that bond with a child." There was a lull. I could see he was trying to find a way to backtrack from this uncomfortable conversation.

"I've asked Estoroc to come hunting with me," I said.

"Good, good. He'll be delighted. He admires you so much."

"Really?"

"Of course. You're his leader after all."

Flattery always appealed to me and I thought it would be quite nice to spend more time with the other young people in our settlement. Presivin's woman had born him four children and I took the eldest two, a boy and a girl, with me on the same hunting trip as I took Estoroc. They were friends already – a little social circle which I observed with fascination. Estoroc and the girl, Invas, were the same age and poked light-hearted taunts at each other as they tried to pick up animal tracks. Invas's older brother, Masga, shook his head with mock impatience and tried to join with me in some kind of shared adult condescension towards the pair, but I was having none of his snooty pretensions. By the time we returned from that trip, Presivin's cautious eldest son had relaxed and the three were all easier in their bearing with me. I didn't want to command constant deference from them. I remembered that people showed my father great respect whilst being at ease in his presence and that he could enjoy their company without losing his authority.

Three days before the next council meeting, Masga came to see me.

"Given my age," he said, after a polite hello, "I think I should be able to attend the meeting. My father is a council member, my grandfather before him was a respected elder and probably I shall be a proper part of the council one day too."

Despite my new fondness for some of the young people in our settlement, I hesitated at this rather forward request. In the past decade, the tensions and fragilities that bound our council of elders together had eased into common understanding, tolerance and like-mindedness. Davit's war-hunger had faded, Presivin's shyness had abated, Antikia had more or less stopped playing her careful word games and Vellocatus had found his feet. The times we had lived through continued to shape our manner with each other and I could not imagine upsetting that well-developed balance after all this time. Namandea was one of the most recent people to gain status on the council and, even with her quiet, considered attitude, it had taken us time to adapt to a newcomer in the circle. How could a boy who barely remembered the battles with Venutius, who had no memory of a time before Roman occupancy, hope to understand the context that coloured all our decision-making? The council had often contained warriors or craftspeople or seers who were young, but these were positions exceptionally earned and offered, rather than presumptuously demanded as some kind of right. People on the council were either advisers or elders and this boy in front of me resembled neither.

"Masga, age alone doesn't bestow entrance to the council. When we have a free and open meeting, you can be present, but this coming meeting is one of elders and advisers only and I cannot allow you to attend." I smiled in what I hoped was a suitably sympathetic manner.

"Then I respectfully insist that I be considered eligible for the council as an adviser." The ridge of Masga's high cheekbones had begun to turn pinkish and his eyes were piercing. He hadn't visited me on a whim; he was quite determined.

"That won't be possible at this stage. I'm afraid you're too young with not enough experience. Someone entering the council usually has experience of warfare, travel, trading or the like. They can offer a viewpoint that will add to my own knowledge. When you are a few years older, then you'll be more ready for such a role."

"You were younger than I am and without any experience," he challenged, the flushing spreading down over his collarbones.

"I was Kesaven's daughter and we were in very turbulent times," I answered.

"These are turbulent times," he countered, trying to keep his voice steady.

"That is enough," I said. "I've given you my answer."

"Yes, you have," he said, with a slight bow of the head.

After he left, I fretted over the turn our conversation had taken. With so much past unrest within our tribe, I hardly wanted to let some slight insult nurse itself into a festering resentment, and I had seen that look of Masga's before. I had seen it on Venutius, every time he wore one of my refusals to bestow more power. Look where that had led! But what was I to do with this child? I spoke to Presivin about the conversation when I next encountered him.

"I gathered something had been said," he told me, "by the moody way that Masga has been behaving."

"He's holding a grudge?" I asked, alarmed and also offended.

"Nothing so adult," Presivin chuckled, "but I think his pride is a bit dented."

"I couldn't let him into the council."

"I know, I wouldn't have let him in myself, and the little brat should have asked me before he came to you anyway. I'm glad you knocked him back. It'll teach him a lesson."

Presivin kicked at the ground with the toe of his sandal and looked away. I had the sense that he didn't really know or understand his eldest son. I guessed it must be a sore point.

"How is Invas? I haven't seen her for a while."

"Always busy. She was up and out early this morning. Probably going up the stream to splash about and try catching some fish." He smiled as he spoke of his second-born child.

"She's a lovely girl. I think Estoroc is taking a lot of interest in her."

"They've always been close. They were born near the same time, you know, so they've grown up together. Perhaps they'll settle for each other." He shrugged. "Well, I'll be off."

He had left me with an image that hooked painfully at my own memories for the rest of the day.

AUTUMN AD67

A trader came, towards the end of the year when the wind was blowing a gale and scattering honey-coloured leaves all over the fields. He carried blankets and rolls of slim, woven fabric, packed tight into a box cart. I inspected his goods and chose a beautiful thick woollen piece that would add to our bedding at night. Vellocatus was complaining of the cold, even though the temperature had a long way yet to plummet through our dark, northern winter. I made up the bed with the cloth laid under a tanned leather square and a large fox-fur blanket that had been gifted to me once. With all those covers and a roaring fire, I would be roasted but the aches and pains Vellocatus suffered would hopefully subside.

"I'm sorry I'm such a nuisance," he said, shuffling about, seating himself by the flames with a drink of warmed ale.

"You're no nuisance to me," I answered. "How are you feeling? Are you in pain?"

He gazed into the fire as if he hadn't heard me. I went to sit by him.

"Are you very ill, do you think?" I half-whispered the question because I didn't really want to hear the answer. Vellocatus had always been so stoic and present. Now he felt almost intangible, waning away beside me. I put an arm around him and he curled against me like a child.

"I'm going to struggle through this winter," he said, closing his eyes. I bit hard at the inside of my lip. I didn't like to cry, but the tears pressed sharply at my eyes and I had to force down a heaving in my chest.

"Amelan can make you some more tonic. We'll keep this fire going all the time and you're not to go out any more. No walking or riding, not while it's cold like this."

He gave no argument, just made a sound of acquiescence. He fell asleep against me and I stayed next to him, to keep him warm and comfortable. I tried to sleep, but there was a nagging in me, a biting feeling that I had left something undone, or ill-done. My mind rolled around, touching on the years and all the mess of a life I had left behind. As I rested there beside Vellocatus, I knew what it was I wanted, what we had to do. When he came to, I told him.

"I'm going to make a formal separation from Venutius."

"Why? It would cause so many problems."

"Why should it? It makes no difference. He's still leader of the Carvettii, with or without me. He gains nothing from being bound to me. It must hold him back as much as it does me."

"I don't think that's how he will see it."

"Nevertheless, I'm decided. I'm declaring myself free of him, and announcing my union with you, officially."

"Before I die," Vellocatus added, blackly humourous.

"Something like that," I replied, with a sad smile.

"I don't need you to do that for me," he said.

"I know. I'm the one who needs it." And I did need it. I can't say why, but it was suddenly so important to get this right, to have something that was clear-cut and true to how I felt. Venutius and I had made such a mess of things, but what Vellocatus and I had was solid and right. It needed that final blessing, that recognition to complete it. I can't explain it more than that.

The messenger went the next day. Poor man, he had a grim set of fear on his mouth, for he knew what he carried and had no idea how Venutius would respond. I had written one sentence. It said "We are no longer bound together." In a leather draw-string pouch I had placed the jewellery he had given me when we married, in case he was in any doubt. I had consulted the council and they had assented to my wishes, though with great trepidation. No one would argue because they could all see how ill Vellocatus was. Whatever people had thought about our relationship at the beginning, they had all come to accept and respect him in the intervening years.

As we watched the messenger head out, over the meadow path to the north-west, Antikia came to me.

"Shall I organise the ceremony?" She asked.

I nodded. The wind whipped past us, sharp as a horse lash. Antikia gave a shudder. Her cloak hung loose around her frame which was slightly stooped these days. She was fifty eight years of age, to my forty six. The years had fallen around us, crisp and used up.

"Try and keep it calm, simple. I know we'll have to invite the legate and inform governor Maximus but Vellocatus won't want a big show."

"No," Antikia concurred. "Maybe that's just as well. You don't want to rub Venutius's face in it."

"It would be hard for me to care less about Venutius," I answered.

There was a lull in the wind followed by the frantic chirruping of a bird. Smudges of cloud sailed overhead, casting dismal shadows. I turned back towards my roundhouse, stifling the sigh of resigned misery that threatened to erupt. I could feel Antikia's eyes on my back, her words left unsaid. As I've aged, I've noticed how all the missed opportunities, the mistakes, the omissions seem to accumulate and destabilize a life. You wish you could have lived perfectly, always saying and doing the right thing at the right time, and even though you know that was never possible, still you carry the pain and guilt for failing to achieve it. Or maybe that's just me. I turned back to my aunt then and reached out my arms to her, trying to get at least that one moment right.

"This is the way it has to be," I said, as she held me. "whatever comes of it."

"You must do what you have to," she replied into my hair, planting a firm kiss on my head.

"Thank you. For everything. For all of it."

"It's what I'm here for." She rubbed my back briskly and released me. The messenger was out of sight, carrying the one simple sentence that would in turn bring on all our fates.

The Roman presence at the joining ritual was limited, in the end. They had their hands full still, fighting small pockets of resistance and consolidating southern towns and defences that had clawed their way back from the Boudicca's wrath. Since Maximus had taken over as governor some four or so years previous, I had hardly corresponded with him, except for brief and impersonal official missives that I was obliged to send every now and then. I informed him that I was dissolving my personal union with Venutius and taking a new mate, but I phrased it all carefully so as not to alarm him and indeed, being unfamiliar with the precise details and implications of our recent history, he probed no further. If any of his own staff had bothered to properly inform themselves and their Governor of the short but bloody war between myself and Venutius, perhaps he would have taken some action or at least interest. As it was, rather than being piqued at their sniggering contempt for our internal politics, I was simply satisfied that we could continue with our plans unimpeded and Maximus, in his ignorance, was happy to leave us to it.

Strictly speaking, there was an impedance, though not from the Roman direction. A small deputation arrived from the Carvettii, carrying with them a reply from Venutius. I had hoped he would not reply at all, but at least thanked my stars that he had not travelled personally to address me. He did not even send any family or long-serving council members, perhaps remembering what I had done last time such a group entered my territory uninvited. Instead a rather homely looking man of middling years, in a coarse robe the colour of dust and with hair and beard to match, came riding in with a few companions claiming to be an accomplished seer and with great delicacy and subservience, relayed an impassioned account from Venutius that a binding such as ours could not so easily be broken and that I should consider the unity of our great tribe. Our blood bond, conveyed the messenger (and I winced at the term, since we had produced no children to justify it) was what held our people together. It had been desired by our ancestors and our councils and was not for any one person to throw over. Venutius, through his humble mouthpiece, did not accuse or attack me directly, but appealed as if to my better nature to recognise the benefits of our existing arrangements. It was a strangely deadening attempt to persuade me, since it drew to light, rather than denied, the sterile, mechanical and doomed nature of our relationship. I ignored it. I fed and housed the party overnight and sent them back, wordless, to their council and Venutius. For better or for worse, you might say.

Davit and Estoroc tracked the group as they headed home over the hills, just to make sure they really were going back to the Carvettii. Estoroc was maturing quickly, and with the passage of just a few years, much of the defiance Davit had once observed in his son had faded into a resilient if tempered ambition. The pair spent a lot of time together and I had grown to like the boy and the fresh, if naive, opinions he offered. He no longer played and hunted with Invas, whose attentions seemed focused on another boy, but I had seen him watch her from afar and sometimes thought I saw her return his glances. These youthful romances made me sentimental but I bit my tongue and kept out of it. Masga remained the only fly in the ointment and I felt my skin crawl whenever he was around. Poor Presivin, to have raised that young man! I don't know how it happened that an honourable and quiet council elder spawned such a bitter and presumptuous offshoot. Masga made a pretence of deference to me, but he betrayed himself constantly with the ticks, grimaces and eye darts that passed over his countenance when he thought I wasn't looking. He truly resented being refused access to the council and clearly couldn't understand my reasoning. When I saw him with his group of friends, I felt discomforted. It was on my mind to remove the lot of them from the royal stronghold, but I couldn't quite bring myself to inflict that insult upon Presivin.

We didn't wait long to marry. Vellocatus continued to ache and suffer, so we held our ceremony just before autumn swept into winter, while the trees still held their scarlet and bronze tresses and the mist left a glossy hue on the fields. Antikia supervised the feast, which was extensive at over twice the size her own had been. The smell of cooking hung over the whole homestead for several days in advance, and great platters of cured meats and flavoured breads stood under cloths waiting for consumption. The legate residing nearest to us arrived with a small entourage the day before and brought with him a gift of a cartload of amphorae - half of wine and half of oil. It was a kind gesture, though not entirely selfless since they consumed a good amount of the former before they left. Heads of the smaller tribes arrived throughout the days leading up to it and brought with them all kinds of presents, some of Roman origin and some of native craftsmanship. I had enough Samian bowls and jugs to sink a small ship, their rich red colour so befitting the season that I had them used to serve much of the food. I saw faces I had not seen for many years - including the odd person who remembered me as a child or recalled one or other of my parents from way back down the years. It was good to see so many old friends and loyal Brigantians.

On the day of our wedding, the sun rose white and splendid behind thin veils of cloud, coating the morning with a cool lustre. A slight wind brushed the skies clean by mid-morning and though it was cool, the sun shone down and put us all in good spirits. We sat out in the meadow for the ceremony itself, so all could see and hear us, as we presided on large carved wooden chairs and had our hands bound together with dyed and plaited rope. I called on the gods and goddesses to look upon our union and bless it with their approval and in the white-gold sunshine of that special day, I believed that they did. The crowd stayed respectfully silent as I spoke and as Vellocatus offered his own invocation to the deities and then they clapped and cheered and hastened us to the feast, which, at a wedding, is all anybody really cares about anyway.

Shamatin gave us a beautiful gift of ornate paired swords which he had fashioned himself over many moons and which had precious stones embedded in the hilts. I have never seen such pretty blades before or since and I still do not know if he had created them with myself and Vellocatus in mind. Namandea rose as we ate and sang a tale she had composed herself of our love, which was perhaps a little sickly-sweet, but very tuneful. Antikia presented us with an olive tree, gnarled and peculiar, that she had obtained by covert and persistent communications with an importer in Londinium. The day was on the whole a peaceful and happy one.

As we listened to music and watched a dance in the afternoon, Patissa who had travelled from her Tectoverdian settlement to the north, came to talk with me. I had not seen her since the leaders of Brigantia's tribes had met to agree a course of action with respect to the Roman invasion of Mona and she looked wizened beyond her years, with deep creases around her eyes and barely any of her thin hair left on her head. She had a tattoo of brown pin-pricks running between the remaining plaited threads, giving her an almost feral appearance. She briefly congratulated me and wished me health and happiness.

"Thank you Patissa," I said and enquired after her own family.

"They're well enough. I have grandchildren grown now. But they go their own way." She lifted her shoulders in contented resignation. I nodded, having no real comment of my own to add.

"We had one of your tribe with us for some time," she continued, as if it were a natural progression of the conversation. "Gorlensa. Your wise old woman."

I felt my breath solidify in my chest and a prickly heat spread over my forehead and neck.

"Had? Is she no longer with you?" I asked, clearing my throat.

"She died, two winters back. She was so ancient, I'm amazed she lasted that long but she was a tough woman. Very steadfast."

"We didn't know where she had gone," I said. "She left us as we returned from the war host."

"Ah really? She didn't join us until many moons later." There was a pause as we each considered.

"She left us under the cloud of the Mona decision. How was she when she came to you?" I had made to walk away from the revelry and Patissa followed me to a quieter spot, away from the roundhouse and the dancing.

"She was disturbed. Even when she settled in with us, she made many trips to different places, alone. Rivers, streams, waterfalls. I think she was speaking to the deities of all those places, but whether to ask their help or to further glimpse the future, I can't say."

"Probably both," I answered. "She was very unhappy with our decision. We assumed that was why she left. Why did no one send a message to us that she was there?"

"We didn't know it was necessary, that she had left without your knowledge. If we had, we wouldn't have felt it was our place." Patissa looked uncomfortable. "She was capable of contacting you if she wanted, but I think she must have needed the separation. I suppose she chose to come to us because we, the elders of our tribe at least, shared her view. Though we acceded naturally to the majority, being a faithful tribe of Brigantia."

"There's no question about that," I reassured her. "But it is a shame she left people to worry after her. Her niece, Namandea, found it hard to lose her. We all did."

"If it helps, I think she found some peace, towards the end. People seem to accept things, when they know the end is near."

"Thank you for telling me all this," I said, "Perhaps you could speak to Namandea?"

"Of course," Patissa said, "I'll find her now, and leave you to enjoy the rest of your day."

She gripped my hand firmly for a moment and then wandered back into the throng of people. I was left standing alone, discomforted by the revelation. I was happy to know that Gorlensa had lived out her days in safety among like-minded people, but it hurt that she had cut herself so cleanly away from us, like a healer slices the diseased flesh from the healthy. She must have actually instructed people not to reveal her presence and perhaps even hidden herself when those who might recognise her visited the Tectoverdi.

I saw Vellocatus looking for me and conscious of his continued ill-health, which had only just withstood the outdoor ceremony, I went to him and guided him back inside where the fire and dancing kept everyone warm in the fading autumn day.

"Patissa told me Gorlensa lived with them after she left us," I explained, as we took our seats behind the feast table. "She died peacefully, after spending her days communing with the gods and goddesses, but never wanted to contact us."

"Ah," breathed Vellocatus, "Well at least we know now."

"Yes," I said, with more confidence than I felt.

"It's in the past," he said, taking my hand. "It's all in the past and we've played our parts as best as any of us could. There's no more to worry about. Let's just enjoy today."

The load in my chest seemed to lift off like a flock of birds alighting. He always had that power over me. I turned my heart and mind back to my wedding, with the shackles of history thrown, for the time being, to one side.

SUMMER AD68

We passed through the winter unscathed, by which I mean that Vellocatus did not die nor deteriorate. He kept inside, by the fire and took his various medicines and rubbed on his various ointments as instructed and we held each other close and talked for hours. It was the beginning of the end for us, but we were both determined to savour and prolong every last drop. Wrapped up in our snow-bound stronghold, we lost sight of the world outside and little cared for it. There was nothing for me beyond the confines of our homestead and in my increasing age, I sometimes thought about the burden of governance and how I would take little persuading to put it aside. They were the short, dark days of winter, when the heart naturally closes in and shores up its defences and the body retreats and rests. By the time the buds sprang from the branches I was recovering a little from my hibernation and returning to the more active duties of the tribal chief and client queen. We had strange and confused accounts of Rome and Nero, but they passed through so many mouths we could barely trust what rumours we heard and there had always been foul gossip about the leaders of Rome anyway, so we paid no mind. Back, then, to counting out taxes and paying our local representatives of the Governor.

We admitted, that Spring, new blood to our council. In the past few years, Estoroc had impressed everyone with his general abilities, from the old, largely recreational skills of hunting and tracking, to the newer ones of communicating diplomatically with our Roman allies and increasing the import and export trade. He had even spent time in the north, dealing with our old border issues that still niggled from time to time. He was invited along with two others to take a permanent seat in the council of elders, though I regret to say that poor Masga was not among this fortunate trio. He had spoiled his chances long before and never recovered himself. The friendships he had nurtured with other rebellious people of his age continued unchecked as his parents looked on helplessly. Presivin had given up trying any influence with his eldest son, putting more effort into his younger offspring. After the council expanded without him, Masga's pride took him from us. He left, with a group of others, after a cursory goodbye to his mother and father. I had misgivings about it, even whilst I was glad to be rid of his supercilious attitude, since I hated to make enemies and even more so, hated for them to be out of my sight and control.

Still, onwards we went, through the green leafy year towards the summer, where all my world began to dissolve. It began firstly with a visit from the legate, who had so cheerfully consumed the wine at my wedding. He was weary and confused as he sat with us to run through the usual business - tax, trade issues, boundary problems; anything, in short, that our Roman masters should know about.

"We've heard terrible news from Rome," he admitted at last, "Emperor Nero is dead, of his own hand."

"No!" I clapped a hand to my mouth, "What will happen now?" Much as I hated our enforced obedience, any instability in Rome could be considered contagious to our own tribal health.

"It will be resolved," he answered and was unwilling to speak more on the topic. Indeed, I think he had wished to stay entirely silent and just could not help but divulge the grave news which was causing him so much concern. Without a strong leader and a clear heading, the tiny chinks and gaps in the huge Roman empire would come under strain and our far-off isles were full of chinks and gaps. It occurred to me that if significant parts of our occupying Roman forces were recalled home to deal with civil strife, then it would be as if all the game pieces had been tossed in the air again and we could face rebellion and tribal warfare as everyone took advantage of the turn of events. I had just enraged Venutius with my marriage. It was not a good time for my Roman protectors to be experiencing turmoil.

Out walking in the summer sun, with the chirruping and clicking of birds and insects all around, it was hard to imagine that we might be at the start of such an awful load of trouble and when I wandered alone across my old paths and quiet places, I shut my mind off from all of it. I walked alone these days because Vellocatus did not have the energy to accompany me. Through winter I had not minded staying close by him all the time, but now the restorative heat and sweet, perfumed breezes were upon us, I had the need in me to set out sometimes and escape into the woods or fields. I needed the time alone to think and to prepare. We both knew I would lose him and be left alone, probably until the end of my days. With the clement weather, I hardly thought it would happen so soon.

Yet, always the blow comes when it is least expected and sure enough, just after midsummer, Vellocatus started to slip away. He kept to our bed and hardly ate any food. I sat by him and tried to make him sip drinks and broth. When he complained of being cold, I put blankets over him, though it was warm enough in the roundhouse to make me sweat.

After so many years in each others company, you'd expect we'd have been entirely comfortable speaking openly with each other, but somehow both of us were constrained by the threat of death and neither of us talked directly of it. I was scared that to speak of it would encourage him towards it and I suppose he was scared that to speak of it would distress me, so we talked about pointless things instead. We almost pretended it wasn't happening.

Six days after becoming so poorly, he finally let go. In the afternoon he asked me if I would be able to cope and I said not to worry about me, I would be fine. I wanted to say more. I wanted to ask him so many things, but he was exhausted and his face, once so golden with youth, was white and lined with age and pain. I stroked his forehead and kissed him on the lips. He held my hand as his breathing became ragged and uneven. On it went, his breath stopping and starting and at some point his eyes closed and did not open again. I laid my cheek against his chest and waited there until at last it failed to rise again. When Amelan touched my shoulder to bring me back to myself, I lifted my head up and was surprised to see the gaunt, middle-aged man on my bed, when in my mind I had been gazing at a tall boy with tanned arms lying next to me in a grassy meadow. I pressed my fingers to my eyes and wailed, then wrapped my arms around his body, so still and heavy, and held him for a long time.

People had begun to gather outside. I could hear the murmuring and shuffling but I wanted no part in it. Amelan, good girl, went to the entrance and shooed them all away. I was alone in my grief. I had lost what had made me whole and I knew, as I held him, that I was losing a part of myself. With my mother and father both dead and Venutius and his family gone from me, I had no one left to anchor me in the world, no one who knew my whole history and my place in it. I am alone, the voice in my head cried. Then Antikia came beside me and placed her age-spotted hand over mine. My faithful aunt, always there, always guiding me. I left off holding Vellocatus and clung instead to her as she drew me away and sat me down, asking Amelan to bring me a tonic of valerian and camomile.

"It hurts so much," I cried, by way of an apology for my useless state.

"Of course it does," she answered, "Just let the grief in so it can do its worst and leave again."

When Amelan brought my drink, Antikia held it to my mouth and made me swallow it, then held me against her, where I sobbed until the herbal medicine did its job and sent me off to sleep.

★

"We should let her sleep, she'll feel better for it." A voice from far away, drifting in my mind.

"I say wake her up. We must deal with the body, given the heat today." A hot day, my mind noted. A hot summer day. Why was I sleeping? I stirred, unwillingly.

"Ah, she's coming to, anyway," the second voice approved.

I sat up with my eyes still sealed, hardly able to bear the pain of opening them and facing the world. For a few seconds I couldn't remember what agonies I was so afraid of encountering.

"Is it any wonder?" grumbled Antikia. "You made enough of a noise about it."

"What did you give me the sleeping drink for, if you were going to disturb me so soon?" I groaned bitterly. "Couldn't you just let me be for a little while."

Davit leaned towards me and put a heavy hand on my shoulder.

"We must move Vellocatus," he said. "The platform is ready and the sun is already past the tree-line. We should move him now, while it's light."

I drew in a long, ragged breath. I wanted to be sick. Instead I rose and went to my dead lover. I stroked his forehead and the soft hair that fell back from it.

"You can move him," I answered. "He's long gone now."

Davit came towards me, looking as if he was going to say something, but I silenced him with an upheld palm and stepped past him, to sit back down.

"If anyone is still outside, move them away," I said. "Tell them to keep a distance, from me and him."

Davit nodded, then with his usual briskness, he fetched others – Shamatin, Presivin and I think Estoroc – to help carry Vellocatus out to the platform. I watched them move him onto a woollen blanket and, taking a corner each, lift him up and heave him out of the roundhouse.

I'll pass over all the mourning and grieving that followed, since it remains too close and painful for me still. Suffice to say,

319

he was laid out, just as I had laid out my parents so many years before, for nature to do its job and dispose of his body. I would have remained in my forlorn misery for a longer time, but the wolf was once more rattling the gate and I had no sooner said goodbye to Vellocatus than Venutius appeared on our horizon once more.

His council requested a meeting with our own, to discuss recent events, by which they meant my binding to Vellocatus. I assumed they had heard of his death and I found their communication with me distasteful and provocative so I ignored it. Perhaps I was being short-sighted – certainly my own council started to think so, for they brought pressure to bear on me before the summer of my great loss was even over.

"We must meet with them and find a way to pacify the Carvettii," argued Shamatin at a tense and uncomfortable meeting of elders.

"What way is there," I replied, "other than to deny my bond with Vellocatus?"

"Maybe that is the way," he persisted. "After all, with Vellocatus now sadly gone, maybe the lesser evil is to reaffirm ties with Venutius."

I scoffed at him, finding the suggestion ridiculous, but everyone else was silent. Even Antikia had averted her eyes from me.

"What? You think I should do this?" I asked them all.

"You might put us all in danger if you don't," said Namandea. "The legions are preoccupied. If Venutius invades again, we'll receive no support and we are ill-prepared for an attack."

"Venutius won't invade," I said, with more confidence than I felt. "He has too much to lose."

"Or maybe he sees that with Rome in disarray, he has much to gain," she answered. "If he deposes you while the Governor looks the other way, will Rome much care if it is him they have the client agreement with rather than you?"

"They will if it means strife and rebellion within their territory, and that is what would happen. Brigantia won't just fall happily under Venutius and his Carvettii upstarts."

"Are you sure?" asked Shamatin. "I hear Venutius has put some effort into cultivating friendships in the north. We already know that the Tectoverdi were terribly unhappy with our decision over Mona–"

"Patissa is a friend," I said, affronted, "and Venutius was against defending Mona as well."

"Yes, he was back then, but he may be making all kinds of offers and promises now - maybe with no intention of fulfilling them, but if it gains him allies, he'll say anything."

"Patissa isn't that stupid," I said.

"Patissa is an old woman," Namandea answered, "and the younger members of her council may well side with Venutius, if he is believable enough. Look how that old fox, Caratacus, had people eating out of his hand, fighting wars for him."

"Do you think Venutius is that cunning?" I asked with some scorn, "and that my own people are so disloyal?"

"Some of them may be swaying to him," Antikia spoke up at last, "because they are unhappy with your recent actions. Many will have disagreed with you binding to Vellocatus and over-turning a long-standing tribal pact that was supposed to unite Brigantia."

Silence fell like a knife between us all. It had taken Antikia to say what none of them dared to voice. I bit back anger that roared up within me like fire, stood up and walked away.

I talked to none of them for days. Amelan moved quietly about me, as she had since Vellocatus died, and the rest had the sense to stay well away. I had lost weight because I wasn't eating and as the temperature began to drop and the hunter's moon appeared huge and round in the daytime sky, my body ached and my head seemed permanently held in a fist of pain. I was losing my grip on everything - my friends, my people, my land and even my own life. It spiralled away from me at that point and even in the depth of my grief I had a sense that I would never, no matter how hard I tried, be able to drag it all back to me. Every day seemed increasingly hopeless, until at last Davit fractured the shield of my self-imposed exile and pulled me a little way back into the world.

I found him sitting waiting for me, after I stumbled back from a slow, pointless walk, and I almost ordered him out.

"Amelan left this," he said, holding out a bowl of stew. "You need to eat it. You look terrible."

I was famished so I took the bowl from him and slumped down into my seat.

"Do you ever think back to what a fool I used to be?" he said, smiling. "How headstrong! I was up for a fight all the time. But now, ha!" He settled back and threw his arms up with a laugh, patting his thinning hair. "You disliked me back then," he remembered.

"Yes I did," I replied, in an intolerant mood. "You wasted council time more than once."

"And could have put us in danger, if anyone had owned the bad sense to listen to me."

"You talked reason sometimes," I said, grudgingly.

"Just occasionally."

"You didn't speak at the last meeting." I took a mouthful of warm pork, boiled till tender and stewed in a mix of spices with chunks of flat bread soaking in the gravy.

"I had nothing sensible to say," he answered, in mock seriousness.

"Tell me what you think," I said, brushing away his light-heartedness.

"Does it matter what I think?"

"What's the point of having you on the council if you won't answer me," I snapped.

"None at all. A council has to be able to speak, and speak freely," he agreed.

"All right, you've made your point," I groaned. "Just get on with it."

"I think they're right to be worried. Venutius has some heavy activity going on, and the northern parts seem receptive to it. He's presenting this as some kind of final opportunity to thwart Rome, while her back is turned."

"You know, that's what we encouraged the southern rebels to do long ago when the governors were changing over. They acted at the wrong time," I recalled.

"You did what?" Davit looked perplexed and I recalled that I had not taken the council fully into my confidence at that time.

"It doesn't matter, all water under the bridge now. You were saying about Venutius?"

"He's playing on this split between you, arguing that you're defying the old ways, breaking bonds of union and casting off the sub-tribes to whom you owe your protection."

"That's rubbish. I'm not casting any of them off."

"But see through their eyes, Cartimandua. You fill the slave quotas by taking from the smaller tribes on the outskirts of our lands. Querns through the land run empty when we have to provide grain for the legions, but ours remain half-full. People feel they're suffering while you and your own are protected. There's a natural hierarchy in Brigantia and Venutius is playing on it to draw people to his side. Circumstances are favourable to him and he's taking his last chance, before he gets too old to act."

"Then how will reaffirming my bond to him help, if he is so determined to make a last stand against Rome and I?"

"Beyond taking the moral sting from some of his passionate diatribes against you? Not at all, I suspect."

"So you don't agree that I should capitulate on this," I said.

"I think your time would be better spent preparing for war.

Call a host, smash Venutius down before he gains any ground." Davit's eyes gleamed as he spoke, but his face was drawn and serious.

"I don't think I can," I answered. "I haven't got any fight left in me."

"Then find it, or you truly will lose everything," he said, with more compassion than I would have expected. "We've all suffered losses, but a chief can't let personal grief wreck a whole tribe. It's not fair, but that's the way it is for you."

I laughed, making Davit jump.

"I don't need you to tell me that. Haven't I spent a lifetime learning the truth of what you've just said?"

"Then what will you do?" he persisted.

I sighed and stood up.

"I thought this part was all over years ago," I said, walking around the great circular central room of my grand house. "How can I face going into battle at my age?"

"We've had peace for a while, it's true, but nothing lasts. If anything, we should be grateful for the good times we've had."

I felt this comment as a rebuke.

"Vellocatus has been dead such a short while and you want me to be happy and grateful already?"

"No, of course not. I just meant that, in this world, upheaval seems more common than peace and so war has inevitably rolled back round again. We may as well moan at the winds and rains of autumn as complain of war in Brigantia."

I knew he was right and that he was being as careful and tactful with me as possible. Deep down inside me, I also knew that Davit's gentle prodding was the precursor to the enormous kick in the backside I was going to have to give myself. I reached up to my temples and found with my fingertips the black feathers I had braided in with my hair. They laid smooth and waxy against my own increasingly silvery brown hair. I tugged at the pointed shafts and drew them slowly out. My father had faced this same challenge once, not altogether successfully, and I would face it too. The time had arrived to put my grief to one side and get on with living.

I had risen from my mourning slumber not a moment too soon and perhaps a good deal too late. The following day, my homestead was hit by the terrible shock that several council members had deserted us, travelling away like cowards in the middle of the night. Davit and Antikia came to me trembling and whey-faced.

"We've lost Namandea and her family. Presivin is gone too, with his woman and children," said Antikia, swallowing hard.

"Gone to Venutius?" I asked, with a plummeting stomach.

"We think so. They may have been in contact with Presivin's boy, Masga. Our guess is that Masga and his friends travelled to the Carvettii and then persuaded Presivin to follow."

"Presivin? I can't believe it," I said. "He's always stood by me. He didn't even like Masga!"

"A father's feelings for an eldest son can't be so easily destroyed," said Davit. "Presivin loves Masga. And Namandea has always held a grudge for the loss of her aunt."

"She sang at my wedding," I said, incredulously, "She was happy for me and she agreed with the decision not to defend Mona!"

"Ah well, sometimes people just jump out when they think a boat is sinking," he replied. "A lot of people are worried that Venutius may have the strength to defeat you now while Rome is worrying about itself and you're in mourning."

"Oh for the sake of the goddess," I cried, "How can I fight him, if the people closest to me are turning away?"

"It's only two people," soothed Antikia. "The rest of us are still here and most people still see you as rightful chief."

"Can we be sure of that?" I asked, wildly, "I mean, the south of our lands still bear the grudge of the rebellion, when they watched their leaders crucified. The Tectoverdians to our north resent the decision over Mona and you said yourselves that my old relationship with Patissa would count for nothing as the younger blood takes over her council. Then in the north west, there's the old hatred for Rome, from people who've felt none of the benefit of our alliance because I've been too busy taking their people as slaves for the emperor. Venutius must be having a wonderful time, gathering in all the families who have either a problem with me or a problem with Rome. How large is his army already? Where is he, even? For all I know, he could be marching upon me now and I'm all but defenceless!" I was out of breath, almost gasping, as the situation hit me like an axe in the head.

"He's not marching," said Davit. "But he is in the north. You're right that he's taking advantage of whatever ill-feeling he can find."

"Why didn't we see that this was happening?" I asked, "How could we miss it?"

"It's all come on so fast," said Antikia. "The binding to Vellocatus obviously offended Venutius greatly and then for Nero to die so unexpectedly and Vellocatus to die also, leaving you bereaved, weaker, well, it all just adds up to give Venutius the best opportunity he's ever likely to get. We couldn't have seen this coming."

"But I should have been more prepared," I said, "My father ran Brigantia through the relationships he built with hundreds of families across the land and I've let it all of it slip. What if they all desert me now?"

Antikia and Davit stayed silent.

"Call the war host," I commanded. "We have to find out how bad this is."

The call went out. My messengers travelled at lightning speed through Brigantia, issuing notice that the war host was summoned and must report immediately to my royal fortress. I did not send any kind of message into Carvettii territory, though Antikia was still hopeful that I might try to pacify Venutius.

"There's no point," I told her. "He's moving against me; the signs are plain to see. This time it's all or nothing for him. He'll take my tribe or die trying. I can feel it in my blood."

Indeed, word was travelling from the north west that the Carvettii had mounted a defensive line of warriors at all the passable routes into their lands and that large groups had been seen travelling in that direction from northern and north-eastern Brigantia. I wanted to set up my own defensive line, to prevent traders from the south and east from reaching the Carvettii as I knew they would be storing up weapons and other supplies. I planned to intercept any such trade and take it by force for our own needs. I sent an urgent message to the Roman governor, explaining the current situation and requesting that assistance be provided if war erupted. It was a difficult and delicate message to craft because I wanted to be sure of some legionary support but I didn't want to alarm the governor into taking action against the whole of Brigantia.

An atmosphere of grim trepidation had entered my serene royal enclave and in my solitary moments, I cursed Venutius for plunging us into this turmoil. My pretty little garden, with its Mediterranean fruits and herbs, looked all at once exposed and vulnerable. I fingered the little jewels and ornaments that my association with Rome had brought me and felt how fragile and ephemeral they were. I had been careless. While I was re-building my own life with Vellocatus and managing relations with Rome, I had neglected the people who really mattered - my large and disparate tribe who ultimately had the power to maintain me as chief or cast me aside.

I waited two days and finally the war host descended. They stormed in on horses and chariots, on foot and by cart. Wearing heavy torques and my most exquisite gold chains and broaches, I made sure to hold myself tall and confident, greeting personally as many people as I could. The crowds were heartening but I could see gaps. The Tectoverdi had not sent any representatives and many of the other border tribes to the north had not responded either. Still, we surely had more in number than Venutius.

Estoroc had built a platform to shoulder height in the open grassland so I could stand and address the assembled warriors and councillors from a position of clear superiority. He and his friends had worked fast to put it together and I supposed that the labour took his mind off the loss of Invas, Presivin's daughter, whom he had loved for a long time and who had recently turned her attentions back to him, after flirtations with other boys. I understood the need to keep busy and not dwell on the pain of abandonment, because I felt it too, whenever I thought of Namandea and Presivin and of course I felt it whenever my mind skipped past all the mental walls I had built and touched on Vellocatus.

I wasted no time in stepping up onto that wooden structure and having my servants call everyone's attention to me. As heads turned and people pressed closer to hear, I began to speak, keeping it as brief and confident as I could. No weakness, no fear. If I showed either, I knew I was lost. I had to keep every last one of these men and women in my service.

"I've summoned you here to tell you we must go to war against the Carvettii again. Venutius is gathering an army and will invade Brigantia. He hopes to rule Brigantia and pretends he will overthrow our Roman governors. But we all know that is a lie. If he seizes power, he will resume his bond with those old fellow soldiers of his and be a far crueller leader to you than any of you could think I have been. Either that, or Rome will crush him like a beetle and sweep into our world to strip you of your weapons, land and freedom. Believe me, what we have now is freedom indeed compared to the south. You may resent the taxes; I do too, but they are the price we pay to keep our way of life. We cannot let Venutius destroy that. I lived with him a long time, I know him and I know that what he wants is power and riches. He may love his little Carvettii homeland, but he cares nothing for any of you or your land. Be ready to fight with me, when I call upon you and together we can hold Brigantia strong, in the face of all its enemies!"

All the upturned faces were grim, still and silent. My heart beat hard against my chest and I felt damp under my arms. People began to shuffle and glance at each other. Then, with only a second or two having passed, they erupted into a cheer and clanged their weapons. The noise spread across the fields and relief flooded into my tensed body. I had sounded the right note. I cannot say how many were teetering on the brink of deserting me and joining Venutius, but I knew as I looked around me that my chances of losing them had just diminished considerably. For a few moments I experienced genuine happiness and then I glanced around to catch Vellocatus's face to see what he thought of my speech. My smile died in my eyes. For the sake of all the expectant people watching, I made sure I kept it frozen onto my lips.

SPRING AD69

I wonder if you can feel it in the telling, the way I could feel it then – the slow, steady plod of time moving on and the end coming nearer. From the day Vellocatus died, the rising and setting of every sun seemed to drag me further away from him and inexorably on towards some inevitable, dreadful conclusion. It is fair to say that, for those privy to my more personal moments when these thoughts were at the fore, I was not a joy to be around.

After my rousing speech in the fields, I broke bread with the heads and elders and elite warriors and planned a course of action. We confirmed and agreed territorial control so that we could stem the supply of goods reaching Venutius. We estimated the levels of our weapons reserves and set a target for increased spear and arrow production. I let Davit and Antikia take control of most of the discussions – indeed the remainder of my council were steadfast and organised, despite the blow they had taken at the loss of two members. When all the plans were made, most of the war host left, but a hand-picked group of warriors stayed behind, to add to those we already had guarding the royal enclosure.

And then the winds came, followed by the frosts and the snow storms and we passed into the year you know as the 69th. It's hard to separate the complicated feelings I was experiencing. I don't know, even now, whether I was governed by my grief for Vellocatus or my fear of Venutius, or whether it was some dark brew of both that had seeped into me and filled me with so much misery and foreboding. As winter dragged on, the beauty of the white meadow, the icy trees and the blessedly impassable hill tracks settled somewhere in my consciousness, such that I can remember them now, but at the time, did not appreciate them at all. I had days, I must admit, when I seemed to live again. A conversation or a song or some gift or act of kindness would lift me up and remind me of a life worth living. Those days were few, but they were the stepping stones out of the current of sadness that had threatened to sweep me away.

When the birds began to chirrup once more, and the frosts receded, the word finally came. Venutius had breached the border of his land and was advancing with his army into Brigantia. From the frozen stillness of winter, we were thrust into the frantic expectation of summer warfare. I had patrols out in as much force as I could manage, with instructions to report to me or their closest noble superiors any suspicious activities or indeed overt campaigning. As reports filtered back, I called my immediate council together to share the overall impression of Venutius's progress.

"He's moving across the north, keeping close to the borders and leaving a defensive line behind him as he goes," I confirmed. "We know his council are moving with him and that he's bestowing rank and privilege on family heads who join him. They presumably agree to answer directly to him. In that way, he's securing the land as he goes."

"How very Roman," observed Antikia with a curled lip. The thought had occurred to me also, but rather than being amused at Venutius aping his supposed hated enemies, I was horrified that he had learned his lessons so well.

"What about numbers?" asked Estoroc.

"He's fast equalling our own," said Davit.

Outside, a breeze picked up and the drawn leather hanging over the entrance gave a gentle flap. Though summer was on the way, it was still cool enough to require a fire in the daytime. Shamatin poked at the one flickering in the centre of our gathering and sent a little shower of sparks scuttling over the floor. He withdrew his stick.

"Have we stopped the traders getting through to him?" he asked.

"I don't believe so," I answered with a sigh. "Delayed them,

331

perhaps, but he has too many friends now and they are providing safe routes."

We were all quiet as we contemplated the worrying state of affairs.

"I've been thinking," ventured Antikia, "that we should move further south. No, no, hear me out. We've always felt safe and protected here, but Venutius is making much more progress than we'd expected and our position puts us right on the front line. As Venutius gathers forces to the north, and gains new friends in the south, we'll be squeezed from both sides and forced to fight on his terms. If we fall back now to a position further away from him, we have a better chance of controlling the situation. The people in the south of Brigantia have become more accustomed to Roman occupation than those in the north and will more readily host and support us. We'll be closer to Roman assistance if we should need it and we can avoid any serious surprises to our rear."

"Leave my home?" I said, appalled. "This is where the bones of my family rest. I won't surrender this place. It would give the signal to everyone that I am frightened and have fled. I can't do it."

"There is that drawback, it's true. But think on it, Cartimandua. In the meantime, we must pull on all the ties your father and my father created in order to hold our war host together. Venutius is intent on ripping the tribal alliance apart and re-moulding it to suit himself, but he doesn't realise the enormous skill it takes to bind so many separate little tribes together. He hasn't the diplomatic skill of my brother Kesaven, nor the stony heart and brutal power of my father and he will realise that when his own shaky alliance fails, be it sooner or later. Cartimandua, you have to mobilise all of our forces in the south, in person if necessary. We must defeat him or he'll ruin everything our family have created."

After the council meeting, I packed my battle dress and weapons, without which I would travel nowhere. I stroked my horse and watched Davit supervise the bodyguard of men and women that would escort me. I walked to a place in the meadow where I felt Vellocatus's breath on my cheek and I asked him to give me his strength.

"I can't go back there," I murmured, into the wind, "Not without your help. Why aren't you with me for all this?" A tear rolled down my face before I could stop it and the grief welled up again so strong I thought I would fall to the ground. I remembered how he had been there for me, beside me, when all those Brigantian rebels had been crucified. Returning to the south always brought back the fear, the sadness and the guilt of that time and I avoided going there if I could. And yet, as I heard often, the constant interaction with Roman patrols, camps and passing legions on the southern borders had changed the prevailing mood into one of tolerance, if not quite acceptance of the Roman presence. It helped that these border tribes had an increased and improved level of both import and export trade. Antikia was right, I had to exploit whatever pro-Roman feelings existed and I also had to pull into my war host anyone whom Venutius had not yet coerced. There, in the dreamy green meadow of my long-gone youth, I dwelt on all of this, and my grief subsided. I heard Vellocatus telling me I was right. I felt his hand in mine and his mouth against my cheek. I carried him with me as I rode my horse south with Antikia in the desperate search for allies.

"We can't take too long convincing them," said Antikia as we led our horses through a dank forest path towards a settlement on the south-eastern edge of Brigantia. "It's making me uneasy being away from home with Venutius on the move."

"I know. I feel the same." She was right to be concerned – Venutius could strike at any time and our attempt to enlarge our war host could prove to be an arrow in our own foot if he stormed on the royal stronghold while we were away. Still, I couldn't help adding, wickedly, "Are you yearning for your comfy old bed, aunt?"

"Huh, you wait till you get to my age!"

We emerged from the trees and followed the track as it looped round a hillside. The tops of a group of roundhouses came into view and our guards cantered on ahead to announce our arrival. By the time we dismounted, a number of men and women had gathered and were eyeing us deferentially. I smiled and let them draw near me whilst my guards formed a half-circle behind me. Antikia stood on my left, two paces back. I wore my armlets and a throat-full of gold and jet. Antikia had her war paint streaked across her cheekbones and white, bloodied feathers in her plaited hair.

"Saviel, it's good to see you and your family looking so well," I said to the man who headed this clan. I knew him vaguely. My father had known his uncle.

"Thank you, we're very happy to see you in good health also," he answered. "We know you have had trying times."

"It's the fate of a leader," I laughed, deflecting any hint of a reference to my own personal loss. "I'll come to the point, Saviel. I'm sure you know why I'm here." He inclined his head as I spoke and I continued. "Venutius is mounting a war host in the north with the aim of invading Brigantia. If he succeeds, he'll destroy the whole tribal alliance and provoke direct conflict with Rome. I already have my own war host ready, but I need every small clan and tribe to join me to be sure Venutius has no chance of winning. I'm asking you to fight with me."

"With the Brigantian war host summoned, I doubt you'll need us," he answered with feigned humility.

"We need everyone," I said. "It's not enough to hold Venutius off. We must completely destroy this threat, or Rome may simply invade and take care of him themselves. Then we'd all lose everything."

"They'd never remove you as queen, not after the loyalty you showed many years ago," he answered with half-lidded eyes and the people with him shuffled uncomfortably.

"It's a dangerous balance with Rome. Put a foot wrong and we end up like the Iceni, or the Druids, or the Catuvellauni. I could go on, but you must see my point. You live quite happily now, don't you? Trade is good, you eat well? If Venutius succeeds, Rome will invade through your border territory and flatten everything in its path." I grinned. "It's really me or nothing."

"You can always count on our support. That has never been in question," he replied, still wearing that funny expression.

"Good!" I moved forward and took his arm triumphantly. "Some of my men here will take a head count and see that anyone who can fight travels north immediately. I must leave you now, but we'll no doubt see each other soon on the battlefield."

I strode back to my horse. Antikia was already mounted. We kicked into a gallop, sending clods of earth flying. Our guards followed, all except a handful picked to enforce the conditions we had just set. There was an element of coercion, I must admit, but I had spoken the truth - these people had no choice but to support me or Venutius would ruin their way of life. I truly believed that and so forcing people into the war host gave me no sleepless nights. It was for their own good.

We'd already descended on fifteen, maybe twenty small settlements in the previous two days and planned to travel north close to the border visiting as many more as possible before nightfall. Then the following day we would ride hard for home. I had worried that my trip would alert Roman outposts to the seriousness of the situation but found that the Roman presence had diminished since I had last been near the borders. It was helpful in the short-term, but if the legions were so stretched, I began to harbour a gnawing concern that no help would be forthcoming from them if I really needed it.

As it happened, my time for gathering warriors was over. As we headed north, two messengers, sweating and exhausted, intercepted us with the inevitable news. Venutius had begun his march on my stronghold. The final war with my old lover had begun.

SUMMER AD69

The call had gone out and my war host had responded. The landscape around my home was a heaving sea of warriors, tribal elders and their families. Most were long-standing and loyal followers of the Brigantian alliance that my father and grandfather had created. Some were there under the pressures we had been exerting in the south. My army was a good size and I was pleased. Venutius may think he had made progress but he surely could not have matched my numbers.

Organising, sheltering and feeding a war host is a huge undertaking and much of our early work was concerned with these basic necessities. Heads of the smaller tribes and families, along with council members of the larger ones came together with my own immediate circle of advisers to form a new emergency council and we met several times daily to manage the needs of the war host and to share the latest reports of Venutius and his movements. The situation was eased by most warriors being accompanied by extended families who cooked and cared for them and who had, for the most part, brought their own supplies of food, but we were conscious that this preparedness could only last a limited time and that Venutius may play a tactical game of keeping us waiting until morale and supplies ebbed.

These were the matters that occupied me in those fast and frantic weeks. The royal stronghold was throng with activity and my days were busy from start to finish. Antikia kept close to me, as did Davit. Our council was tightly knit and we talked often, privately, away from all the other nobles and leaders who laid claim to our time. In the days of war, my family was Antikia, Shamatin, Davit and Estoroc.

"None of us will fight," I told them. "I need you by my side."

"I'm too old to be any use on the field anyway," said Antikia, dismissively. "We can all do more good by commanding from the rear."

"But not me," Estoroc interrupted, "I'll be fighting."

"No," I insisted, "I need you with me."

"You can't stop me fighting! What will everyone think, if I cower at the back and never even make a kill?" His cheeks had flushed with colour. Estoroc hated to challenge me and I saw that he was in a difficult position. I sighed. Of course I couldn't stop a young man proving himself in battle. If I forbade it, he'd just have to disobey me and I didn't want to force him into that.

"Fine. You can fight, But no one else." I glared at Davit. "We don't know how long this war will last and I can't lose my council right at the start."

Venutius made his move days later. A patrol notified us that the Carvettii were leading their war host directly towards us at a fast pace. I was in the roundhouse we used for meetings, at the bottom of the meadow, with various heads of families.

"This is it, then," I told them, rising from my seat. "Send word out to all the others and let's start moving."

People were running before I even finished my sentence. They'd had enough of waiting and they were all ready to fight. I understood that feeling a little better - I'd felt the bloodlust on me when Venutius and I battled years before - but as I'd aged, my distaste for death and destruction had grown again. I wanted to defeat that self-serving man who'd shared my bed, but when I watched so many men and women taking up arms, mounting horses, dragging out chariots, I felt sickened that many of them would die painful, brutal deaths. Once, I could have shared my troubling ambivalence with Vellocatus, but now I dared not speak frankly to anyone. I had to inspire everyone around me with unfailing courage, for we were standing on the brink and a faltering step from me would plunge us all down.

"Cartimandua, the royal chariot is ready." Antikia was breathless, leaning over as she ran towards me. I took her arm.

338

"You should stay here," I whispered.

"No chance," she said. "I'll be riding with Shamatin. I'll keep myself safe, don't worry."

I nodded and we hugged. I couldn't stop her coming, just like I couldn't stop Estoroc fighting. For a moment, my complete lack of real control in the face of destiny overwhelmed me. I saw myself as a tiny being caught in a swirl of chaos. It brought me terror and then an odd calm. I could only follow my fate. Perhaps if Vellocatus had been there, that's the kind of thing he would have said to me. I laughed a little, at this thought, as I stepped up into my chariot and began the short journey into hell.

My formal chariot was a huge bronzed affair and had actually been my father's travelling vehicle when he was a young man. I hadn't used it in the previous troubles we'd had when I was younger, because I wanted a chariot I could handle easily and fight well in. Now, at my age, it was more important to create a visual impression both on my own side and the enemy. Over the years it had been enlarged, with new leather pieces added and even some gold working and new bronze-covered iron fittings that had been inlaid with jet and coral. It shone beautifully as it caught the light and was equipped with a double seat, so I could stand or perch as required and have a companion with me. I made a splendid spectacle as I led the war host up over the hills, shining like the sun itself in the centre of a hand-picked escort of ferocious, painted, armed warriors. The day was fine with a warm wind and the dry paths were easy, if bumpy, for the passage of wheels and feet.

"My back hurts," I grumbled to Davit. "This thing needs cushions in it."

Davit snorted and passed me a bladder of ale.

"This might take the edge off," he said, still laughing, "it's a strong brew."

I had a quick gulp and handed it back.

"Where's Estoroc?" I asked.

"Keeping some of the southern families in order," he replied. "Somewhere near the back. He'll find us when we get there."

"He's a good boy."

"A man, now. Yes, he's turned out well."

"You want to fight alongside him, don't you?"

Davit sighed and turned his face to me.

"I have to. I'd be failing as a father if I didn't."

"You'll be failing me if you get yourself killed," I countered, but I sounded petulant even to my own ears.

"I'll try not to get myself killed then." His face creased into another grin, the bristles of his beard shining grey in the sunlight.

I took his hand and gave it a squeeze.

We came to the brow of a hill and took a dog-legged track down to the west through woodland that had been partially cleared. It brought us to flattish land that gave a long view north and that was when we gained our first sight of the opposing army.

They carried banners just as we did and the colours and symbols fluttered in the wind, like vivid flowers on the horizon. Beneath the pretty canopy marched the grim, grey swarm of a war host, a mess of men, women, chariots and horses. Our own reflection.

"Keep moving," I shouted, "We'll stop when we've reached that pasture." As planned, my order went echoing through a line of command, from one appointed voice to another and so we marched on, as one. I stood in my chariot, so that I might be seen, erect and unafraid, and give heart to the many people willing to lay down their lives for me. The distance seemed infinite, the fields rolling on and on and the warm wind blowing all the time like the expectant breath of the gods and goddesses. Finally we drew to a halt and proceeded to arrange ourselves into the attack formation we had discussed. I remained out at the front the whole while. Antikia and Shamatin had drawn their chariot level with mine. Estoroc came and found his father and we all dismounted and stood together for the last time.

It's frustrating, but I can't remember what any of us said. I can't even take a guess, as I have done with other, sketchier parts of my memories. All I remember is that the wind blew even warmer and that the clamour of a multitude of warriors filled the air and we embraced each other. Then our little group grew as more elders and heads joined us for the final preparations. Those that were fighting embraced those that were not and then the latter moved back, through the throng, behind the host. One of the warriors from my guard mounted my chariot to drive me to the rear line where I would remain as battle commenced. I recoiled instinctively as he took the reins and panicked, looking for Davit and Estoroc who were taking to smaller, serious fighting chariots. The speed of events was overtaking me. I clenched my fist, thinking of how I had held Davit's hand what felt like a moment ago but was already almost half a day away. And his boy, not really a man, not when measured against my age, fastening himself into that metal death-trap, tying the reins around his waist to leave his hands free for wielding his great sword. I raised my arm to them as my chariot wheeled around and they saw and responded heartily, full of the fight, while my own throat was choked with sadness. All about them I saw faces I knew, faces I cared for, men and women who I had known for many years. And beyond them, faces who were familiar to me, people with whom I had discussed taxes, carried out trade, shared meals. These people were the lifeblood of my land. They were Brigantia and they were fighting to hold onto our hard-won federation in my name, in my father's name, in my grandfather's name.

The chariot whipped through an opening in the masses and we sped through to safer ground, halfway between our army and the caravan of family and followers who had set up a basic camp on the higher ground. Shamatin drew his chariot level with mine once more. He had followed us and I was pathetically glad to have my aunt and her husband close by me. We had a guard stationed around us also, and various other nobility were taking up positions alongside, avoiding the dangers of the battlefield. In my grandfather's time, I'm sure such action would have been considered cowardly, if not completely bizarre, but many of us could not see the point in potentially losing all our ruling elite in one fell swoop. Some would fight - those for whom the blood-lust was all-powerful, as it had been once with Alabas, or those who felt they had something to prove - but not us. Oddly, being protected at the rear of my war host left me more anxious and fearful than I remembered being years before when I was out there fighting. Back then, the rage took me over and I simply got on with fighting and killing. Now, waiting there for the battle to be decided, I had time to think and to worry and, worse, I had time to watch and appreciate the full-scale horror of warfare.

There was another sight that bit into my heart also. I caught glimpses of Venutius, visible by his plates of metal armour that shone unnaturally brightly and the size and might of his chariot though mostly he stayed back, cautious as I was. Yet near him at times were his inner circle - his brother Iticus, no doubt, and Carvettii council members. And added to their number was a female form that I recognised and whose face I pictured even though I could not possibly have seen it at that distance. Namandea, her proud stance never more evident. I wondered if she glanced towards me and felt the same tug of pain. I wondered, also, where Presivin was - fighting by his son Masga, just as Davit fought beside Estoroc, perhaps? And what of Invas? If she was fighting too and came face to face with her beloved Estoroc, would she cut him down, or he her? The splitting of mine and Venutius's union had rent asunder so many lands, families and relationships and now I had to watch as it literally rent apart the bodies of hundreds of Brigantians.

I cannot think more on it. I can hardly bear to dwell on the outcome either, but I must because it's important. Our army struggled, and seemed at one point to be forced back, but they broke through eventually and the Carvettii banners receded then disappeared. Once they had been overcome, they retreated as fast as possible and I knew their tactic was to regroup. The land at our feet was soaked in blood and held many bodies from both sides. There was a huge mess to clean up and those who had not fought – elderly onlookers, children, mothers – went out into the fields to search out our wounded, strip goods from our enemies and carry back our dead. I rode my chariot far enough back from the scene so that my nostrils would not have to suffer the metallic tang of blood and baser scents of bodily excretions that happen during slaughter. Away from the carnage, we began to assess the costs of the battle and evaluate Venutius's own army, whilst heads of families and nobles who had been fighting came to us with numbers of their dead. Amelan had organised our food and brought us cold meat and bread and a hot broth for me to drink that she whispered in my ear would restore my nerves.

It was whilst we sat there in the fading warmth with our hastily prepared food, that Shamatin gave a cry and leapt up, bounding away towards the tumult of activity on the battlefield.

"What is it?" I asked no one in particular, standing up to see what had caught Shamatin's eye and then I saw him grasp onto the side of a chariot that was making slow progress in our direction. He pulled the staggering war pony to a halt and reached for the collapsed figure inside the vehicle.

"Oh no," breathed Antikia.

"That's Davit's chariot," I said, breaking past men and women seated around me. "Amelan, get someone to fetch a stretcher and bring your medicines." I was yelling over my shoulder as I hurried after Shamatin. I caught up with him as he lifted the man from the chariot, laying him down on the grass. It was

Estoroc, not Davit, his plaited hair damp and shining against his skull and his breath coming in ragged gasps.

"Are you wounded?" I panicked, "Where are you hurt?"

Shamatin was already looking over the boy.

"It's a slice to his side," he answered. "Long but not deep. Amelan will be able to clean and bind it."

Estoroc shuddered and moaned. I took off the light cloak I was wearing and covered him with it.

"Where is Davit?" I asked him, but the boy only moaned again and then fell into a sleep. Amelan came to my side with her leather bag of medicines and was followed by some of my personal guard carrying a large leather piece to use as a stretcher. I moved aside and they loaded him onto it and heaved him away towards the other wounded, with Amelan walking beside him. Shamatin began to unharness the war pony, checking it for wounds.

"Is he still on the field?" I asked, pacing and looking out over the wasteland of bodies and people stepping slowly amongst them, retrieving valuables. "Is he helping carry the wounded back?"

Shamatin straightened up, giving the pony a little pat.

"I'll go and look for him," he said. The corners of his mouth were fixed grimly downwards as he handed me the pony's reins and plodded off. I led the little beast away, towards our council gathering, where someone found it a bowl of water and I rejoined Antikia who had remained with the others.

"Is Estoroc badly injured?" she asked and a few people looked up, mildly concerned.

"Slice to the side. He'll mend," I answered. "But we don't know where Davit is. Shamatin has gone to look for him."

"Oh." Antikia gazed out to where her husband had wandered. We could just pick out his form, moving in and amongst the dead, bending sometimes.

"Have I missed anything?"

"Not much," Antikia replied. "Venutius is decamping to a place not far north of here. You can see their smoke. The scouts are watching them." She was still looking out onto the field. Birds were circling above, dark flutters against the fading sky. On the eastern side of the field, a grisly pile of dead warriors was growing as our followers retrieved unidentified bodies believed to be ours. Those whose family could name them might be carted off to their homesteads for a more ceremonial end. The rest would burn here, on the site of battle. The dead from the Carvettii army would be left in the fields to rot. Soon, we, like Venutius, would leave this place and camp in a more hospitable location. Some had already gone ahead to erect shelters and start fires.

"He's picking someone up," said Antikia.

We watched, waiting in silence, as Shamatin's vague figure lumbered towards us. He had hoisted the body up over his shoulder and was staggering slightly under the weight. The body was limp, the clothes stained with blood. The arms and legs swung heavily, purposeless.

"Help him," I barked at one of my guards and he sprang forward instantly, running into the distance to meet Shamatin and relieve him of the load. Then suddenly there were more men and a stretcher, made of leather bound to two wooden poles, and with the body on that they moved swiftly towards us. I instinctively stepped backwards. I was not ready to see, but they were upon me and there was no where to go but forward to face death in the eye again.

Davit lay awkwardly on the floor where they had carefully placed him. His eyes were closed – maybe Shamatin's doing, for warriors usually die with their eyes wide open. His mouth was partly open and twisted, as if he had called out in a final agony. He had a gash to one side of his face and his sword arm was bent, probably broken. There were wounds to his torso, where his lifeblood had drained from him.

"You were supposed to take care," I said, with a sob, "How can I fight a war without my best warrior?"

Shamatin and Antikia stood close, with my guards behind them, to shield me from onlookers. The Brigantian nobility were an unsentimental breed and would not look sympathetically on my sadness, especially not at this time. I knelt down and kissed the forehead of my father's cousin's son and remembered him as a hot-headed young fool who wanted to fight the Romans. I blessed him for staying always loyal to me and I straightened his arm and his face and stroked his dirty, bearded cheek. Shamatin took a sword out from his own belt.

"I found his sword by him," he said, passing it to me. I laid it on Davit's body and lifted up his hands to hold the hilt.

As I was about to order my guards to carry him away, there was a cry from behind me and Davit's wife pushed blindly past, clutching her face. She sank over his body, crying as her younger children followed with frozen faces. I put my hands on their shoulders, thankful that I'd had time to tidy him up a little before they saw him.

"Do you have a cart?" I asked the eldest child, a girl with Davit's eyes and her mother's chestnut hair.

She nodded mutely.

"Your brother is over there with Amelan, wounded but not too badly. You'd do best to get them both home tomorrow, when Estoroc has had a night to rest."

I sent her with one of my guards to fetch the cart and then we moved away to leave Davit's woman to grieve over him.

"It's time to leave," I ordered, walking back to the gathered heads and councillors. "We have another battle to prepare for."

Amelan had returned, with my cloak which she hung around my shoulders. Someone brought my golden chariot to my side and I mounted it and started the two horses into motion without looking back.

★

We decamped a short distance to the south west, setting up leather tents for ourselves and pens for the animals. When I arrived, a larger structure had been erected for myself and my immediate family and council. The other tribal leaders were putting up tents nearby. All across the hillside small fires burned, the smell of roasting meat drifted in the air and gritted wails from the injured echoed and dissipated in the hubbub of camp activity. Whenever we gathered the war host, for meetings or for actual battle, I was struck by the celebratory atmosphere that resulted. Ordinarily, it was rare to find groups of more than four or five families living together. To have so many people in one place at the same time was unusual and exciting and we were all infected with it. I called out for some food and had a large fire set in front of my tent. Before long I was engaged in long conversations with my allies, planning our next offensive against Venutius.

You could say we were optimistic, given that the first battle had gone our way. There is a spirit that takes you over at times of peril and that is what I lived on over the next few days. There isn't time to ponder on what has happened or to dwell on mistakes made. I think I saw Davit's family leaving. Or maybe I imagined afterwards that I had seen them go. In any case, they left and we carried on. After a few nights at our makeshift base, we upped sticks and set off on the offensive. We thought we had the advantage – indeed, based on what we had seen during that first battle, it was a reasonable assumption. But none of us had anticipated Venutius's next move.

As we moved our army in a north-west arc to attack the remnants of the Carvettii force, the message ran like wildfire among us that Venutius was attacking from the south-east.

"That's impossible," scoffed Shamatin, "We know he's with his army just north of here."

"So what's the meaning of this news?" I considered aloud.

"Maybe he's spreading lies to confuse us or slow us down. He could have spies planted in our war host who are starting these rumours." Antikia looked back at Shamatin and he shrugged.

"No. There's more to it." We were resting in a clearing and the senior Brigantians were all nearby, taking food and ale. "Council!" I yelled and raised my arm to draw all the important people to me.

"We're going to wait here until I get more news from the south-east," I told them all, as they approached. "Send messengers ahead to halt the whole war host. Nobody goes any further."

"We'll lose our chance if you do this," argued one of the men. "We must attack while Venutius is weak."

"No. I'm not discussing it. We stay here." I walked away to stop any conversation. It was enough that I had given an order. I was not about to waste time justifying my gut feelings to a bunch of petty leaders. Antikia followed me away from the crowd.

"What is it you're thinking?" she asked.

"I think Venutius is a dangerous enemy and the situation is more complicated than it appears. Either he didn't sustain the losses we thought he did or he's found more support from elsewhere. Either way, I think we're in danger of being forced to fight on two fronts."

"Where would he find more support? We rode the south ourselves and found no evidence of an army. The Parisi are traders with no interest in joining the fight against Rome. The Corieltauvi hardly even exist any more and the strangers in the far north wouldn't ally themselves with the Carvettii unless they desperately needed to, which they don't. So where would he find more warriors?"

"I don't know. Maybe from further afield? Over the sea? There are places where Rome has squeezed the people very hard. They might not take much persuasion to flee and join an army that thinks it can defeat the Romans."

"Gaul?"

"Perhaps. Venutius spent some time there, I believe, when he was forced into the Roman army. He may know people there."

"It's possible." Antkia drummed two fingers against her lips. She looked towards the council, shuffling and grumbling and scowling in our direction. "You may have a problem there," she warned me.

"They'll thank me later."

I kept to myself for a day, avoiding the dissenters and the querulous voices that muttered ever louder that we should move north and attack. As we waited, the mood became more nervous and agitated, teetering between the belief that Venutius was on our tail and the belief that we were losing our big opportunity to ensnare him. Finally, answers came.

Venutius had done exactly as I'd feared. Even the guess about Gaul was correct. Somehow, that infuriating man had dredged up a large army of angry foreigners, all willing to swear some kind of allegiance to the Carvettii cause. No doubt he'd promised them land, goods or women to entice them over the water to fight his war. It was annoying and somehow insulting to my sense of this whole feud as an old-fashioned northern territory war, but I couldn't fault his tactics on a practical level. He was determined to win the war, at any cost. We were locked in between his battered but still-standing alliance who were camped just to our north and his Gaulish auxiliaries to the east.

I swung our whole war host around and headed back to the royal stronghold. That, I knew, was where the Gaulish force was heading. If they could take it, they would strike a spiritual blow to my war host and to me. I had known Venutius long and deep enough to guess at his intentions. As we stormed back at full speed to my home, the chills of danger prickled my skin. I was desperate all the way to be back on the ground I knew and loved, to be sure that it had not yet been stepped on by hired fighters to whom the sacred land meant nothing, not to mention the urgency I felt to protect the people who had stayed behind or returned after battle - the old, the weak, the injured, the young.

349

I got there in time. For that, I was grateful - to the gods or to my own instincts I'm not sure. The first person I picked out of the crowd when we arrived was Estoroc. He was heavily bandaged around his waist and used a large staff to support him as he walked slowly towards me.

"You're up!" I cried, holding my arms out to him. We hugged lightly; I was conscious of his obvious pain, but he brushed off my concern, saying the wound was more superficial that first thought and that he was healing. I didn't altogether believe him, but there wasn't time to argue.

"The second army is marching on us," he said, "We've started organising more defences but I'm glad you've returned. When we found out the rumours were true, we didn't know if you'd come back or sacrifice us."

"What faith you have in me!" I said, only slightly offended.

I called a meeting immediately. The council gathered in the ceremonial roundhouse at the bottom of the meadow, still dusty and tired from the ride. As I looked at their exhausted faces, I understood that we had gone from being the victors to being on the back foot. Venutius had turned the whole war around. Perhaps he had planned it this way and our first battlefield success was actually a tactical withdrawal on his part to lull us into a more exposed position. I think someone said as much during that very meeting, but I didn't let them elaborate. It would only crush any remaining confidence to ponder more on that possibility. Instead, we concentrated on a plan for defending my stronghold. I kept the whole thing brief. We couldn't waste time talking.

Afterwards, I walked out to the north-eastern perimeter of my homestead. Venutius was approaching, like a double-faced monster, from two directions, but they would converge on this corner of my home. The banks were being raised and the ditches deepened all around this section by people who would not be fighting - young girls and boys, older men and women. The warriors were eating, resting, preparing their weapons and saving their strength. Some were walking the old paths, whispering with the gods and goddesses and laying offerings at the sacred places. The stream through the woods would glint with daggers and arrows that night. On the hills and in the fields, people were working and patrolling and to see the usually quiet landscape so full of human activity was unsettling. It didn't feel like home.

A few tired boys walked along the path in my direction. They'd downed tools and were heading back. I glanced them over with disinterest, thinking only that it was a shame they were not a few years older and ready to fight. There was another person on the path behind them. In her faded green dress she was hard to notice at a distance and I hadn't seen her as she made her way over the far hill, though it was obvious from her weary gait and the travelling pack she carried that she must have been walking a long time. I watched her come ever closer and I saw her halt as she saw me. Her eyes met mine and my instant reaction, before the angry questions clouded my mind, was joy. She repositioned her pack and continued on towards me. One of my guards, ever present, though they tried to be discreet, came to my side.

"My chief, is that woman known to you?"

"Yes, she is Invas, daughter of Presivin who deserted us to join Venutius."

The guard drew out his sword and made to step in front of me.

"There's no need for that," I said, staying his arm. "I don't believe she means me any harm. But stay nearby and if you see any other travellers approaching, notify me."

"The patrols will pick up anyone coming this way," he said, confidently.

"They didn't pick up Invas," I pointed out. He backed away and began a hurried conversation with more of my guards, who then dispersed in a flurry of activity. They were ever so concerned for me, those loyal men and women.

As Invas came within calling distance, she slowed uncertainly.

"You can approach," I motioned.

"I don't expect to be welcomed back, but please would you hear what I have to say?" she asked me. Her eyes were black as nightfall and her mouth sat in a miserable little frown.

"I'll hear it," I answered, not unkindly.

"When my father left to go after Masga, I went because I thought he would bring my brother back. But if that was ever his intention, he changed his mind. Now he believes, like Masga, that Venutius should rule Brigantia. I don't think he really believes Venutius will be any better a leader than you, but he does believe that Masga will thrive more under Venutius. Masga is already on the war council and Venutius seems to have some regard for him. So you see, for my father this is about under which star our family will shine brightest."

"I never took your father to be so fickle," I said. "Perhaps age has made him vain."

"I think he just wants to be sure his son has the best chances."

"Masga's best chance would have been to stay here and learn about real leadership," I said. "But he was too impatient and foolish for that. So why have you returned? Didn't you want to shine under Venutius?"

"I feel I've been torn in two. I wished to be with my family, but I never wanted to leave my home or the man I love. It was so hard to go against them but after a while I realised there was nothing there for me. My father became so concerned for Masga, he forgot about what was best for me."

"So it was Estoroc who pulled you back, not loyalty to your true queen?"

"Second to my own mother, you have been the most important woman to me as I've grown up. I hated to be on the opposite side to you, even though I did not fight. But I can't deny that my need for Estoroc was what gave me the courage to return."

"That's a good enough answer, I suppose." I took her arm, in a warrior's greeting, and she folded, unexpectedly, into my body like a fallen flower.

"Now then, don't cry," I told her, patting her clumsily. Few people ever displayed this kind of affection with me and it threw me for a moment. She straightened up and took hold of herself.

"Anyway," I continued, "you should save your strength for Estoroc."

"Why, what's happened?" she cried, stricken.

"He has a wound to his side, not deep but certainly painful. And his father died on the battlefield."

"No," she gasped, "Not Davit." There was genuine distress in her eyes and it opened my mind for a moment to a sliver of the many hurts I was storing up inside my own heart. I pressed them back within.

"You should go to him now. It will do him a great deal of good to see you."

"Thank you," she started to hurry away, then stopped and came back. "There's something else. I can't believe I nearly forgot to say." She looked sheepish and I raised an eyebrow.

"Masga knew I was returning. He let me go because he wanted me to pass a message to you. He says if you surrender now and leave Brigantia, Venutius will spare all your supporters if they agree to follow him. He says Venutius won't track you down. He'll let you go free if you give up power to him."

A rage swept over me. Insidious Masga with his pathetic little offer.

"I'll never give up power to Venutius. Is your brother expecting some kind of reply?"

"No," said Invas, shaking her head. "If you send no word, Venutius will attack, as planned. I'm so sorry to be the one to bring this message."

I nodded my understanding and she took her leave. My

guards closed around me. They had heard the conversation and saw my anger.

"You can escort me back to my roundhouse," I said. "I need a drink."

I sent a message that same night to the nearest legionary camp. I had already sent some information to the governor in Londinium with dilute requests for assistance, hoping we might get some auxiliaries but anxious not to agitate my relationship with the authorities by admitting any vulnerability in my position. Now I saw we were past the time for such caution. In my brief missive I outlined the tactical advantage Venutius had created and insisted that Brigantia received the military support it was owed under the client agreement. The message would travel by a relay system and I could only hope that it would not arrive too late to be of any use and that the legion would act upon it.

In my roundhouse through that evening, we sat and drank and planned. There were many leaders to speak with and so much to think about that it made my head ache and eventually I sent them all away. I wanted to sit with people I loved and trusted and to hear their considered opinions and advice but there were so few of those people left. One by one, over the years, they had come and gone - Vellocatus, my parents, Tantoban, Fistoc, Gorlensa, Namandea, Presivin, Davit, even Risha, Tyrius and Venutius. I had taken each of them for granted at one time and now they were gone. As the old families and friends of the Brigantian alliance died or drifted away, the bonds loosened and my status wavered. I had begun my leadership of the tribe at the centre of a huge web and now I was clutching at fewer and fewer strands, watching new generations grow, all with their own ideas and ambitions. Watching how Estoroc had welcomed back his lost love and how it seemed to fill him with life again, I felt ever older, as if their youth and vitality inversely mirrored my age and irrelevance. In my lifetime, the whole lands had changed immeasurably and my mother had been right once when she said we could sooner hold back the tide than stop the changes that were coming. I had kept abreast of the incoming wave for a long time, but now it was rolling away from me, washing away the structures on which my life was based. In the dark heart of the late summer night I could dwell on these philosophical sadnesses, but when morning came, the single-minded worry I had was how to hold onto my home, my land, my people and my power. I was not ready to be parted from my material wealth and status just yet.

When the two armies appeared on the horizon converging together like some swirling mass of insects, we pushed out from the boundaries of my royal fortress and established a rear defensive line which we hoped would not be broken, no matter how bad fighting became. I fell back to within the compound, along with the key council members. In addition, I had Estoroc, who was not yet recovered enough to fight and Invas, whose offer to fight I had resolutely turned down. We sent out all our brave men and women, and probably, inadvertently, some children too, to push back the enormous Carvettiian threat whilst we waited in our stronghold and hoped for a response from the Roman legion. The battle raged and the valleys echoed with clashes and howls. Then came the news I had been dreading - Venutius was beginning to break us.

"I'm going out onto the battlefield now," I told the assembled leaders. "They need to see me. Perhaps my presence will inspire them to fight harder."

"No, no, it's far too risky. What if Venutius captures you? Or cuts you down?" Some noble, a man I didn't know well. It didn't escape me that none of my close circle objected.

"That's the risk, but if the alternative is that Venutius breaches our defences, then what is the difference? You all may join me or remain here, as you wish, but I would say the time for us all to take up arms has arrived."

There was a general clambering about, arranging horses and chariots and swords. Estoroc set off intently.

"Where are you going?" I shouted.

He didn't bother answering, but faintly rolled his eyes.

"You can't fight in that state," I pressed.

"It's really not that bad," he said, pulling his tunic round to conceal where the blood had soaked though his bandages and caked into scabs. I puffed air through my nose in frustration.

"You'll just be a liability to me out there. Come here." I led him away from the crowds, towards my little garden, still standing so delicately in the midst of all the ugliness. Invas hovered near us. "I have another job for you. I need you to pack my things. Anything valuable; use your judgement and be discriminating. If it comes to it, we won't be able to take much. Anything you decide against taking, bury somewhere. I don't want Venutius handling my things. If I return, you must be ready to lead us south. If I don't, then take my possessions out of the reach of that man. You need to keep an eye on what is happening out on the field. If it's looking very bleak, order the people out of here. Venutius may show little mercy. Invas, you must help him with all this. Concentrate on our own people. The other tribes will take care of themselves if this all falls apart. Do you both understand?"

They nodded and Estoroc said yes, he would do what I asked. In short, heart-pounding minutes I found myself in the great bronze chariot heading out for the front line, clearly visible to my hard-pressed fighters who were being pushed back even more fiercely than we had anticipated. In my chariot, standing behind me, was Strisen, that little nephew of Mandulay, who was now truly the best and most terrifying warrior we had, with his enormous bunched muscles and bared teeth and the blood of scores of our enemy already streaked over his clothes and skin. Shamatin came too, in his own chariot, but he made Antikia stay behind. She was too old and though she might have taken down a few of the enemy with her beautiful dark grey sword, just swinging the weapon would have exhausted her in a short while. Reluctantly she stayed put, but she travelled out a little way to be our eyes at the rear. She had the experience and knowledge of battle to assess the situation and would know when Estoroc should begin evacuating our homestead.

We raced to the killing place at the front of our war host in a frenzy, the war ponies foaming as they do when they are raring for action. My stomach churned with fear, for myself and for the whole cause. I was doing the right thing, I told myself, but I wished and wished I could have closed myself in behind my soft, leather hangings in my grand old roundhouse and stretched out on the covered hay bunk with the smell of herbs rising from the filling. These fields, splattered with blood, guts and limbs were not mine. They were a vision from another world. I didn't recognise the hills with their chanting, shrieking onlookers or the people in their war paint stabbing their spears and blades into other human flesh. And then, for a second only, I saw the face I did recognise and would always recognise; the face that would haunt me and remonstrate with me and pain me forever. With his hair wild and scattered with plaits and feathers and blood, and cheeks striped with woad and black soot, Venutius pulled his sword out of an unlucky opponent and brought it up high to smash down again on another who had sidled around his chariot. He caught my stare as he swept the weapon through the air and barely let his eyes leave mine as he cut open the man's throat. Then he was gone, the chariot subsumed in the thick of fighting, blocked also by the warriors of my own war host who had flocked near to cheer me and protect me.

It went on, as battles do, for an eternity. I fought when I could, though Strisen took care of most attackers with violent efficiency. We worked reasonably well as a team and there were only a few times when blades whistled slightly too close to my person for comfort. The benefit of my great chariot was that because of its size, it was hard for anyone on foot to get close before we despatched them. Other chariots and riders were harder to deal with, but on we went, just slicing and fighting and thinking only of how many Carvettii people and their allies we could kill. When dusk began to settle, there was a retreat on both sides. With the fading light, cold air and tired warriors, Venutius would have to wait another day to break us, but he could be patient, since he was winning.

My home was now full of wounded, dying and dead people. There was no comfort in returning to it, save the physical ease of resting my muscles. I knew that in a day or two, I would feel the burn right into my bones, if I lived that long. Antikia hugged me tight when I dismounted.

"Shamatin?"

"He's alright. Resting," she said, leading me to my roundhouse, "just as you should be. There is a message from the legion."

"What does he say?" My chest constricted.

"They'll be here within a half day. There won't be many, but it's the best they can do. The legate also advises your speedy retreat from Brigantia as he can't guarantee your safety."

"Ah. We could have done with better news. At least it's help. I thought they might not send any." Still, my heart sank and suddenly all I wanted was to sleep. My eyes felt so heavy. But if I slept, the morning would come faster, and with it, undoubtedly more fighting. If the Romans weren't here in time... An awful thought hit me.

"Antikia, did the messenger say whether the Romans would travel through the night?"

"Yes, he said they would travel as soon as ordered."

"Good. That is something. By tomorrow's noon, it could all be over otherwise. We just don't have the numbers against Venutius. Everywhere I look, his bloody Gauls are trampling on my fighters, more than two to one." I shook my head. "I raised everyone's spirits today, but we can't win a war on that."

"No," she agreed. "My assessment was much the same as yours. We're outnumbered and it's only our slightly better location and supplies that are giving us the edge. Another day and he will break us. There's no question."

"So," I continued, as we ducked inside my roundhouse and joined the small gathering of top people, "it all depends how many soldiers the legate sends."

"We'll know in the morning. As soon as we seen them, we'll know," said Antikia, "whether we are doomed or saved."

That was my last night in my home, my last night in the roundhouse where I grew up and where I lived with Kesaven and Metassia, my father and mother. It was the last evening when I walked through the plants and trees in my garden and returned to the bed I had shared once with Venutius and later with Vellocatus. In the roundhouse that had once served my immediate family and its servants, and which I had lovingly rebuilt and expanded, I now looked on Antikia and Shamatin, Estoroc and Invas, and six other nobles of the largest sub-tribes of Brigantia. I had invited Estoroc's mother and siblings to join us, but she kept to the home she had shared with Davit and I was not surprised. There was Amelan also, quietly mending her tunic by the firelight, staying by me because she was too traumatised and overwhelmed to go out and tend the many wounded. I would not have asked it of her; there were enough other people skilled in the healing ways, even if their concoctions were not as potent as those Amelan brewed. Strisen was elsewhere, though he had been to see his sister. He preferred to keep himself separate as he prepared himself for further fighting.

My roundhouse felt like a safe place that night, if I kept my mind closed to the horrors outside. I stayed awake a long time, working very hard to close my mind and imagine that I was just passing another uneventful night that would lead to a happy and contented day. So many nights I had taken that for granted and I bitterly wished for them back so I could treasure them a little more. Sleep overcame me, as it always does and then morning arrived bringing with it the hammering of feet.

We were up and out, ready to meet and greet the Roman auxiliaries, hoping against hope that there were enough of them to push Venutius and his Gaulish helpers back into the north. A column of men, weary and dishevelled, paraded in, headed by a middle-aged man who recognised me, though I didn't remember him. He came towards me and affected a slight bow.

"Cartimandua, we have been sent to your assistance in the understanding that you are fighting against Venutius? Can you see to the service of my men so they might be ready to fight when called upon?"

"Certainly," I said, though it was through gritted teeth. They had not brought enough of their own supplies, though they already took such high taxes from us in grains and other commodities. It obviously had not occurred to them that we already had a large army to feed and care for and that our own supplies might be limited too. I also noted with concern that most of the men did not look like they would be capable of fighting a war that day, after their long trek through the night.

"Have they rested at all?" I asked.

"A short while in the darkest hours. Enough to see them on," he said.

The Roman, Espulus, himself a Gaul, sat with me while I explained the situation in detail. He had several of his men present and they kept conferring on what seemed to me to be minor points and distractions. All the while, as we talked, I watched the sun edging up above the horizon and wondered what Venutius was doing.

"Surely we should prepare for battle now," I said, very anxious that we would be attacked while we sat discussing tactics.

"Yes, yes. I think your old lover will have hesitated today, knowing of our arrival, but from what you say, that won't hold him for long. I would prefer if you stayed out of battle though. I understand you fought yesterday, but I am charged with your safe-keeping. The governor takes his responsibilities under the client contract very seriously."

"That contract was to preserve my role as queen, not just my life," I commented, but took it no further. I had not intended to go out fighting anyway. I had watched Antikia's face as she took in the Roman force we had been sent and I saw in her eyes what I already knew. It was not enough. It was too small a force, even with all the ingenious tactics and regimented methods they would employ. It was too small, especially against an opponent who was himself experienced in Roman tactics. "I'll keep back and let you do your job," I said.

"Right, then it's time we went out there." We parted and I went to my own people to advise them of how to fight with the Romans. It was a strange thing, to have a war host of Brigantian warriors expected to fit in with the completely foreign ways of the Roman army but we had settled on an approach of having the Romans drive the attack so the Brigantians could defend the rear and flanks. It was similar to how we had worked with Septimus Avarasi long ago, to force Venutius into submission. I ordered Shamatin and Antikia to remain with me, along with Estoroc and Invas. We went to the boundary of our homeland to see our people and the Romans into battle and we watched for a short time. Enough time to know that defeat was inevitable. On the horizon, the crowds of our enemy dwarfed the remains of my war host.

"We must fall back now," said Antikia. "This is not our time. We'll die if we stay."

"Is that what I should do? Shouldn't I go out there and die with my war host?" I asked her.

"When I was younger, I would have said yes. But now, I

know that some things must continue. They cannot be allowed to die out. Our family is one such thing and as long as you live, you preserve the memory of your father, my brother. While you live, there is a hope for Brigantia. That's why we must fall back now."

"I'm not sure there is any real hope," I said, looking at the tatters of my war host, "but we'll go, as planned."

We went back through my stronghold, back through the pastures and along by the woods, past the foot of the stream - the stream where I had seen Antikia and Tyrius making love, before everything soured for them. We passed the meadow and I looked out over it, thinking of the boy Venutius running off in anger and coming face to face with a pack of wolves. Everywhere there were memories. For a moment, I wished I had been killed the day before and been saved the pain of leaving all this. Then, self-preservation took over and we were preparing the carts and the few horses we had held back. Invas began the work of encouraging the remaining people to leave, though many would not because they were nursing injured fighters. Estoroc helped his mother to get on her way with his younger sister and brothers. Soon enough, as if a force I could not see or feel had pushed me there, I was on my horse, trotting south. Somewhere over the next hill, I realised what that force was. It was time, just time, pushing me on, inexorably moving us all on and the thought comforted me.

AUTUMN AD69

Here we are, back where I started, on a hillside with barely a clan to my name. Even a mighty oak has to fall eventually, but the grief of loss is undiminished by this inevitability. Oh yes, I had felt relief when we arrived at the strange, solitary hill fort known in Brigantia as Camulodunum, but I only felt the warmth of temporary safety for a few moments and then the scale of my failure began to dawn on me. We had come a long way south, almost to the limits of Brigantia, and Venutius had not followed us. I knew his plans, even before stragglers and survivors turned up with their own accounts. Strisen was one, making his way to us with a wound to his skull and to his back. He never even made a sound when his sister stitched him up with a fine bone needle and the thinnest thread she could find. I knew even as Strisen staggered into our new settlement that Venutius would consolidate his position at my stronghold and re-group his forces. Then, when his hold in the north was secure, he would track me down and remove the only real threat to his power. My war host was crushed – many dead, others seduced to Venutius's side and yet more scattered in terror back to their outlying homesteads where they would ride out the storm of the take-over in anonymity. I had no chance of gathering another army. I had done my very best, but the spell my grandfather and father had cast over all the Brigantian tribes had faded. The federation they had built had crumbled against the dissension instigated by Venutius. I did not believe he had constructed anything so strong in its place. I felt I had failed the memory of my ancestors by allowing the fall of their empire. But then the words of my mother would hum in my ears, telling me there were worse forces than the Catuvellauni and that you could not hold back the tide. Maybe my father and grandfather too would have failed as I did if they'd had to see out these years of Roman occupation.

It was late summer when we came to that hillside and autumn quickly descended, bringing wind and mist and rain. We built up a solid encampment, with a large cluster of roundhouses that were small but serviceable and effective against the weather. The hunting on the valley floor was good and we had brought a small herd of livestock so we ate reasonably from that, but the food was nothing like as fancy as I was used to. Amelan, who still served me, apologised daily for the quality and I lied and said it was absolutely fine and that I enjoyed the simple tastes of food that she was forced to prepare in basic conditions with very limited ingredients. The other people with me included the pure Brigantian element of my personal guards and everyone from my royal homestead. The warriors from the sub-tribes had either stayed to fight until the end or simply gone home. Their loyalty to me had been true, but limited. At the end of it all, I was a Brigantian, but they all considered themselves to be something else first and foremost – whether Gabrantovice, Lopocare or any one of the many smaller tribes.

We had only been on the summit for four or five nights when the Roman auxiliaries passed us, falling back from their encounters with Venutius. I had ridden out to meet them, having sighted their banners over the hilltops – that was the advantage of our current location. Espulus was still in control, but the numbers he commanded were much reduced and he had a sorry tale to tell.

"We held them off for a few days," he explained, "and your people fought with us for a time. When we judged you were far enough away, we abandoned the site and retreated, following your tracks. I'd lost enough men and it was hopeless to continue. I hope you can see that we've done our bit, we've fought as hard as we can but your husband has too much support."

"He's not my husband," I corrected. "What about the royal enclosure and the people there?"

"We assume Venutius has taken control. I did assist some of

your people to safety, but others wanted to remain. I think," he paused and pursed his mouth up in distaste, "that some of your own people mean to join with him now that he has been proved the victor."

"They just want to stay on their land and continue with their lives. This dispute is not of their making and I can understand why they don't want their whole lives turned upside down by it." I felt loyal to them even though they'd turned from me and didn't like the simplistic, judgemental tone that Espulus had used.

"What are your plans now? We cannot assist you further in this war but we can escort you well away from Brigantia."

"No, I'm going to stay here until I've fully understood Venutius's intentions."

"Well, we cannot wait. We intend to march to a camp south east of here where we will be based until after the winter. We will not return here, but you can join us and expect to receive an escort to Londinium in the spring." He'd had enough. After losing many of his own men, I couldn't be surprised that his patience with me was limited.

"Thank you. I will correspond with Bolanus regarding my plans."

Espulus had tipped his head at me and wished me well as he left, taking his ragged band of auxiliaries away.

So here we were in the middle of autumn. Our sanctuary had become a fully-functioning camp for almost a hundred people and I heard definite confirmation that Venutius was based at my home, that he lived in my roundhouse and that all his council attended him there, while his large army camped on the land surrounding him. We truly had swapped roles. I passed my days in the pursuit of necessity, ruling over my small band of people to control food and other supplies and agreeing trades with passing merchants and hesitant local inhabitants. I sent messages to Bolanus with any traders and travellers going south and also sent two of my own people to deliver a detailed supplication and request for assistance.

"Is it worth travelling there yourself, to make a personal appeal?" Antikia asked me. "You could go before the bad weather arrives. Your father always said that it was better to do something like that in person than trust it to others. He liked to speak face-to-face with whoever he was dealing with."

"I can't step off this land," I said. I didn't add my reasons – that I felt if I stayed I was still queen, but if I left I was nothing; that I was scared Venutius would prevent my return and I would never claim this land my own again; that I was afraid of the humiliation of asking Bolanus for help and being refused.

"I could go in your place," she suggested, but I said no. I sent a man and woman I trusted to pass on my exact words.

Then, for many days and nights, I continued my humble little existence on the fringe of Brigantia, looking out from my lofty position over the misty valleys and distant hills, walking on the ancient, ruined ramparts and sitting on the stubs of burned wood where a huge fortress once stood before it fell in cinders and ash. I sat on the grassy banks which dipped away into prickly gorse and brambles and I mended blankets and clothes or twined spindly wood into untidy, useless baskets or simply gazed into the distance wondering what strange new sights lay to the south where the Romans were rebuilding the towns destroyed by Boudicca.

WINTER AD69

The nights drew in bitterly and my days were no longer spent out on the hillside, but inside my little roundhouse keeping a constant fire burning. Food was harder to find and our limited supplies of beef, oats and barley were low. The best hunters went out to supplement our stocks and we had a pack of well-trained dogs to chase down prey also. I ate small animals that were foul to me. But beggars cannot be choosers and like the poorest people in my lands, I had to eat what was available or starve, though I admit that before long I insisted on trading some of our possessions for cattle to slaughter, so I could at least have beef. I longed for pork soaked in honey wine and roasted slowly over a low fire, just like Mandulay would once have cooked for me. I yearned for the sharp and complicated taste of the wine we had imported from over the seas for so many years.

I wore my long woollen dress and my thick cloak and on a night my bed was covered with blankets and topped with my best leather. I was glad to have salvaged some of my things when we escaped and felt only mildly guilty that the others around me had far less than I did. I was still chief – it was my place to have those things. I kept in reasonable health which surprised me. Given the harsher life I was now living, I would have expected the aches and pains of age to grind me down but instead I felt far more robust. Maybe the leaner meats and thinner drinks agreed more with me. Antikia stayed well also, even though she was a lot older than me, but Shamatin was slower and greyer than he had been. I watched him sometimes, jealous that Antikia still had her man to lean on but also desperately worried for how she would cope when he died. They seemed to have had such little time to enjoy each other before our world had caved in.

One day, the sky threatened snow. It was plain white and the air was still and very cold and the land shone a little as if a hand had reached down from above and painted it the colour of the clouds. I was walking on the southern rim of the hill – I had not been down the hillside into the valley for eight days – when I saw travellers approaching.

"Estoroc," I shouted after realising they were heading directly towards us, and we watched the progress of the two figures together.

"Massina and Ret," Estoroc said. "Back from Londinium."

"So it is," I said, now recognising the pair.

They cantered their horses on, along the path through the valley floor, disappearing at times beneath the trees and the dense foliage. Up on our high hillside, others had noticed our messengers returning and they were beginning to gather, hovering at the entrance between the high ramparts. I joined them, to wait for the news, only half-listening to the chattered conversation in the cold about what help Bolanus might have offered to give. People were speculating that he would send more help after the winter had passed. Those of us in more senior positions kept quiet. I had seen the slow, steady pace that Massina and Ret maintained on their approach – no final spurt of speed as they came near the desperate remnants of their tribe. I knew already there was no good news. I had known all along that this was the end.

As the pair rounded the twisting track that brought them into our encampment, everyone greeted them, helping them with their meagre travelling packs and passing them cups of ale. In the air of expectancy, I asked the required question.

"What news do you bring from Bolanus?" As I spoke, everyone fell silent. Ret moved forward to me and Massina stood behind him looking down.

"Bolanus says he can send no help. The legions are still over-stretched and they have much trouble at home. They say they cannot afford to fight our war and that the best they can offer is to take yourself and your family away from Brigantia. Bolanus advises you to travel immediately to Espulus and let him escort you to Londinium in the spring." Ret's voice was low and colourless.

"There is no help coming," I echoed, confirming it to myself as well as the disbelieving crowd. "Ret, Massina, come to my roundhouse now and we'll talk further." I motioned to the other important people, my ragged council, to join us and I led the way inside. Behind us, a kind of chatter resumed, but it was muted and hollow. I wondered that they could have held out any hope at all or even that I had also nursed a secret belief that anything could be salvaged, when it was as clear as the ice crystals that hang from the branches in the depths of the year that we had lost, undeniably and irretrievably, and that there was no way back.

Inside, the travelling pair warmed themselves at the fire and ate watery barley porridge. Despite the news they brought, they were in reasonable spirits and talked at length about their experience.

"Bolanus gave us these," said Massina, fingering the thick, woollen cloak that she had slipped from her shoulders. Ret wore a similar one. "He treated us very well. We stayed in his house, in the part where his slaves sleep, but it was comfortable and we ate good food while we were there. He had our horses looked after."

"He gave us a kind welcome," agreed Ret, "but it was the least he could do since the news he had for us was so bad. We described the battles and we explained the dispute in exactly the words you gave us – he had only a very rough idea and in fact believed that you and Venutius were still married – but for all the pleas we made he could only say that he had no legions to spare. He led us to believe that if the situation in Rome is not sorted out soon, large numbers of auxiliaries may have to be sent back and that the very occupation of the whole of these lands is under threat. When we pointed out that with Venutius in control they wouldn't receive any taxes, he laughed and said it wouldn't matter if there was no one here to collect them."

"Venutius certainly picked a good time to attack," I said. "What about the southern tribes? Are others taking advantage of this lull in Roman activity?"

"Not that we saw or heard," answered Ret, "But few tribes to our south have the kind of power we've retained so even with this opportunity, they just don't have the weapons or even the governing structure to rebel effectively. Venutius is in a fairly unique position. The Iceni, the Trinovantes, the last fragments of the Catuvellauni have been all but wiped out. The people remain, but the leaders, the councils, the weapons are all gone." His voice was tinged with sadness, even though those tribes had never been our friends. Yet the notion of any tribal power disintegrating devastated us all because it was the truth at the heart of our own situation.

"Londinium was a very busy place," said Massina, lightening the mood. "Lots of building work going on and people everywhere. I felt quite frightened when we got near because you can hear all the noise before you even see it. There are streets, not tracks and houses with walls made of stone - no roundhouses at all, except for right out on the edges of the town and further upstream."

"Upstream?" Estoroc asked.

"A great rivers twists and turns through Londinium, all the way from the sea. That's why the Romans are building there. It means they can fetch all their trade in that way. There are boats all over the river and big wooden platforms that reach out into the water so boats can moor up and unload. Then, not far away from where they unload everything, there are the markets where all the goods are laid out and everyone goes to buy things. They all use coins there. Everyone carries pouches of money, tied to their belts."

"Money, I've only seen that once before," mused Invas, while I thought about a single coin I had once found out on the southern Brigantian marshes that my father had thrown away, calling it foolish. He had been wrong about that. Money was the future after all.

"They have entertainment places as well," said Ret, "where you can see gladiators, although people say it's not as good as in Rome. And there are other places where you can go and buy meals and wine and sit there while slaves serve you."

"It all costs money," added Massina, "so we didn't go to those places, but the smells were amazing – all different scents wafting through the streets and as many languages to go with them."

"How does anyone understand each other?" Antikia asked.

"Ah, they all understand the language of money," answered Ret, knowingly. "The traders hold up their fingers, two coins, three coins maybe and the buyers shake their heads and hold up one finger and so on. People understand each other enough to get by."

"It sounds like a different world," said Antikia, shaking her head in the manner of an old woman who doesn't understand the dawning age and has no desire to. "You cannot possibly want to go there, Cartimandua?"

Spoken at last, the question that they all had wanted to ask me - would I take the advice of Bolanus and escape south? I fingered the gold bangle on my wrist and pictured the far away streets of Londinium.

"I'll have to consider it, but not for a while. Let's get through the winter and see if the storm in Rome blows over. Who knows, by then Bolanus may be able to spare some help for us." It was a long shot, but a tribe needs its leader to give them hope. My answer found its way round the loyal people residing on my exposed hill-top and we all let the matter rest.

The start of the truly ice-cold weather began, when the days, although short, were even more of a struggle and we had a light smattering of snow. Life was more hand-to-mouth than I would have liked, given that we had not been able to stockpile and preserve enough grain and meat, but we were coping. Then, over the pale valley and shining winter moors came the danger we had not expected until Spring. Venutius marched south on us, fetching a small but deadly force that moved incessantly through the hostile frozen land. I had believed he would consolidate in the north and not bother hunting me down until his position was fully established but instead he acted while his star was in the ascendancy. He tracked me down to remove me while Rome could offer no help. It was a risky strategy on his part, leaving the majority of his war host surrounding the royal stronghold, where rival clan leaders might fight and vie for supremacy and break apart his fragile confederacy while he was not there to manage them. He could not bring the whole army on such an expedition in the winter-time and yet he had decided not to send assassins but to come himself. He didn't steal upon us silently but camped in an obvious position where he knew he would be seen – if not by us then by someone who would pass word on to us. Why didn't he just send someone sneaking in to kill me? Perhaps he did not trust assassins to do the job properly or perhaps he had enough respect for me that he wanted the final encounter to be between us. I cannot say, but when I saw them coming, the banners flickering on the horizon, I knew it was over. I had nowhere left to run to within my borders. My war host was scattered, my star had faded.

My people took up their arms when the menace on the northern front was identified. They panicked and began packing their meagre possessions once more. They lined the northern defences of our solitary tor and watched fearfully as the camp fires burned on the distant hill. For that day, we sat tight and waited. When night fell, some people stayed out to keep watch. They half-believed Venutius would come in the dark hours and ambush us in our sleep, though it was not the warrior's way to attack in such a cowardly manner.

The moon was a fat sliver in the sky as I left my roundhouse as silently as I could. Those close to me, whose attention I could not escape, spoke urgently, in whispers.

"You can't go there, he'll kill you," said Estoroc, and Antikia, who had once run in desperate fear for her life from this enemy's father, nodded in agreement. Amelan hovered anxiously and bit at her lips while Shamatin stayed wearily quiet. I put on my cloak and my sword and ignored them all, ordering that no one should follow me and that if I was not back by midday or if the enemy camp moved, they all should run. Antikia threw her bony arms around me and hugged me tightly then thrust me away before I could see the tears I knew were shining in her old, raven-like eyes. I went for my horse while Shamatin caused some diversion to prevent anyone else seeing me leave. Then I led the animal down the hillside and prepared to ride into the night.

I was so afraid, I thought I would be sick. The slice of moon threw enough light for me to see my way, but still the shadows seemed so black and the woods were like an army of giants waiting to close in on me. I had not ridden alone for a very long time. Without my escort of guards, I felt very vulnerable and keenly aware that I was riding into utmost danger with no knowledge of how Venutius would respond to my requests. My only hope was that he would afford me some final dignity on account of our long, if troubled history. I told myself, on that tortuous ride, that it didn't matter what happened to me but only what I could negotiate for the people who had been loyal to me. Even so, it's natural to cling to life, to cling to hope and self-interest and that turned the journey into quite an ordeal. I passed through woodland and over old pasture land where the moors had steadily seeped in, taking over from farmers of ancient times and replacing their crops with heather, bracken and gorse. I followed a track that took me roughly in the right direction and after a while I saw quite clearly the camp fires they had left burning for warmth and heard the snuffling noises that a group of people and animals make at night.

I cantered my pony more slowly towards the glow and considered how to approach. If I startled the wrong person – a glory-seeking fool – I might be murdered before I could even speak with Venutius. I could see a larger tent that I presumed may be his, but there were men sleeping all around and I had no hope of getting closer without disturbing the whole encampment. I dismounted and tethered the pony to a tree. Then I walked as quietly as I could around the outer edge of the camp, into thicker woodland where I was better concealed but closer to the large tent. As I walked, I startled a bird that swooped up out of the undergrowth and threw out a warbling cry, fixing me to the spot in panic, but no one rose to investigate and it gave me an idea. I swallowed hard and then let out a primal howl, imitating as best I could a hunting wolf. I let a moment go by, then gave another howl and another. If that didn't wake Venutius, nothing would. I knew the things that prickled him.

Sure enough, he emerged, pulling a heavy cloak around him because the night was frosty. There was some conversation with men around his tent. They all looked towards the trees, suspiciously and I stood very still, behind a thick trunk. One of the men made as if to come closer, picking up a bow and sheath of arrows, but Venutius stayed him with a hand to the shoulder and though I couldn't hear more than a hint of their voices, it was clear he was telling his man not to bother and to go back to sleep. They all settled back down, but Venutius hovered, then he moved further in my direction fiddled with his clothing and aimed a piss against a tree. I gave him a moment to finish, then took a chance and called his name, low and soft. His head came up sharply and I moved out from behind my tree so he could pick out my shadow among the dryads. We stood for what seemed a very long time, facing each other at a distance until finally he came towards me and I began to move towards him. It was an eerie dance in the chill, wan night with the trees framing our moves and the space between us shrinking.

When we came to a point at which our fingertips might just have touched if we stretched out our arms, we both stopped. I searched the changed face in front of me, much as I am sure he searched mine. It had been years since we had been in each others presence and we were both greatly altered. The hair on his head was a dark silver and his dense beard had lightened to match it. At the far corners of his eyes, wrinkles forked out like furrows and the circular indentations around the corners of his mouth had deepened. The combined effect gave him maturity and a sinister jocularity – the look of an unbeaten fighting man. He was still muscular, but I could sense the sagging that lay behind his thick cloak. It showed itself under his chin and beneath his eyes, where the skin had drooped with age. He looked back at much the same sight – my hair, too, was changed in colour to mostly white and the lines criss-crossed over my once-fine face. Like my mother and my aunt, I still retained strength of features, with my high cheekbones and straight forehead but I was undeniably old. I was nearly fifty – about the same age my mother had died.

"I'm going to flatten your new settlement," he said, finding an uncompromising tone in which to address me. "Brigantia is mine and I will remove you."

"You could take me away in chains right now," I conceded. "But you have hesitated. Will you listen to my terms?"

"You're in no position to state terms, but I'll hear your final pleas." Curiously, he took no obvious pleasure in the words he had waited so long to say, but uttered them in an emotionless monotone.

"So be it," I said. "I accept your victory. I have lost my hold on these lands, and though I dread that you will lose your grip and Rome will triumph, I accept that I can do nothing about that. The people who follow you cannot see this danger. If only they understood, they would not have flocked to you so readily."

"Is this a plea for mercy or just a speech to annoy me?" He had raised his hands up onto his hips and I feared he would call out for men to tie me up. I wondered that he had not done so already.

"I'm saying this now to warn you, Venutius. Bolanus is struggling now, but Rome will right itself and when that happens, they'll renew their campaign here and you'll be the first target. For pity's sake, make sure you have a firm grip on the reins of Brigantia. For all that I hate what you've done to me, I wouldn't see you lose what rightly belongs to us."

"I need no advice from you on that subject," he scoffed.

"Then perhaps you'll see the reason in pardoning all my supporters - the few here and the many who have returned to their settlements. If they agree to fall under your tribal rule, then please don't persecute them. You'll lose numbers you'll sorely need against Rome and you know in your heart that they are good people who will fight to protect their land, even if they must support you to do it. You know I have no chance of regaining my power here. I'm too old and have been proved weaker in battle. I'll leave and never trouble you again if you can make this oath to me now, that you will not kill the people who have supported me." I stopped to take a breath and realised that was in fact all I had to say. It was my only request. He kept on looking at me with that same blank expression.

"At last you are speaking some sense," he said. "You are too old and too powerless to stop me now. I could strangle you here and be done with it all." A feverish tingle started on the back of my neck and worked its way over my shoulder blades and down under my armpits where I grew damp. "Having said that, some of my best advice now comes from people who once followed you. Your Namandea is quite helpful in many ways."

He said it to hurt me but though there was a ghost of pain in my chest, I had suffered too many hurts and losses to feel her betrayal keenly any more. I waited.

"It would be a condition that you would go overseas and never return," he said, at last. "If you and your family go, then yes, I'll pardon and accept all those who willingly come to me."

"Thank you," I said, "But Antikia may not be able to go with me. You know how old she is now. I ask that she may stay if she chooses."

"After what she did to my father?"

"She did what I commanded, and only because he had hurt her badly in the past. When she escaped from you both, she was in a terrible state."

"Ah well, I don't care much either way. He was an old fool for her, that's why what she got to him so badly. She can stay if she chooses. If she causes me trouble, she will be easy enough to remove."

"Thank you," I said. I didn't know what Antikia would choose but at least she had the decision to make.

"Is that all?"

"That's all," I answered. "I'll leave tomorrow and join what remains of the legion to the south east. They will escort me to Bolanus in the spring, when he will undoubtedly package me off on an outward bound ship."

"You could be like Caratacus and live a famous and happy life in Rome," he said, half-mocking.

"I think I'll request somewhere quieter. I've got no interest in what Rome has to offer."

"Vellocatus died in the summer, did he?" asked Venutius without preamble, though he must have known the answer and had no need to bring it up.

"He did, yes," I said, wanting suddenly to weep.

"I didn't expect it. I thought I'd see him again. It's funny, even though I would have killed him, I imagined breaking bread with him and sharing another jug of ale by the fire."

I felt dizzy and thought I would fall. Venutius must have seen it and he roughly grasped my arm.

"Don't faint now," he ordered, "you've got the ride back to manage yet."

"Why haven't you just killed me?" I asked, stupidly. I should have been on my pony and away.

"I've got no desire to kill a tired, sad, old woman," he said plainly. "On the field, it would have been different. Here, it would be a messy end to things. Better that you go. Besides, my mother had some surprisingly good things to say about you, not least that you deserved my gratitude for caring for her. Ironic, really, since she was only with you because you imprisoned her. Still, I owed her something. I didn't do much for her while she was alive but I can honour her with this small mercy now she's gone."

"Did she pass well?" I asked, genuinely wanting to know.

"She died in her sleep," he supplied. "Peacefully. My father died from a wound gone bad. That was not so good but lots of ale and the sleeping herbs made it easier."

I nodded.

"Davit was killed, in the battle," I said and shrugged. "Like so many."

"We've all suffered losses," he said. "It's time now to move on."

I broke myself out of the sleepy nostalgia my mind had wandered into. Venutius still had his hand on my arm. I placed my hand over it.

"You were my husband once and I did love you. I hope that now you have what you wanted. I am sorry we could not rule together." I peeled his fingers from my arm and walked away, leaving him there in the broken moonlight. If I had stayed, might he have said something equally conciliatory? Probably not. It was not his nature to admit mistakes or confess to enfeebling emotions but I thought as I took the final look into his dark eyes that I saw the shadow of remorse, just the barest flicker.

To strengthen my heart as I rode away, I reminded myself of the peace I had negotiated and of the calm release of that last conversation, where I had spoken a simple truth and done justice to the memory of our early years together. It was a dangling thread that had needed weaving back into the piece and now it was done.

The pearl-coloured night was shimmering away into a grey dawn when I rode back into my meagre settlement. People watched me return with anxious stares, their eyes wide and full of trepidation. Presumably they had been relieved when they picked out my form coming through the valley but by the time I arrived, the fact that I was still alive had been overshadowed by a fear of what might have been agreed. I was tired from my night without rest, but I addressed them immediately to save them from the agonies of speculation. Men and women not already manning the ramparts and busying about with the start of the uncertain day came hurrying out of their little huts to hear my news, which I delivered at the southern tip of the hill, where the ancient earth bulged out like a ship's hull and faced in the opposite direction to the ominous force on the northern horizon.

"I have arranged terms for you all," I said. "Our fight is over. You are all free to remain in Brigantia though you must recognise Venutius as your chieftain now. He will accept your loyalty and will not exact any revenge upon you. The same is agreed for all those within our once-mighty war host."

"What about you?" came the clamour, "What of Cartimandua, our queen?"

"I am no more. I must leave. I'll go south with the legion and then overseas as soon as Bolanus can arrange it." There was a collective recoiling gasp, yet I think they all knew this day was coming. There was no response of angry outrage, just a terribly sad acceptance that followed the shock, and that felt worse, for me anyway. "I'll leave later today. I cannot stay longer or I'll put you all at risk."

I left them to go and eat and rest. Inside my roundhouse, Amelan unhappily served me a dish of food while Antikia paced about.

"I'll pack my things," she began saying and I cut her words off.

"You're not coming. Venutius agreed to you staying here, as long as you live quietly, uninvolved in the politics."

"Not coming?" she shrieked. "Ridiculous! Of course I'm coming. I've been with you my whole life. I won't abandon you now."

"I won't be alone," I said quietly. "Estoroc and Invas will come with me. There's no future for them here now, Masga will see to that, but they're young enough to make a new life somewhere else. You're not, dear aunt. You're too old to face the challenges that are coming for me. You should stay here, on the soil you know and keep a home fire burning for me. Amelan will remain as well, with her brother. I won't rip any of you from the place you belong." Amelan put her hands to her face and gave a sob of relief and sadness.

"I'll never see you again," Antikia cried. "You'll be so far away, over the deep waters in foreign lands."

It was true and it broke my heart. I couldn't answer for fear I'd start crying and not be able to stop. I held her bony old body and let her sobbing diminish. When her chest had finished heaving, I put her from me.

"I will be all right. This will be an adventure for me and a release from all the strains of leadership. Don't think of it as my exile, think of it as my new life. I'll miss you more than you can imagine, Antikia, but you must go on with your own life here and not worry for me." I smiled at her and got a weak reflection in return.

All those years, Antikia had been there to guide me. Even

when I outgrew her authority, I leaned on her advice and opinions. She was the constant in the torrent of my life though often I had not realised it. I think that's what I learned at the end - that the people around us and the little day-to-day things are what matter most and that though we try not to take them for granted, we inevitably do. Then, when they are gone, we mourn for them deeply. I mourned, not just for the people I had lost or the places I would never again see, but for the whole of my past, the stories I could not change, the decisions I could not revise and the experiences that would die with me because those who were not there could never truly appreciate them.

I took a last walk around that strange hill that we called Camulodunum, surveying my vast lands that stretched out in all directions. I ignored the blot of Venutius and his army and gazed past them, over the hills and moor, trees and valleys to my beautiful homestead that lay beyond. It was out of my sight, but would always be in my heart. Estoroc and Invas had the cart loaded and fastened up to a pony, leaving my gilded chariot to Venutius, the new chief of Brigantia. Strisen tried to insist on escorting me himself, but I forbade it and pressed him back to his sister, entrusting her to his protection. She cried again as I gave her a hug.

Finally, Antikia came to me and held me again.

"Be brave," she said, with her cheek against mine. "Go with my love."

"I'll send news when I can. I love you, aunt," I said,

Then I rode out from our hill, down the path and into the valley, leaving all of my inheritance behind me.

EPILOGUE AD75

Some years later, when I was sitting out on the pillared veranda of my sun-baked villa, drinking cold grape juice, I received a guest. He was from my old islands, though from the southern parts, but his trade work took him all over the empire. The conquest had been exceptionally good for his business. Whilst travelling through the Iberian peninsula he had made a stop at one of the tiny places in the village that sold food and drink and there he'd heard of the strange lady from Prittain who spoke Latin with a funny accent. He encountered his own kind overseas now and then, but often in the capacity of slaves, so he eagerly sought me out. I invited him to sit with me for a drink and he happily fell into telling me tales of our homeland.

"I'm from the south west originally, although my parents were from different tribes so I never really belonged anywhere. We travelled a lot - my parents were traders too - but it's changing so much that you go away one year, come back the next and it's all different! Londinium is so crowded now," he exclaimed, his shaggy brown hair falling from behind his ears where he habitually rammed it. "They're building huge bridges and laying stone roads and houses just spring up everywhere. It's quite a sight. Which part did you say you were from?"

"The north," I answered, vaguely, "Up in the hills."

"Ah, Brigantia? Well, you must have heard what's happening there. No? The ninth legion have broken Venutius. His whole war host has been torn apart. Poor man, poor man." He shook his head and the ragged locks swung around his face. He pushed them back behind his ears again and sighed. "Cerialis was very determined. They really do bear a grudge, when some little king or queen turns against them. It was just a matter of time before they got up the strength again to really take over Brigantia properly. A lot of people haven't got much sympathy for Venutius. He could have carried on with the good life, under client rule, but instead he's dragged his whole tribe into a war that's got them all killed. When did you leave anyway? You never said."

He was the kind of man that kept on talking apparently oblivious to the reactions of his listener, so he hadn't seen the colour fade from my face or the shake in my wrist as I replaced my drink on the table.

"Oh, a while ago. I got out when it all started to go downhill," I said, brushing off the question and he nodded sagely as if we were both wise ones. "So was the fighting very bloody?"

"They say so, yes. You know the Romans - they get a lot of the killing done by machine, like those terrible ones that throw the spears? But in Brigantia I heard there was a lot of close-up fighting. Then after, Cerialis made sure that they cut down all the warriors that were still alive and I believe they took a good lot of the others away as slaves. As they do." He took a long slurp of his drink.

"And what's become of Venutius?"

"Dead on the battlefield, they say. And with his queen tidily out of the way some years back, that leaves the hills wide open to the ninth. They'll colonise the whole place, even if they have to run their stone roads straight over the the highest hills and moors to do it. You have to admire them, nothing stops them. They've been building forts all over the south of Brigantia for years now, ever since Cartimandua left and Venutius holed up in the north. He should have taken the advantage then and moved his war host down to retake the southern border of the land. That's what I think. But he stayed up in the north, where the tribal chiefs always lived, apparently."

"For three generations, more if you count the original Brigantes, before the war federation was formed," I murmured, sickened by everything I was hearing.

"Ah, you know your tribal history, then! No one knows much about your hill folk. You Brigantians are a mysterious lot."

"So tell me about your travels. Where do you go next?" I asked quickly, taking him away from the dangerous subject of my heritage. He began to tell me how he would continue into the south of Hispania and catch a trading ship from one of the ports in another moon or two's time. I pretended to listen to his explanations of the itinerary he had to follow and his descriptions of previous ship journeys, riddled with sea storms and sickness. Instead of imagining his experiences, my mind was skipping backwards, to the events of five years previous, when I had fled my forlorn territory to join the legion heading to Londinium. I remembered Espulus's face, creased with satisfaction and relief, when I arrived at his fort. I remembered living out the rest of winter in a cold, stone bunker, with Estoroc and Invas attending me and serving up food taken from our provisions supplied by the legion. The quality of the food was even worse than on Camulodunum, because at least there I had the best on offer. Now I was just another mouth to feed. When the ice subsided and the wind was not so biting, the march to Londinium began and I viewed the world from a bouncing, uncomfortable cart, adapted from a legionary vehicle to suit a fallen queen – a hint of ceremony in the fancy wheels and curtained supports, but no real grandeur. We rolled steadily on away from my hills and moors, until we were marooned in a sea of flatlands and marshes, endless forests and swathes of cultivated fields. We stomped through new towns, travelling on new roads and witnessed the building of ever more forts. At settlements of roundhouses, people came out to watch us pass, morbidly excited to see the huge column of a legion marching by. Children waved to the soldiers and ran alongside the auxiliaries, copying their monotonous rhythm and adults glanced towards my cart with interest. I pulled the curtains around me, unwilling to display openly my departure from Brigantia. That journey went on and on, through weather which was, though not hostile, very inclement. When finally we came within sight of the grand new market town that straddled the twisting river, all I could think of was having a warm meal and a decent night's sleep. Even the strange smells, clamouring noises and wondrous sights hardly stirred me at all. I was lost in homesickness and weariness. My instinct was to grab a fast horse from somewhere and ride hard back to my homeland.

Instead I redressed in a suitably ceremonial outfit, decked in bangles and torques of gold and wearing my amber pendant over a rich tunic of dark red and a heavy cloak of brown leather and I allowed myself to be presented to Vettius Bolanus, the governor who had refused to send more aid. He received me in his ornate villa - the home that Ret and Massina had described to me. His manner was apologetic but disinterested. He gave me the same explanations for reneging on the client contract as he had given my two messengers and quickly swept me into some anterior wing of his home to be fed and watered. Then he arranged a room for myself and Estoroc and Invas at an inn and asked me to consider where I might like to settle. I could travel to Rome, he suggested, but the situation there was volatile, so I might choose to reside in one of the established areas of the empire. As long as there was a vessel sailing my way, it didn't much matter where I picked. I told him I would go wherever the first boat was headed, as long as it was not Rome - I had no desire to be caught up in further turmoil. So be it, he declared happily and thus I was shipped off to Hispania.

I was lucky to have a calm crossing, as so early in the season it was often treacherous, but even so, the swells and heaves of the ship made my stomach lurch and poor Invas suffered more so, vomiting over the side every time she tried to eat. When we landed on foreign soil, we were provided with transport, rough and ready but serviceable, to take us the many miles to a villa that local colonial officials agreed I might take as my own. Before I left the port, I had a message written out on a slice of wood, to be transported back to Brigantia by whatever passing traders could take it. It was for Antikia, by way of Mesuvian, the woman with the Roman husband who was still stationed in one of Brigantia's Roman forts, south of the defensive line established by Governor Gallus on our land and which I believed Venutius would never retake. I stated that we had arrived safely and were travelling to our villa, nothing more. I didn't sign it. There was no need.

We travelled through a strange and unforgiving land, where dry mountains rose up from wide, open expanses and the sky seemed vast and nameless, stretching like an enormous bowl overhead. The trees were gnarled and stunted and though it was still cold in Londinium, here the heat of summer was breathing in through the wind. The Hispanic tribes whose old land I was passing through were said to be very savage and violent, but I saw little sign of this. The Roman occupation of this territory was more comprehensive than in my home islands and the tribes were mostly under control. When I came to the dusty village that would be my nearest community, a deputation of several tribal elders emerged to greet me and though they were brief and impassive, they spoke clear Latin to me and directed me to my new home with good grace, explaining some of their local customs and rules before they did so.

I came to my villa and stood before it with a dawning feeling of peace upon me. I had feared for a long time the worst that could happen to me. This was it, and, as horrific outcomes go, it wasn't so bad. Estoroc, on the other hand, was suffering a bad case of homesickness and disappointment.

"This is an empty, dying place," he fumed. "What kind of lives can we lead here?" But Invas quietened him, afraid of making me feel guilty and responsible for their strange and unexpected fate. I stepped past them into my building of stone, with its creeping plants entwined round the pillars and its echoing rooms furnished with sparse items left by the previous occupant. The back of the house opened onto a flat, dried-out garden with pathways that divided it into four squares. There were stone troughs that held dying plants and a couple of statues of figures, gods maybe. A new garden, with new plants to learn about – this was how I would spend my time and forget my past.

We lived there into the summer, enough time for me to acclimatise to this new world and make the links with local people that I would need in order to survive and then I ordered Invas and Estoroc away.

"You're not happy here," I commiserated with them, "and I don't want you to throw your lives away. Travel on to one of the bigger cities, even Rome if you like. You can send word back to me and perhaps even return to visit me."

They cried, both of them, like children in my arms, for they knew if they left, they would never see me again. It was more than that, though, that brought forth their tears. They cried to leave behind the woman who was their last remaining link to all that had been and all that had ended. To leave me was to cut the thin thread that tied them back to their fathers, Davit and Presivin. On the nights before they left, we sat deep into the darkness, them listening to my stories of the past. I told them everything I could remember of their families, of my family and of all the history we shared. How many noble family lines had been ravaged by the Roman invasion? Cunobelinus's sons scattered to the winds, Boudicca's daughters killed in battle, the Druids murdered to the last one, the Corieltauvi dual magistracy thrust aside and my own intended destiny manipulated, thwarted and cut short. The Romans had their historians and their writers but we only had the tribal line and the living council to string our stories through the ages. Now the strings had all been cut. I could tell these stories to Invas and Estoroc and perhaps they would tell them to their own children, but within a few generations they would fizzle out, suffocated in a foreign land, surrounded by a completely different culture, denied the necessary sustenance of the dark Brigantian hills.

I was sad to wave goodbye to the pair, who had been such

devoted servants to me, excepting, of course, Invas's brief desertion. Yet, it was a relief also, not to be responsible for them any more. I had come to understand, if only slightly, the nature of the burden of parental responsibility that Vellocatus once talked of and it didn't sit well with me at all. It was easier to be alone and to think solely of my own needs. That is what I had done, these many seasons since they had left and until the shaggy-haired trader arrived on my veranda.

After he'd gone, I sat thinking for a very long time. I wrapped a blanket around me and watched the sun go down behind the golden hills, casting long shadows that crept like night over the landscape. I could see the rooftops of the little village, with smoke drifting up into the evening air, and beyond them, the sweep of pasture land that stretched away towards a large grove of olive trees. The stars began to twinkle in the dusky blue sky, radiant as dew drops against their darkening canopy. They were the same stars I had often gazed towards at home; I recognized the same groupings and clusters. When I watched their slow travels across the sky, they seemed to mark a pathway, as if they were calling me to return. I longed to view those stars from my own beautiful home once more. Hispania had been a safe and peaceful haven for me and I had spent many quiet times cultivating my new garden and encouraging it back to life, but it could never warm my soul the way the hills and valleys of Brigantia could.

Now in my fifty fourth year, my white hair curled and thinned to wisps as it reached my shoulders. My skin had tanned in the sun and the wrinkles had grown deeper and more numerous as a consequence. I was barely recognisable as the queen I had once been. The seed of an idea was germinating in my mind, a foolish plan that became more certain as the night set in.

I slept fitfully, dreaming of battles and of Venutius. First I was fighting against him, then alongside him until it was all a confusion of blades and arrows, dirt and blood. Then a mist descended and I was alone. I woke distressed, then dropped back off to dream of Antikia smiling and calling out to me and Vellocatus standing with her. Before dawn broke, I was wide awake, my mind darting between so many memories of so many people. I found myself thinking of Tantoban, that old warrior who had cared for me so tenderly, and of Risha who had begun as a dreadful foe and ended as a confidant, and of my great aunt, Gorlensa, whose wise counsel I'd lost forever when I had to ignore her warnings about the Druids. I thought of my parents and the way they had raised me, so carefully and kindly after they had lost my sister, their eldest daughter, and how my father balanced that love for me and my mother with a ruthless ability to lead his massive tribe. I thought of his father before him, who had died long before I was born and who wove so many different little tribes into the formidable alliance of Brigantes. I thought of Tyrius, who had been another father figure to me and whose selfish desire for my aunt had turned from honest passion to his own undoing, rendering him a bitter fool.

As I remembered all these people, I wondered how others would remember me. The clever queen who held the Romans at bay for so long? The chief who lost control of her tribe? The woman who broke with her husband to marry his armour-bearer? Once, it had mattered to me what people thought. Once I worried about my name being remembered for the right reasons. Now, in my old age and my wisdom, I didn't care about my name being remembered at all. All I cared about was going home.

I packed my things – just those things I had brought with me from Brigantia – and I ordered one of the slave girls who helped run my household to go into the village and hire a cart and driver. She mutely obeyed, fearful of her unpredictable mistress, and by midday I was on a cart heading towards the coast. At the busy port, I mingled with the crowds, amongst traders and travellers, livestock and slaves, until I heard about a small vessel bound for the Cassiterides. It was a Parisi boat, heading for one of their northern ports and I almost wept for joy to be able to secure my passage on it, when I had expected to wait ages and then only get passage to Londinium. We were supposed to leave within a few days, but travel was delayed because the consignment of oil and wine was not complete. I lodged in a stinking tavern as an anonymous traveller until the moon had waxed and waned and then finally the forty amphorae the ship master was waiting for arrived and we set sail. There was a small group of passengers – a young man, a couple, myself and a middle-aged woman, crammed into a small bunk. It was worse than my first crossing and a longer route, but I hardly cared. When the boat docked on a Parisi shoreline, I traded one of my fat gold bangles for a good cart, a strong little pony and a supply of cured meat, salted flatbread and three amphorae of wine. If the man was curious how I came to be in possession of such a glorious bangle, he did not show it, but instead quietly pocketed the valuable item and no doubt counted himself lucky. I was not sad to lose it. I had no more use for it and anyway, I had three more.

With my possessions loaded on the cart, I coaxed the pony into a trot and began my journey west, into southern Brigantia. I cannot describe the emotions that overcame me as I rode into sight of a horizon I recognised. All my arduous travelling, the years of exile, the previous burdens of ruling the tribe, melted into nothing as I experienced that clear pleasure of being home. Everything felt perfect to me – the smell of the air, the colour of the hills, the sounds of the birds. Even all the Roman forts and outposts I passed could not remove the joy I felt in being back.

I heard on the road of a huge new fort near Camulodunum. The Romans had chosen not to colonise the old hill because it was too small and difficult to access. I was pleased – it would remain as it was and not be defaced by the imposition of the Roman military. I headed towards it because it was the last place

I had seen my people. It was my only link to Antikia. When I got there, it was deserted. From the summit I could see the road leading to the new fort and the old settlements that lay in the valley, but no one had been on the hillside recently. My delight faded and the blackness began to sneak in. Was there no one left who would know me? I stayed there for a few days and nights, in the weather-beaten remains of a hut, gathering my strength to face the final part of my journey north, towards my true home.

On the third day, a young woman came up the pathway. She startled me in my hut, coming to the entrance and speaking in a small voice.

"Do you need any help? I have grain and meat if you have anything to trade? I can take coins."

"No, I'm fine," I said, trying to place her vaguely familiar features. She took a step inside, though I hadn't invited her, and my puzzlement mirrored itself on her face. A few long seconds passed.

"Is it you?" She asked. "I thought, when I first saw you come, there was something about you..." She let her words hang.

"Who are you?"

"My mother is Essalea. I am Davitia. I live with her in the valley."

"Davit's daughter?" I breathed, amazed.

"Cartimandua?"

I nodded and she rushed to me, helping me to sit and kneeling down before me in an attitude of servility.

"Is my brother Estoroc returning too?" she asked, "Do you know anything of him?"

"Only that he and Invas travelled away to make a new life for themselves. I never heard from them after they left Hispania. I can't tell you any more than that."

"Oh." She was despondent. "We had a message that he was in Etruria and was well, but that was a long time ago. Still, I'm glad he found a better life."

"Can you tell me," I began, hesitantly, "anything of Antikia, or her man, Shamatin."

"Oh yes," she nodded, "yes I can. They lived in this valley near to us. They couldn't return north to the royal settlement because Venutius had taken it, so they stayed here. My mother spent a lot of time with them. But, I am so sorry to say, they died, shortly before Cerialis began his campaign. Antikia had become very unwell in her chest, coughing and feeling weak and Shamatin died a few moons after her."

"Oh, my aunt," I cried, "How I wish I could see her again." Davitia looked uncomfortable, as young people do when confronted by grief, then a smile broke over her pretty face.

"We have her things," she said, triumphantly. "Would you like them? Mother wasn't sure what to do with them."

I nodded, tears falling unashamed from my cheeks. She scampered away and when she returned a long time later, her mother accompanied her and the two of them carried a large folded blanket that contained my aunt's possessions. They laid it on the floor for me and stepped back, flushed with nervous pride. I pulled back the blanket to reveal Antikia's jewellery, her polished agate mirror and her little dagger. There were other items as well, but beneath them all, one caught my attention. It was a flat piece of wood, pale but dirtied with fingermarks and dents. When I turned it over, I saw my own message, cut by a scribe in a Gaulish port, telling my aunt I was safely overseas. I let out a loud sob.

"I never knew if she got this," I said.

"Oh yes," said Essalea, "she was very relieved to know you were in Hispania. She missed you very much, but she was happier knowing you were safe."

"How was she, at the end?" I asked.

"She was ready. She knew it was time and she wasn't alone. I nursed her and Shamatin never left her side."

I spent some time with Essalea and Davitia, on the hillside.

They invited me to their settlement, but I decided it would be best not to be widely recognised and declined their offer.

"Where will you go, will you be welcome anywhere?" asked Davitia, who was more forthright than her mother - her father's trait shining through her honest, young features.

"I'll go north, to see my old home. Do you know what's happened to it?"

"I think it's been badly trampled," said Essalea. "Venutius used it as his own homestead, as you know, and we heard that after the last battle, the ninth legion did a lot of damage to prevent any remaining supporters moving in. But they're not using it themselves. Will you return here once you've seen it?"

"I don't know. I'll see where the winds blow me."

So it remained only for me to say goodbye to mother and daughter and to wish them well. I left Antikia's belongings with Essalea and Davitia, since they seemed worthy recipients and would surely care for the precious objects. They waved to me as I drove my cart and pony north, two slim figures on the stark hillside. The last time I had taken this route was when I went to speak with Venutius that final time and when I passed the place where I remembered his camp to be, I got down from the cart and picked some wild flowers. I bundled them with a strong piece of grass and set them down on the ground. I gave myself a few moments to openly mourn that happy little boy who became such an angry, determined man and then I set off again before I could be overwhelmed. Grief is like a stream held back by a dam of self-control. You can glance on the pooling black waters from time to time, but let go of yourself for too long, and the deluge will flood out and drown you. I went onwards, sustained by the excitement of coming home, no matter what damage I might find.

And damage there was - not a roundhouse left standing and many of the carefully built walls knocked over. Crops had been burned and possessions broken and scattered. I left the cart hidden and walked on foot into the old settlement, in case I should find anyone, but it was truly abandoned - a place of ghosts. Until Cerialis can implement the extensive plans he has for Brigantia, this place will stay just as it is for no Brigantian would want to enter ground so touched by disaster and destruction. He will come eventually though, with roads and forts and towns and more will come after him to continue his work, stretching Roman occupation further and further north.

I return for my pony and cart and bring them up through the royal enclosure, its large circle still evident though the fences have been smashed down. The garden is gone. A pause and then on, up into the meadow, blessedly unchanged, and on to the woods with their whispering branches. Here the stream comes out, gurgling and fresh and I unharness the pony and let her drink before she wanders away. I put my hand in to taste the cold, clear water. The grass grows thick and green by the edges, giving way to bracken and bramble as I walk into the forest. It's a shorter walk than I remember to reach the little waterfall and the flat, cool rocks, or perhaps time is moving faster for me now. There are two leather necklaces, faded and old, hanging from a branch, and a sparrow fidgets next to them. I feel so tired after my long, long journey and I lie down to close my eyes for a while, my heart pounding too heavy in my chest and a pain blossoming like fire in the side of my head. The daylight shines red through my eyelids, making me think of hot summer days and endless sun and my golden-haired Vellocatus. I breathe the sweet air, see his face, and cast my life and memories to the winds.

Lightning Source UK Ltd.
Milton Keynes UK
UKOW042330021212

203070UK00001B/1/P